A WONDERLAND WISH ON
EVER AFTER STREET

JAIMIE ADMANS

Boldwood

First published in Great Britain in 2024 by Boldwood Books Ltd.

Copyright © Jaimie Admans, 2024

Cover Design by Alexandra Allden

Cover photography: iStock and Shutterstock

A CIP catalogue record for this book is available from the British Library.

Paperback ISBN 978-1-80483-881-5

Large Print ISBN 978-1-80483-880-8

Hardback ISBN 978-1-80483-882-2

Ebook ISBN 978-1-80483-879-2

Kindle ISBN 978-1-80483-878-5

Audio CD ISBN 978-1-80483-885-3

MP3 CD ISBN 978-1-80483-887-7

Digital audio download ISBN 978-1-80483-883-9

Boldwood Books Ltd
23 Bowerdean Street
London SW6 3TN
www.boldwoodbooks.com

For everyone who's ever been told they were too much. Or not enough. Or too weird. Or too different. Keep being you. The world needs more spectacular nuts!

1

'Is it currently your birthday?'

'No.' The man in the smart suit who is interviewing me looks bemused by my question.

'Then "Happy Unbirthday" to you.' I take a cupcake off the platter I'm carrying and place it on the desk in front of him, poke a candle into the icing, lean across to light it with a long-reach lighter, and breathe a sigh of relief when the flame dances into life with no incendiary incidents. Hurrah. That had all the potential to go horribly wrong. Open flames and me are never a good mix.

'It's from *Alice in Wonderland*,' I continue when the interview board look at me blankly. 'The Mad Hatter and the March Hare celebrate every day that *isn't* their birthday. Why should you only get to celebrate on your birthday itself? Isn't life worth celebrating every day?'

Mr Hastings, the smart-suited man who's leading the interview, flicks a fingernail at the swirl of icing atop the cupcake and then peers down at the bit he's flicked off. The three interviewers are all wearing sharp suits and have stern looks on their faces, but his is the sharpest and sternest of them all. Their table is on a platform at the end of a big meeting room in the council offices, and I feel like they're all looking down at me, and I wish that, like Alice, I had a piece of cake I could nibble to make me grow taller *and* be less intimidated by their sophisticated stares. It feels like going for an audition, except they have a big heavy desk in front of them with lots of important-looking papers laid out on it, and I just have a row of plastic chairs at the other end of the room where I had to dump my bag and wonkily balance my platter of cupcakes while I smoothed my hair down and tried to get myself prepared for this interview.

'That's what I'll do if you let me take over the tearoom on Ever After Street. I'll theme it after Wonderland – lots of red and black, chequerboard flooring, card suits and clocks everywhere, and Mad-Hatter-style tables piled high with decorative teacups and teapots. We'll do tea parties and Alice-themed afternoon teas where we serve dainty finger sandwiches and cupcakes and tarts, and I'll offer "Unbirthday parties" every day of the year. Children and adults alike will be able to celebrate a Wonderland-style "Unbirthday" on any day they want.'

They don't seem very impressed.

Maybe putting on the blue Alice dress and black headband was overkill. I thought I was being fun and quirky, but I feel more like a child, auditioning for a part in a school play while the headmaster watches on thinking, 'Who is this overgrown toddler, and why does she keep swinging around a cake stand?'

I've been pacing as I talk and on a particularly sharp turn, the cakes nearly go flying off my cake stand, so I put it down on the desk in front of them. Even their desk is severe and intimidating. If inanimate objects can frown, it is definitely frowning at me.

'Well, I can see the exploitative potential in daily birthday parties...' Mr Hastings huffs as he talks and accidentally blows out the candle in the cupcake. I could've done with that to make a wish.

I wish for them to say yes. I wish for this tearoom. It feels like a second chance – a chance to start undoing everything that's gone wrong in my life lately.

Exploitative potential doesn't sound like a good thing. 'It's something they do in the Lewis Carroll books. I think it would be nice for children to be able to have a tea party on any day of the year simply because it *isn't* their birthday.'

'And there's definite money to be made. Our previous owner only earned money from birthday parties on one day a year from any singular customer, but here you are with a solution that makes *every* day a potential birthday party.' The man on the left never introduced himself, and now he elbows Mr Hastings with a chuckle and gets a glare for his troubles. 'This "Unbirthday" thing is quite a clever concept, no?'

I'm not sure whether I'm supposed to agree or not. Maybe it's better if they think I'm some kind of business-minded entrepreneur, who should be appearing on *Dragon's Den* rather than letting them see my knees knocking under my white knee-length socks. I've dreamed of owning a tearoom my entire life, like my family did many moons ago, and I want this interview to go right more than I've ever wanted anything to go right before.

The interview board is made up of the two men and a woman who has introduced herself as Mrs Willetts, and she leans forward and takes a cupcake off the stand. She holds it by the paper case and turns it around in her hand, admiring the pink and yellow swirls of rose-shaped icing piped on top. 'And these are homemade, yes?'

'Yes, of course.' I gulp and try to cover it by sounding easy-breezy and laidback.

It's not a lie.

They *are* homemade.

By the bakery I passed on my way here.

But who needs to know that teeny-tiny detail? They haven't asked me to specify *whose* home they were made in, have they?

It wasn't planned, but I drove past a little family-run bakery on my way to the council offices and thought it would be an icebreaker if I brought a platter of cupcakes with me. God knows what the poor woman in the bakery must've thought when I ran inside, dressed as Alice, spotted her rose cupcakes and begged her to let me pay an extra tenner and take her display cake stand with me too.

It's only in that moment that I realise they think *I* made the cakes myself. I wasn't intending to mislead them, but Mrs Willetts actually looks very impressed with the cake, and nothing I've done so far has made any impression whatsoever, and this dream is sure to die if I admit that I bought them on the way here, and it's not *exactly* the sample of the cakes I'd make if I took over the tearoom.

I mean, it's not *that* much of a lie. If they let me rent the tearoom on Ever After Street, I *will* be making my own cupcakes to serve to customers. I *can* do it. My nan and my mum ran a family teashop together when I was growing up, until my mum walked out on us, so it was just my nan and me, keeping it ticking over, hoping that Mum would come back one day...

And now I know that she never will, and my nan has gone too. And I have always wanted to step into their shoes. Tearoom ownership is in my blood. From the moment I heard the rumours at the end of last autumn about the tearoom on Ever After Street needing a new owner, I felt like it was meant for me, and now it's mid-March, Lilith who used to own the tearoom has retired, and it's up to the council to fill the empty space on our fairy-tale-themed shopping street in the heart of the Wye Valley.

I can't let this opportunity pass by because of some unfortunate baking incidents in recent years. My ex-landlord's angry face flashes before my eyes. The blue strobe lights of the fire engine. The soot-blackened kitchen and the eviction notice that soon followed.

I still love baking... It just hasn't loved me back lately. And all right, the last time I tried to bake, I promised the fire brigade that I never would again, but this is different. I have something to bake *for* now, a renewed purpose, actually a double dream – both owning a teashop and working on Ever After Street. I've barely been outside for the past couple of years, and I need to do something to shake my life up, take back control, and claw back the shattered pieces from the last time I tried to make this dream a reality.

Mrs Willetts contemplates the cupcake for a few moments before peeling back the paper case and taking a bite.

I hold my breath. *Please let it be as good as it looks.*

'Oh wow.' She holds a hand up to cover her mouth. 'That is delightful. Truly delightful.'

She looks at both the men pointedly, and Mr Hastings peers down at the cupcake already in front of him, while the other man eagerly reaches over to pluck one from the stand and gobbles it down in three large bites.

'Oh yes, very good.' He brushes crumbs from the desk. 'You're very talented.'

I blush at the compliment, even though it's not *me* they're complimenting.

Mr Hastings picks off a piece of the cupcake and deposits it into his mouth. He looks like he's intending to be unimpressed, but as he chews thoughtfully like some kind of professional cake taster, his face softens.

'I wish more interviewees tried to bribe us with cake.' Mrs Willetts takes another one.

'Oh, I wasn't—'

She laughs. 'I know, Miss Jordan, I was just joking. I must admit that the cakes have swung it for me. You're our best candidate so far, and not *just* because none of the others thought to bring us treats.'

Hope races through my body, and then quickly fizzles out again when Mr Hastings speaks and the unimpressed look is firmly back on his face.

'You are very late, however. The deadline for applicants passed two hours before your application was received. How do you explain that tardiness and why it should inspire confidence in you, given that you cannot follow simple guidelines?'

I don't know how to answer that. The honest answer is that I went back and forth with myself so much.

This is a *terrible* idea.

This is the best idea you've ever had.

You can't do this.

You've *got* this.

It was like Rapunzel in *Tangled* when she first leaves her tower. I didn't know which way to turn. I filled in the application form and pitched my idea, but when it came to actually pressing send... I doubted myself. Applications closed at 12 p.m. on Monday, so I continued doubting myself while watching the clock, waiting for 12 p.m. to tick by, and then when it did, I was filled with regret and mentally kicked myself for not just getting on with it.

And then Marnie came by to make sure I'd sent it, and she yelled at me for not doing it and made me send it anyway, even though the deadline had passed. She persuaded me that I had nothing to lose and the worst they could say was that it was too late.

'I lost track of time. I was helping my friend Marnie out at the Tale As Old As Time bookshop and we had a lunchtime rush and the deadline passed without me realising it.' It's not exactly a lie, it's just leaving out the bit about crippling self-doubt. No job interviewer needs to hear that.

I was more surprised than anyone to receive an email inviting me for this interview. And I realised this had to be a 'go big or go home' moment. I had to do something that would get their attention and make me stand out from the crowd, which is where the Alice-inspired outfit and cakes came in. The kind of thing that could go very, very right, or hideously, awfully wrong. Metaphorically blow their socks off. I give the lighter a wary glance. Maybe literally blow their socks off, and a few other bits too, if that had gone awry.

'Well, that shows a dedication to work, doesn't it?' Mrs Willetts says kindly. She's eyeing-up another cupcake. It's possible those cupcakes are loaded with genuine magical powers.

'The only reason you're here at all, Miss Jordan, is because I was *persuaded* to look over your application, despite the fact that rules are rules and, contrary to popular belief, they are *not* made to be broken, not even by those who already work for us.' Mr Hastings' sternness obliterates all my positive thoughts. If there's magic in those cupcakes, it's definitely not *that* strong.

'Ah, yes, you do have experience of Ever After Street itself, don't you? You already work there on a casual basis?' The nameless man also helps himself to another cupcake.

'I've been helping Marnie on and off since the autumn. When I heard about Lilith retiring from the tearoom, I knew it was what I wanted to do straight away. I grew up with family who owned a tearoom and, a couple of years ago, I was going to—'

'And yet you still couldn't get your application in on time,' Mr Hastings mutters, cutting me off from further oversharing, which is probably just as well.

'Oh, stop grousing, it was close enough,' Mrs Willetts says as she goes for another cupcake and I wonder if it was her who persuaded him to begrudgingly look at my application. 'We're not going to split hairs over an hour or two when this is clearly the best application we've had. Lilith has been in that spot for many decades and leaves big shoes to fill, and you, Miss Jordan...' She nods down to my Alice-style black Mary Janes, which are pinching a bit, if I'm honest. 'I think you're just the bright spark we need. Anyone who can make cakes like this definitely belongs on Ever After Street. It's a good job the council offices aren't nearer or I'd be popping by every day for one or two of these!'

Oh dear. Those cupcakes have gone a bit far now. I mean, I *can* make cupcakes. I used to be able to make cupcakes. Just because no baking has gone right for me lately, doesn't mean I can't do it. It doesn't mean that every attempt will turn out like my last attempt – flat, semi-burnt buttons with curdled butter icing, and not exactly the soft and fluffy vanilla flavour of these beauties, with lashings of delicate icing perfectly piped in a rosebud shape, but I try not to think about it because it sounds like I might be winning them over. Well, the cupcakes are winning them over. The nameless man has got a smile on his face now too, although Mr Hastings is still glaring at me.

'And you'd dress up like this every day, would you?' he demands.

'I think it could be fun. I'd give the tearoom a makeover to make it as much like entering Wonderland as possible, so why shouldn't customers be served by someone dressed as Alice? It would add to the fantastical feeling and surrealism of all things Wonderland. An immersive experience for every visitor. Tea and Alice go hand in hand, don't they? The books are much-loved classics, and children everywhere connect to Wonderland and the characters encountered there, and...' I lose the train of thought on where I was trying to go. 'It would be a perfect fit for Ever After Street. Every shop is themed after one fairy tale or another. Until now, the tearoom has been the only establishment that's not themed. It would be nice to tie it in with the rest of the street, don't you think?'

'Hmm.' They all make varying noises of agreement and Mr

Hastings spins the cake stand around, admiring the few remaining cupcakes left on it.

'You're in luck, Miss Jordan. It just so happens that my daughter is a huge fan of *Alice in Wonderland*, and in her younger years, I was subjected to watching the Disney film hundreds of times and reading the books for her bedtime story on many, many nights. I must admit this is quite an inspired idea.'

'Yes,' Mrs Willetts chimes in. '*Alice in Wonderland* is something that's sorely missing from Ever After Street. I can't think of anything being a better fit for an Alice-inspired business than a tearoom. Especially with these delicious cakes.'

Maybe it's a sugar high. Maybe this is where I've gone wrong in job interviews before – by *not* getting the interviewers so hopped up on sugar that they can't think straight, and offer me the job in a haze of cake-related endorphins.

'Your passion is inspiring and your dedication to Alice is enchanting. And your vision for the tearoom is by far the most imaginative one we've heard.' Mr Hastings' brash voice ricochets through the room. He pushes his chair back, and the three of them glance at each other knowingly. 'I don't think we even need to discuss it. This will be the first time there's ever been Alice representation on Ever After Street, and it's well past due. Herefordshire Council would be delighted to offer you a three-month trial, Miss Jordan.'

'But what about...' Mrs Willetts gives Mr Hastings a sharp look. 'The decision has already been made.'

Mr Hastings waves a dismissive hand in her direction. 'You let me worry about that. It won't be a problem.'

I don't know what that means but it's best not to question it. I'm too busy trying not to hyperventilate *or* jump for joy, or do some disturbing mix of the two. I can't *believe* this went my way. I thought they were going to laugh me and my blue Alice dress out of the room, and without those cupcakes and Mr Hastings' daughter, they probably would have.

'We will provide a small budget to cover the costs of reimagining the tearoom,' the imposing man continues. 'You may start work immediately. Once you are ready to open, the trial period will begin. You can expect regular assessments and we will expect your full sales reports delivered weekly to make sure things are moving in the right direction. Online customer reviews will be monitored. When the trial period is up, *if* we decide that your establishment is an asset to Ever After Street, we will consider extending your lease for a much longer period of time. Any questions?'

Billions. But the main question is – am I brave enough to ask any of them? What if I ask something stupid and let slip that I don't know the first thing about business ownership? What if I accidentally admit that I'm slightly worried about how badly my attempts at baking have gone lately? I gulp. 'Nope. All seems pretty clear to me.'

'Jolly good. We'll get the paperwork sent over ASAP.' He pronounces it ay-sap, which was enough to set my teeth on edge without his next question. 'Can I just query one thing about your address? It says The Old Rustbucket, and the address you've given matches the address of Marnie Platt, the Ever After Street bookseller... Are you staying with Miss Platt?'

'Well, no, er, not exactly... I mean, just temporarily. There was an issue with my post and everything is forwarded to her. It's no big deal, really. The post office are sorting it out.' I wave my hand so fast that they must see nothing but a motion blur. 'The Rustbucket is just an old caravan on her driveway where my mail gets delivered to save it being muddled up.'

Why did I put The Old Rustbucket in my address in the first place? What if they judge me if they find out that I *do* live in a caravan? The last thing I want is these extremely put-together people getting a hint of how un-put-together I am.

'Thanks for your time. I'm excited to get started. I won't let you down.' I sound like I'm parroting the 'what to say in job interviews' book I flicked through in A Tale As Old As Time the other day.

Mr Hastings makes a doubtful noise, and Mrs Willetts tells me to have a good afternoon. 'And Miss Jordan? Please do leave the cake stand.'

Dammit. I was hoping to scoff a cake or two on the way home. And I just spent a tenner on that stand. I give them a bright grin. 'With pleasure. Plenty more where they came from.'

I cringe as I say it. While I'm sure there *are* plenty more in that little bakery, that was an expensive trip there this afternoon – there's no way I can afford to buy cupcakes from there every day, and there's probably some law against taking someone else's work and passing it off as your own, even when it comes to baked goods.

'We'll be in touch.' Mr Hastings indicates towards the door, letting me know it's long past time I left. 'Welcome to Ever After Street. On a temporary basis only.'

Temporary. A word that has haunted my life in recent years. Everything seems to be temporary these days. Friends, boyfriends, jobs, places to call home... but still, temporary is better than nothing. I need this. I've hidden away from life in the past couple of years. After my ex pulling out of the tearoom we were going to run together in the most humiliating way possible, I've shut myself away. I need to get back out there and learn to live again. Now all I have to do is turn a tearoom into Wonderland, remember *how* to bake the things I used to be able to bake, and metaphorically knock their socks off.

Definitely, definitely *not* literally.

2

'Oh, Cleo, that's brilliant! I'm so happy for you!' Marnie squeals when I tell her how the interview went and wraps me in a massive hug. 'I *knew* that tearoom was meant for you!'

That evening, we're standing by the caravan that's parked on the driveway outside her cottage. My nan left it to me when she died, and I *had* a flat with decent driveway space where I could park it, but there was that whole 'accidentally setting the kitchen on fire' incident and I got evicted, and now the caravan is the only place I've got to live. Marnie took pity on me and let me bring it here. Her boyfriend, Darcy, who runs the flower shop on Ever After Street, alongside starting up gardening classes with a focus on mental wellbeing, was injured late last year and he moved in with her, and... well, he intended to move out but they're so happy together that he never did, so his truck, The Old Rustbucket, and my knackered old car are all jammed into Marnie's driveway and dragging down the quaint neighbourhood aesthetic. Marnie is too nice to tell me that the neighbours have started complaining about the caravan, but the neighbours *have* started complaining about the caravan.

I've been looking for a flat, but the availability of one I can afford, is nearby, and has parking space would be the holy grail of house-hunting and so far has proved impossible to find. My previous landlord would *not* be on-board with writing a reference letter, which also complicates matters.

I feel deflated rather than excited tonight, like I cheated at the interview by pretending those cupcakes were mine. I'm overwhelmed with fear that I won't be able to create anything even vaguely similar. I used to be able to bake, but I feel like I've forgotten how to, and everything I try goes disastrously wrong. What if the pressure of the tearoom makes that worse rather than better?

'This is what you've always wanted!' Marnie can tell there's something wrong and is trying to cheer me up.

And she's right. Marnie's bookshop is *Beauty and the Beast*-themed, and since the moment I saw it, I wanted to do something like that but with my favourite book, *Alice in Wonderland*. The tearoom is a perfect fit. An ideal second chance for the tearoom I never got to own before, but better this time around, as I won't have to trust someone else not to let me down.

After Mum left when I was ten, and Nan was running the tearoom alone, I'd sit in there after school to do my homework and she'd keep filling up my teacup and would deposit a little cake on my table every time she walked by, until she closed up at five and we'd go home together. She was the centre of the little town where we lived. Everyone knew her – and everyone went to our tearoom. The place was always filled with laughter and chatter, and the ding of clinking teacups was the soundtrack to my childhood. Like my mum had been too, my nan was an incredible cook. Our family tearoom offered breakfasts and lunches as well as cakes, tarts, and a selection of teas, coffee, or hot chocolate. I grew up thinking I'd step into her apron and sensible shoes one day.

And then, when I was in my twenties, she died. And a few years later, I got word that Mum had died too, and life turned upside down.

Nan hadn't told me the tearoom was in trouble, and it had to be sold to pay off debts, but the one thing she left to me was her beloved caravan. It's definitely showing its age these days, but it's also been a lifeline. Without the caravan, what would I have done? Accept the offer of Marnie's spare room and encroach on even more of her alone time with Darcy? They're a few months into a new relationship – even though they both insist I'm welcome, the last thing they *really* want is a third wheel.

'You can use my kitchen anytime,' Marnie is saying. 'I know you're nervous about the cooking aspect, and you haven't got much room in there.'

She knows I was kicked out of my flat for causing a fire. She doesn't know I've led my interviewers to believe that I'm a female version of Paul Hollywood minus the affinity for double denim and random handshakes. I'll be okay on the sandwich front. I can make a sandwich. I can make tea. The problem is that people coming to a tearoom are going to expect a slightly more extensive menu than a sandwich and a cuppa. Unbirthday parties and Wonderland-themed afternoon teas make you think of Mad-Hatter-style tables, piled high with delicate-looking delicious treats, and it feels like my baking ability has been lost to grief. There were family recipes, secret ingredients that were never written down, but passed from my nan to my mum and then to me, and I've forgotten them all. I can't remember what the secret to my mum's soft cakes was. I can't remember what my nan used to put into scones to make people travel for miles to get them. I wrack my brain, stare at the ceiling for hours when I should be sleeping, but all the memories of my childhood are fuzzy, like I'm looking back through a screen of water. I can see my mum in her Laura Ashley floral apron. I can see her blushing as customers complimented her bakes. I see her smiling down at me as she showed me how to use the kitchen scale. I *know* she shared our family recipes with me. I just can't remember anything about them. When she died, I wanted to own a tearoom as a tribute to both her and my nan. It was what we had always planned – I thought it might make them proud, wherever they are now. And I hope that finally fulfilling the dream I came so close to a couple of years ago will unlock something inside of me. If I force myself back out into the world, try to take control of my life again... will I get back to who I used to be?

'I'll manage in here.' I pat the caravan on the side – carefully, in case any more bits of her fall off. There's a small gas stove and a tiny bit of unit space with a sink at one end – the extent of my kitchen. 'Besides, there will be a kitchen at the tearoom. I can use that. It'll be fine. *Fine.*' My effort to reassure her ventures into Ross from *Friends* territory, but one of us has to believe it, and I'm terrified that *I* don't.

Marnie invites me in for a celebratory drink, and it's pouring by the time I open her door to leave and make a dash for the caravan. It's dark and nearly midnight, but both Marnie and Darcy's enthusiasm has cheered me right up.

This is my dream. Owning a tearoom like I grew up thinking I would, and to combine that with something I love as much as *Alice in Wonderland* is more than I could have ever hoped for, and even better, it's on Ever After Street – a few doors up and opposite where my best friend works. Ever After Street is really special to me. Not only would I never have met Marnie without it, but as soon as I went there, it felt like somewhere I fitted and I'd never felt that before. I've barely ventured outside in the past couple of years. Since my nan died, and then Mum, and then my ex left too, I've hidden away. I've shut out the world and lived like a house goblin in my flat.

Life carried on outside my curtains and I just... got stuck. I couldn't see a way to move forward, until I pushed myself to start visiting A Tale As Old As Time every week and made friends with Marnie. While helping out in the bookshop, I've become friends with the other shopkeepers too. It will be a thrill to work alongside them properly and be a real part of Team Ever After Street.

So what if I've told one teeny-tiny little white lie to a stern man who I'll probably never see again? It's not like I'm going to be serving seven-course meals to lords and ladyships and battling for Michelin stars. All I have to do is bake a few simple things and practise enough to get really good at it. I have to unchain the creativity that I once had and get back to who I was before life imploded in grief and despair.

I can't keep living like this. I lay in the pull-out bed with the caravan rocking side to side as the wind batters it and rain beats so hard against the roof that it's surely going to drip through one of the many patch-ups this poor old thing has had over the years to keep it watertight. I need to change my life and *make* something stick. I want somewhere stable, somewhere that's mine, something constant and reliable. My jobs until now have been uninteresting sorts of jobs. Cleaning office buildings after hours. Restocking supermarket shelves. Packing online orders in soulless warehouses. Waitressing. Factories. Just a cog in a wheel that no one ever notices or values. I want to feel like I matter to someone. I want people to walk into a spectacular tearoom on Ever After Street that's all *me*. I want to stay, and since I found Ever After Street, I've had the feeling that it wanted me to stay too, and I don't want to let it down.

I roll over and wriggle around to get comfortable on the thin mattress. It's definitely time for sleep when I'm talking about a street being sentient.

* * *

A few days later, the council have sent a commercial lease, the keys, and a contractor with a very small budget. It's my first time getting to look around inside properly, and I follow him through the tearoom as he measures up the space, dodging stacked up chairs, and tables covered with dustsheets.

'That's too much,' he says for the thousandth time, a sneer on his face at every suggestion I make for the tearoom makeover.

'How about—'

'Overbudget!' he barks, not even letting me finish the sentence.

It's very hard to transform a tearoom into Wonderland when the council have allocated you approximately £3.50.

All right, they've been a tad more generous than that, and I try to think logically while the contractor puts more numbers into his tablet and sits at a table I've hastily uncovered, muttering under his breath about how soon his next appointment is.

One thing I love is crafting. Give me a hot glue gun and a stack of paper to bend and shape into something new and I'm happy. A good chunk of the limited space in my caravan is taken up by storage boxes of my crafting materials, which are something I consider essential, even though other people may suggest clothes or food would be a better use of my storage space. But there is nothing I love more than sitting down at a table and losing myself in making something.

I'm good at painting too, so I can repaint the fading tearoom walls myself. I want to fill the place with Wonderland touches, like teapots and teacups, hats, clocks, mushrooms, and my beloved paper flowers, and I won't need a contractor for that either.

'Can you retile the floor?' I ask as inspiration strikes for something I can't do myself. 'Black and white square tiles so it looks like a chequerboard?'

The contractor has already pointed out a couple of broken floor tiles at the edges of the room, and at my suggestion, he keys a few more numbers into his tablet screen.

'Essential replacement,' he mutters begrudgingly. 'Within budget.'

Hurrah! It was starting to feel like those words weren't in his vocabulary.

'How about the shop sign? Right now it just says "Tearooms", but I want to call it The Wonderland Teapot.'

The contractor jabs at his tablet screen again but doesn't say anything, which presumably means it's also within budget.

'Can I have some pots of paint and someone to cut giant chess piece shapes out of wood?'

He raises an eyebrow at the tablet screen without bothering to look at me, and then turns it around. 'We'll replace the floor and repaint the sign. This is the remaining budget to do what you want with. Send your receipts to Mr Hastings and he'll reimburse your outgoings. Don't try to get clever. Hastings is a stickler when it comes to money. You won't be able to pull a fast one on him.'

'Wouldn't dream of it.' The thought of getting on the bad side of the scary man from the interview sends a chill down my spine.

'Good. My men will start on Monday. Will that be all?' His tone leaves me with no doubt that it *will* be all, whether I like it or not.

'Wait, you didn't check the kitchen. I want to be sure the appliances are up to date and health and safety checked.' God knows, I need all the health and safety I can get when it comes to baking.

'Kitchen? Appliances?' His face screws up like he's wondering what planet I've recently landed from. 'You have a food preparation area. There's a fridge for keeping things cold and a kettle for making water hot.'

'That's it?' I look over my shoulder at the doorway to the back room. I'd assumed it was a kitchen, but the contractor was waiting outside when I arrived this morning and I didn't have time to investigate. 'But this is a tearoom. Where am I supposed to make the food?'

'The previous owner made everything at home and brought it in. Is that a problem?'

'No... just unexpected. I, er...'

'As far as I'm aware, you're only here on a trial. Hastings won't be approving any rewiring of the kitchen or purchase of appliances without a long-term lease and a *very* good reason.'

Brilliant. Now what am I supposed to do? I have no kitchen. The one-hob stove in the caravan isn't going to get me far, and I can't encroach on Marnie's kindness for much longer. Running a tearoom is going to involve a lot of early-morning and late-night baking to get everything ready for the day ahead – I can't do that in someone else's house.

The contractor is on his way out the door without giving me a chance to ask anything else. 'Cheerio,' he says, despite being the least cheerful person I've met in recent months. 'And good luck.'

The silent 'you're going to need it' is etched in the smirk on his face, and the fear that he's right follows me like a cloud as I go inside and look around my oven-less kitchen. There's a fridge, an industrial sized kettle, and a four-slice extra-wide toaster on the unit. There's plenty of counter space for food preparation, a large sink area with drying racks and a draining board, bread bins and cupboards for food storage, and a walk-in cupboard with plates and cutlery stacked inside, and that's it.

I was expecting a kitchen like you'd find behind the scenes in a restaurant. I assumed there would be at least some way of cooking food. I'd never thought about how or where Lilith prepared her food. I just assumed it was all done in this little room that was off-limits to customers.

Have I bitten off more than I can chew? Assumed that having a tearoom of my own will magically unlock all the recipes I can't remember and turn me into a younger version of Mary Berry, when the most complicated thing I've successfully cooked in recent years has been cheese on toast? I can feel panic rising and I fight it by concentrating on the things I *can* control, like turning this little space into an all-singing, all-dancing Wonderland to inspire awe in children and adults alike. There has to be a solution to the kitchen issue. I don't know what it is yet but something will come to me. It *has* to.

* * *

Two weeks later and The Wonderland Teapot on Ever After Street is ready to open. Contractors came and broke up the old floor tiles and replaced them with a black and white chessboard of shiny new squares. The boring sign on the shopfront has been repainted with an iridescent white background, and 'The Wonderland Teapot' is painted in swirly lettering of eye-catching pink and purple Cheshire-Cat-style stripes.

The interior of the tearoom is decked out with Lilith's vintage chairs and tables, and I've gone through a million glue sticks and should've bought shares in a fabric paint company. I've stencilled roman numerals around the edges of each tablecloth and put hands in the centre so each table looks like the face of a clock, and each one has got a centrepiece of a bouquet of roses, made from playing cards, displayed in mismatched teapots.

I've painted the wall on the left red and stood a row of black and white wooden chess pieces along it, each one about five-foot high, apart from the king and queen, which are suitably taller, and there are the giant paper flowers I've been making. They're all the height of an adult, with stick-on googly eyes in an array of bright colours like the talking flowers Alice encounters in the Disney movie. The counter is along the far side of the shop floor, and I've painstakingly stencilled my favourite Wonderland quote on the wall behind it – *Alice had begun to think that very few things indeed were really impossible* – and it's surrounded by a hotch-potch of different size flowers in a rainbow of colours, and on the other side of the counter is the door to the customer bathroom, where I've added pieces of wood around the handle and painted them with a face, so it looks like the talking doorknob Alice first meets when she falls down the rabbit hole.

On the right-hand side of the room, I've shifted the nearest tables inwards and created a space for a game of flamingo croquet. There's a strip of artificial grass, and pink plastic flamingo-shaped clubs for little ones to have a go at knocking the hedgehog-shaped balls through the playing card arches.

I've turned broken teacups and teapots into decorative planters at every opportunity, and the display case at the front of the counter will be filled with delicious, dainty treats... that I made.

Okay, that I made *if* anyone asks.

The reality is that I've been so busy with making the tearoom look like Tweedle Dum and Tweedle Dee have exploded in it that practising any kind of baking has had to come second, and it's *very* hard to bake anything with the single hob in the caravan.

Which is why it's now 11 p.m. and I'm walking around the local supermarket, desperately looking for things to serve my customers on opening day, which is in... approximately ten hours.

It's not like I haven't tried. The other night in the caravan, I followed a child's recipe to make chocolate fairy cakes and took the results up to the house for Marnie and Darcy to try. Darcy wasn't brave enough, and Marnie took one tiny nibble and politely suggested that the caravan stove might be on the blink. I used to be able to make fairy cakes, and now... no matter how hard I try, something always goes wrong. My tearoom dream depends on me being able to get it right, and I'm just... not.

So I've had an idea. I can buy things from the supermarket, unpack them, decorate them for my own unique Wonderland twist, and serve them in the tearoom, and no one will be any the wiser.

I'm not proud of it, but needs must. And it's not like the local supermarket is going to mind, is it? And it's only temporary – until I can afford to rent another flat with a kitchen. Until then, absolutely no one is going to know, and if I add my own spin to things, it's not *exactly* like taking someone else's work and passing it off as my own.

I fill a trolley with the regular things I'll need to buy anyway. Loaves of bread and tubs of butter and other sandwich fillings, and then I add a few boxes of cupcakes with swirls of icing on top, tray-bake brownies that I can cut up, packages of scones, crumpets, and custard tarts.

'Ooh, someone's having a party,' the checkout woman exclaims as I pile my goodies onto the checkout belt.

I give her a tight grin and make a mental note to use the self-service checkouts in future. She might get suspicious if she sees me buying this amount of stuff again.

I lug home bags of shopping and pass one of my Cheshire Cat signs in a tree on the way. I bought wooden outlines of the cat's face and tail, painted them in pink and purple stripes, and strategically placed them in trees and hedges around Ever After Street and the surrounding area, intended to look like the cat has started to disappear, like he does in the films. I've attached laminated tags to them, advertising the opening of The Wonderland Teapot. I got posters printed up and every shop has got one displayed in their windows for me, and I also got some postcards printed and every shopkeeper took a handful and promised to pop them into the bags with every customer's purchase.

I just hope it will be enough because I've never wanted anything to be a success more than I want this to. This opportunity is perfect for me – I just need to be perfect for *it*.

3

It's opening day and I've been here since 7 a.m., unpacking everything I bought last night and decorating it. There are the trays of brownies that I've cut into individual squares and affixed rice paper 'Eat Me' tags to. Red velvet cupcakes with swirls of cream cheese icing on top that I've showered with red heart sprinkles. The scones have been given a dusting of edible glitter. I got circle-shaped shortbread biscuits, added cat ears made out of pretzels, and iced them in pink and purple stripes.

As I finish each item, I arrange them on my homemade cake stands, made by gluing upside-down teacups between plates that decrease in size as they go upwards, and display them in the glass case in front of the counter where I've stood many times and chosen which of Lilith's treats to devour that day.

A part of the wall beside the counter is painted with chalkboard paint, and I've added sandwich options in a rainbow of colourful chalk writing, alongside tearoom staples like toasted teacakes, crumpets, hot buttered toast, and scones with clotted cream.

I'm cutting apples into thin slices to form a rose shape to put on top of each custard tart, when there's a knock at the door. It's half past eight. Who on earth is that going to be? Early customers? I can see a flash of colour standing outside the frosted glass panels in the door, and I pull it slightly ajar and peer out.

'Twinkle twinkle, little bat, how I wonder what you're at.' Standing on the cobblestones outside is the Mad Hatter, who winks at me with a grin that's as bright as the rest of his *exceptionally* bright outfit.

I recognise the quote from Wonderland immediately, and the costume the man is wearing is unmistakably inspired by the Hatter, from his lime green jacket to his blue spiky hair and the stack of top hats sitting on his head. What on earth is this? Are eager customers dressing up now? I hadn't considered others might embrace the Alice theme with such dedication.

Unfortunately this one is a bit *too* eager and I'm going to have to put him off. 'I'm sorry, we're not open yet. If you could come back in half an hour...'

'ello! Mad Hatter reporting for duty.' He salutes me by raising a hand to the second of the stack of three top hats balanced on his very bright head of hair.

I'm unsure of what he's going on about but I try to be as polite as possible as I close the door. I really need to get those apple rose tarts finished, I can't let a customer in at this time of day. 'As I said, we're not open ye—'

His hand shoots out and holds the door. His voice, which was high-pitched and childlike, drops to a more normal tone. 'I'm not a customer. I'm supposed to be starting work here today? I'm the Mad Hatter, in case it wasn't obvious.'

Work here? *What*? He must be confused. Or the 'mad' bit of Mad Hatter is alarmingly appropriate. 'I'm the owner. I think I'd know if I'd hired a Mad Hatter. You must be in the wrong place.' Even as I say it, I wonder how many *Alice in Wonderland*-themed establishments there *are* in the area. It's not like he's going to be starting at *another* Alice-themed tearoom, is it? It sets off an uneasy feeling in my stomach because this is a bit too much of a coincidence.

'Oh, for the good ferret's sake, don't tell me they didn't tell you?' He throws his hands up and looks skywards, annoyed at an unknown someone.

'Tell me what?' The uneasy feeling grows.

'The council. They're getting behind your *Alice in Wonderland* theme and thought The Wonderland Teapot needed more than just Alice.' He indicates to what little he can see of me through the gap in the door, which I'm still holding ajar because it's quite scary to see someone so *bright* at this time in the morning. And unexpected. And I'm not entirely sure this isn't some kind of elaborate joke, or possible robbery attempt. Although what a potential burglar would expect to get *before* opening time is debateable, and burglars tend to go for more understated costumes than this guy, who can almost definitely be seen from space, if not further. Also, knocking on the front door would be a new approach to burglary.

'They've hired me to play the Hatter. I'm also a magician.' He holds a hand up and clicks his fingers, and a playing card appears between them, ostensibly from thin air but clearly from a hidden pocket in his sleeve or something similar. 'I'm here to entertain the diners and help to give them a real mind-boggling experience, complete with Wonderland-style bonkersness.' He hands the card to me. 'You can keep that.'

I look down at the card in my hand. The Queen of Hearts. How fitting.

Taking the card has meant I've opened the door further and I can't help looking at him. He's got on black cargo trousers with an array of pockets all around them, and a button-down shirt with a pattern so loud you can almost *hear* it screaming underneath the green faux-leather jacket. His hair is the brightest shade of electric blue, sticking out in hairsprayed spikes, almost like you'd see on a cartoon character who'd just been electrocuted. There are silver hoops through each of his pierced earlobes, and his eyes are outlined with thick black eyeliner. I thought I'd done well with my blue short-sleeved Alice dress and white pinafore with card suits painted on it, and my hair is blonde and past my shoulders anyway, so all I had to do was add a black bow headband, but his outfit really is impressive.

'Am I allowed to come in?' His question makes me realise I've been staring at him for an abnormally long time.

'Oh. I... er...' Am I supposed to take his word for it? Let this stranger into my tearoom? While I'm debating internally, he must realise how uneasy this has made me because he's pulled his phone from one of the many pockets of his trousers.

'Ahh, I get it. Who the heck *would* let this weird bananagram into their shop without some kind of confirmation, right?' He's already putting a number into the phone. 'Just a tick, we can get this straightened out with a quick call.'

I stand in the doorway watching him, the stack of hats on his head bouncing around every time he looks down at the phone. The three top hats are in Disney's animated Hatter colours. The biggest one that rests on top of his blue hair is dark green and the Hatter's infamous 'In this style, 10/6' is written on a card and tucked into the wide yellow ribbon that runs around the brim. On top of that hat is a smaller top hat in a light green colour, and on top of that one is a smaller one again, in bright yellow this time.

''ello, treacle,' Hatter says into the phone when it's answered. 'Yeah, it's me. Can you patch me through?' There's a pause and then it sounds like he interrupts the person on the other end. 'I don't care if he's in a meeting, this is important. Yes, *important*. No, not my usual kind of "important".' His brown eyes meet mine and he rolls them at the phone and turns around to face the street, and I can hear faint hold music coming through the handset.

Eventually the music clicks off and there are the strains of an angry voice on the other end.

'Good morning to you too,' Hatter says into the phone with a cheery-sounding voice. 'Yeah, I've just arrived at the tearoom and the poor woman who works here…' He turns back to me. 'It's Cleo, isn't it?'

I nod. How does he know my name? Is that a sign that this is legit?

'Cleo wasn't expecting me,' he continues into the phone. 'You wouldn't happen to have forgotten to tell her, would you?'

I'm assuming the person on the other end says something along the lines of 'you tell her', because the Hatter says, 'I have told her, but would *you* trust a random guy turning up on your doorstep at half eight in the morning dressed as the Mad Hatter?' There's a pause while the other person speaks again, and then the Hatter holds the phone out to me.

I take it gingerly and hold it up to my ear, wondering who the heck is going to be on the other end.

'Miss Jordan.'

I yelp in surprise. I'd recognise that smug voice and tone dripping with sarcasm anywhere. It's Mr Hastings from the interview. This guy has got his direct number? This guy can seemingly interrupt meetings and be put directly through to scary Mr Hastings? No one ever gave me his number *or* invited contact if needed.

'I see you're already having issues and you're not even open yet. Not quite off to a flying start, are we?'

'Er, not issues as such, Mr Hastings,' I stutter out. There's something about this man that turns me into a wibbling wreck. Someone so confident and self-assured only serves to highlight how unconfident and un-self-assured *I* am. 'Only I didn't know there was supposed to be a Mad Hatter working here. I thought...' I swallow hard and force myself into a modicum of assertiveness. 'I thought it was the sort of thing that would be up to me, or at the very least, that someone might discuss with me first.'

'We're all busy, Miss Jordan,' Mr Hastings huffs into the phone. 'You bear no responsibility for hiring employees during the trial period. The council decided to take your theme and run with it. I spoke to my daughter – you remember I told you about her – and we decided that the Mad Hatter is the most recognisable character after Alice herself and no Wonderland would be complete without him.'

'Well, yes, but...' I try to summon the courage to tell him that I would've liked a say in who works in the tearoom that I'm supposed to be running. This is my idea, my project, and I certainly wasn't expecting someone else to be part of it.

Mr Hastings carries on as if I haven't spoken. 'And we realised we had the perfect candidate already working for us, and all it took is a quick reshuffling of staff, and Bob's yer uncle, one *Mad* Hatter who does some kind of nonsense with card tricks. Kiddies will love it.'

The emphasis he puts on 'mad' makes me feel slightly alarmed and I look over at the guy who is scuffing his bright yellow boots against each other as he stands outside.

'Afternoon tea with a touch of magic will add a whole new dimension to your quirky theme. I can only apologise for the over-sight in failing to mention it to you.' It sounds like he begrudges even having to use the word 'apologise', God forbid he actually had to say sorry for anything. 'Good luck with... it.'

That 'it' does *not* sound like he's talking about the tearoom in a general sense. 'Him?' I ask, wondering if it's a good idea to question the boss.

He laughs. 'Oh, I suspect by the end of the day, "it" will be your chosen form of address too. Now if you don't mind, Miss Jordan, I really am too busy for this needless interruption.'

'I didn't—' The dial tone sounds in my ear before I can protest that *I* didn't interrupt anything.

'He's hung up.' I pass the phone back to the Mad Hatter.

'He does that.'

The awkwardness is tangible. I didn't expect him and he didn't expect to be so unexpected, and now he's standing with his hands in his pockets, waiting for me to invite him in.

My instinct is to tell him where to go. I don't want or need any additional employees, particularly ones that I didn't know about until five minutes ago, but I don't think I can argue with Mr Hastings. And all right, a Mad Hatter in Wonderland is actually a very good idea, I'm just annoyed that no one thought to even consult me about it.

In my mind, I frantically scan across the food preparation area. I can't be caught serving supermarket-bought goods, not by anyone. Have I left any packaging strewn around? Any hint that those goodies filling the display case were *not* baked by me?

'Sorry about all this. Clapping eyes on me first thing in the morning must be a shock for anyone. Can we start over? I'm Bram.' He holds a hand out for me to shake.

I transfer the playing card into my other hand and reach out to shake his. He's got warm hands with long nimble fingers, if the speed at which he produced the playing card earlier is anything to go by. 'Bram? I've never heard that name before. Short for... Bramble? Bramley Apple?'

He laughs. 'Abraham. But no one's called me that since the day I was born, other than my father. And I'm sure you're heard of Bram Stoker, the nineteenth century writer of *Dracula*, which was also short for Abraham.'

'Well, aren't you brimming with fun facts?' I say, despite the fact it had never before occurred to me that Bram Stoker was short for anything and that's actually quite interesting. I'm still trying to remember if I've left any incriminating evidence lying around. It's bad enough that I'll be bluffing my way through Unbirthday parties and afternoon teas, the absolute last thing I needed was to have to cover it up in front of another staff member as well, particularly one who has clearly got contacts at the council. It's even more of a liability that he will discover my sordid supermarket secret and report back to them about my underhanded misrepresentations.

Speaking of underhanded misrepresentations, it's now quarter to nine and I really need to get back to mine. 'It's getting late, you'd better come in.'

'You know what they say – gotta make fudge while the sun shines!'

'Hay. Make hay while the sun shines.'

'Who'd want to make hay unless they're a horse?' His face screws up in confusion and then he peers at me and narrows his eyes. '*Are* you a horse?'

'Do I look like a— You know what, don't answer that.' I pull the door open and he stops to tip his hat to me. The stack of three hats on his head must be sewn together because when he lifts the bottom one, the other two stay attached, and it's the most bizarre sight that makes me smile despite my misgivings about this arrangement.

I can't help watching him in amused confusion as he stops in the middle of the room and looks around in wonder. 'Oh, my fur and whiskers, look at this!'

It's another Wonderland-ism that the White Rabbit says in the book, and if nothing else, I can appreciate someone who knows my favourite book as well as I do.

He spins around in a circle like he doesn't know where to look first. He reaches up to touch one of the teapots I've got hanging from the ceiling with colourful ribbons pouring out of their spouts. They're above head height, but apparently not too far up that they can't be fiddled with.

'Can you not—'

Before I've had a chance to ask him not to touch the decorations, he's bent down and picked up a wooden mushroom. They're cheap garden ornaments, but I painted their caps red and added glow-in-the-dark white spots. He turns it around between his hands, and— 'Flamingo croquet!'

He drops the mushroom and *races* across to the strip of artificial grass and picks up a flamingo club. They're not adult size and he has to bend over to hold it and putt the hedgehog ball through the playing card arch. He misses and it rolls across the room.

I huff and go over to get it, intending to confiscate it before he tries again, but he's already put the club down and is now taking a selfie with one of the giant paper flowers.

'Holy frogs and donkeys, this place is *amazing*.' He's still looking around in awe, and his eyelinered brown eyes fall on me. 'Did you do all this yourself? Because I've seen the council restoration budgets and they're not *that* generous.'

'Yeah, mostly. I love crafting and I love *Alice in Wonderland*, so...'

'It was a match made in heaven. This is *gorgeous*.'

'Thank you.' I can't help blushing because he sounds genuinely bowled over and it gives me a little thrill of hope that customers will feel the same way. Apart from Marnie and Darcy and a couple of the other shopkeepers who have brought things over, no one's really seen inside yet. He's the first stranger with no biased reason for being kind.

'Wow. I feel like I could work here for a week and I still wouldn't have seen everything.' Now he's twirling the red and black card suit bunting that's hanging in the front window, and then he turns back to the painted lettering on the wall behind the counter. 'Good choice of quote. I would've gone with "we're all mad here".'

'Not all of us are mad...'

'Ahh, some of us are mad enough for everyone.' He gives me a lopsided grin that seems like a well-practised response to something he's heard many times.

That word again. Everything seems to be coming back to that word this morning. '*Are* you mad?'

'Oh, undoubtedly so. Completely bonkers. Team Basketcase all the way. As barking as a box of soapy frogs. Barmy as the March Hare. Got a kangaroo loose in the top paddock. An aardvark in my arcade. But I wouldn't be much of a Mad Hatter if I wasn't.' He inclines his head towards me and his stack of hats slip forward. 'At your service.'

I don't intend to smile at this uninvited man who's just invaded my business, but I can't help it.

'But I'll tell you a secret...' His voice has risen to that higher pitch again.

'All the best people are?' I offer.

'Ah ha! That's what I was going to say. High fi—' He goes to high five me but pulls his hand back sharply. 'I'm sorry, I was going to suggest a high five but I momentarily forgot that I'm not currently entertaining children and no adult with an ounce of decorum would do a high five. My deepest apologies for being so painfully uncool.'

His look of shame makes me laugh. 'I'm a thirty-four-year-old dressed as Alice. We passed uncool long ago.'

'Your costume looks great. This whole thing is so... clever. Unusual. People will come from miles around. It'll be a real success.'

'I hope so.' His words give rise to a fear that I've tried not to think about. What if Alice is *too* quirky for most people? What if people liked Lilith's non-fairy-tale-themed tearoom as a break from all the Disney-ish shops on Ever After Street? What if grinning cats and over-sized flowers are scary for little ones and people don't want to come here? What if I've put all this work in and it falls flat on its face within days?

When I blink back from the anxious thoughts, Bram has shrugged his bag off his shoulder and is holding it out in the direction of the kitchen area. 'All right to go through? I'll just put this out of the way.' He disappears through the staff-only door without waiting for an answer.

'It's upstai—'

'I know,' he calls back from halfway up the stairs. 'I used to help Lilith out all the time.'

Did he? Is that what Mr Hastings meant by someone who already works for them? I glance at one of the many clocks dotted around the walls. I don't have time to think about it. It's ten minutes to opening time and I've still got roses made from apples to arrange on top of supermarket-bought custard tarts.

There's a teapot sculpture on the counter, one that Mickey from The Mermaid's Treasure Trove gave me for nothing because it had a chip in it. I've arranged it on a fancy plate, glued fake grass around it and added foam roses coming out of its spout, and there's a spray of playing cards arranged on wire so it looks like they're bursting out of the open lid. I tuck the Queen of Hearts card he gave me in amongst them, wash my hands, and return to what I was doing before the unexpected interruption.

Within a few minutes, Bram comes back downstairs and he can probably see the concentration on my face as I manipulate thin strips of apple into a shape that starts to resemble a rose because he stays mercifully quiet as he watches me.

'Now *that's* magic.' His tone sounds genuinely appreciative as I finish one off with a sprinkle of edible glitter and slide it onto the cake stand display. 'Did you make all this yourself?'

'Yes!' I bark a bit too sharply.

'Wow. You must've been baking since 3 a.m.'

'Something like that,' I mutter. My own defensiveness is going to give me away faster than anything else at this rate. He has no reason to suspect I *haven't* made all of this stuff myself – it's me who feels guilty about it and I'm projecting that guilt onto everyone else.

'Can I help?'

'No, thank you. I don't need your help. I don't know why the council thinks I do.' I'm trying not to let my feelings cloud my judgement, but I'm hurt and feeling undermined that Mr Hastings and his cronies have so little faith in me that they've sent in some kind of tearoom babysitter. This was supposed to be my venture, something that I was going to do on my own, for me. I had no intention of hiring any staff. I've been let down before when it comes to running a tearoom, because that's what other people always do – they let you down.

'They don't.'

I finish another apple rose on another custard tart and slide it onto the display stand and then start the next one. It takes me a second to realise he's answering my previous sentence and not the thought in my head. 'No? Then what exactly are you doing here?'

'Anything you want me to. You're the boss. I'm just an entertainer, here to amuse the customers with card tricks and bonkersness. I can help wait tables or serve people when it's busy, and I'll even do the washing up if you like.'

I let out a reluctant laugh. 'I don't know if anyone has ever uttered a more alluring line than that.'

'Washing up wins everyone over in the end.' He laughs too. 'Look at what you've done with this place. The one thing that's blatantly obvious is that you don't need *any* help whatsoever. I won't get in the way, I promise. You won't even know I'm here.'

I look at him. Just under six foot of blaring colour, blue hair, and three hats. This is *not* someone who is going to blend into the background and let me get on with things.

'Hey, maybe it'll be so busy that you'll need my help. So many customers that one person can't keep up. That's what every business owner on Ever After Street wants, right?'

Am I a business owner on Ever After Street? I thought I was, but him turning up has left me feeling like I'm subject to the council's every whim, and I clearly have no say whatsoever until I pass this three-month trial. Right now, I'm an employee of the council. It's only when they extend my lease that I'll get any autonomy over my own business, and who knows what could go wrong in that time.

'Come on, Hatter and Alice serving tea and cake. It'll be fun.'

'Why do I think you'd say that about things like jumping out of a plane attached to a bungee cord or eating the world's hottest chilli pepper?' I concentrate on another apple rose rather than looking at him in all his overly jolly brightness.

'Nah. I don't like heights. Or flying. Or spicy food, for that matter. I'm quite boring really.'

Now *that*, I do not believe.

At my lack of response, he disappears through the doorway into the back room and I hear the kettle click on. 'What are you doing?'

'Tea?' His voice sounds confused from the food preparation room.

'It's...' I glance at the many clocks on the wall. The clocks were a terrible idea. Each one says a slightly different time. I take an average and guess. '...8.57 a.m.!'

'Always time for tea!' he calls back in that cheery, high-pitched Hatter voice again.

'There's no one here.'

'It's not for the no one who's not here.'

By the time I've tried to untangle that riddle of a sentence, he's returned to the shop floor and he puts a mug on the counter in front of me.

'Oh. Thanks.' I hadn't realised he was making tea for *me* and I feel guilty for being so hard on him, although my benevolent feelings don't last long when he opens the display case and helps himself to a red velvet cupcake. 'Oi!'

'I'm making them look popular.' A dimple dents only his left cheek as he gives me a grin and bites into the cake, and then lifts his mug to cover his mouth and carries on talking. 'Think of how many people will come in and go "they're going fast, they must be *really* good, I'll have to try one of those!"'

'That's not how it works,' I huff in annoyance. Eating the stock before opening time does not equate with his aforementioned promise of not knowing he's here.

He swallows the mouthful and slurps down more tea. 'Look, there's *no* point in working in a tearoom if I can't have tea and cake for breakfast. You can always nip home and make more if we run out.'

No. No, I can't. But I can't tell him that, of course.

'Ooh, that's nice,' he says after another mouthful. 'That tastes like—'

'It doesn't taste *like* anything. It's original.' Knowing my luck, he will have eaten those cupcakes from the supermarket before and will recognise the taste.

He raises both eyebrows at the tone in my voice, and finishes the rest of the cupcake in merciful silence, and guilt needles at me for being too harsh. The last thing I needed was someone taste-testing the stock, and my fear of being found out is growing by the minute. How could I ever explain to someone that I've *forgotten* how to bake? How could I expect anyone to understand that I don't have a kitchen to even be able to try?

He downs the last of his tea at the same time as I finish the last apple rose, sprinkle the custard tart with glitter and put it into the display case, closing the door with a pointed click in case he gets any ideas about eating more of my limited stock.

'Nearly opening time.' He looks around the clocks on the wall. 'Well, by three of the clocks anyway. They don't all agree. You know what they say – a person with one clock knows the time, a person with seventy-two is always late.'

'I don't think anyone's ever said that.'

'Well, I like to be different.' He does that happy shrug again. 'You want to do the honours?'

He's standing by the door, inviting me to open it, and I can't help thinking that it's quite considerate to let me open the doors on the first day. I just hope it's the first of many.

4

Far from hordes of Gryphons and Mock Turtles waiting outside at opening time, customers have been trickling in over the course of the morning. It started off with a couple of old ladies wanting hot buttered toast and being quite alarmed at the changes since the last time they were here, then came harried parents having dropped kids off at school, and curious people who had seen my Cheshire Cat advertising signs or heard about The Wonderland Teapot in other ways. I didn't expect to be fending off armies of customers clamouring for tea, and for a first morning, the shop hasn't been empty once, although it hasn't been full either.

A couple come in with a young boy, probably around the age of four. He's got eyes that are red from crying and a frowny face that looks like he might be mid-tantrum, but from the moment they open the door, he can't take his eyes off Bram. The parents order sandwiches, and the young lad jabs angrily at a cupcake in the display unit, and Bram notices the extra attention. They sit down as I make their cheese and ham sandwiches, and he goes over to introduce himself. The boy stares at him in awe, and Bram kneels on the floor to be at the same height, shaking the boy's hand, keeping up a constant conversation, flitting between talking to the kid and the adults with ease. When I've put their sandwiches on a tray and added the pot of tea they ordered, he scrambles up and comes to get it with a conspiratorial wink.

He carries the tray over and unloads the teapot, cups, and sandwiches onto the table, but when he gets to the little boy's cake, his hands move so fast that I barely see them move at all, but the plate he puts down is empty. The boy stares at it open-mouthed and then at Bram, who matches his open-mouthed shock.

'You've eaten it already!' It's his squeakyish Hatter voice again, the one that sounds childlike and unthreatening.

'You!' The boy points at Bram, clearly knowing he's done something with the cake.

'It was right there!' Bram consults the parents. 'You saw it, right?'

The parents play along and Bram scratches his head. Well, his hat. 'Now, where could it have gone?' He looks around the tearoom like someone might've taken it. 'If you haven't eaten it, maybe the White Rabbit took it? Did anyone see a Mad March Hare running off with it?'

He kneels down again. 'Oh no, wait, I can see exactly where it's gone.' He reaches behind the boy's head and extracts the cake, seemingly from behind his ear. A trick as old as time, but usually completed with a fifty-pence piece rather than baked goods. 'Now why did you put it behind there?'

The boy clutches his fingers for it, and Bram goes to hand it to him and then pulls it away again. 'Maybe the cake doesn't want to be eaten! Maybe it's going to disappear again!' He waves a hand between the cake and the boy, and sure enough, the cake disappears. I mean, it doesn't *really* disappear, but I can't work out where he's stashed it.

The boy gasps in surprise, laughing with glee, his tantrum long forgotten. 'Again!'

This time Bram does another hand movement and the cake reappears on his palm, and the boy is rigid with sheer delight, and squeals joyfully when Bram waves his hand and makes the cake disappear yet again. I have *never* seen anyone move their hands so fast.

Bram stands up and looks around, like he's looking for the missing cake, and then he spots it again, and kneels to extract it from behind the boy's ear again. 'Now it's behind the other ear! You've got to stop hiding food round there, you know. You'll have columns of ants following you everywhere you go. Look, here comes one now!'

He points to an invisible something on the floor and when the boy looks, he removes the cake again, twirls around behind him, and replaces it from the other side. Once the cake is safely on the plate in front of him, Bram bows and tips his hats to the family, but the lad is far more interested in Bram himself. The parents invite him to sit, which he does, and makes easy conversation for a few minutes. He takes the stack of hats off and messes his hair up, making it even crazier than it was anyway, and dipping his head to let the curious boy touch his blue hair.

The dad takes a photo of them together, and when they leave, the boy runs back and hugs Bram, and as they walk away, he's waving all the way down the street until they get out of sight, and Bram waves back from the doorway.

My elbows hurting makes me I realise I've been leaning on the counter, mesmerised by the scene in front of me. I can feel my heart melting. I couldn't have done that. My Alice costume didn't even register on the young lad's radar, but Bram captured his imagination from the first moment. He gave him his full undivided attention and did exactly what was needed to turn his frown upside down.

And Bram kind of... came to life. For someone so colourful, when he was entertaining that little lad, he lit up brighter than a planet in the night sky.

He comes back inside and starts clearing the table without being asked.

'You're very good at that.' It feels like the first nice thing I've said to him all morning.

'Clearing tables?'

'No.' I glance at the empty cups and plates he's loading onto a tray. 'Well, that too, but I'm not sure that's much of an acquired skill. What you just did. Doing magic. Entertaining kids.' He's done a couple of card tricks for other customers so far this morning, but nothing like that. 'You knew exactly what that lad needed.'

'Was that a compliment?' he asks without looking up.

Usually, when faced with a question like that, my natural instinct is to say something sarcastic and turn it into a joke, but I decide to stand by it. 'Yes, it was. That little boy *loved* you.'

'Just trying to make someone's day a bit brighter. If you can make someone smile when they otherwise wouldn't have smiled then that's a day well spent. Doesn't matter if they're four or eighty-four – everyone needs a smile sometimes.' It's his normal voice again. In a few short hours, I've noticed the difference between how he speaks when he's in character and how he speaks when he isn't.

I didn't know what to expect with the lunchtime rush, but it starts picking up as we get closer to midday, and there are orders for sandwiches and tea from the menu, and the display case is looking decidedly decimated by the time Marnie stops by in the early afternoon.

'This place looks amazing,' she says, even though she's helped me with decorating and has seen it many times before. 'I couldn't help noticing the steady stream of customers coming in all morning too. How's it—' She catches sight of Bram when he stands up from where he was crouching to tidy the flamingo croquet area and she gives him a wave. He tips his hat stack to her and she smiles fondly.

'Why didn't you tell me you'd got Bram working here?' She leans over the counter and whispers to avoid being overheard.

'I didn't *know* I'd got Bram working here,' I mutter, trying to cobble together a sandwich for my own lunch but I think I've got the ratio of cream cheese to cucumber wrong. Never mind my baking skills, even my sandwich-making skills are threatening to desert me now. 'Who is he, anyway? Do you know him?'

'Cleo! He's the eyelinered magician who operates the carousel!'

'Oh! *That's* what Mr Hastings meant by someone who already works for them.' It's such a Homer Simpson moment that I should have shouted 'D'oh!' out loud.

'Did the eyeliner and magician bit not give it away?'

I glance over at him. 'I think I was blinded by the blue hair and green jacket.'

'I can't believe you two are working together. He was born to play the Mad Hatter. You'll love him. He's a spectacular nut.'

I can't help laughing at the description. Despite having only met him this morning, it seems accurate.

'Anyway, I can't stop. Darcy's running his "gardening for mental wellbeing" class at the castle and I've left Mrs Potts on her own, and honestly, cats are terrible bookshop assistants. She'd sell books in exchange for Dreamies.' She points to a salted caramel cupcake in the display unit. 'I can't leave without trying one of those though.'

I use the tongs to get one out and she grabs it before I've had a chance to put it on one of the spiral patterned napkins that are stacked under the counter.

'Oh my God,' she says with a mouthful. 'That's gorgeous. *How* did you go from that chocolate thing you forced me into tasting the other night to being able to bake things like this?'

'That was bad luck,' I mumble. My cheeks have flared red. Even to Marnie, I haven't admitted that I'm stocking the tearoom with definitely *not* home-baked goods, and there's no way Bram hasn't overheard this conversation.

'I knew that stove was on the blink.' She raises the cake in a toast. 'Here, give me two more, will you, I'll have another and take one back for Darcy.'

We've got pop-up cardboard boxes for takeaways and I grab one and load two cakes into it, and refuse the ten-pound note Marnie gets out of her pocket. 'Opening day special for best friends who happen to work on Ever After Street.'

'Awww.' Marnie admonishes me but takes the box appreciatively and rushes back over the road to A Tale As Old As Time.

I continue making my sandwich, aware of Bram's presence. 'Don't tell me off for giving my friend a couple of cakes on the house. I wouldn't be working here if it wasn't for Marnie. She's helped me out so much. The least she deserves is a couple of cakes.'

'Marnie's great. She runs a bookshop – it's humanly impossible to dislike someone who runs a bookshop.' He looks up and tries to catch my eyes. 'I'm not here to judge anyone for anything. I don't know why you think I am.'

'I don't.' I didn't intend to look into his eyes, especially when I'm telling a lie, but they're deep and brown and impossible to look away from. That whole direct line to the head of the local council thing has made me think he's going to report back to them. If I do something I shouldn't, he's going to mention it, isn't he? And if he finds out I'm serving supermarket-bought cakes, it would be the end of this dream for good.

The shop is empty for the first time today, and this is the first opportunity I've had to eat something resembling lunch, and I press the upper slice of bread onto my sandwich, cut it in half, and turn around to throw the knife into the sink, and in the seconds that my back is turned, a hand sneaks out and steals half of it.

'Bram!'

He shoves it into his mouth and grins around it. 'Cheers!'

'You cheeky beggar,' I mutter, pretending to be angrier than I am. He hasn't had lunch yet either, and his mischievous grin makes it impossible to scold him without laughing.

He sits on one of the stools and leans his elbows on the counter and takes a more civilised bite, and I back up to lean against the unit behind the counter opposite him.

'Marnie made me realise who you are,' I say casually. 'The magician who operates the carousel and entertains bored children while their parents are busy shopping, which explains how you were so good with that lad this morning.'

'My father would tell you I'm good with kids because I have a similar mental age. To be fair, that four-year-old was probably a *lot* more mature than I am.'

The underlying bitterness in his tone intrigues me. It sounds like he's trying to make a joke out of something he doesn't find funny.

I've seen him from a distance. I've always really wanted to go on the carousel, but every time I've thought about it, it's been full of screaming children and I've felt too old. 'Your hair is usually dark, isn't it?'

'It is.' He twists a finger of his free hand around one of his blue spikes. 'But if you can't have blue hair when playing the Mad Hatter, when can you?'

I don't know why it makes me laugh, but it does. 'Fair point.'

'A few vats of colour stripper and bleach later, here we are. My hair is blue and no one told me how much blue dye bleeds, so now *everything* else in my house is also blue. My bathroom looks like

Eiffel 65 live there. You know, "Blue (Da Ba Dee)"?' He sings the earworm song from the Nineties, which will now undoubtedly be stuck in my head for the rest of the week.

I know he goes to the Ever After Street staff meetings because Marnie's mentioned him, but my involvement with the street until now has only ever been casual, helping out if the bookshop is busy, so I've never been to one of the meetings where everyone who works here gathers outside and there's tea and cake. 'Why have you left the carousel?'

He thinks before answering. 'My plans changed. I was going to do something else but it fell through at the last minute and they'd already hired my replacement, so I couldn't go back either. The council were looking for a Mad Hatter, and I'm the obvious choice, you know, being totally mad and all that.' He winks at me, although I'm not sure that being first choice for a character who's known for being off their rocker is the greatest compliment.

'Will you miss the carousel?'

'Yes and no. I love the old-fashioned magic of the ride, the way something so simple creates such wonder, no matter your age. But the hours are long and unpredictable. I don't close until long after the shops do, and I've got to be "always on", you know? I'm there to entertain anyone who wants to be entertained, whenever they want to be entertained. Some days can leave you feeling like a commodity being pawed at from all sides. I've been doing it for a couple of years now and I was ready for a change. Something a bit more serious.' He flashes both dark eyebrows at me. 'Something to keep me out of trouble.'

It makes me feel like a headteacher dealing with a naughty schoolboy who's been sent to my office for the umpteenth time. 'Do you get in trouble a lot?'

His grin is as bright as his lime green jacket, and when he

answers, it's the nasally Hatter voice again. 'Depends on who's asking and whether they want me to.'

He's got crinkles and smile lines around his eyes, making him look like he smiles and laughs a lot, and I can't help smiling at his cheekiness. 'I think we'll have enough trouble around here without you causing more.'

'I'll be on my best behaviour, I promise.' It's said with that overly cheerful pitch again that does absolutely nothing to reassure me.

Somehow, I think we might have very different definitions of 'best behaviour'.

5

Bram stayed late last night, washing up while I mopped the floor and wiped down all the tables and chairs until long after closing time, and unsurprisingly there's no sign of him when I arrive before 7 a.m., with bags of shopping over my shoulder, bought on a clandestine trek around the local supermarket late last night.

There isn't space to do much in the caravan, but the space in the food preparation area in the tearoom is generous and I have plenty of room to make packet after packet of supermarket-bought goods look homemade.

I've bought mini carrot cakes and I'm adding my Wonderland twist by making carrots out of fondant and adding a white fondant rabbit and a clock made out of a white chocolate button that I've drawn hands on with edible ink. I'm filling a crystal plate in the display case as I go, a couple of different things today in case we have any return customers who'd like to try something different.

I shouldn't be doing this. I *have* to get a handle on baking if I want to keep The Wonderland Teapot, because of the dishonesty, and because of the money too. Supermarket goods are *expensive*. I spent much more at the checkout last night than I took from customers throughout the day. And this is the furthest thing from what I wanted to do when I had a tearoom of my own. My entire livelihood now depends on me being able to summon some vestiges of the baker I used to be, but I keep failing. Last night, Marnie and Darcy went on a date and she let me use her kitchen, and what I made was... Well, I put the resulting banana bread out for the birds this morning and even they didn't want it.

At five to nine, I go over to pull the net curtains back and hopefully welcome customers in.

''ello!'

I let out a yelp of surprise. Bram must've been sitting on the pavement because he suddenly pops up outside the door. I fiddle with the keys until I can yank it open. 'What are you doing down there?'

'Coming to work, I wouldn't wonder.' He looks around in confusion, like I might genuinely not realise why he's here.

'Knocking is a foreign concept?'

'I could see the light on out the back. Figured you were busy and wouldn't want to be disturbed.' He gives me a jovial shrug. 'It's a nice April morning. Sitting outside for a while is no hardship.'

He's right there – I wouldn't have wanted to be *disturbed* in the middle of my underhanded misrepresentations. But he puts an intonation on the word and I have to shrug off the feeling that he *knows*. I'm projecting again. He couldn't possibly know. No one could.

'Still, I'm here now. You know what they say – the early bird gets the worm. But actually, so does the lunchtime bird, and the mid-afternoon bird, and the late-evening bird. There are always plenty of worms to go round when it's raining.'

I look past him as he comes in. It's not raining. 'This is a tearoom. Can we not talk about worms?'

He ignores me and his aftershave instantly fills the café with a bright and lively sherbet-like scent as he stops in front of the glass display full of delectable looking goodies. 'Ooh, some changes, excellent. Going to yell at me for sampling one for breakfast?'

I give him a non-committal grunt because whether I say yes or no, he will anyway. 'You're unnervingly cheerful this morning.'

'Why shouldn't I be cheerful?'

'Because it's unnerving,' I mutter, well aware that I sound like a real grump in comparison.

'It's only unnerving to un-cheerful people.' He turns around and grins at me. 'I'm still alive. I get to go to work. That's worth celebrating. Not everyone is that lucky.'

'That's both surprisingly sunny and alarmingly macabre.'

Behind the lashings of black eyeliner, his twinkling brown eyes suggest that's exactly what he was aiming for. 'I'm healthy. I've got a job and a roof over my head and food in my fridge. People underestimate the privilege of having an average life, but if you're well and warm, what more can you want?'

I notice that he didn't say happy. Most people would say 'healthy and happy'. Bram did not. It makes me wonder about his life and who the *real* Bram is behind the Hatter costume. Is he happy? Or is this just a front he's putting on? 'Another fair point.'

'I know.' He gives me that grin again, the one that turns arrogance into mischievousness and makes him impossible to dislike, even if you really, really want to.

Today he's wearing an electric blue shirt that's almost the exact same colour as his hair, and the same lime green pleather jacket and stack of three top hats. He takes his bag upstairs, taking the stairs in sets of two, his neon yellow boots thunking on each step.

I'm folding napkins into rose shapes when he comes back down and starts making us a cup of tea each without being asked. He sets a mug down in front of me, opens the display case and peers in.

'There's so much choice that I don't know which to go for. It's like browsing the shelves of a supermarket.'

Again, it sounds sarcastic, and my stomach plummets. I have to repeat to myself that there's no way he could *know*.

I can feel his eyes on me as he takes a Black Forest cupcake without a word and closes the doors of the display case quietly. He's mercifully silent as he eats it and we both down our tea with further awkward glugging. It's like he knows he's said something wrong, but he can't possibly know what. He takes the empty mugs through to the back while I open the door for customers, but like yesterday, there's not exactly a horde clamouring to get in. Ever After Street is quiet at this time of day.

'Sorry. I'm always putting my foot in it and saying something I shouldn't.' Bram returns from the so-called kitchen and we skirt around each other as he goes to tidy tables that are already tidy and I squeeze in behind the counter. 'People pay no attention to me. You shouldn't either.' He switches into his Mad Hatter voice for that bit, and it makes me wonder why. That voice seems like a façade, and I can't help thinking about what it's covering.

'Let me make it up to you.' He comes up to the counter and produces a deck of playing cards from one of his many trouser pockets.

'How?' I raise a dubious eyebrow, watching as he shuffles them like a card-shuffling master.

He looks up and waits until I meet his eyes to wink at me. 'By making you believe in magic.'

I laugh. From anyone else, it would sound horrifically cheesy and egotistical, but from him, with that twinkle in his eyes and his Mad Hatter voice on again, it sounds kind of endearing. Even though it will take more than a magician in eyeliner to make *me* believe in magic. The magic disappeared from my world long ago.

'Pick a card, look at it, but don't let me see it.' He fans the cards out face down in his hand and then turns to the side and looks away while I select a card and cup it in my hand. The Three of Diamonds.

From a pocket, he produces a biro and holds it out to me. 'Sign your initials on it, fold it into quarters, and hold it between your thumb and forefinger.'

I do as he says and he turns back, splices the deck of cards together and shuffles them, and then spreads them across the counter and taps his finger on one and slides it out. 'Is this your card?'

It's an Eight of Spades. 'No. Considering I'm still holding my card, it would be highly unlikely.'

'Oh, okay, this has gone wrong already. Let me try again.' There's a hint of teasing in his voice that suggests this is deliberate misdirection and I play along, because whatever trick he's trying, it's not going to work on me.

He reshuffles the cards and pulls out another one and then sighs when I confirm that it, once again, is not the card I'm still holding. 'Oh well, I'd better give up then.' He gathers a handful of cards and throws them up in the air and they glide down and land in disarray on the counter, and then he suddenly holds a finger up. 'Ah, I know where it's got to.'

His hands go to his hat, and from behind the 'ten shillings and sixpence' sign, he pulls out a folded playing card and holds it up in front of me, making a show of deliberately unfolding it. 'Is *this* your card?'

Even though I'm surprised when he unfolds the Three of Diamonds and points out the *CJ* I signed in the corner, I try to keep a neutral look on my face. Okay, so he's got duplicate cards in that deck or something. I'm going to need a closer look at those initials. It's probably one he prepared earlier. The point is that I'm still holding my card. 'Yes, it is.'

He does a mocking gasp of surprise. 'Well, if *this* is your card, what card are you holding?'

I unfold it and have a look because he's not fooling me that easi — 'Oh, come *on*! That's not... I mean, that wasn't... *How* did you...'

He grins at me with that audacious beam, because the card I'm holding is a folded-up Jack of Hearts.

'I haven't let go of that card once! How could you possibly have switched it?'

'Magic.'

'It wasn't magic.' I want to be disparaging, but I'm absolutely flummoxed by how he did that. My thumb and index finger have been on that card the whole time. I can't explain how it's suddenly turned into a different card, and like most things I can't explain, it leaves me feeling an exhilarating mix of nerves, awkwardness, and disbelief, and I have no idea how to deal with it, so I start laughing. '*How*?'

He laughs too. 'Magic circle. A magician can't reveal his secrets.'

'You can't do that and then not tell me what wizard-y sorcery this is!' I know it was a trick of some sort, some kind of sleight of hand thing where he switched out the card while I was looking at something else, but I can't deny he's bloody good.

'Worked, didn't it?'

'Hmm?' Without realising it, I'm watching him gather up the cards from the counter and tap them back into a neat pile, hypnotised by how fast his fingers move and it takes me a moment to understand what he's getting at. 'Oh, you haven't made me believe in magic. You've distracted me with trying to work out how you did that.'

'Near enough.' He's still grinning and now he shrugs too. 'That's the first time I've seen you smile since I came in, so it was worth it.'

'I don't like tricks – they're intended to make a fool out of others,' I snap at him, and then feel ridiculously guilty. He did make me smile, and lately, there haven't been many people in my life who *want* to make me smile, and I like that he tried so hard. 'Sorry, I didn't mean that. That was very clever. You're…'

I make the mistake of looking up into his brown eyes and my mouth goes dry and my brain sputters to a halt. I wet my lips to prise them apart with my tongue. Words are rushing in my head, racing with each other for attention. That is a sentence with too many possible endings. He might be a bit bright and lively, but he doesn't deserve another insult. His eyes are glinting, challenging me to say something flattering.

'…magnetic,' I finish eventually, and of all the words I was thinking of, *that* wasn't one of them. Where did that come from? Why did it come out of my mouth?

He grins and drops eye contact. 'Well, stick me on a fridge and call me Trevor. I *thought* I heard a compliment from you yesterday but now I've definitely heard one. Thanks!'

I glare at his sarcasm and hold out the Jack of Hearts card, and his fingertips brush against mine as he takes it and tucks it into the teapot display next to the Queen of Hearts card he gave me yesterday.

I have a feeling they're the first of many.

That afternoon brings our first Unbirthday party. It's a mum bringing in her two daughters, and she explains that it's the older of the two girls' first school day after a long illness, and she promised to bring them both in for a little celebration as a reward for over-coming her first-day-back nerves. This is what I've always wanted to do. My first thoughts of an Alice-themed tearoom were about throwing Unbirthday parties, and I don't know who's more excited – the girls or me.

While the family choose their cakes and order sandwiches from the menu, Bram sets up a table in the corner. I've made a selection of props for occasions like this. There are placemats made of artificial grass, vases of paper roses, and brightly coloured broken teacups glued together in stacks and decorated with ribbons and faux flowers, and teapots everywhere, their spouts pointing in all different directions. It's chaotic and fun and the most Mad Hatter-style tea party I could create with a box of broken china from Mickey in The Mermaid's Treasure Trove shop and my beloved hot glue gun.

I put together ham and mustard sandwiches for the mum, and jam sandwiches for the two girls and cut them out with cookie cutters, so each sandwich is crustless and flower shaped, and garnished with a fresh mint leaf. I do a teapot of tea for the mum, and another teapot of orange squash for the two girls, because no one should miss out on the teapot experience, even if they're not drinking tea. I tie 'Drink Me' tags around the handles of their teacups, and carry over the first tray, and Bram goes over to pick up the drinks tray and bring it over.

My idea for Unbirthday parties was always that 'Alice' could join them if they wanted company, so I look around to check there aren't many other customers, and apart from one woman typing on a laptop who looks thoroughly unimpressed with all things Wonderland, and Mrs Moreno, an elderly lady who also came in yesterday for a toasted teacake, there aren't any. 'What a coincidence, it's my Unbirthday too. Can I join you?'

The girls nod enthusiastically, and I take a seat at their table, and then glance up at Bram. 'How about you, Hatter? It's your Unbirthday as well, isn't it?'

'It is.' He looks confused for a moment, like he wasn't expecting me to get involved, and then he covers it with his familiar grin. 'And no Mad Hatter ever says no to a tea party!'

I'm keeping an eye on the shop too, but it's fun to introduce myself as Alice and tell them I fell down a rabbit hole and ended up here. I ask them about school and what they like to read and watch, and Bram starts doing magic tricks – ones more aimed at children, like making things disappear, and that thing where the magician pours water into a teacup but it disappears, and then he turns the cup into a handful of paper shapes. Makes it *look* like it turns into paper shapes, I tell myself as he throws the paper in the air and scraps of it float down and settle on the table, and the girls pick up pieces of it in awe. They genuinely believe he's got magic powers and, although I'm a bit old for believing in magic powers, I can't help being impressed as I fiddle with a bit of paper too, unable to comprehend how he did that.

After a while, I declare that everyone must move one place on, like the Mad Hatter and March Hare do in the book, and all five of us stand up and shuffle around the table to take each other's seats. It's a bit barmy, but it makes the girls laugh, and Unbirthday parties were invented for a bit of barmy-ness. After that, we try to find the Dormouse in a teapot, which results in much giggling and clinking of china lids.

I have to jump up a couple of times and rush over to serve customers, while the party finish their sandwiches and cakes, and Bram's next trick is to take his hat off and produce two balloons from underneath it. He blows them up and gives one to each of the girls and invites them for a game of flamingo croquet. They run across the tearoom and start trying to swing the hedgehog balls through the playing card arches. I couldn't get round balls and had to go with hedgehog stress balls that aren't quite spherical, which makes it a bit harder, but at least they don't get up and walk off like they do in the book.

When the game is over and their mum starts gathering their things to leave, Bram bounces over to me, takes hold of my wrist and drags me out from behind the counter. 'It wouldn't be an Unbirthday party without "The Unbirthday Song". Come on, *Alice*.'

At first I go to protest that I'm not singing, but there's something about Bram, the way he's so carefree and authentically himself, that makes me remember why I wanted to do this in the first place and reminds me that you can't open a Wonderland-themed tearoom without throwing caution to the wind once in a while.

He takes my hand and starts dancing around the girls, dragging me with him, and launches into a version of the Mad Hatter and March Hare's song from the 1951 Disney movie. The girls clap and cheer and join in the song too, and the look on Bram's face is so infectious that there's no way I'm *not* joining in as well.

'Best day ever!' the oldest daughter declares when we've finished singing. If you could call it singing. Yowling might be more appropriate.

'Can we come again tomorrow?' the younger one asks.

'Can't get higher praise than that,' the mum says to me as she comes over to pay and I hurry back to the safety of the counter. 'We'll be back! You two are brilliant.'

In one final trick, Bram produces a handful of glittery confetti from thin air and huffs it all over both the girls and they squeal in delight. They're still giggling as Bram waves them off with a cheery goodbye and comes back to the counter. He drags a stool over and sits on it, leaning his upper body over the counter like he really is exhausted, and his stack of hats falls off. 'That was brilliant. I'm knackered.'

I'm knackered too. I haven't had much contact with people recently and that was the most social thing I've done in a long time, and I... surprisingly enjoyed it, and Bram is a whirlwind of colour and fun, and impossible to take your eyes off, even if you want to. Anything would be enjoyable in his company.

I've started clearing the table, and there's still tea left in the teapot. He reaches over for it, adds a splash of milk, and drinks from the spout, and I watch him in horror because I've never seen a teapot violated in such a way before. Teapots are generally civilised things, and I'm fairly sure I could evict him for such a crime again kitchenware. 'You really are as mad as a hatter, aren't you?'

He grins when he realises it doesn't sound like an insult. '*Exatically*.'

It's another quote from *Alice in Wonderland* and his smile gets even wider when he realises I recognise it too. 'That's my life goal. To be so mad that it makes other people happy. Hat makers used to use mercury to stiffen felt for hats and the prolonged exposure would give them mercury poisoning. That's where the saying comes from. Luckily also achievable without deadly mind-altering drugs.'

'And what am I supposed to do about the confetti?' I try to sound stern, but he's utterly impossible to stay mad at. 'How are we going to get that cleared up before it gets trodden into the floor tiles for all eternity? Glitter gets everywhere. Customers will be complaining about eating the stuff.'

'And now for my next trick.' He holds up a 'stay there' finger, slides off the stool and goes out the back. There's the sound of a door opening, and then he reappears from the cupboard under the stairs holding a floor sweeper. 'Ta da!'

It probably shouldn't make me laugh as much as it does, but it's like the final straw of all the hilarious things he's done in the last half an hour, and I can't help watching as he sweeps up the confetti, treating the sweeper like a dance partner, spinning it and twirling it, moving tables aside to get every last bit, unaware that the customers are watching him too.

I carry on clearing props off the Unbirthday table and returning them to the back room, and he goes to empty the sweeper and then stashes it back in the cupboard it came from and sits back on the stool in front of the counter.

'I did not expect you to get involved in that. You seem too...' He falters, like he's realised too late that this sentence can only be ended with an insult. '...uptight,' he finishes after a moment, like it's taken him a while to choose the least offensive option. 'It was nice to see your fun side. I didn't know you had one.'

'I don't. Didn't. I mean, I used to, once, but...'

'What happened?' He pulls the stack of hats over and starts fiddling with them on the counter.

Instinctively, I want to tell him to mind his own business, but he sounds genuinely interested, and I like his straightforwardness in simply asking. I meet his eyes and, for once, it feels like I'm talking to the real Bram, like all the layers of bright clothing and eyeliner are stripped away and this is a rare glimpse into the person behind the costume, and I decide to be straightforward too.

'Life,' I say with a sigh. 'Or, more specifically, death. My nan who raised me died. Then my mum died and I hadn't seen her for years. Then an ex let me down at the last minute, and I... shut myself away in my flat. I haven't really been part of the world for the past couple of years, and this tearoom is my way of forcing myself headfirst back into life and clawing back the control I lost...'

'And then I turned up without your say-so or agreement. Not a good start for taking back control.' He grimaces in a sympathetic way, like he realises how undermined I felt by Mr Hastings' lack of upfrontness.

'Well, maybe it wasn't the *worst* idea he's ever had...'

'It's a good thing I'm already sitting down because I'm almost positive this might be leading to another compliment.' He looks up and the seriousness in his eyes melts into a twinkle and a soft smile makes his lips quirk up.

I could snap something sarcastic and cutting, but he seems quiet and open, different without his stack of hats on, more like the real

Bram than the character he plays, and it's almost like he *needs* to hear something nice. 'You were brilliant today. Those two girls adored you. You knew exactly how to make their Unbirthday special,' I say, because I've noticed that about him – he's excellent at reading people. He seems to instinctively know which kind of trick will impress people the most and his approach is individual to every person who comes in.

'And yet, I would never have thought of joining them if you hadn't invited me. There might be a slim chance yet that Hatter and Alice actually work well together in a Wonderland setting.'

I smile without knowing why I'm smiling. The last thing I wanted was anyone else involved in this, not least because of what he might find out about the definitely-*not*-homemade goodies I'm serving, but tonight, it feels like no Wonderland would be complete without a Mad Hatter, and *that* is more important than my hang-ups from years ago that have nothing to do with Bram. 'How about you? How does a carousel operator become first in line to play a character who's barking mad?'

'Ahh, it's a long and complicated process of becoming the black sheep of the family.' He scrunches a hand in his hair and then holds a blue spike out and looks at it. 'Well, maybe the blue sheep of the family. I haven't followed the path that my father set out for me, and now my family wishes I was someone I'm not – may as well play the part of someone else entirely.'

I knew his sunny smile was hiding more beneath the surface, and I get the feeling he's simplifying something that goes a *lot* deeper.

'This wasn't my initial plan, but I believe in making the best of things and embracing what life throws at you, so maybe we can help each other here. No better place than Wonderland to find the joy in life again?'

I find myself smiling as I look at him. I want to believe that, but in recent years, it's felt like getting my spark for life back is... 'An insurmountable challenge that only a fool would take on.'

'One fool at your service.' He replaces the stack of hats on his head solely so he can tip them in my direction.

It's impossible not to laugh. He makes the world seem brighter than it has for a while now, and I don't think it's *just* the electric-blue hair and lime green jacket.

6

'Don't you ever eat your own creations?' Bram asks the following morning when he comes in from the back room, carrying two cups of tea and places one on the counter in front of me.

Today's selections are Millionaire's shortbreads, sticky toffee pudding tarts, and lemon cakes that I'm currently adding lemon butter icing to, and Bram opens the display case and takes his usual pick for breakfast. I'm still decorating the last of the cakes and he pulls the stool up to the counter again and sits opposite me, using a spiral patterned serviette as a makeshift plate.

He's wearing a shirt with colourful clocks printed all over it, and I can't help noticing that he hasn't shaved today, and the added stubble makes him look sexier than usual.

'Yes,' I lie. The truth is that I've been avoiding it, both scared of running out of stock and not wanting to break the illusion that they taste as good as they look. What if I try one and they really are dried-up pre-packaged supermarket stock that someone's gone to town with butter icing on?

'Go on, have cake for breakfast, live large,' he says. 'There's a slim possibility that you might enjoy it. If cake for breakfast can't improve even the darkest of days, there really is no hope.'

He looks so earnest as he sits there, and apart from a few finger swipes of the icing I'm putting on, I haven't eaten anything else yet today. And I have been given a cup of tea, and it does feel a bit wrong to obstinately refuse the cake when it's right next to me. 'Fine.'

'Never has anyone had to be persuaded to eat cake before. You are a strange and unusual phenomenon to mankind, Cleo Jordan.'

'You can talk,' I mutter as I take one of the lemon cakes I'm icing and take a bite. 'Happy now?'

'Ecstatic. So overjoyed that my hardened little soul may *burst* with delight.' On the word 'burst', he pulls a hand out from nowhere and—

'Don't you dare!'

It's too late. He throws a handful of glitter over both of us.

I make a noise of frustration. 'What is *wrong* with you?'

'A question that has puzzled many renowned scientists for decades, but no one has ever come up with an answer. They've eventually had to agree that I really am just a bit of a weirdo.'

'You can say that again,' I grumble.

'Oh, thank you.' He clears his throat. 'I really am just a bit of a weirdo.'

He's doing it deliberately now. He knows it's winding me up. After what I said about glitter yesterday, he *knew* the one thing that would drive me mad was *more* glitter.

'And you can relax, by the way.' He swipes a finger through the glitter covering the counter and sucks it clean. 'It's edible glitter. So no one can complain about eating it.'

I make that noise of frustration again. Spending time with Bram seems to lead to nothing *but* noises of frustration. 'That doesn't mean I want it in my hair,' I mutter, trying to shake my blonde locks out over the floor. 'Or my tea! Bram!'

He peers into my cup and then his own. 'You should serve that. Who wouldn't want to drink sparkly tea? It screams Wonderland.'

'Someone is certainly screaming *something* around here.' I'm still trying to brush glitter off the shoulders of my dress. While I appreciate his forethought in making it edible glitter, even edible glitter should be used sparingly. Although the sparkly tea thing is not a bad idea. I could line each teacup with a pinch of glitter so it's ready when people pour their tea in...

Bram ignores me trying to blow glitter off my cake before I plonk myself down on a stool and take another big, frustrated bite.

'I'm going to need the recipe for these. They're so good. You could make a fortune if you got the local supermarket to stock them.'

I choke on that big, frustrated bite. He suspects, I'm sure he does. The silence between us is punctuated only by my hacking breaths as I try to claw air back into my lungs. Maybe I should be honest with him. His body language is laidback and easy, like he's inviting me to say something, and he seemed so open last night, like he'd be kind and understanding, and the guilt is weighing me down. Maybe if I told *someone*...

'I'm sure,' I mumble eventually. I can't say anything. He's got a direct line to the local council. There's no way he's not going to tell them something like this.

His eyes sink downwards and he looks disappointed, like he was expecting me to spill the beans, but he continues picking pieces off his now-glittery cake and poking them into his mouth.

'So, Dora or Patra?' The next time he looks up, he's got a carefully schooled grin on his face, as though the previous few minutes didn't happen.

'What?' I ask in confusion. If it's not frustration with Bram then it's almost always confusion.

'What's Cleo short for – Cleodora or Cleopatra?'

I stifle a laugh at the randomness of it. 'Neither. It's not a nickname, it's just my name. Abraham.'

'You know what they say about people who live in glass houses – they should put up curtains.' He laughs. 'Fair point, well made, Cleonardo.'

I try not to laugh, but once I start, I can't stop. 'Every conversation with you is like a trip to Wonderland where everyone talks in riddles and every encounter leaves you feeling turned-around and upside-down.'

'Pleasure to be of service.' He tips the stack of hats again, that indomitable grin back on his face, and we finish our tea in slightly less awkward silence.

'So when are you going to start the sparkly tea thing – today or tomorrow?'

'I'm not.'

He raises two dark eyebrows as high as they can possibly go. 'Sparkly tea is a must for Wonderland. We both know it.'

I hold his gaze for a moment, intending to stick to my guns, but his eyes have a glint to them that makes it impossible to hang onto my resolve. 'All right, as ideas go, it's not the worst I've ever heard.' I take a piece of chalk over to the chalkboard menu on the wall, and add an asterix and 'with extra sparkle' underneath the tea options, because edible glitter might not be to everyone's tastes. 'Happy *now*?'

'You could just say, "Thank you for brightening up my day, Bram." Contrariwise, I don't exist solely to annoy you.' He lifts his teacup and drains the last of his glittery tea, and I do the same without another word, because, to be fair, these past few days would have been a lot less successful if he hadn't come along. Where would Wonderland be without a very, very Mad Hatter?

* * *

That morning is our first afternoon tea, ironically at 11 a.m., a birthday treat for three middle-aged sisters, and Bram entertains with card tricks while I make smoked salmon and cream cheese and egg and cress sandwiches and put them on a serving platter, and then load up one of my handmade cake stands with glittery scones, fairy cakes, and butterfly-shaped slices of lemon loaf cake that I've cut out with a cookie cutter, and serve it with pots of tea and a selection of mismatched dainty teacups. They requested the extra sparkle, so each teacup has a pinch of edible silver glitter inside.

After they leave, lunchtime brings a rush with it for the first time, and although it's not *busy*-busy, there seem to be customers in for most of the day, and by the time I flip the open sign over to closed at five o'clock that evening, my feet are killing me and my back is protesting about not having had a sit down all day.

'I guess word is spreading.' Bram's clearing tables as I walk back across the shop floor. I take a tray from him and carry it to the back room and start loading plates into a sink full of hot water, because Lilith never had anything as modern as a dishwasher.

'I'll do that in a minute.' He comes out with another loaded tray. True to his word, he's been wonderful at keeping on top of the washing up without a single complaint. I've never met anyone who *enjoys* washing up before, and yet he whistles to himself and breezes through it. 'Right now, there are cakes in the display case that are going to end up in the bin if we don't do our duty as responsible citizens to save landfill and scoff the lot. Tea?'

'Bram, it's…' I glance at a clock. It's after five and all I want to do is go home. Well, back to the caravan. You can't really call a rustbox on my friend's driveway a home, can you?

'Always time for tea!' he says brightly, a sentence that I hear at least three times a day, usually said at the moments when it really is *not* a good time for tea.

'You've been on your feet all day. Go and choose what you want because I'm going to *ransack* that display case in a minute.'

'You've been on your feet as long as I have.'

'Ah, but I haven't been up since the early hours baking a teashop full of delicious goodies.'

That guilt again. I didn't plan this, but I certainly never planned on sharing a workplace with someone who would think I baked them myself. I thought hiding it from customers would be a breeze, but it's harder to outright lie to someone who seems so utterly open. There's something about Bram that's unflinchingly straightforward, and my guilt is giving way to panic that I *still* haven't magically become the baker I used to be. I still can't remember my old family recipes. What if I *never* do? How much longer can I go on like this? Sooner or later, am I going to have to admit defeat?

I go through to the shop and sit down on the stool behind the counter, and lean over to take a fairy cake with added Cheshire Cat-style pink and purple sprinkles from the display case, and Bram comes out with two large mugs of tea and a plate. He puts a mug down by me and one on the opposite side of the counter, then opens the glass doors of the display case and proceeds to load his plate up with one of everything that's left until there are six cakes on his plate.

'Moderation?'

'Nah. I could get hit by a froose tomorrow. You know that Bon Jovi song, "I'll Sleep When I'm Dead"? Well, I'll eat cake in moderation when I'm dead. I quite like sleeping while I'm alive.'

It's hard to imagine him ever being quiet enough to sleep. 'What's a froose?'

'I dunno. Cross between a frog and a goose?'

I don't intend to laugh, but sometimes I'm so bewildered by what he's going to come out with next that laughter is the only response. 'How is it possible that even *you* can't make sense of the things that come out of your own mouth?'

'All part of the fun.' He drops onto the stool, lets out a long sigh, and his shoulders droop. 'Ah, the holy grail of life. A cup of tea, a cake, and a nice sit down. Is there anything better?'

'You're looking very good for your apparent age of ninety-three. I thought it was illegal to utter a sentence like that unless you're collecting your pension.'

He laughs. 'Age is just a number. You are never too young to enjoy the simple things in life, nor too old to enjoy the fun things life has to offer. Even better with the good company of people who barely tolerate you. Cheers.' He lifts his teacup and clinks it against mine.

I feel that shot of guilt again. It's not that I barely tolerate him. He's quite tolerable sometimes. And quite intolerable at other times. Unfortunately both of those times seem to coincide and he is both tolerable and intolerable at the same moment. The Schrödinger's cat of human beings.

He blows on his tea to cool it and then takes a big bite of his Victoria sponge slice. 'Tell me something,' he says conversationally, with his mouth full. 'Why do you put preservatives in these?'

'I don't...' I say slowly. *Are* there preservatives in them? I'd never even thought about it.

'I'm just wondering why you'd want to pump freshly baked cakes full of chemicals when they're intended to be eaten on the same day and not, oh I don't know, just as a wild example, sit in packages on shop shelves with a best-before date approximately three weeks from now.' He fixes me with a pointed look and one dark eyebrow pings into an arch.

The cake I was eating turns to rock in my mouth. I don't say anything because one wrong word is going to give my secret away, and I have a sinking feeling that he knows anyway. By sinking, I mean *drowning*.

'The jam in this' – he lifts the slice in his hand like he's making a toast and then takes another bite. Apparently preservatives aren't enough to deter him from cake – 'is packed with artificial sweeteners, which jam has no need for, and these cakes have got enough additives in them that you could dig them up in three-thousand years' time and they'd still be edible, like that honey they found in the Egyptian pyramids.'

'You're full of... something a lot less pleasant than three-thousand-year-old honey.'

'I can also taste the E numbers...' He clears his throat and pulls something from his pocket. A card to read from? No. It's something that rustles, concealed in his palm.

'There are no E numbers in the cakes.' I speak over him as he rattles off the list of E numbers.

'Oh, come on, Cleo.' He sighs. 'I *know*.'

'Know what?' I'm not falling into that trap and giving myself away. That's a trick as old as time – bluffing about knowing something to fool someone into admitting something they weren't ready to admit.

He places his palm down flat on the counter, the rustling thing underneath it, and pushes it towards me before lifting his hand off with a flourish. On the counter is a list of ingredients on a cut-out piece of plastic packaging. Familiar plastic packaging that I've been stripping off 'my' bakes every day.

'While I appreciate your environmental conscience when it comes to recycling, when unwrapping supermarket-bought goods and trying to pass them off as your own, might I suggest that when you recycle the packaging, you put it in a recycling bin at home rather than out the back here where anyone else who also enjoys recycling may see it should they go to put something in said recycling bin?'

Oh, sweet mother of missing socks. I was so unprepared for sharing a workspace that I hadn't even *thought* of that.

'Who *enjoys* recycling?' I go for deflection instead of admitting to anything. I'm trying to ignore my suddenly pounding heart. The whirlpool of panic has turned into a tidal wave. This is it. Now everyone is going to know I'm a fraud. Everyone is going to know that I took on a tearoom when I've forgotten how to bloody bake. Mr Hastings is going to—

'Why shouldn't household jobs be enjoyable?' He sounds like his usual cheery self, but there's a look of steel in his brown eyes that suggests he isn't going to let this go. 'If you can have the time of your life while hoovering, you can conquer the world.'

He laughs, looking like he's expecting me to do the same, and then sighs when I don't. 'What I don't get is why you're trying so hard to hide it? You're not doing anything wrong. I'm sure lots of cafés and tearooms do the same, even without the fancy decoration that you add. Why won't you tell me? I know I'm a bit much sometimes, but what have I done to make you think I'm some kind of enemy?'

'How long have you known?' I say, instead of answering properly. The fact he knows he's a bit much punches me in the chest because he sounds sad and resigned, like it's something he's been told many times before. *He* hasn't really done anything – it's me. I've become someone who only expects the worst these days.

'Since the first day. The first bite – I'm a connoisseur of shop-bought bakes. I recognised it instantly. I didn't say anything because I hoped that I wasn't *so* offensive to you that you'd tell me. It was only today that I came across the packaging and thought it was time to lay my cards on the table, so to speak.' He clicks his fingers and a playing card appears between them, and he holds it out to me. An Ace of Diamonds.

'An ace up the sleeve – very clever.' It was obviously stashed inside his jacket sleeve or *somewhere*. It didn't just appear out of thin air, even though that's what he was going for.

He sighs when I don't take it, and then leans over to tuck it into the teapot display with the others. 'I'm not your enemy. I'm a bit of an amateur baker myself, maybe I can help?'

I don't intend to scoff quite so harshly, but I do it so violently that it hurts my throat, and he looks remarkably upset, and I feel guiltier again. 'You have a direct line to the council, Bram. Like you're not going to report back on me.'

His face falls and, for the first time since I met him, the Hatter's mad grin is a thing of history. 'Oh. That.'

'I can't let them find out about this. At the interview, I got these cakes from a bakery on the way, and I didn't *intend* for them to think I'd made them, but that's what they thought and I didn't correct them. I've always wanted to run a tearoom and I've always wanted to do something to share my love of Alice, and this was my one chance. If they find out now, they'll fire me instantly.'

'Is *that* why you hate me so much? Because you think I'm going to report back to them?'

'I don't hate you.' I feel a stone of dismay settle in my stomach again. I hate the fact I've been so wrapped up in prolonging this lie that I've made him think that. 'How could anyone hate you, Bram? You're...'

We keep running into this problem – sentences with too many possible endings, and almost none of them are going to go well. What is he? He's talented. Quick-witted. Charismatic. Delightfully bonkers. He's holding my gaze and I feel like he sees every option flicker past before I settle on redirecting the sentence. 'You work here. You've worked here for years. You're obviously thick as thieves with the council. Why *wouldn't* you tell them that I've deliberately misled them?'

'Because I'm not like that, maybe?' He sighs when I don't reply. 'Cleo, this place is amazing. The *last* thing I'm going to do is try to undermine you. I phoned Mr Hastings because he's—' He sighs and shakes his head before continuing. 'I'm an employee here, just like you.'

'I wasn't supposed to be an employee. This business was supposed to be my own.'

'And it will be. But the council are fiercely protective of Ever After Street and they have to make sure every establishment betters the area as a whole. Do you know how many requests they get to rent premises here? Some of them are terrible. One of them was a Disney-themed sex toy shop! There were Dumbo-shaped... you-know-whats with the ears and the trunk.' He makes a phallic shape with his hands. 'I mean, fun in its own way, of course, each to their own, but certainly not suitable for a place where children come to believe in magic. We try to keep scarring for life to a minimum.'

'The point is, Bram, that *you* know that. I do not know that. Marnie doesn't know that. Mr Hastings is one of the most intimidating people I've ever met and you've got a direct line to interrupt meetings. By reporting me, you'd have a one-way ticket to getting on his good side.'

'Ever After Street wouldn't be the same if anyone who wanted to monetise this place was given free run. Everyone starts with a three-month trial unless they own their own shops, like Sadie in The Cinderella Shop, or rent from a private landlord like Marnie used to. I started on a three-month trial run at the carousel. I was constantly monitored to ensure I didn't make any small children cry or take any wooden horses out for joyrides. We all have to go through it. I'm no different.'

No different. Here is a human who is different in *every* way.

'Yes, Ever After Street is an amalgamation of different shops, but it has to work as a whole. It's a business – it *has* to attract visitors and make money. Either way, that's nothing to do with me and not something I'd be involved in. And if it was, I'd say The Wonderland Teapot is a perfect fit for Ever After Street, no matter where the cakes come from.'

'And I've pretended to be a good baker when I'm clearly not any more. You'd certainly get brownie points for telling them that the brownies themselves come from a supermarket.' I down the rest of my tea, ram the remaining fairy cake down my throat, and march through to the back. 'Excuse me, I have work to do.'

The unit is piled high with dishes and they clatter and clink as I plunge my hands into the hot water and wash each dish with such force that I might as well be trying to scrub the pattern itself off.

This is exactly what I was dreading. He's going to have a field day with this. He must think it's hilarious. The woman who's opened a homemade tearoom despite not being able to bake *and* not having a home. He'll have a whale of a time telling his council buddies about that, won't he? And then everyone will know. The other shopkeepers who I've grown to love and respect will know I can't be trusted. Mr Hastings will sack me instantly. There'll probably be some kind of mark on my CV for the rest of my life. I didn't think things could get any worse than the last time I got close to fulfilling my tearoom dream, but this will beat it hands-down. The emotions of that day come rushing in all at once, and the thought that history is repeating itself makes tears well up, and the more frustrated I get with myself for getting emotional, the harder it is to push them down.

Bram appears in the doorway.

'Oh, for God's sake, just go away. You weren't supposed to be here. I didn't want you here. This wouldn't be a problem if you weren't here.'

'Oh, if you knew how many times I've heard that in my life.' For just one second, something sad flickers across his face, lingering for long enough to intrigue me before he covers it with his Mad Hatter grin. 'I'll dry.'

He picks up a tea towel and comes over to the sink where he prises the very, very clean plate from my rigid fingers and wipes it up. I hear his sharp inhale when he catches sight of the tears I'm desperately trying to stifle, and I appreciate the fact that he doesn't say anything. I've always been weak in the face of help with household tasks, so I carry on washing up, piling soapy plates and cutlery on the draining board for him to dry.

'Cleo, you didn't get this job because of the cakes. You got it because your idea was outstanding. It stood out by a town mile.'

I'm about to snap that he's got that wrong when he whispers, 'That's like a country mile, but longer. The Wonderland Teapot blew all the other pitches out of the water. Don't underestimate that.'

His voice is gentle and kind, and he sounds so genuine that it makes me feel even more choked up.

He's quiet as we wash and dry. He's *never* quiet. In the three days we've worked together, he's shut up for approximately two and a half minutes collectively. If he's not yakking to customers, then he's singing out-of-tune songs with misheard lyrics or tapping his feet and clicking his fingers to a beat heard only in his own head, and it means a lot that he understands the need for silence right now.

When the washing and drying is finished and put away, he crosses the kitchen and jumps up to sit on the unit opposite me. He takes his hats off and stands them on the unit, then pushes a hand through his blue hair, scruffing it up, getting rid of the hat hair by making it look like he's been pulled backwards *and* forwards through a hedge several times. His brown eyes find mine and his look is one of real concern that softens my heart towards him. 'What's the problem? Tell me, please? I can't help if you don't tell me. I'd like to think we're kind of in this together?' He sounds questioning and unsure, the complete opposite of bright and confident Hatter.

The idea of sharing this burden is a nice one. I can't tell Marnie, she's got her own business to run and her own mortgage to pay now she owns the shop, and she's got Darcy. She's helping me out enough with giving me somewhere to park my caravan, I can't burden her with my issues too.

And he knows anyway. Trying to hide it has been unexpectedly exhausting.

He can tell I'm wavering. 'Is it a time issue? Have you been so busy preparing the shop itself that you haven't had time to cook anything? Because I get it. We're open nine to five. And everyone knows that nine means much earlier than nine and five means much later than five. It's a lot of pressure to work full-time *and* have a life outside of work, not that I'd know anything about lives outside of work, but to get a shop full of cakes baked, you'd be up most of the night, right?'

'I... um...' I twist my fingers together.

'Is it a skill issue then?' he asks, and I get the feeling that he can see through me as well as Alice could see through the Looking Glass.

'I'm kind of...' I swallow hard, trying to think of a way to put it, '...between kitchens at the moment.'

His head tilts to the side. 'I say a lot of strange things, but I've never heard that one before. What does "between kitchens" mean?'

I intend to give a carefully constructed answer, but my mouth moves without my permission. 'Last time I tried to bake something at home, I accidentally set the kitchen on fire and got myself evicted and now I'm living in a caravan on Marnie's driveway and the kitchen consists of one tiny work surface and a gas hob that I'm scared to turn on in case it blows up.'

The sentence comes out so fast that it's all squashed together and jumbled and it takes him a minute to untangle it. 'You're homeless?'

'I'm not homeless. I have a caravan and an address. I have slightly too much money to claim a benefit but not enough to be able to afford rent, and I'm a terrible prospect for landlords. If I can make this a full-time sustainable job, then I'll be able to rent another flat and get a handle on the baking thing, but I *need* to get through this three-month trial. If you would just, please, not tell anyone, and—'

'Get a handle on it? *Can* you bake at all?'

'Yes!' I huff in annoyance, but mainly annoyance that my attempts to be nonchalant are so transparent. 'All right, no, not... not recently. I used to be able to. A couple of years ago, my ex and I were going to go into business together with a teashop, but it didn't work out, and between that and the grief, it's like... I've forgotten how. Every time I get near a kitchen, I go blank. I used to throw ingredients in with abandon and somehow they'd work out. My nan always said I had a sixth sense about what flavours went well together, but... I stopped baking, and now, I follow recipes to the letter and they still go wrong. I thought The Wonderland Teapot would unlock whatever part of my soul has gone missing, and I really, *really* thought it had its own kitchen, but it doesn't, and I don't, and...' I trail off as my voice breaks. I didn't intend to tell anyone that, but saying it aloud for the first time makes it feel like a weight has gone from my shoulders, and I almost sag against the unit, feeling like I need to catch my breath.

'What's wrong with serving supermarket-bought cakes then?

There's no law against it. Hastings and Co. would never know. He's got the taste buds of a jellyfish.'

'Because it's not honest, is it? It's someone else's work that I'm pretending is my own.'

'I'm sure the factory machines will be mortally offended.'

I laugh and then sigh. 'My mum and nan ran a tearoom together when I was little. It was magical in there... but then she left, when I was ten. My nan took over – both the tearoom and raising me – and I helped out as much as she'd let me. Everything was homemade. Uneven and messy. Rustic would be the polite way of putting it, but everything was made with love. She was like the whole town's nan. Customers would come in and ask if she had any of a certain type of cake and if she didn't, she'd tell them to come back in a couple of hours and nip out the back to whip up a batch. I wanted that. I thought there'd be a proper kitchen here and I'd have time and space to get things right, but...' I throw my hands out to the sides, indicating the units all around me.

'Plenty of space to prepare food, nowhere to actually cook it.' He finishes the sentence for me.

'Both her and my mum taught me everything they knew about baking. I always thought I'd take over their tearoom one day, but... my nan aged. I didn't know until after she died that it had got too much for her and the shop was drowning in debt. There was no way out but to sell up, and then...' I shake my head. I already told him too much last night. 'Cut to now. I thought baking would come back instinctively. Like muscle memory. Second nature because owning a tearoom is in my DNA... but when I heard about Lilith and this place and went back to the kitchen in my flat... the resulting cake ended up being decorated by the foam out of a fireman's hose.'

'Never the ideal end to a bake.'

'And every time since then, it's just got worse. I don't *want* to serve preservative-filled cakes that I've unwrapped and slapped some icing on. I want to be authentic. I can do it. I just need to—'

'Don't say get through this three-month trial again.' He cuts me off. 'That isn't the answer. You need to concentrate on the here and now. Buying this stuff must cost a fortune. It's counterproductive because you want money coming in but you're spending more than you're earning, and you're clearly spending most of your days terrified and wound-up about someone finding out, and honestly, Cleo, people *are* going to find out.'

'Because you're going to tell them, of course you are.'

'N—'

'You've got something to hold over me now. Something you can have a good laugh about, tell all our colleagues so they'll think less of me.'

He jumps down from the unit and his yellow boots hit the floor with a loud smack. 'Why do you think I'm that kind of person?'

'Because that's what people do. They let you down. They let you come within touching distance of your wish and then rip the rug out from underneath you. They say one thing and then do something different.'

'The wrong people. Selfish people. I'd like to think I'm not like that.'

'What are you going to do then?'

'I'd like to help.'

It's... unexpected and I struggle to come up with a response. 'And why would you do that when...' I start off snappy, but I look up and meet his eyes across the room, kind, genuine, dark but with a sadness in them that catches me off-guard. '...when I've been nothing but horrible to you?' I finish the question in a very different way than I intended to.

'It's okay, I deserve it,' he says with a nonchalant shrug. 'I'm a bit too weird for most people. If they don't realise it straight away, they do soon enough.'

That gets to me. No one *deserves* people to be horrible to them. Sure, he's a little bit out-there, but other than turn up unexpectedly, has he actually done anything to suggest he's a terrible person? He's known about the bakes since day one. He could've disgraced me publicly with his knowledge but he hasn't, and in the face of his attentive eyes, I can't remember what exactly I'm holding against him.

I swallow hard again, for a different reason this time. 'No one ever said weirdness is a bad thing. Even the most sensible people have weird little souls inside, waiting to get out. I've always liked people who are a bit weird. They make me feel better for being a bit weird too.'

'Well, I wear my weird little soul on my sleeve, and it makes a lot of people uncomfortable. And that's fine, but I'm not going to change to make other people happy.'

His words have a sense of weariness about them, like this is a conclusion he's come to after many years of soul-searching and has had to use as justification more than a few times. I try to think of what I know about him. He's obviously brilliant with children and an incredible magician. He helped Marnie out with the book festival she threw last year by keeping the carousel running for festival attendees, long after it was meant to be closed. He obviously helped Lilith out when she used to run the tearoom too. The carousel is a hugely popular part of Ever After Street and I wouldn't mind betting that's a lot to do with him. Even with his normal dark hair, he's got the upbeat type of personality that draws people to him.

Literally, it seems. I come back to my senses to realise I've drifted across the room towards him. I shake my head and take a step backwards so sharply that I catch my hip on the corner of the unit and make myself jump.

'Use my kitchen.'

I almost laugh at the absurdity of it. 'Oh yeah, right. Very funny.'

'Oh, yeah, *right*,' he repeats pointedly, putting an emphasis on the sentence to let me know he's not joking. 'I have a massive kitchen and I bake often so there's a ton of ingredients in. I only live a short drive away. You're more than welcome to come over after work. If you want help, I can help. If you don't, I can stay out of the way. It's no problem.'

'I'm sure your girlfriend will love that.'

'If you wanted to know my relationship status, you could have just asked.'

'I don't—' I start, but he cuts me off before I can protest that it *really* wasn't about that.

'You'll be pleased to know I'm single. Can you imagine anyone being daft enough to put up with me for long?' He says it in his up-tempo Hatter voice, but there's a waver in it and a hint of sadness behind his words. 'I live alone. You're more than welcome to use my kitchen as often as you need. And don't worry, I have a fire extinguisher. Between the two of us, we'll have a better chance of monitoring for all flame-related activity.'

'Flame-related activity' makes me burst out laughing and he grins that wide Hatter grin again. 'So that's a yes, then. Let me give you directions.'

He holds his hand out for my phone, and I get a little shiver when our fingers brush as I give it to him. I watch him typing something and wonder just how wrong I've got this man. Just like last night, when he took those hats off, I think he let me see a bit of who he is when he's not playing a character. And it was someone quite different. Someone I actually quite like.

7

I've never been to the affluent part of Herefordshire before. It's not far from Ever After Street and the surrounding villages, but as my old car clunks along the smooth road that's *not* filled with potholes, I have a feeling that someone is about to pull me over and politely point out a 'no peasants allowed' sign. This is a seriously *nice* neighbourhood. Houses seem to have a minimum of eight bedrooms, pretty flowerbeds, neat lawns, and trimmed hedges. At least one motorhome parked outside massive double-garages. Some even have fountains in their driveways. Fountains, for goodness' sake. Have I taken a wrong turn? Surely Bram doesn't live somewhere like this? The trees are swathed in masses of white and pink spring blossom and neatly pruned into wine glass shapes. Who the heck worries about what shape a tree is in?

I pull over at the gate of a large house and double-check the instructions he put in my phone. The house in front of me is set so far back in the grounds that it looks quite small from this distance. This cannot be Bram's house. It's got to be a joke.

On one of the imposing gateposts, there's a security camera with a screen, showing my car in the gateway and my face when I get out and peer at it, but while I'm still trying to figure out which button I need to press on the intercom, it buzzes and the iron gates slide open to let me in.

'Thanks,' I say to the screen and get back in the car and drive through, and they close automatically behind me.

It feels more like driving into a country park than a house. The gravel driveway is bordered by freshly cut grass on either side and there's not a weed in sight. I don't think I've ever *seen* a lawn without dandelions and buttercups popping up all over it. There are trees dotted around covered in fresh green leaves that have sprung open for spring and the ever-present fizz of blossom.

I'm driving painstakingly slowly, leaning forwards so I can see the mansion as it comes into view. Maybe it's not exactly a mansion. There's probably some rule about how many rooms a house has to have to qualify for mansion status, and this probably just misses out, but it's a *very* nice house.

There's the most beautiful magnolia tree I've ever seen in the middle of the courtyard, its branches are weighed down with two-tone magenta pink flowers and they extend over the neat gravel area where there's a car parked.

Bram's car? It's completely out of place with this manor of a house – a dinged-up old blue thing that makes mine look modern when I stop next to it, parking underneath the branches of the magnolia tree, the scent of blossom strong in the air. Sandy-coloured gravel crunches under my feet as I grab my bag of ingredients and swing my legs out of the car, wishing I'd worn something a bit more formal than the jeans and oversized T-shirt I changed into after work.

There's a bumper sticker on the back of the car that's got a silhouette of the White Rabbit with his trumpet and the *Alice in Wonderland* quote – '*Why, sometimes I've believed as many as six impossible things before breakfast.*' Definitely Bram's car then.

I'm admiring the stone planters of colour-coordinated pastel tulips when the front door opens to reveal... a totally different person.

'Good lord, I really *am* in the wrong place,' I say as I crunch across the gravel towards the steps leading up to the door. Because the man who has answered it is so far removed from the Mad Hatter that I genuinely do have to squint and discreetly double-check that it's actually Bram and not a brother or cousin or something.

He's wearing black jogging bottoms and nothing but white socks on his feet. A plain grey marl T-shirt, no hat in sight, and no eyeliner. He's still got his earrings in, and instead of sticking out in a thousand directions and spiked with product, his blue hair is soft-looking and close to his head, the ends starting to turn wavy where it's still drying after being washed.

''ello,' he says in that high-pitched nasally voice that I'd recognise anywhere.

'You look so different,' I say in response, because it's really thrown me. At work, I *know* Bram is playing a role, but I'd never considered what he might look like at other times. 'You are full of surprises.'

'Thought I was full of something a lot more unpleasant than three-thousand-year-old honey.'

'Oh, you are.' I reach the top of the steps and look up into his gentle dark eyes. 'But you've got some surprises in there too.'

He smiles, a soft smile that's nothing like his megawatt Hatter grin, and something flutters inside me so I look away quickly and continue admiring the sweeping gardens. 'I feel like I should have brought something. Like champagne and caviar, or a yacht or something.'

He laughs. 'Terrible choices. I'm vegetarian and I don't drink. And a yacht would never have fitted in your car.'

'Me too! And me neither!' I say, surprised we have that much in common. 'I've been a vegetarian for years, and I can't really afford to drink these days, so it feels better to make it a choice. Besides, I'm old now, the thought of getting rat-arsed and then spending all day nursing a hangover loses its appeal by your mid-twenties, I think.'

'I'm weird enough without being drunk. And I'm really boring and spend most evenings eating too much cake and dozing off in front of the TV. I hate the vulnerability of being drunk and I morally object to doing things you're "supposed" to do just to fit in.'

Why have I never noticed what a cracking outlook he's got before? A teetotal vegetarian with eyeliner, two pierced ears, blue hair, and a really massive house, who is also refreshingly honest. He really is full of surprises, and so far today, they've been good ones.

He steps back and holds a hand out towards the entranceway. 'Come in. You didn't have to bring anything.'

He nods to the bag I'm carrying, because even though Bram said he had plenty of ingredients, it felt wrong not to bring my own. 'It's bad enough that you're letting me use your kitchen.'

'What's bad about it?'

'I'm thirty-four and don't have a kitchen of my own, Bram!'

'That's not bad, it's just the way the cards fall sometimes – forgive the pun *and* the fact I don't have a deck of cards on me to perform a visual representation. Life isn't easy and sometimes it's harder than at other times. Besides, you're just "between kitchens" at the moment.' He points to a mat inside the door, where his neon yellow boots are, plus a pair of muddy wellies, and a pair of trainers, wordlessly telling me to take my shoes off. 'All bad things pass eventually. Pretty soon kitchens will be between *you*.'

'That sounds remarkably uncomfortable.' I toe my trainers off and shift them onto the mat beside his yellow boots, and look up at the high ceiling and wide hallway. I instantly see why I had to take them off. We're in a large hall that's decorated in shades of cream and white, with gold accents. Under my feet is fluffy cream carpet, the walls are cream and hung with gold-framed prints of geometric shapes that look like placeholder pictures when you buy an empty photo frame.

'Kitchen's through here. Although feel free to look around, you won't find much mischief to get into.'

'I'm not a mischief type, Bram.'

'That just means you haven't met the right people to make mischief with. Everyone's got a five-year-old child inside just waiting to get out. It can usually be coaxed out with silly string, party poppers, or a pack of crayons.'

I can't imagine this pristine house has ever had a *sniff* of a party popper, much less a crayon.

I can't resist peering through the doorless doorways of other rooms we pass. A living room with oversized white leather sofas, grey accents, a cream carpet. A dining room with an imposing mahogany table and eight chairs. A conservatory with arguably more light coming in through its enormous windows than there is outside. They're all decorated in the same colourless colour scheme – a thousand shades of pale, and everything looks ultra-modern. Bram seems more of a colourful vintage type, but this could be something straight from an *Ideal Home* brochure.

'Tea?' His voice floats back down the hallway. I've dawdled and he's disappeared.

'You're not in work now, you know.'

'Always time for tea!' he calls in that cheery Hatter voice and I follow it to find my way. Imagine having such a big house that you have to *hunt* for the kitchen. I follow the sound of china clinking and a kettle boiling and come to a large arched doorway that leads into a vast room.

'Oh my God. Now *this* is a kitchen.' I intend to look around in awe, but the first thing I see is a large red fire extinguisher, deliberately placed on the marble worktop opposite the doorway. 'Very funny.'

He laughs without looking up from the kettle he's pouring. 'I was trying to rig it up to open the door by itself, but you arrived before I could figure it out. Thought it might make you feel better if you knew where it was.'

The kitchen is as awe-inspiring as the other rooms. The floor tiles are shiny mirror-glazed white, the cupboard doors are white with gold handles, and the work surface around the units must be pure marble, glistening white with flecks of gold sparkling through it. There's a fridge and a freezer side by side, both taller than me, and an oven with a screen and so many buttons that you can probably earn some sort of engineering degree just by learning to operate it.

The only bit of colour is a large rectangular magnet on the front of the refrigerator with a slogan on it in a rainbow of blocky letters. It reads 'this kitchen is for dancing'. 'Is it?'

'I'm not much of a rules person, but it's my one and only rule.'

'I hope it doesn't apply to me because I can't dance.'

'Neither can I. That's what makes it fun.'

I suppose I should've known that. He can't sing either, and that really, really doesn't stop him.

'So what do you think? Can you make use of it?'

'Bram, it's...' I look at him. His hair is the only thing that's colourful about him tonight, but the kitchen is so astoundingly plain. I've never been to any home that was more unfitting of its owner. Bram is bright in every way, but this house has been to Magnolia Town and hit every branch of the cream tree on the way back. Bram is chaotic. Colourful. Lively. Loud. His house is bland, bland, bland. Everything looks so perfectly positioned that I expect it to be superglued in place, like it belongs in a photoshoot. 'Yeah, of course. The thing is... I make a mess when I cook.'

'Messes can be cleaned up,' he says with a carefree shrug as he places a mug of tea on the unit and nudges it towards me, making the tea swish-swash in the cup and come perilously close to sploshing over the edges.

'I know, it's just... you could perform surgery in here, it's so clinical. Operating theatres aren't as pristine as this.'

At first, I think he might be offended, but then he grins and says, 'Oh, so *that's* what the team of scrubbed-up surgeons were doing here earlier.'

It's a joke, but I can't help feeling slightly uneasy that his house is so big, you could genuinely lose a team of surgeons inside it.

'Have you eaten?'

I had a sandwich this afternoon in work, but nothing since. 'By the time I'd got home and showered and changed...'

'Me neither. Would you like a blueberry flower tart that I made last night?' He's already crossed the kitchen floor and opened the giant silver fridge, and when I go to protest, my stomach rumbles instead.

He comes back with a cake tin and opens the lid to reveal a beautiful display of tarts. I didn't know what a blueberry flower tart was, but it's a normal blueberry tart where the pastry case has been carefully split into petals and cooked in the shape of a flower, decorated with a big swirl of fresh cream and has a blueberry on the top. It's simple and yet incredibly effective.

They're small so I take two and he does the same, and it feels like he's waiting for my verdict when I bite into one, and they taste as good as they look. The tartness of the blueberry filling perfectly balances the sweetness of the sugared cream and the pastry is buttery and melt-in-the-mouth.

The noise I make must convey how good it is because he bites into his own with a look of satisfaction. He seems so quiet tonight, everything about him is a world away from his usual exasperating self.

He invites me into the living room, but given the colour of his carpets and my unrivalled ability for staining light-coloured things, it's best to stay put with tea and blueberry tarts. He reaches over to pull up a blind, revealing a window that looks out onto the park-like grounds and greenery surrounding his house, and leans on his elbows, looking out.

There's nowhere to sit, so I do the same. The light is on inside and it's getting dark outside, so the reflections block a lot of the view, but I can see neatly mowed grass and flower borders filled with waving daffodils, and a lawn with crocuses growing in it. A bird feeder with birds flying back and forth to it, and a pond in the distance with a trickling water feature. The only thing it's missing is a few grazing fawns and wandering peacocks to make it into a real country park.

'It's not mine, by the way.'

'What?'

'The house. If you were wondering how a magician can afford a place like this. It's my father's property. He bought it years ago, spent a lot of money making it over, intending to sell it for a huge profit, and then the market crashed and it wasn't worth selling. People are less likely to break in if it's occupied, so I live here as a burglar deterrent. I was living in a really run-down hellhole of a block of flats. There was one too many stabbings in the stairwell and my mum took pity on me and persuaded my father that it made sense for me to move in here so the place wouldn't be standing empty.'

I didn't realise how relieved I'd be to hear that. 'Thank God for that. This house is so not you. It's so scarily different from you. I was starting to think you'd stolen the place from an IKEA catalogue.

That makes so much more sense. I *knew* you wouldn't voluntarily live somewhere so un-colourful.'

'I think there's a compliment buried in there somewhere.' He tries to hide his grin behind taking a sip of tea. 'My ex thought I was an embarrassment for being basically a glorified housesitter.'

It's the first time he's mentioned an ex or a relationship of any sort, and I can't help being intrigued by what sort of person Bram would date. 'I live in a rusty, leaky caravan on my friend's driveway. I judge no one when it comes to living quarters. Whatever it takes to get through each day, right?'

'Right.' His eyes flick to mine and he gives me a small smile that's full of understanding, and I *like* how different he is without his Mad Hatter walls up.

When we've finished eating, he puts the empty plates and mugs into an under-counter dishwasher, and pushes himself up to sit on the kitchen unit.

My veins are thrumming with nerves. I couldn't bake in Marnie's kitchen by myself the other night. Surely trying to do anything in an unfamiliar kitchen with Bram watching can only end in disaster.

There's a couple of bookshelves on one wall, packed with beautiful recipe books, and he's put out a pile of baking equipment, from mixing bowls to spatulas and measuring cups and cupcake cases, baking tins and oven trays, and keeps telling me to help myself to anything.

I brought a recipe with me, because I'm determined not to fail this time. A recipe for a batch of basic fairy cakes. The kind of recipe that *can't* go wrong. *Children* make fairy cakes. *I* made fairy cakes with my mum when I was about six. I cannot have been better at baking at six than I am at thirty-four.

'It must've been nice to grow up with a family tearoom...' It's clearly a leading sentence, and I'm sure he can sense my nerves and is trying to distract me.

I'm not sure how to answer him, but I measure out butter and sugar and cream them together, and the noise of the electric whisk convinces me that he won't be able to hear what I'm saying anyway. 'It's what I've always wanted to do. Mum hosted an Unbirthday party for me – ironically on the day it actually was my tenth birthday. She invited all my school friends to the tearoom, and she'd made a real Unbirthday cake, exactly like the pink one with blue flowers the Mad Hatter gives Alice in the animated film. When I blew out the candles, I made a wish that life would always be as magical as it was then and that I'd be like my mum when I grew up too. That was the last birthday before she left and life changed drastically.'

I stir in eggs and vanilla flavouring, and then fold in flour. 'I overshared the rest earlier. I thought that cosy family tearoom would be my life. Never really considered that I would do anything else, and then when Nan died and it had to be sold, I found myself adrift. I've been adrift ever since.'

When the batter is smooth, I spoon it into cake cases. 'And when I heard about Lilith and the tearooms, it sparked something inside me, and I *wanted* to bake again... and then I couldn't.'

'I'm sorry,' he says gently. 'It sounds like you've had a rough few years. Enough to make anyone lose their spark...'

'Alice has always been my comfort book. When I was little, my mum used to read it to me, and after she left, I was drawn to it again. I escaped into Wonderland. In my real life, nothing made sense, and reading a book where nothing made sense made it better somehow. Alice felt as lost as I was. I identified with her. I longed to wake up on a riverbank one day and discover it had all been a dream. Alice made me believe it was okay if things didn't make sense and that things would be better soon, that one day I'd find the exit to my confusing, spiralling world too. I feel more like *me* than I have for years at The Wonderland Teapot. I'm finally doing something that would make my nan and mum proud, something that was meant for me, I want to make the things they used to make using our family recipes, and...' I trail off. There isn't any point finishing the sentence. He knows as well as I do that this is only ever going to be temporary if I can't pull myself together and actually remember what those family recipes *were*.

The oven heats up in record time and I slide the baking tray into it while Bram loads the equipment I've used into the dishwasher and then invites me into the living room to wait.

'I'm going to stay here and keep watch. Things go wrong when ovens are on.'

'Okay.' Without a moment of hesitation, he sits down cross-legged on the floor in front of the oven.

'What are you doing?'

'Keeping watch.'

'Bram...'

'There's a David Attenborough documentary on the TV that I've seen several times before. This is far more interesting. It's like *The Great British Bake Off* but I get to be Paul Hollywood *and* Prue Leith, minus the interesting jewellery choices. All we need now is Noel Fielding making bad jokes.'

I can't help looking at him as he sits there, his elbows on his knees, his hands steepled under his chin with his head resting on them. 'You don't need to—'

'You know what they say – good things come to those who...'

'Wait?' I offer.

'...Make sizeable donations to the right politicians, but both are correct.' He's got a familiar cheeky grin on his face when he looks up at me with a one-shouldered shrug, and it makes me laugh much harder than it should do.

I sit down beside him and cross my legs under me. I'm intending to watch the cake batter start to rise in the lit-up oven interior, but I find my gaze being drawn back to the man beside me. I've sat close enough that my knee is touching his. Usually he smells of citrusy aftershave, but tonight it's just shampoo and laundry fabric softener, and only the swish of the dishwasher and the fan of the oven fills the silence between us.

'So, magic, huh?' It sounds sharp and awkward and it's increasingly obvious that in my two years of avoiding life, I've totally forgotten how to talk to other humans.

'It's just an oven.' He holds a hand out in front of him, indicating the glass door we're both looking through. 'A mix of certain ingredients produce a chemical reaction when exposed to heat and do that thing known as "cooking". Science, not magic.'

'Oh, you're a riot tonight,' I mutter, even though I'm fighting not to laugh. At work, I think he's trying too hard and I *try* not to find him funny, but tonight everything about him seems natural, and he's hilarious without intending to be. 'You know what I meant. I've never met a magician before... how long have you been doing magic?'

He looks over at me curiously, like he's trying to work out if there's an ulterior motive behind the question, and I feel bad again that this is the first time I've actually asked him anything about himself. It's the first time I've needed to, because at The Wonderland Teapot, he keeps up a constant litany of chatter, and I'm always wishing he'd shut up, and definitely not encouraging him to talk *more*.

'I started when I was twelve,' he says eventually. 'I didn't have the easiest time growing up, and an uncle bought me one of those children's magic kits for Christmas one year, and... it was everything I didn't know I needed. It spoke to me. Back then, they were just basic tricks like balls under cups and linking and unlinking steel rings, the kind of thing that anyone could do, but I focused on perfecting those tricks and while I was concentrating on them, I forgot everything else that was going on. I learned harder and more difficult things. It was the first thing I really connected with. The first thing that made me feel like *me*. Magic gave me a sense of place in the world. I went from being too shy to put my hand up in class when a teacher asked a question to performing magic in front of school assemblies. It's an ice breaker. I learned to separate the tricks from myself. I was awkward and terrible at communicating. I was always frozen by crippling shyness and if I bumbled my way through meeting someone, I was too embarrassed to ever talk to them again, but if I did a trick, I could tell myself that if they hadn't liked my trick, that didn't mean they didn't like *me*, and it did so much for my confidence. It changed my childhood completely. It takes a *lot* for me to feel like I'm good at something, but I knew I was good at magic.'

I'm surprised by his passion and openness, and by the emotion in his voice. He's obviously very good at what he does, but it had never occurred to me that it means *that* much to him, or that it could have such an enormous effect on a child.

'Now I'm still shy and awkward and haven't got a clue how to talk to people, but magic is an ice breaker.' He holds his hand out, inviting me to shake it, and when I do, his long fingers curl around mine and he shakes my hand like we're meeting for the first time. 'Nowadays I don't have to walk up to people and say, "Hi, I'm Bram, the least memorable human in the history of the world and you'll have forgotten me before your next blink." I can do a trick instead and make an impression, whether good or bad.'

I stifle another snort. Of all the strange things he says, *that* has got to be one of the strangest. 'You? *Shy*? You, the Mad Hatter who yaks all day? *You* struggle to talk to people?'

'Yes, actually.' He lets go of my fingers and pulls his hand away like I've hurt him. 'Is that really so hard to believe?'

I didn't expect his sharp response, and I realise what's just happened. He's opened up to me, told me something that I doubt many other people know, and I've done exactly what he expected me to. 'In the shop, yes. Tonight... no, it isn't. I'm sorry. I try not to judge people based on their appearance, but I've been doing that since I met you.'

'You know what they say,' he says with a shrug. 'Never judge a duvet by its cover.'

It's his squeaky Mad Hatter voice again, the one he uses while playing the character, and it makes me wonder how much deeper this goes. More and more, I get the feeling that he plays a character in public to hide very real insecurities.

'The one thing you're not is unmemorable.' I bite my lip. 'You make an unforgettable impression on everyone you meet.'

'Hatter does. The alternative-type magician I've played at the carousel does. But me? I don't stand out in any way. I'm quiet. I like watching nature documentaries and reading books. I play video games. I'm not into sports. If I go out, it's for a walk in the country-side. Sometimes the highlight of my day is a nice nap.'

I laugh even though I didn't intend to because it feels like a serious moment. 'If it helps, while Hatter has his good points, I think this side of you is the most intriguing one yet.'

I probably shouldn't, but his knee is *right there*, next to mine, and I reach across and touch the back of my hand to it, his jogging bottoms well-worn and soft under my fingers.

He looks down at my hand and then his dark eyes flick up and meet mine. 'Thank you.'

We hold each other's gaze. I've become terrible at eye contact lately, but for once, I don't want to look away, I want him to know that I see *him* tonight... and he's nothing like I imagined he would be.

My hand is against his knee and he hasn't dropped my gaze, and everything around us has gone very still and quiet and it's like a magnet is pulling me towards him. It's a tingle I haven't felt for a very long time and I let out a breath, and in the stillness that was so fragile, it's enough to break the spell.

He blinks and looks away. 'You should check the cakes.'

'Cakes! Yes!' I scramble to my feet. God knows what I'm thinking, looking into Bram's eyes and feeling tingles. He might be different than I thought, but just getting out the door every morning is a hard enough life achievement at the moment, without thinking about adding further complications. I don't do things like looking into people's eyes any more. That only ever leads to trouble.

He's got to his feet too and he hands me an oven glove and a skewer, and I open the oven door and slide the skewer into one of the cakes. It comes out clean and they look the right shade of golden brown, so I get them out.

'And you say you can't cook.' Bram elbows my arm gently as we look at the steaming tray of cakes on the unit. 'They look amazing.'

Maybe it *is* just a kitchen issue after all. Maybe every previous disaster has been down to bad luck or fluke coincidences that couldn't have been avoided in any set of circumstances, and a beautiful modern kitchen is the key to unlocking my potential. 'Maybe you're my lucky charm.'

'Awwwww.' He reaches out to take a cake. 'Now that's definitely the nicest thing you've ever said to me.'

'Oi! You can't have one yet, they need to cool down and be iced!'

'If you think I've sat in front of an oven for twenty minutes just so I can wait another hour for decoration, you're as sorely mistaken as my glutes are after sitting on the floor for so long. Besides, it's a fact of life that nothing will ever taste as good as when you're burning your mouth on it, mere seconds after it comes out of the oven.'

I want to be annoyed but I appreciate his enthusiasm, and there are sixteen of them, so more than enough for us to sample one now and then decorate them later. My head is filled with visions of tomorrow being the very first day that I serve customers genuine homemade cakes, lovingly made from scratch and exquisitely decorated. It will be the start of what I wanted to do with the tearoom from the beginning.

He's already peeling the cake case off, and he keeps shifting the cake around and shaking his fingers because it's too hot, but as I'm coming to learn, there's not much that can deter Bram from cake.

I take one too and flap my hand to disperse the steam, and I can't help watching as he takes a big bite of his.

'Oh my God,' he says around a mouthful.

'That good?' I can feel my face light up as I get the case off mine and take a bite too. 'Oh my God.'

I echo his words but it is *not* the good kind of 'oh my God'. What the heck *is* that? Because I've eaten many cakes over the course of my life, and that doesn't resemble *any* of them.

Bram's face shifts to revulsion and he speaks with his mouth stuffed. 'I'm going to need a crowbar to prise my teeth out of this.'

It does tend to take to your teeth and form a bond with them, a bit like denture fixative in edible form. I'm trying to inch it out of my mouth without taking any fillings with it, and he's trying not to gag as he leans over to spit the unfortunate bit he'd bitten off into the bin.

'Crikey, that was like eating an armchair.' At least he's laughing as he throws the remaining cake into the bin too. 'What did you do to this?'

'I don't know!' I say helplessly. 'I followed the recipe! You watched me!'

'Was one of the ingredients Polyfilla? Did it call for butter, sugar, and four tablespoons of wallpaper paste? When you went to buy your ingredients, did the shop have a big sign saying "B&Q" outside?'

He makes me laugh even though I *want* to cry. How can a simple cake go so very, very wrong? 'I used to be able to do this with my eyes closed.'

'*Did* you have your eyes closed? Because that could explain a lot...' He takes another cake and pokes at it. 'I'm actually very impressed that anyone can make a fairy cake go *that* horribly wrong. That's a skill in itself.'

'Maybe they'll be better when they've cooled down?' I say hopefully.

'When they've cooled down, you'll be able to send them to warzones and substitute them for cannonballs.'

He's being kind there.

'Place them very gently in the bin, lest they crack the floor tiles and go straight through to the magma of the earth's core.'

I make a noise of frustration and drop my head into my hands. 'I did exactly as it said.'

'Never mind. We'll try again. Come over tomorrow night and I'll help, see if we can figure out where you're going wrong. At a guess, I'd say you got to the part where it says to fold in the flour and then accidentally transferred it into a cement mixer...'

'This is hopeless,' I mutter without lifting my head. 'This is what happens every time I get near a kitchen now, and it's *so* disheartening. Everything comes out tasting like this – or worse.'

'There's no such thing as hopeless.' He reaches out to give my shoulder a squeeze. 'You know what they say – practice makes better. Frustrated, but ultimately, better.'

For once, his habit of getting sayings wrong actually makes sense. 'Not perfect?'

'I don't think anyone's perfect, are they?'

I lift my head and look over my shoulder at him. 'Very insightful.'

He'd been leaning on the unit too, and he pushes himself up, sweeps the remaining cakes into the bin with a comment about not recycling anything so potentially hazardous to public health, and heads for the kitchen door. 'I'll come to the supermarket with you to choose tomorrow's Wonderland options. There's one ten minutes away from here. It's good to mix it up, make sure you don't arouse suspicion in your regular one by buying enough baked goods to feed an army every day.'

'Bram, you don't have—'

'I want to.' He cuts off my protest. 'Come on, we can take my car, we'll be there in a jiffy. And when we get back, you can help me make another batch of those blueberry flower tarts, so at least there'll be *something* homemade to offer tomorrow.'

'I didn't want to get you involved in this.' I follow him out into the hallway. There's something lovely about how easy-going he is and how he takes everything in his stride.

'It's okay. Between us, we've got customers to feed and entertain, and a bit of crossover never hurt anybody.'

At the front door, he shoves his feet into well-worn trainers and I tug mine back on, and watch in fascination as he steps over to a mirror and pulls on a grey knitted beanie hat, and tucks his hair underneath it, pushing the blue locks up and pulling the hat down until every strand of hair is hidden. He takes a baseball cap and pulls that on over the top.

'It's not that much of an incognito mission.'

'I know.' His eyes flick to mine in the mirror. 'But having blue hair makes people look at you and sometimes I don't feel like being looked at.'

Now *that* I understand. My extrovert Hatter is more of an introvert than I imagined.

He picks up a set of car keys and opens the front door, and I step out and stand aside as he locks up.

'You're really different than I thought you'd be,' I say as we walk down the steps.

And right on cue, he jumps off the steps from the third up, lands with a pirouette and a splash of gravel under his feet and spins around. 'I'm still going to drive you up the wall at work tomorrow.'

I meet his eyes and smile. 'Wouldn't have it any other way.'

He walks backwards across the courtyard without dropping eye contact as he grins at me, and this time, it's very much a Bram grin and not a Hatter one.

8

'How can there be someone new starting?' Bram says when I fill him in on the phone call from Mr Hastings last night, informing me that he'd hired a new member of staff for the tearoom and to expect them today. 'Doing what? Playing another character?'

'I don't know, but at least he told me this time,' I say, even though an unexpected call from Mr Hastings on a Sunday evening did nothing for my cardiac health. We don't need a new member of staff – Bram and I have been managing just fine, but Mr Hastings was unnervingly cagey when I tried to question him, and now it's Monday morning and I'm wondering what he's got lined up for us.

The Wonderland Teapot has been open for two weeks today. The days are whizzing past and I simultaneously can't believe it's been two weeks already and that it's only been two weeks, because it's starting to feel like I've never *not* been here, in a good way.

I've hidden away from life for so long and not met many people. I wasn't sure about how well I'd cope with being thrust headfirst into a customer-facing role, but it's been a welcome reminder of the times when I used to be happy, and how much I loved the tearoom I grew up in. Our customers are lovely. Almost everyone has embraced the madness of The Wonderland Teapot and been very complimentary, from people who love the books and films and get all the references in the décor, to people who just pop in for a cup of tea and don't expect the sensory assault of colour and weird things, and leave saying it's inspired them to read the book.

And then there's Bram, who makes every day pass in a blur of colour and jokes and producing things from the bottomless caverns that seem to exist behind most people's ears.

There have been afternoon teas and a couple more Unbirthday parties, and he's let me come over each night and use his kitchen, with varying degrees of disaster. I seem to be the exception to the 'practice makes better' idea, although he hasn't given up on me yet.

Between us, we made an apple pie and a batch of butterfly cakes yesterday, but not enough to fill the entire display case, so we're still relying on supermarket-bought goods too. It's quarter to nine and we're standing side by side, decorating the raspberry and white chocolate cupcakes we bought last night. I've got a piping bag of red butter icing, and he's got one in white, and we're piping rose-shaped swirls onto each one, and it's been surprisingly nice to share the burden with someone. It really has started to feel like we're in this together and I have a niggling feeling that The Wonderland Teapot is only as special as it is because of what the Mad Hatter brings to it. I'm just a woman wearing an Alice dress, but he *is* the Mad Hatter. I struggle to find the confidence to engage with people like he does, but he's got time for every customer, and I'm starting to wonder how I would ever have done this without him.

'At least they're early,' I say at the sound of a knock on the door and go over to open it, trying to ignore the uneasy feeling of Mr Hastings hiring yet another employee without my permission. Having the decency to inform me beforehand only makes me feel slightly less undermined than last time.

The woman standing outside the door is wearing a ruffled red ballgown, poorly hidden under a jacket, with a bright red wig and a gold crown. 'Let me guess, the Queen of Hearts?'

'Hello. Tabby. I believe you're expecting me?' She does a curtsey for me to admire her huge dress, and holds a hand out. At first I think she's inviting me to kiss it, but really she's showing off her red-jewelled rings and the red heart-shaped tips on her stiletto-pointed false nails. 'Off with everyone's heads!'

'Indeed.' Everything about her has set me on edge, and I can't help feeling annoyed that I, once again, don't have any control over who works in *my* shop. Are random people playing Wonderland characters just going to keep rocking up until the Teapot is so full with employees that there won't be any space for the customers?

'You'd better come in.' I have to give her a chance, don't I? I thought Bram wouldn't be an asset at first too, and I was wrong on that front. Customers are loving the Mad Hatter, maybe they'll also love the Queen of Hearts and enjoy the fully immersive Wonderland experience.

Tabby follows me into the café and stops to look around, and I'm reminded of Bram's reaction on the first day, his glee and joyfulness, and how it's the complete opposite of the sneer that darkens her face.

'Oh, how charming.' It's said with a patronising tone and sounds like the way she might critique a nursery school child's proudly presented first finger painting.

Bram's gone out the back and stops abruptly when he comes back in, and a stormy look instantly clouds his face. 'Tabby? What the *hell* are you doing here?' His face turns from a storm cloud to confusion. 'Are you here to see me?'

'I work here now.' She smiles a smug smile in his direction. 'Part time. I'm far too busy to commit to a full-time role.'

'You... work... here?' His mouth opens and closes like he doesn't know what to say. Quite a feat for someone who chats non-stop, whether there's anyone listening or not. 'Since when?'

'Since this morning. Mr Hastings hired me.' Tabby shrugs the jacket off her shoulders and then holds it out to me, like she's expecting me to hang it up for her.

'The staffroom and bathroom are upstairs.' I pretend not to have understood her hint, and she huffs the layered fringe of her red wig upwards.

'Did you know I'd be here?' Bram asks her.

'Of course. Your father told me.'

'Why the hell are you still in touch with my father? We broke up two years ago!'

Ahh, and there was me, just about to ask how they know each other. I might have wondered about what kind of person Bram would date, but I didn't want to actually meet one, live in living colour. Is this the same ex he mentioned the other night? Because she didn't sound great, to be fair...

'I can still be civil to people from the past, Bram. He was nearly my father-in-law. Relationships don't simply disappear on your whims.'

'He wasn't nearly your anything.' Bram's hands are in such tight fists that it looks like his nails are cutting through his palms and I've never seen his mouth set in such a hard line before.

'So you two know each other?' I try to ease the tension that's shot through the room, so tight that it feels like you could pluck the air with a guitar pick.

'She's my...'

'We were engaged.' Tabby finishes the sentence that Bram seems unable to complete, and then she clearly appraises him. She makes no secret of looking him up and down, and I can see him squaring his shoulders and standing straighter.

Her nose turns up. 'Why would you do that to your hair? You look like an electrocuted Smurf.'

He plasters on his Mad Hatter smile and gives her a false grin. 'Because I knew it would drive people like you and my father absolutely crackers.'

'He wants me to get back with you, you know. Luckily I have a wonderful new boyfriend now, but your father still wants me to see if I can straighten you out.' She gives him a look of scrutiny. 'Seems it might be beyond even my powers.'

It rubs me up the wrong way. I might have had plenty of reasons to get annoyed with Bram myself, but no one comes into *my* tearoom and insults *my* Hatter. 'Bram is the best Mad Hatter I've ever met. Absolutely no one gets to straighten him out on my watch.'

'Have you met many Mad Hatters?'

'Enough to know when I've got a good one.' I dodge around her and go back to the counter. 'Now, if you'll excuse us, we still have work to do before opening time. If you're going to work here, you'll need to muck-in.'

'Muck-in? Me?' She looks so horrified that she must think there's actual muck involved. 'Oh, no no. I take my orders from Mr Hastings. He said nothing of the sort. I am to play a Queen. Can you imagine what people would think if they saw a Queen waiting tables?'

'You can help us cle—'

'*Orf* with your head!' she cries before I've finished the word 'clean'. 'See? I'm playing a character who would have servants to clean and I am fully committed to the role. I'm sure you can appreciate that, *Alice*.' She gives me the same appraising look she gave Bram earlier and it makes me stand taller too.

What the heck is going on here? First I get Bram dumped on me unexpectedly, which hasn't been an altogether bad thing, then his ex-fiancée turns up, and she's already got my hackles up.

Instead of letting Tabby's critical gaze get to me, I pick up the bag of icing I'd put down earlier and continue icing the cakes. Bram and I are working like a well-oiled team. He passes a tray over, spins around me to collect the ones I've just finished and place them on the stands in the display unit, and she watches us for a moment. 'I'm going to freshen up. Bathroom?'

I point out the door to the back room. 'Through there and up the stairs, you can't miss it. You can leave your coat up there too.'

Bram watches the doorway, and when she disappears, he jerks his head to get me to step closer to him, and he bends until his mouth is right next to my ear, and his fruity aftershave fills my nose.

'I won't tell anyone our secret, but she will *delight* in it. Be very careful.'

Oh, great. It was hard enough keeping it a secret from him, but now he knows, life has been so much easier. And I trust him, but the thought of someone else working here and finding out my little secret sends my thoughts spiralling. Just when things were starting to go well, I'm once again left in a spin of panic that my little white lie is going to get back to Mr Hastings and he'll fire me on the spot. 'Did you know she was coming?'

'Heck no. Holy green tomatoes, she's someone I never wanted to clap eyes on again, never mind work alongside.' He sounds like he's *trying* to sound upbeat and jokey to cover how much her appearance has thrown him. 'Seriously thinking of quit—'

'Don't you dare!' I reach out and grab his forearm, my fingers curling tightly around the sleeve of his lime green jacket. 'The Wonderland Teapot wouldn't be the same without you. You're not allowed to go anywhere, ever.'

He seems flummoxed for a minute, and then his face breaks

into the most genuine smile I've seen so far this morning. 'Awww. And all this time, I thought you barely tolerated me.'

'I barely tolerate you pulling things out from behind my ear. When you're being yourself, you're marginally okay.'

'Be still, my dusty old heart.' He puts a hand on his chest and gives me a sarcastic grin. 'And on that note, I'm going to go and empty the recycling bin in case she pokes her nose in there.'

'Did you see her nails? There's no way she's ever been near a recycling bin in her life.'

He lets out a loud unexpected laugh and his shoulders loosen for the first time since she came in. 'Remarkably accurate. Back in a tick.' He goes to walk out and then turns back. 'Cleo? Thanks for saying that about straightening me out. Much appreciated.'

For just a second, he looks insecure and vulnerable, and I think I've just got a glimpse of *why* he hides so much of himself behind a character.

Having taken the supermarket packaging to his car, Bram is back inside by the time Tabby glides into the shop in her ridiculously oversized red ballgown. 'What are you really doing here? Don't forget I know you well enough to know that you'd never deign yourself to work in a tearoom if there wasn't something in it for you.'

'I'm just here to show willing. I put in an application to take over this building myself, you know. A wellness retreat. I think it would've been the perfect fit.'

'A wellness retreat on Ever After Street?' I say incredulously. Of all the things Ever After Street needs, I can't think of anything more misplaced.

'You know something's a terrible idea when it rhymes,' Bram interjects.

'Well, my bid was unfortunately rejected, and as Mr Hastings was telling me about this place, I thought that what any Wonderland needs is a Queen of Hearts, and I wanted to show Mr Hastings there are no hard feelings and that I can be a valuable asset to Ever After Street too, and maybe next time, my bid won't be rejected when an opening comes up on the street.'

'You're trying to prove you can play nice with other children,' Bram says. 'I don't know what you think you're going to get out of this. They'll never agree to a wellness retreat here, it's the least fitting thing I can possibly imagine for Ever After Street. This is a place where children come to believe in magic. Children are *not* the target audience for yoga and spa days. Acupuncture for five-year-olds will never catch on. Chemical peels? Eyebrow threading? Back waxes for seven-year-olds?'

'You are never too young to start looking after yourself,' she trills. 'Mr Hastings thinks it's a wonderful idea but he was outvoted by his fellow councillors.'

She puts a strange emphasis on 'Mr Hastings' every time she says his name and I'm not sure why. 'I agree with Bram, it's—'

'No one has *ever* agreed with Bram.'

I glance up at him. The Hatter grin is plastered onto his face and it looks like he's fighting to keep it there. Discomfort and defensiveness are pouring off him in waves. He's still standing near enough that I can nudge my foot against his behind the counter without her noticing. 'Well, I do. We have Rapunzel's hair salon – they have a niche of doing Disney princess hairstyles for children and doing adult haircuts as well. A wellness retreat is an adult thing. It would never work on Ever After Street.'

'We'll see. I have plenty of ideas. I'm a trained beauty therapist and yoga practitioner, and this place is an untapped customer base. Think of how many knackered parents come here. They must be crying out for beauty treatments. Parents always forget to take care of their own needs and deserve a bit of pampering. For a price, of course.'

'Are you also going to open a childcare centre? Because most of those knackered parents have got youngsters in tow and there's nowhere to leave them and pop off for a quick hour of relaxation.'

'I don't know,' she says with a huff.

'You can burn that bridge when you come to it,' Bram mutters, another mixed-up saying that might have made me laugh if the tension wasn't so severe.

'Oh, what a surprise, look at you being discouraging and negative. You never did support my dreams. That's what comes from having the ambition of frogspawn.'

Negative and discouraging. That's the *last* thing Bram is. And ambition? Admittedly I don't know much about him, but he *loves* magic, and I know you don't get *that* good at it without a lot more ambition than frogspawn.

A gentle knock on the door makes me realise it's past 9 a.m., and before I have a chance to go over and open it, Tabby gets in first.

'Off with your heads!' She screeches at the two elderly ladies outside the door, and they step back in alarm.

'Don't mind her!' I rush over to reassure the two regular customers who have been coming in for tea and toast most mornings. 'This is the Queen of Hearts, a new addition from today who *won't* be using that greeting on a regular basis. Come in, come in, make yourselves comfortable. The usual? Extra sparkle in your tea?'

They nod and when I go to start it, Bram has already gone to boil the kettle and put bread in the toaster. Because he's helpful and encouraging, and although all relationships end with a degree of bitterness, he seems nothing like Tabby says, and she seems like the type of person who becomes an ex for many good reasons.

9

'Well, it's not *bad*,' Bram says kindly.

We're in his kitchen again and I've made a lemon drizzle loaf cake, hoping to be able to put slices of it out in the tearoom tomorrow. Which was definitely overly optimistic. After doing this for over a week now, I had hoped I might be improving slightly, but I'm still just as bad as ever.

'I think you might've misinterpreted the context of "sponge" because it's like eating a lemon flavoured bathroom sponge.' Even so, he digs his fork into the cake tin again. 'I've had worse this week. And it's only Monday evening.'

He's leaning on the unit and I'm sitting on it, with the loaf tin between us. I dig my fork into my end again too. It's definitely got a spongey texture to it... as in, the cake tries to push your fork back out when you dig it in. A similar level of bounce to a trampoline.

'The drizzle is nice though.'

'You made the drizzle!' I can't help laughing.

Bram's looking like himself again tonight. Freshly washed hair, no eyeliner, black jogging bottoms and a white T-shirt with Snoopy on it. There might be something about him when he's playing

Hatter, but there's even more about him when he's his natural quiet self, and I'm thoroughly enjoying our evenings in his kitchen, no matter the quality of the resulting bakes. And some of them could barely be termed that, and definitely shouldn't have the word 'quality' attached to them.

We both work our way towards the middle of the loaf tin, no matter how much resistance the cake puts up. 'Why are we eating this?'

'Comfort food,' he says with a mouthful.

I suck on my fork thoughtfully because it's an ideal opening to bring up Tabby, a topic he has meticulously avoided so far tonight. 'Does that mean you're in need of comfort after today?'

He glances at me. 'No comment.'

I sigh. 'Come on, Bram. How long are you going to avoid telling me about Tabby? All of tonight or a good chunk of the next two and a half months that's left of our trial too?'

Our trial. I didn't mean to say that. There's a growing feeling that Bram and I are in this together, but it's *me* who's ultimately accountable, and I need to remember that.

'It's still early, why don't we make something else?' He looks up at the clock on the wall to avoid looking at me.

'Never mind the elephant, you're avoiding the Jabberwock in the room.'

'I vote for making something else. I have a great idea for Alice-themed cookies to serve in the shop. Shall we try them? You can be my sous-chef. Watch and observe to avoid any more sponge misinterpretations.' He digs his fork into the lemon drizzle again and shoves a huge piece of cake into his mouth, undoubtedly to fill it up so much that he *can't* talk.

'Bram!' I say in frustration. 'Your ex has just turned up in my tearoom. The least you can do is give me an explanation. I didn't know you'd ever been engaged.'

'We've never talked about stuff like that. I see no reason to start now.' He puts a hand up to cover his mouth and his words are muffled around the cake he's still chewing.

'Do you want to get back with her?' I clear my throat because my voice breaks as I say it. I hadn't realised how nervous I am about what his answer might be. What if he's being so coy because he wants her back? It shouldn't matter to me. It *doesn't* matter to me, but the thought of Bram with someone so condescending is an uncomfortable one.

'No! Crikey, no. Are you as mad as the March Hare?' He can't chew the cake up fast enough to answer properly. 'There aren't enough variations of the word "no" to cover that one.'

'I get the impression things didn't end happily...' I prod at the cake like I'm trying to prod at him.

'Cleo...' he mutters, drawing my name out as though he's asking me not to push any further, and when I fix him with a stern, unrelenting look, he sighs and swallows the last of the lemon drizzle mouthful. 'Fine. I can bake and talk.'

The kitchen scale is still on the unit, the bags of sugar and flour haven't been put away yet, and he dries up the mixing bowl and gets another one out of the cupboard. Whatever these cookies are, they're complicated enough to need two mixing bowls. He weighs out two lots of butter and sugar and starts creaming them with the electric whisk.

'Tabby never wanted to date me.' He speaks over the noise of the whirring whisk. 'She wanted to date my father.'

'That strikes me as quite an age gap...'

'Not literally.' He laughs, but it's a taut laugh. 'My father is... He's kind of a big deal around here. Someone with a lot of sway on his side. If he gets behind your business idea, you're unlikely to run into any problems along the way, if you get my drift. A lot of people would like a way of getting "in" with him, and Tabby fancies herself as a bit of an entrepreneur. The wellness retreat is just one in a long line of "bright ideas" that she wanted my father's backing for. And I was just a means to that end.'

He adds salt and vanilla extract to both bowls and starts mixing flour into one gradually with a wooden spoon.

'Did your father know that?' I prompt.

'I don't think my father much cared. We have a... complicated relationship. I'm not the corporate ladder climbing type, and Tabby is, and he thought her influence would be good for me. Between them, they tag-teamed in an attempt to turn me into what my father has always wished I was. Some kind of businessman who wears boring suits and talks about businessy things like profit margins and loss leaders and carries a briefcase and wears a tie.'

He puts one bowl of dough in the freezer to chill, and then starts mixing flour into the second bowl, but also adds cocoa powder to this one.

'It's got all the hallmarks of a *really* healthy relationship so far.'

He lets out a sarcastic bark of a laugh. 'It was always two against one. Three, when we got together as a family and they got my sister involved too. Also a corporate ladder climbing solicitor. We're the most unalike two siblings have ever been.'

I watch him adding flour and cocoa powder gradually, folding it in as opposed to beating it in, which is what I've been doing. 'You said your father isn't happy with your career choice...'

'My father isn't happy with *anything* about me. You know when you're feeling criticised from all angles? Some people would withdraw, but it made me even more determined to be the opposite of what they wanted me to be. I leant further into my eccentricities. I grew my hair out. Dyed it dark. Got my ears pierced. Put eyeliner on. Did a card trick instead of listening whenever anyone tried to talk to me about my life choices. Used humour to laugh off spiteful comments, rather than let anyone see how much they hurt. Things

I knew would drive them mad. I wanted to make them realise that I was never going to be like them.'

It reminds me of when he first arrived at the tearoom. The obnoxious Hatter act – a shield to hide this softer, quieter side of himself that not many people get to see.

When the cocoa powder is mixed in with the flour, he puts the second bowl in the freezer too, cracks two eggs into another bowl and separates the whites, and then cleans and dries the unit and sprinkles flour on the surface, ready for rolling out the dough.

'Were you and Tabby together for long?'

'Five years.' He goes over to get the vanilla dough out of the freezer.

'Five years?' I'd taken another forkful of cake and I promptly choke on it. Which is marginally more appetising than eating it. 'She doesn't seem like the kind of person you could spend five years with. To be honest, five hours at work was more than enough today. She doesn't seem like your type at all.'

He scoffs as he rolls out the dough. 'Doesn't seem like the type who'd put up with me, you mean.'

Judging by his sharp movements and the way he thwacks the dough around, I've touched a nerve with that comment. I think before answering. 'She seems like the type who'd make you think that people have got to "put up with you" rather than just liking you and enjoying your company.'

His hands go still on the rolling pin, and he looks into the distance through the window, like he needs a moment to think it over. 'I don't know if that was a compliment or not, but it made me feel really nice.' I'm still sitting on the unit and he sidesteps and nudges his elbow against my knee and looks up to meet my eyes. 'Thank you.'

I like his openness. Most men don't say things like that, but Bram wears his heart on his sleeve in an endearing way.

Once he's rolled the vanilla dough into a rectangle, he gets the chocolate dough out and starts rolling that into the same shape.

'It didn't start off bad.' He pushes the rolling pin like a pro. Every time I try to roll anything out, the dough clumps up and sticks to the rolling pin. 'Things were great at first, as relationships usually are. She was the first person I could really see a future with. But things started to change – slowly at first, then faster. I started to feel like her child rather than her partner. Every time we left the house, she had something to scold me for.' He does an impression of her haughty voice. '"Do you have to wear *that*? Why don't you cut your hair? Ugh, the eyeliner *again*? *Two* earrings, what will people think?"' He brushes the egg white across the top of the rolled-out chocolate dough and then lays the vanilla dough on top of it, and I still haven't worked out exactly what he's making. 'After I moved in here, she wanted me to propose because she thought my father would give us this house as a wedding gift. I did because… I thought things might change if I gave her what she wanted.'

'Didn't work?' I ask gently because he sounds humiliated, and it's easy to tell this isn't something he talks about often.

'Made it worse. She became obsessed with the wedding and making sure I wouldn't do anything to embarrass her on the big day. She was ashamed to be marrying me.' He's concentrating on cutting the joined two-colour dough into strips. 'When I realised that, I broke things off. She never understood why. Neither did my family. But why would I want to marry someone who was embarrassed by me? I was only acceptable to her if I wasn't myself.'

I bite my lip because he seems so downtrodden when he talks about it, and every word sounds like a struggle and I'm not sure if he's going to clam up completely if I keep questioning him.

He starts assembling the strips of dough in alternating colours, almost like a Battenberg cake…

'Chequerboard cookies!' I suddenly realise what he's doing. 'God, you're clever.'

It makes him laugh out loud and his cheeks redden at the compliment. 'This is what happens when people make me talk. I can only do it if I'm distracted by baking.'

'I'm going to keep that in mind.' I grin at him and then, because I'm fighting a sudden urge to give him a hug, I reach my leg out until my big toe can poke his thigh. 'Why is it so hard to talk about? Relationships end. We've all been there.'

He continues stacking strips of dough in alternate colours until he's built a square roll of four-by-four vanilla and chocolate squares, lining them up perfectly, gluing each strip to the one next to it with a brush of egg white. 'Relationships are hard to get out of. When you've been with someone for a long time, so long that they've become part of your family, it's hard to admit that it isn't working, and I felt too small and insignificant to do anything about it. Relationships are supposed to be about love and support and lifting each other up, and ours was the opposite. She picked holes in everything I did, everything I said, everything I wore, everything I thought...' He starts a list that sounds like it could go on for a lot longer. 'I tried to change, but nothing I did was good enough because *I* wasn't good enough, and I let it beat me down until my confidence was zapped to nothing, and looking back now, I don't know how I let it get so far.'

'*Because* your confidence was zapped so much,' I say quietly. That much is obvious. 'Because that's what people like Tabby do. They denigrate those around them to build up their own importance. But now look at you. Rising like a blue-haired phoenix from the ashes.'

He tucks his head against his shoulder and turns away. The blue hair is just for show. It's part of the shield he shows the world. A physical representation of the bright personality he spent years suppressing.

'I got the carousel job after the relationship ended, and getting to do magic again, getting to entertain kids and make adults gasp in disbelief... it gave me my self-worth back. I got to be myself at the carousel, and being liked by kids, being looked up to for everything I'd felt was so wrong about me... it gave me a much bigger sense of self. I regained my confidence. Realised I'll never compromise myself again. I'll never be bothered by whether I fit in with what people think I "should" be. Not for dating though. I don't know how I'll ever let anyone in again.'

I watch him slice the chequerboard log of dough into squares and place them on an oven tray. 'You will because you're a spectacular nut. You just need someone who understands that the spectacular bit complements the nut bit.'

He laughs out loud again. 'Please, Cleo, I beg you to stop drowning me in such unfettered compliments.'

I wait until he looks up and meets my eyes. 'You wouldn't be you without both aspects and that would be a bad thing.'

He holds eye contact and a soft smile pulls at his mouth, and then he blinks and looks away. 'I'll remind you of that when I pull a playing card out from behind your ear tomorrow.'

He puts the oven tray in the freezer to chill for a few minutes while he tidies up and loads the dishwasher, refusing my offers to help. Instead, he holds a hand out to help me down from my spot on the counter top.

It's a quick drop to the floor and I don't need any assistance, but he's laid himself bare in a way I never thought he would and something is pulling at me to touch him, even for a moment, so I brace one hand against the counter and slip my other hand into his.

His long, exceptionally talented fingers fold around mine and he gives them a gentle squeeze and waits for me to look at him again. 'Thank you.'

Another moment passes as I look into his shining brown eyes, a reminder that you never know what someone has been through, and scratching the brightly coloured surface can reveal so much depth that it rivals the rabbit hole Alice fell down.

'Right, you know what's unfair, me talking that much about myself and you not returning the gesture.' He drops my hand, collects the oven tray from the freezer and slides it into the waiting oven. 'These need twelve minutes to cook, therefore you've got twelve minutes to spill your deepest secrets.' He presses an imaginary stopwatch in his hand. 'Go!'

He sits down cross-legged on the floor, his back against one of the under-counter cupboard doors, and although I trust Bram's bakes not to spontaneously combust in the oven, I do the same and sit in front of the oven door, opposite him, watching the cookies start to rise.

'You had a complicated relationship with your mum too?' It's Bram's turn to prompt me now. I liked getting him to open up, but I've never intended to tell anyone this much about myself.

'That Unbirthday party she threw for me was the last one before my dad announced he was in love with someone else, they were having a baby together, and disappeared from our lives for good. Mum didn't cope well. Looking back now, I can see that she had some kind of emotional breakdown, but I didn't understand that at the time. She thought he'd replaced her with a younger model and became obsessed with her age. She had cosmetic treatments that did more harm than good, and the bathroom was full of hideously expensive anti-ageing lotions and potions, and then a few months later, she went on a "girls' holiday" to Greece and didn't come back. She met some Greek God out there who made her feel young and decided to stay. I only saw her a handful of times after that. And then a couple of years ago, I got a phone call from one of her Greek friends, saying she'd passed away, and the grief hit me like a truck. I lost my job. I was working in a shop at the time, and I constantly messed things up. I snapped at a customer. I was struggling to sleep at night so I was always oversleeping in the mornings and arriving late. They fired me, rightfully so. Then there was the ex and that whole debacle, and after that, I kind of closed myself off from the world. I barely left the flat. My friends were supportive at first, but they got tired of trying to coerce me into going out with them, and you know what they say... a friend in need is a bloody nuisance.'

He lets out a loud laugh at the tribute to his own fondness for mixed-up idioms.

'It's hard to face the world when you haven't for a while...' I look over at him again, and his understanding smile and kind eyes are reassuring somehow. 'I saw something online about A Tale As Old As Time, and I've always loved books and bookshops and I pushed myself to go there, just once at first, but then every week. I'd buy a book as a reward, something completely outside of my reading comfort zone – symbolic for stepping outside of my real-life comfort zone too. I got talking to Marnie and we bonded over our love of books. When she got more customers after the Bookishly Ever After festival last year, I started helping out in the shop, and I *loved* Ever After Street so much. It brought me back to life and made me *want* to live again. It reminded me of who I was before and what I wanted in life. When I heard about Lilith and the tearoom, it was like a sign. What I'd always dreamed of doing someday.'

'And still your application didn't go in until after the deadline...'

'And *you* know that.' I fix him with a hard stare. 'How do you know that?'

'Just some overheard gossip.' He does a vague handwave.

'Ignore me, I'm just nosy. You know what they say – curiosity makes the cat knowledgeable and fun to be around.'

The laugh makes my guard drop again. He's leaning back against the cupboard door, his head resting against it, and his easy-goingness and unintentional humour make him so effortless to talk to. 'I doubted myself. I didn't think I could do it. It was Marnie who hit send when I'd ummed and ahhed and watched the deadline tick past.'

'Self-sabotage...'

'I can't bake, Bram! And I no longer have a kitchen! It's not self-sabotage to think those two things might have a negative impact on my ability to run a tearoom.'

'They might make it difficult, but nothing's impossible. Come here whenever you like. Consider my kitchen yours.'

'Bram, that's—' I was about to say how kind that is, but I'm cut off by the oven timer bleeping. 'Well, no more kitchens are burning down on my watch, so one of us is going to have to get them out.'

He rolls his head along the cupboard door until his tired eyes meet mine. 'I would rather they burn than you stop talking.'

I nearly say 'awwww' out loud but I stop myself as he hauls himself to his feet and shoves his hand into a brightly coloured oven glove – one of the little touches of himself that he's brought into this bland house.

I touch a hand to my lips, surprised by what has come out of my own mouth. 'I did not intend to tell you all that.'

'If it's any consolation, I didn't intend to tell you any of what I told you either. Welcome to Oversharing Alley, population: two.'

It doesn't seem like a bad thing when it comes to finding out about this spectacular nut, but I'm not sure it's a good thing when he's also finding out about me. I've hidden away for so long and I never thought it would be this easy to let someone in again, but

Bram has a way of breaking down even the toughest construction of walls.

He puts the hot oven tray on the unit and while he turns around to switch the oven off, I've already prised a cookie off the baking paper and it's on a plate in front of me, even though it's far too hot to touch yet.

'Oi!' He's taking the mick out of all the times I've told him off for grabbing something without letting it cool first.

I put a hand on my hip. 'If you think I'm waiting even a fraction of a second longer than I have to...'

'Contrariwise, I would *never* recommend waiting for something to cool before sampling it. There really is no point in making anything if you don't burn your mouth *and* fingers in your haste to try it.'

'I'm glad we agree.' I turn over the square cookie, which somehow managed to retain its perfectly square shape in the oven instead of expanding and splurging into one mass like my attempts keep turning out. I roll it from edge to edge using my nails until it's cool enough to break a piece off and pop it in my mouth.

'Oh my God,' I murmur, but this time it *is* the good kind of 'oh my God'. The biscuit melts on my tongue in a mix of chocolate and vanilla, with a crunch of sugar and a buttery taste. I quickly pop another bit in. 'These are amazing. How did you *do* that?' It's a rhetorical question because I watched every step and I still can't explain how he can make a few simple ingredients complement each other so well. Before I know it, I've eaten a whole one and taken another one. 'Magic by day, wizardry in the kitchen by night. I don't know why I'm even trying – I should just give up and hire you as the tearoom chef.'

He laughs, but it's an awkward laugh and his cheeks are blazing with redness. I never would've thought that someone who is so cocky as the Mad Hatter would be so bad at taking compliments himself. 'Well, firstly, "wizardry" is pushing it a bit for simple chequerboard cookies, secondly, because I wouldn't stop doing magic for anything, and thirdly, because you don't want to hire a tearoom baker, you want to *be* the tearoom baker, and we're not giving up on that.' He puts another piece of the cookie into his mouth. 'But I'm happy to carry on helping out to supplement the supermarket-bought goods until you don't need them any more.'

I like how much faith he has that that will ever be a possibility. 'These are beyond perfect for The Wonderland Teapot. I've still got some "Eat Me" rice paper tags, I could stick one of those on each with a dob of icing. How did you get to be so good at this?'

'I don't know. It's an outlet.' He gets a Tupperware container out, ready to load the cookies into when they've cooled down. 'I have a limited amount of outgoingness, and when I get home after work, I need to do something to chill out and be alone. I can switch off and concentrate on nothing but measuring and mixing and rolling out with no pressure or expectation to be fun and entertaining. Sometimes it goes wrong, sometimes it goes right, but either way, by the time it comes out of the oven, I feel like me again and I can face another day tomorrow with a spring in my step.'

I'm once again struck by how open he is and how he isn't afraid of his feelings. 'Am I messing that up? Your alone time, your time in the kitchen... I've been here almost every night.'

'No.' He thinks about it for a moment. 'No, you're genuinely not. I still feel like I'm alone when you're here, I'm just less lonely.'

His words make me feel warm and fuzzy inside. 'Was that a compliment?'

'I think so.'

We both laugh, but I see what he's really saying. The front he puts on in public is exhausting, and afterwards, he needs to decompress and just be himself. He hasn't hidden that from me since the moment I arrived, and it means a lot that he can still do that while I'm here.

It's late by the time the cookies have cooled, and the sky outside is dark when Bram walks me to the door and pulls it open.

'Thanks for tonight,' he says without elaborating, but I know what he means. A non-judgemental listening ear makes all the difference sometimes. I feel it too. I didn't tell him much about my mum, but it was more than I've told anyone else in recent years, and the tension that seems to constantly clench around my shoulders feels looser somehow.

'Thanks for the cookies.' I give the Tupperware box I'm holding a gentle rattle.

It feels like he's lingering and I *know* I'm lingering. I've lingered in the kitchen, I've lingered all along the hallway, and now I'm lingering in the open door.

'See you tomorrow?' He sounds hesitant and unsure, even though I most definitely will see him tomorrow.

We both seem uncertain of how to say goodbye tonight, like we've passed some invisible border of friendship by being so open with each other. It feels wrong to just wave goodbye and walk away like I would any other night.

He seems as though he needs a hug. His hand touches my hip like he doesn't know where else to put it, and I reach up and slip the arm not holding the cookies around his neck and awkwardly pull him down. Even though the position is uncomfortable, I feel him exhale and relax, and I can't see his face, but I imagine his eyes slip closed.

It doesn't last anywhere near long enough. Within a few seconds, he's stood back upright and extracted his arm from around me and taken a step as far away as the narrow doorway will allow, and I try to ignore the urge to cling on a bit longer. He gives incredible hugs, but it's not *just* the hug that's making me feel warm and squishy inside tonight.

'So, see you tomorrow, then?' I paste on a smile and step out onto the top step, because if I stand here much longer, I'm likely to hug him again, and that would be a very bad thing.

'With out-of-tune bells on.'

It makes me laugh because I wouldn't have it any other way now, and I wave as I head down the steps.

'Cleo?' he says as I reach the bottom. 'Why didn't you ask me who he is?'

His father. Someone important. Someone with influence. Someone who can afford a house like this. Someone famous, maybe? It never even crossed my mind to question it any further. If Bram wanted to tell me, he would have. 'I don't care who he is. Who *you* are is what's important.'

The smile that crosses his face looks like he couldn't *not* smile if he tried, but his eyes flicker downwards and then he turns serious again. 'I might have to hold you to that one day.'

'You have my word. You'll always be more important than whoever your father is. He sounds like an inflated walking ego with excruciatingly bad taste in décor.'

I can hear his laugh as I crunch across the gravel to my car and he stays leaning against the doorframe as I get in and start up. I meet his eyes across the distance and smile to myself, trying not to look at how the light from the outside lamps catches the blue pigments in his hair and make it look like it's glowing.

The Mad Hatter might be a spectacular nut, but Bram might just be something spectacular.

10

'There's no such thing as a secret ingredient, only an ingredient that hasn't been remembered yet.'

'Well, being both secret *and* forgotten doesn't bode well, does it?' We're in Bram's kitchen again and I'm trying to make scones in the vague hope of them *not* turning out like small lumps of boulder clay this time. 'My nan was famous for her lavender scones. She would put a chalkboard outside and write the time they were due out of the oven on it, and people used to queue up to get them while they were so hot that the butter would start to melt as you put it on... She always swore there was a secret ingredient that must never be written down in case someone found out our family secrets.'

'Tearoom espionage,' he says with a grin. 'That must've been some scone.'

'I watched my nan make them so many times. I've tried to recreate them, but it was like eating a greenhouse. A soapy-tasting greenhouse. And that was my most successful attempt, others have been worse.'

He laughs from where he's sitting on the unit, clearly not realising just how *bad* my attempts at baking have been in recent years.

'It tasted like cloves, but I've tried it with cloves and it was just...' I shudder at the memory. I feel like I've let down my family name, and I'm definitely letting down my own tearoom.

I'm not intending to make my nan's scones tonight because I can't remember that missing ingredient. These will just be plain ones, that hopefully won't go wrong with Bram's supervision. The other day, I made the mistake of trying one of the supermarket-bought scones I've been serving and they really do taste like they come from a supermarket, and The Wonderland Teapot deserves better than that.

I keep thinking I'll remember it. But even with the ingredients set out in front of me and my fingers literally in the mixing bowl, rubbing the butter into the flour, my mind is *still* blank. I remember Nan telling me to add a pinch of something, but no more than a pinch otherwise it would be overpowering. But... what was it? I wrack my brain, getting increasingly annoyed with myself. This is *ridiculous*.

I didn't realise I'd made a noise of frustration until Bram speaks. 'I think you're too worried that you might not remember and your brain is putting up a mental wall. When you're trying *so* hard to remember something, the harder it gets to remember it.'

I'm not sure if that makes sense or if it's one of his nonsense ramblings, but he jumps down and holds a hand out to me. 'Come here.'

'What are you doing?'

He points to the magnet on his fridge and does a little boogie on the spot, and then steps closer, wiggling his fingers to encourage me to take his hand. I hold mine up above the bowl, my fingers coated in butter, which has made the flour stick all over my hands.

He shakes his head, not accepting my excuse, so I hold my flour-coated hand out to call his bluff, and I'm surprised when he slips his clean fingers around the floury mess of my hand.

He pulls me closer and grasps my other hand with his too, and starts leading us through some demented version of a waltz, except *no one* has ever done a waltz like this before.

'You're going to be covered in flour.'

'I don't mind.'

'*Everything* is going to be covered in flour!' With every step, flour is dislodging itself from my fingers and making a new life for itself on the floor.

'Don't worry about it. The more time you spend in the kitchen, the easier things will come back. The more you do it, the more you'll remember. Or not. Maybe you won't remember and you'll have to add your own unique twist instead and you'll come up with something even better.'

I'm busy trying not to cringe at the feeling of butter and flour squelching between our hands. Sometimes I love how *un*-ordinary he is – this is *not* one of those times. 'Do you ever struggle to get magic tricks right?'

'Of course I do.' He lifts my hand up above my head and makes me spin around under it, so flour rains down all over me too.

I shake it out of my hair. 'And dancing is the solution to that, is it?'

'It doesn't hurt. Sometimes the best thing you can do is take a step away and *not* think about it.'

'At the moment, I'm thinking about the flour we're treading into your floor tiles.'

'Stop worrying so much – about the floor tiles *and* the baking. It doesn't matter if you don't remember. What difference does it make if you don't? You won't be in any worse position than you are now. You've got endless time.' He spins me around, pushing me away and pulling me back until I crash into his chest, laughing so hard that it's like it shakes something loose inside me.

'Time! Bram, that's it! Thyme!' I emphasise the *h* sound in the pronunciation. 'Nan had a plant growing on the window ledge at home. A row of herbs she used to use in cooking. Thyme is sort of citrusy, which complements lavender, and it tastes a bit like cloves, doesn't it?' I shake my head at myself, unable to stop grinning. 'It was thyme. I never thought I'd remember.'

I let out a squeal of delight and he darts forwards and wraps his arms around me, lifts me up and spins us around, and I squeal again for a different reason. My hands are still too flour-coated to cling onto him, so I just flap them and squeak. 'Bram! Flour!'

He's laughing as he puts me down. 'Sorry, you looked so happy that I couldn't help myself.'

I hold my hands up uselessly, watching grains of flour drift towards the floor. 'Dammit, I wish I had some lavender and thyme. Now I've thought of it, I want to try it *right now*.'

'Your wish is my command.' He crosses an arm over his chest and bows. 'I have culinary lavender growing in the greenhouse, and there's a thyme plant in the conservatory.'

My mouth falls open in surprise. 'Seriously?'

'Yep. We'll go and get it now. You wash your hands while I grab the mop. Dancing with such floury hands was a terrible idea. I don't know why you didn't say that.'

I can't help giggling at the rueful look on his face and the spark in his eyes. Somehow he knew exactly what I needed... long before I did.

* * *

We step out the back door onto a paved patio, surrounded by decorative planters full of spring colour. The clocks have already gone forward and the evenings are lighter now. The breeze is gentle tonight, and I breathe in the fresh air and revel in the late-evening sunshine. We go down steps and onto a gravel path running along-side a neat lawn, and he offers me his arm. Despite my better judgement, I slip my hand through his elbow and let my fingers curl into his forearm.

The hedgerow beside us is full of chirping birds who disappear into the branches as we pass, and I get the sense that he wants to ask me something.

'What stopped the love of baking?' he says eventually. 'Because you've told me about your mum and your nan, but you haven't told me why you stopped baking.'

I sigh, because it's a memory that I don't like reliving often, and yet it lives rent-free in my mind more often than I'd like to admit. At the same time, I *want* to be open with him. He's so direct about his feelings in a rare way, and he deserves the same in return.

'Losing Mum made me realise life is short and I wasn't doing what I'd always wanted to do – run a quaint little teashop some-where. My ex and I decided to go into it together. We found a gorgeous property over in Ross-on-Wye, close to his flat, and I was going to move in with him. My mum had left me a little bit of money, so he was going to match my investment and we were going to be partners and get a business loan to start up. And then he...' I take a deep breath, because even after so much time has passed, it still isn't easy to think about that day. 'Well, it was a bit like being jilted at the altar, but I was jilted in the local branch of Barclays, with half a business plan that was now irrelevant, and an increas-ingly angry branch manager. While I huddled in a corner and even-tually got through to my ex on the phone, he said the prospect of going into something so permanent with me had made him realise that he'd been unhappy for a while and didn't want to continue – not the business plan or the relationship.'

'I'm sorry.' Bram ducks his head and murmurs the words against my forehead, and I squeeze his arm where my fingers are still curled around it.

'Everything got so mired in grief. I still missed my nan. My relationship with my mum was never repaired, and losing her so unexpectedly threw me totally off-course, and then that sudden end to what I thought was the last relationship I'd be in for the rest of my life... Grief overwhelmed me. I went home and shut myself away. I used the money Mum had left me to live on rather than putting it into the business like I'd intended to, and every time I went near the kitchen, I couldn't face the thought of baking anything. Instead of bringing back happy memories, it reminded me of all the things I'd lost, and I just stopped doing it.'

Bram pulls his arm in, tucking my hand against his side. 'No one could blame you for that.'

I look up at him. 'You must think I'm stupid, to dive into this like I have.'

'I think you're brave. To take a second chance and grasp it with both hands, to overcome self-doubt and trust that you'll be able to do it even when things have been going wrong. To go through all that grief and force yourself back out into the world, even when you want to hide away. It takes courage to follow your dreams, especially when you've been knocked back before.'

It makes me feel flushed all over. He puts such a unique spin on everything, and I wish more people saw the world in the way Bram does. But it also makes me think of what he's said about his own family, and how much he clearly struggles with their lack of approval. 'You hide away too, don't you?'

He pulls back until he can look at me, and I continue. 'My walls were physical, but I can see the way yours go up when you slip into the Mad Hatter act. It's like you pull a shell around yourself.'

At first I think I've pushed him too far. We're wandering through lush green grounds, and I can see the glass roof of a greenhouse in the distance, but his body language is suddenly stiff. I'm not sure if he's about to pull away and throw me out, until he lets out a long sigh. 'You don't grow up around my father without a bit of bullet-proof armour. He's the type of person who thinks that if you don't agree with him, you're wrong, and we've never seen eye to eye, so I've always been "wrong". He had my whole life planned out. I was to go to university to study politics and business management, and then straight into the job he was going to get one of his crony mates to line up for me. The thought of it filled me with a sense of dread and the whole world felt utterly bleak. I couldn't do it, and he's never understood that. Nothing I've done since has been good enough for him.'

'I'm sorry,' I murmur, squeezing his arm. 'People don't realise how complicated families are.'

'You do.' He holds my hand against his side again.

'I do,' I echo. 'So, instead of doing the boring, sensible thing, you...'

He raises an eyebrow at my leading question, before finishing the answer off. '...Became a magician's assistant. Backstage stuff, like setting up tricks and planning his shows, but they were just that – shows. Smoke and mirrors, music, lights, and showmanship. It was flashy, but it wasn't authentic. People left feeling like they'd been to a magic show, not like they'd seen magic. After that, I was a free-lance entertainer for hire – doing magic at parties and corporate events – and I managed a magic shop for a while. We sold all kinds of tricks and props, and I did a lot of teaching people how to use them. I ran a monthly workshop, but also kids would come in and ask me how things worked or how to do certain tricks, and I'd show them. But like most tiny independent shops on high streets every-where, it was a thing of bygone days. There's nothing you can't learn on YouTube or get delivered next day from Amazon now, so people stopped coming, and it was just me, standing in an empty shop, trying to figure out a trick to conjure up some customers.'

'You really loved that?' I ask because it's impossible to take my eyes off his face and the way it's lit up as he talks.

'Almost as much as I love what I do now. I like doing magic, but with only a few people watching, so it's intimate and personal. It's harder to write off if you're seeing it right in front of your eyes. I *love* seeing the disbelief on people's faces when they can't explain what's just happened. It makes me feel invincible. I still have to pinch myself that *I* can do that. My father has always made me feel like I've made the wrong choices, and every little gasp of surprise makes me *know* that I made the right ones for myself.'

I'm holding his arm so tightly that he'll probably have pins and needles from the circulation being cut off. Magic illuminates him. I've never had a job that I *loved* before The Wonderland Teapot. Jobs have always been jobs – do what you're paid to do, get through the day, and go home. His passion is inspiring. Everyone deserves to love what they do *that* much.

We reached the greenhouse a while ago. I was hoping he wouldn't notice because I didn't want him to stop talking, but now there's no avoiding the glass structure in front of us.

His eyes linger on me for a few moments, seeming as reluctant to end this conversation as I am, but eventually he slides the glass door open and invites me to step inside. 'I'm not much of a gardener, but seeing as there's a greenhouse here, I haven't given up trying yet. My mum bought me some culinary herb plants last year. You'll officially be the first person to use them.'

I rub a leaf between my fingers and inhale deeply, instantly transported to my childhood and the lavender plants my nan used to grow in the little garden at home.

He's pottering around, looking for the secateurs to cut some, and I reach out and grab his hand. 'Thank you.'

I hope he knows I mean for more than the plants. 'Even if it goes horribly wrong. Even if thyme isn't the magic ingredient and I accidentally put in enough lavender to fumigate a small country. Just talking to you, feeling like I used to, like I know what I'm doing, even for a moment... Thank you.'

His hand slides over the top of mine and he smiles that soft, muted smile that makes my heart skip a beat and my cheeks feel all tingly as they heat up for no reason.

When we get back, I can't wait to get into the kitchen, and Bram takes his usual seat on the unit and lets me get on with it, and after a while, we're eating scones that taste almost like the ones my nan used to make. They're not perfect, I probably used a touch too much lavender, but it's the closest I've come in years, and I feel on top of the world. This is what I always wanted to do. This is what I used to love.

For the first time in a long time, it feels like it's not too late for me to love it again.

11

Monday morning has a habit of bringing unwanted guests. The tearoom has been open four weeks today, and the number of home-made baked goods are slowly but surely pushing out the supermarket-bought cakes. Today there's a stand of Battenberg slices in the display case, which are the result of how Bram and I spent our Sunday afternoon yesterday.

It's the Easter holidays and there are a few customers in this morning. Bram is entertaining a young family, and has so far impressed them by turning a saucer into a playing card, and then making the dad's watch disappear while the children hunt for it. In about two minutes, it will reappear on the dad's wrist like it was never missing, and I still haven't worked out how he does it.

Tabby is wafting on the sidelines, doing a royal wave and squealing 'off with their heads!' occasionally, but thankfully smiling for selfies with customers and children who are nervous to approach the Queen of Hearts, and I'm just ringing up an elderly couple who have been coming in for tea, crumpets, and cake on a regular basis, when Mr Hastings' imposing shadow fills the doorway.

'Well, well, well,' he booms, letting the door swing shut, only to be stopped by Mrs Willetts, the much nicer woman from the interview, who scurries in behind him and closes it quietly.

'Well, this is a fine sight.' Mr Hastings stops to look around, blocking a child's pathway to the flamingo croquet and not bothering to apologise when he bumps into a seated customer. 'Oh, yes, this is very rabbit-hole-ish. A sterling job.'

Before I can say anything, Tabby inserts herself into the space between Mr Hastings and the counter. 'Hello, sir.' She curtseys to him. Actually curtseys. Which I really hope is part of her act and not how Mr Hastings expects to be greeted. 'I'm so glad you could make it.'

That sounds suspiciously like she was expecting him. Did she know they were coming? I look over at Bram, who has stood up and quickly handed the dad his watch back without the usual fanfare, and is looking on with an alarmingly pale face.

'Oh, Tabby, that's quite an ensemble you've put together there. Don't you look fabulous?' He twists a finger around so Tabby does a twirl for him, and then clicks his fingers towards Bram. 'You think she looks fabulous, don't you?'

'I think someone would behead me if I contradicted your judgment.' He puts on his high-pitched Mad Hatter voice, and I think I'm probably the only one who notices how hard he swallows. Maybe I'm not the only one intimidated by this formidable man.

'Mr Hastings.' I smile through gritted teeth. 'What can we do for you on this fine Monday morning?' I have never sounded more false in my life, and this is rapidly becoming the *least* fine Monday morning ever.

'Just popping by for a quick inspection, Miss Jordan.' He runs a finger along a table and inspects it for crumbs, looking disappointed when he finds none. 'Nothing formal, just a check-in to see how things are going.'

He dresses it up in a casual tone, but I have no doubt that this is a well-planned 'unplanned' inspection, probably hoping to catch us out in some way or another.

'He doesn't mean inspection, dearie.' Mrs Willetts lifts one of the playing cards from the teapot display on the counter and then goes to put it back, but accidentally knocks three more off instead. She hands them to me guiltily. 'We've heard so much chatter about The Wonderland Teapot, and we had some other business in the neighbourhood and thought we'd stop in.'

Whatever the other business was, it sounds like Tabby knew to expect them, because she doesn't seem surprised at all. I noticed her watching the door earlier and didn't think anything of it, but now it seems like she was clearly waiting for them.

Bram is hovering, looking unsure of himself and like he's torn between chiming in and running away.

Mrs Willetts looks between all of us and seems to sense the awkward atmosphere. 'I could murder a cup of tea, couldn't you, Mr Hastings?'

'What? Hmm? Oh, tea, yes. Quite.' Mr Hastings is distracted by the teapots hanging from the ceiling.

'Please don't do—' I start, but he's already pulled a chair out from one of the tables, clambered up on it, and has got his hand wrapped around one of my hanging teapots, giving it a good tug.

'Mr Hastings, health and safety!' Mrs Willetts bellows, making him jump enough that he wobbles on the chair and then glares at it like the chair itself is at fault for not being designed to stand on.

'They're screwed into reinforced board,' I say helpfully as Mrs Willetts tries to help him down and gets barked at for her trouble. 'They aren't coming down, not even if you yank on them.'

A red-faced Mr Hastings dusts his trousers down as though my ribbon-tied teapots are responsible for making him dusty, even though I run my feather duster over them regularly. 'People could hit their heads.'

'If they were seven foot tall!'

He frowns at me and then looks up at the teapots like he's trying to mentally calculate the distance between them and the tallest person's head. 'A child on a parent's shoulders—'

'Would never get through the door in the first place,' I finish for him. I gave a lot of thought to the ceiling teapots. He can't find fault with them, no matter how hard he tries. And I didn't expect him to try quite *this* hard.

He reaches up and tugs one of the ribbons pouring from the spout and shakes his head in disappointment when he fails to dislodge it. 'Teapots in the ceiling. I've never seen anything like it, Miss Jordan. You've certainly got an imagination, I'll give you that.'

It does not sound like a compliment.

'I'll go and make that tea for you, sir.' Tabby, who has never lifted a finger in the two weeks since she started working here, hurries out to the back room as fast as her red ballgown can swish. Does she even know *how* to make a cup of tea?

Mrs Willetts' eyes flick between my face and the doorway Tabby disappeared through. 'I'll lend her a hand,' she says and hurries after her, leaving me with the impression that she has a bit of experience with Tabby.

'So, things going well, are they?' Mr Hastings saunters towards me and slaps his giant hands on the counter. 'It's nice to see it so busy. I must say I'm surprised.'

'Er, thanks.'

'Wouldn't mind knowing where you got permission for those Cheshire Cats you've attached to trees around here, though. If every shop who wanted free advertising were to attach advertising materials to trees, there'd be no trees left. It could be termed littering. Fly-tipping at worst. You could be in big trouble.'

'Fly-tipping? For tying a few wooden cat faces and tails into nearby bushes? Are you seri—'

'They're cable-tied on.' Bram steps up beside me. 'Doing no harm, easily removed. *I* gave Cleo permission to put them there.'

What? He wasn't even on the radar when I put them there. What is going on here? Why would Bram need to give me permission to do anything and why would he pretend he had when he hadn't? A look passes between them and I suddenly get the feeling there really *is* something going on here.

Mr Hastings looks him up and down with a scornful look. 'And you? This job suits you, does it?' His disapproving eyes flick to a child who has just squealed in delight after putting a hedgehog ball through the playing card archway with a plastic flamingo club.

'Best job I've ever had.' Bram is in Mad Hatter mode. He's got a deck of cards and he's shuffling it with one hand, his fingers in constant motion, a nervous habit that's not quite hidden by his false grin.

'Not flaming difficult,' Mr Hastings mutters and then turns to me. 'And you, Miss Jordan? Are you doing good business? Getting good reviews?'

Reviews? I gulp. I know they mentioned reviews at the interview, but I haven't thought about it since. The idea of people reviewing me is *terrifying*.

'The reviews are cracking,' Bram answers for me. 'Look at this place. Anyone who isn't completely devoid of childhood wonder and imagination loves it.'

He knows about the reviews? *Are* there good reviews or is he making it up to impress the boss?

Mr Hastings looks between the two of us with a sneer on his face and his eyes come to rest on me. 'And I see you're putting up with my son?'

'Your...' I feel like someone's pinged me in the chest with a taut elastic band. Of bloody course. My mind replays everything in supersonic speed, from the direct line to Mr Hastings on the day he arrived to everything he's said about his father. Someone important around here. Someone with influence. Someone who makes new businesses glide right through any pesky red tape. Someone who disapproves of him and everything he does.

I look over at Bram. No amount of black eyeliner can disguise the panic in his eyes. No wonder he looked so uneasy just now. No wonder he looked like he wanted to run away. He knew what I was about to find out and there was nothing he could do to stop it.

I could shout. I could yell at Bram and make a scene, demand to know why he didn't tell me, but Mr Hastings is standing there with his sneer still firmly in place, waiting with gleeful anticipation for me to say something derogatory about this man, who so far, has done nothing but stand up for me.

The last thing I want to do is show a split between us. Mr Hastings will take the greatest pleasure in discovering I didn't even *know* he's Bram's father. And I might've just heard the 'my son' bit of that sentence, but I also heard yet another iteration of 'putting up with', and it makes me wonder how many people have made Bram believe that his presence is something people have got to endure.

I swallow hard and paste on another false smile. 'Of course. He's a pleasure to work with. We get on like a house on fire.'

Bram pushes out a held breath. He breaks into his Mad Hatter grin, takes a step closer, and clamps an arm around my shoulders. 'Lots of screaming, shouting, running about. Alarms blaring. Frequent use of a fire extinguisher. You know what they say – familiarity breeds uninhibited joy.'

I can hear how hard he's *trying* to come across as upbeat and carefree, but his voice is missing the usual ease. His fingers are pressing into my upper arm in a tight grip, and I get the feeling it's a silent way of asking me to keep up the pretence and not give his father any further ammunition.

He's still got the deck of cards in his other hand, spinning them on the counter, fanning them out, spreading them into a circle that he can wind out and wind back into a neat stack again with a quick flick of his fingers, like he's nervous and keeping his hands occupied.

Mr Hastings watches what he's doing for a moment, and then almost like he can't bear to watch any longer, he pushes himself off the counter and stalks away to examine the rest of the shop, muttering about the chess pieces being a hazard if they're not screwed down. God forbid there be anything he *doesn't* criticise.

Bram's eyes stay on his father, but his arm squeezes my shoulders without letting go. He turns his head to the side and whispers, 'I'm sorry.'

I want to be angry. I *should* shove his arm off and push him away. He's always seemed so trustworthy, and I know he's opened up to me over our nights in his kitchen... and all the while, he's been hiding this secret. But I also think about everything he said the other night when I didn't ask who his father is. Would he have told me if I had? I think he probably would. The 'I might need to hold you to that one day' when I said I didn't care who his father is. Today is that day.

I reach across and slide my hand over his, stilling the cards he's shuffling. My thumb brushes the back of his hand and his fingers fold around mine and hold them tightly, and he takes a few breaths to centre himself and then he lifts my hand to his mouth and presses his lips to the back of it.

His dark stubble scratching my skin wasn't meant to be hot, but the hand kiss is such a sweet, simple gesture, and it sends an unexpected tingle through me. I'd be lying if I said I hadn't noticed how gorgeous Bram is. He's undeniably sexy while playing Hatter, from the dark eyeliner surrounding cheeky brown eyes to the megawatt grin and constant sense of mischief, but there's something more about him in his kitchen in the evenings. When he lets me see the quieter version of himself, the one who's tired after putting on a show all day, the cheeky eyes and playful grin are still the same, but there's something extra sexy about someone who isn't trying to be something they're not.

I can feel heat rising up my neck, centring in my cheeks, when Mrs Willetts appears, carrying a tray with a teapot and two teacups on it, and Bram drops his arm and takes a giant step away. Tabby gives us a curious look as she swishes out behind Mrs Willetts.

Mr Hastings has got a wooden mushroom under one arm and is scratching at the spots I've painted on it, presumably so he can claim it's poisonous should a child try to eat it. 'It's non-toxic paint,' I call over to ease his many, many fears about how much harm my tearoom could do to the population of Ever After Street. There are a few customers in and his constant nit-picking is doing nothing to reassure them they won't come to any harm in here either.

'Would you like something with your tea?' I ask as Tabby goes to offer Mr Hastings a tour of the back room and Mrs Willetts insists he sit down at the table she's put her tray on.

'None of the rose cupcakes from the interview?' Mrs Willetts peers into the display case.

'All sold out. Could I tempt you with the Battenberg instead?' Bram steps in smoothly while I attempt to stamp on his foot to stop him. For the love of white rabbits, *don't* get them to eat something *I* made. Mr Hastings could find fault with *anything* and this morning has been enough of a disaster as it is.

She reaches over to pat his hand and I get the feeling she's trying to make up for his father's rudeness. 'Oh, Bram, you know full well that *you* could tempt me with anything. Go on then. We'll have a slice of that each.'

Mr Hastings goes to protest and she shuts him up quickly. 'Well, I'll have *two* slices then; pay no mind to the miserable old sourpuss.'

Bram opens the display case, picks up the tongs and slides two slices of the Battenberg onto two plates. 'Take a seat, I'll bring it over.'

'Bram!' I hiss as she goes to persuade Mr Hastings to leave the bunting he's examining for loose threads alone and sit down.

'What?' He grins at me. 'They want to try something *you* made. They came at the right moment.'

'No, don't—'

'He never does listen,' Tabby comments, making me jump because I hadn't realised how near she was standing. How much of that did she hear? What could she deduce from what she did hear? 'The more you tell him to do something, the less likely he is to do it.'

'A man with a mind of his own. How unappealing.' I don't intend to snap at her, but my heart is hammering from how much she made me jump, combined with the fear of what she overheard and the already frayed nerves from Mr Hastings' unexpected intrusion. 'You could have warned me they were coming.'

She gives me an incredulous look. 'Why would I tell you about an unplanned inspection? That would defeat the object, duh.'

'A planned unplanned inspection defeats the object,' I hiss back at her. 'If you're going to continue working here, you could be on our side.'

She scoffs. 'What, like *he* is?'

I glance over at her and her eyes are trained on Bram, who has put the slices of Battenberg on their table, thrown a playing card into the air and turned it into a rose, which he presents to Mrs Willetts with a bow and backs away. 'We'll leave you to discuss how well things are going. The Wonderland Teapot defies expectations, I'm sure. Not a complaint to be found anywhere.' It's his falsely bright Mad Hatter voice again, but I do *not* like the stone that Tabby's words have caused to settle in my stomach. What is she implying? That Bram is somehow *not* on our side?

...*My* side?

I go to question her further, but there's a commotion as the child on the flamingo croquet sends the hedgehog ball flying across the room, hitting a lady's shoe and disappearing beneath her shopping bags under the table, and Bram springs into action. He retrieves the ball with his foot while using his hands to juggle three tangerines he's just pulled out of one of his many pockets, swiftly preventing the tantrum that's nanoseconds away from starting, while the child's parents eat their sandwiches obliviously.

He can juggle. Of course he can juggle. And he carries tangerines around in his pocket for no good reason. I'm constantly impressed by his level of dedication to his craft, and how he handled that as only *he* could. No matter who Mr Hastings is, no one could be a better Mad Hatter in this tearoom, and I'm about to say something to that effect, when the door crashes open.

'Dad! Sadie said I'd find you he— Oh my *God*.' The woman who has just burst in comes to an abrupt halt and looks around in awe.

'Laura!' Tabby squeals at a pitch usually only audible to small rodents.

Bram shuffles up to the counter and inclines his head so I lean over from my side. 'My little sister, Laura.'

I pull back to meet his eyes and raise an eyebrow. 'How many more Hastings are coming to visit today? Is there, perhaps, a slew of first and second cousins about to appear from the basement? Great-uncles three times removed coming down the chimney? Your great-aunt's hairdresser's neighbour shimmying in from up the drainpipe?'

Tabby has raced over to the new arrival and now they're both squealing and exchanging air kisses. I didn't think it was possible to hear the word 'mwah' so many times in one morning. 'Oh my gawd, it's *so* good to see you, Laur! Thank you *so* much for inviting me to the wedding! I've narrowed my dress down to three choices! And I'm so excited about the hen night! I've got *so* much planned for all us girlies!'

'Yes, why *is* my ex invited to your wedding?' Bram asks loudly.

'Because she's *my* ex-sister-in-law, Bram.' Laura glares at him across the shop.

'We were never—'

'It's not my fault that you ended things. We grew close when we were related, that doesn't end because you snap your fingers and turn a playing card into a rabbit.'

'I don't believe in using animals for entertainment.' He gives her a mocking glare.

'You can't expect me to give up *my* friend just because you decide you don't want to play with her any more,' Laura fires back.

'Customers, please!' I say through gritted teeth. 'Can we keep the family disputes for elsewhere?'

'Sorry,' he mumbles to me, and then addresses the rest of the café in his Mad Hatter tone. 'Sorry, ladies and gentlefrogs, please forgive us, we've had a bit too much jam roly-poly today.' He takes his hats off and scruffs his hair up and puts them back on.

Mr Hastings has stood up and is looking worried. 'Everything all right, my dear?'

'Daddy, no! Disaster! I need that!' Laura takes the slice of Battenberg that Mr Hastings hasn't eaten yet and shoves it into her mouth. 'Oh my *God*. That's so good. Is *this* where you're working now?' She turns to Bram. 'Why didn't you tell me how amazing it is here?'

'Because it's not a law office and I don't carry a briefcase so you're generally not interested?' Bram replies sweetly, and I frown at him because this has got all the makings of another family spat.

Laura ignores him and turns back to her father. 'The caterer's pulled out! They had a double-booking, would you believe? Sadie has gone through all her back-up caterers and every single one of them is booked solid. Where are we supposed to find another caterer for four weeks' time?' She takes another mouthful of the Battenberg slice and her face shifts. At first I think it's into revulsion and I wonder what she can taste that no one else has complained about so far today, but I soon realise she's smiling a Cheshire Cat-style cake-filled smile. 'Oh my God! *You* could do it!'

She turns to me. Why is she turning to me? I glance at Bram. He's standing near me, she must be turning to him. Maybe she's got some kind of eye condition or the lighting in here is a bit dodgy. She obviously meant to turn to him. She must know what an incredible baker he is. Of course he could cater her wedding.

Except her eyes stay trained on me as she approaches the counter, tapping the empty plate. 'That was *amazing*. Tabs, can I have...'

Tabby instantly dashes behind the counter and throws the display case open, ready to serve Laura, who's peering in from the front.

'You choose something for me. I know everything will be equally delicious,' she says as Tabby grabs a plate and tongs and considers it for a moment and then picks out a shop-bought chocolate-cherry cupcake and hands the plate to Laura, who rams it into her mouth like she's been on a diet and this is her first sugary thing in six months.

She takes a second bite, which finishes the cake off altogether. Definitely more than six months.

'It's perfect!' she shouts, spraying the counter with crumbs. 'This is fate! We'd just been to see the venue this morning, and then Daddy had to come here on the way back to work, and the caterer called to cancel while he was still on Ever After Street, in a shop themed after my favourite book, no less! Did my dad tell you how much I love *Alice in Wonderland*?'

'He did actually.' What a weird throwback to the interview, a day seven weeks ago that feels like it was simultaneously seven months ago and about seven days ago. If only I could've foreseen that the daughter whose love of Alice helped me get this job in the first place would later rock up and expect me to... cater a wedding? She can't really be suggesting that, can she?

'See? It's fate! We were meant to meet! Today of all days! And you...?'

'Cleo,' I fill in because she's obviously waiting for my name. We've skipped anything as banal as introductions.

'Aww, such a pretty name. You're brilliant. This place is brilliant. These cakes are brilliant. You're exactly what we need, right here in front of me. I'm getting married in a month and the reception is being held in the castle, and the caterers have just let us down at the last minute. I don't know where else to turn. We just need someone to—'

'Look, Cleo *is* brilliant.' Bram can see where this is going as well as I can and interrupts before Laura can get any further. 'But she's *not* a wedding caterer. We've got—'

'We don't need a wedding caterer. We just need someone to knock together a few sandwiches, a bit of finger food, and some delicious cakes and goodies. It'll be no trouble at all. It's a *tiny* wedding. Only a hundred and fifty guests!'

'A hundred and fif...' Maybe I've fainted and this is some sort of unconscious hallucination. I'll probably come round to being revived by a paramedic in a minute and this will all be a terrifying dream.

I hold my very shaky hands up. 'I'm flattered, really, but this is so far beyond my level of expertise that it's not in the same stratosphere. I can't—'

'But you made all these, didn't you?' Laura waves a hand to the cakes on display in the cabinet.

'Er...' I gulp. Bram and I made some of them, but I can't come clean about the ones we didn't *now*, can I? Mr Hastings has started stalking towards us and it feels like he's bearing down on me. He would no doubt *love* to hear that I have, in fact, been lying from the start and can't bake to save my life.

'Exactly that.' Bram waves a hand towards the cakes in the glass cabinet. 'She makes all of these every day. She's incredibly busy here.'

'The wedding is on a Sunday. You're not open on Sundays, are you?' Laura's hands are on her hips and there's a steely set to her mouth. I know she's a solicitor, and I get the impression that this is what her opponents see in court. 'We'll pay you. The other guy isn't getting a penny from me – you can have his fee and extra on top!'

'It's not about the mon—'

'Oh yes yes yes.' Mr Hastings is rubbing his hands together. 'What a perfect solution, and an excellent opportunity for Miss Jordan to prove her worth to Ever After Street.'

'With all due respect, I run a tearoom, not a catering business. This is not something I can do.'

'You have to be versatile!' I think he's trying to be encouraging, but it comes out as a shouty bark. 'With weddings at the castle, this would be an excellent service to offer, and right on the doorstep of the venue too. Brides can buy their wedding dresses at The Cinderella Shop and get their catering sorted out all in one go! And you can't discount the possibility that people will request Alice-themed weddings or milestone birthday parties. Or *Un*birthday parties, ho ho,' he says with a chortle. Got to love a chortle.

'Which will be catered for them by professional caterers. Sadie and Witt are hosting events at the castle – they deal with all that stuff. I'm sure Sadie can find *someone* who will be available that day.

They've got long lists of people who can provide any service an event could possibly need.'

'But "wedding caterer" would be another feather in your cap.' Mr Hastings strokes his chin thoughtfully. 'Which will make you a *much* more attractive prospect to Herefordshire Council when we consider your position here. And as a bonus, it will be a brilliant way to get your name out there.'

'I don't want to get my name out there. I want my name *in* here.' I hadn't intended to snap, but people who refuse to take no for an answer are absolutely exhausting, and this is so ridiculous that neither he nor Laura can continue entertaining this idea for a moment longer.

'Which will never happen if you refuse my daughter's simple request.'

'What?'

'Oh, come on, Dad.' Bram folds his arms, sounding like he saw this coming. 'That's totally unfair. Blackmail, some might say.'

'How else do you think people get what they want in this world, Abraham?' He turns back to me. 'You work for me, Miss Jordan. My daughter has requested *you* to cater her wedding reception. If you are to refuse her request, then your trial period will be terminated immediately and we will find someone far more deserving of this space, someone who fits in with the community spirit of Ever After Street, which you clearly do not.'

'You can't do that. This trial period was dependent on what I bring to the street. Nowhere in my agreement does it say that I'm expected to cater a wedding reception for a hundred and fifty people!'

'This has nothing to do with the tenancy agreement. It's simply me asking you to do my family a small favour.' He drums his fingers along the counter, creating a staccato beat that sounds like a horror movie soundtrack and fills me with a similar sense of dread. 'There's one thing I would like to make crystal clear to you, Miss Jordan. Your application for this tearoom was late. It was received past the deadline. When you were chosen for this position, the tearoom had already been offered to someone else, and we rescinded that offer because your pitch was by far the best option for Ever After Street. We took a chance on you. Don't make us regret that decision.'

'Mr Hastings...' Mrs Willetts starts and receives a look sour enough to stop her saying anything more.

What? Someone else had been given this shop and the council changed their minds because of me? That doesn't sound very professional. Surely you *can't* offer someone a job, presumably a three-month trial like this, and then decide someone better has come along and just... take it away again?

I remember Mrs Willetts' worried question in the interview. Mr Hastings' hushed response that I probably wasn't supposed to hear. *Don't worry about that, it won't be a problem.* Is this what they were referring to?

Insecurity washes through me. The feeling that nothing here is *mine*, and the metaphorical rug could be pulled out from under me at any moment. Talk about out of the frying pan and into the depths of hell, to use one of Bram's malaphors. I look between Mr Hastings and Laura and then over at Mrs Willetts and then at Bram, pleading with my eyes for one of them to throw me a lifeline, to come up with some astoundingly clever excuse as to why I can't do it, but Bram's eyes are wide and he's shaking his head, looking like he's at a loss too.

Time is running out. We've already stood here for an abnormal amount of time before the look on Mr Hastings' face softens a little and he waves a hand towards Bram. 'Abraham enjoys all this baking malarkey too, I understand. You can do it between you. It would be nice for you to be involved in your sister's wedding, wouldn't it, son?'

Even Bram is lost for words in response.

'That's all right with me too,' Laura says. 'A real family affair. I'd like that.'

'I guess so,' I stutter eventually. My voice is unstable and sounds as unhinged as a drunken hyena. Because I have *no* choice about what else to say. The ultimatum is glaringly clear. Agree to the demands or my dream of keeping The Wonderland Teapot is over.

'There, now that's settled.' Mr Hastings claps his hands together like a crack of thunder and then taps on the front of the display case. 'I will have a slice of that Battenberg after all, Tabby, if you don't mind. Laura, tell Cleo what you want. You're writing this down, aren't you, Miss Jordan?'

Writing it down? My head hasn't stopped spinning long enough for me to catch my breath yet, never mind have the forethought to write anything down. This is ridiculous. There's no way I can do it. An orangutan would do a better job of catering her wedding than me.

One thing you can rely on a magician for is to produce things from thin air, and Bram produces a Post-it note and a biro from one of his pockets and hands them to me.

'Oh, I'm not fussy.' Laura huddles closer as though we're good friends and I'm only too happy to do her a massive favour like I had the vaguest bit of choice in the matter. 'Thankfully we'd ordered the wedding cake from a bakery and *they* won't let us down, but the reception itself is a buffet, so everyone can help themselves to whatever they want. Finger food. Sandwiches. Cakes. Nibbles. Bram knows what I like. He can fill you in on all the details. I need to get back to work anyway.'

It's a blur as Laura leaves. Mr Hastings seems to enjoy his cake and then Tabby shows him and Mrs Willetts around, and I let her get on with it, because no inspection is going to make any difference now. If we can't cater a wedding reception for a hundred and fifty people in four weeks' time, it's all over. I may as well give up now. I *should* give up now so Laura's got enough time to find a real caterer, but this is unfair and the injustice of it has made me so angry that I'm not going to admit defeat just yet.

Bram's leaning on the counter with his head in one hand while we wait in silence for them to come back. His other hand is occupied by fanning out and spinning the deck of playing cards again. I can still feel the imprint of his fingers where he squeezed my hand earlier, and I'm fighting the urge to reach over and still those cards again, to touch him in some small way, despite the vague feeling that all this could have been avoided if he'd been honest from the start.

When the inspection party return, Bram walks them to the door. He gives Mrs Willetts a hug, and I see the way she gives him an extra squeeze, and then he goes to shake his father's hand, but Mr Hastings promptly ignores him. Some people might be hurt or affronted, but Bram slips instantaneously into character. He does a little tap dance and whistles a quick tune.

'Thanks for coming!' he says in a deliberately shrill voice, right into Mr Hastings' ear, who puts a hand up like it was painful and frowns at him. 'It was a joy to see you, as always. Have a day that's filled with wonder!'

He produces a fistful of something from his pocket, and I see the horror cross Mr Hastings' face as he realises what he's going to do just one second too late. Bram opens his hand and blows a fistful of sparkly confetti all over his father.

It wasn't intended for Mrs Willetts but she gets caught in the crossfire and brushes glitter off her shoulders good-naturedly, but Mr Hastings isn't so good natured. He glares at Bram without a word, like he's not going to dignify it with a response. It's the personification of 'I'm not mad, I'm disappointed' conveyed in one simple look.

When his face starts to look like it might fracture if he scowls any harder, Mr Hastings huffs, blowing his greying hair upwards and disturbing the array of confetti that had landed on his head and sending a rainbow of paper shapes fluttering to their deaths on the floor. It would be quite comical if you couldn't feel the anger pouring from him in waves. I get the feeling this is far from Mr Hastings' first shower of confetti. Without a word, he gestures for Mrs Willetts to walk in front of him and closes the door from outside with a pointed thud, without taking his glaring eyes off Bram.

Once they've walked far enough down the street to be out of earshot, one of the regular customers who's been coming in for a toasted teacake daily, starts a round of applause. 'Well done, lad. If anyone needs a bit of confetti, it's that stuffy old toadstool!'

Bram takes another bow. 'Exactly my point, Mrs Moreno. It really is a sorry state of affairs when someone's day can't be improved by teeny-tiny colourful paper shapes and sparkle.'

I sigh as he walks back towards the counter. 'Why did you do that? You must've known it would *infuriate* him.'

'Ugh, because he's a manchild!' Tabby wails and stomps out to the back room.

'Because I'm obnoxious.' If the totally false Hatter grin didn't give him away, the wobble in his voice does.

'No, you're not. You're...' I can *see* what he's doing. He's putting on a front, pretending not to be bothered by his father's open display of disdain to hide *how* bothered he is by it. And no matter what, this isn't the time to talk about it. 'You're incorrigible,' I finish instead, trying to be non-judgemental. We've both had enough judgement for one day.

'I like to think so,' he says proudly.

The three playing cards that Mrs Willetts dislodged from my teapot display are still on the counter, and he holds his hand out for them. When I refuse, he reaches over and pulls them out from behind my ear instead.

'Bram!' I snatch them back, but in the blink of an eye, he's switched them, and the three cards I'm holding are not the ones that were there nanoseconds ago. 'How did you do that?'

'Magic,' he says with a grin and sidesteps to the teapot display to put the original ones back in.

'So you're going to tell me that was an empty threat, right?' I watch as he winds the cards onto the strands of wire. 'Just a big joke. Mr Hastings throwing his weight around. He wouldn't actually expect us to cater a wedding, right?' I sound too hopeful for my own good. 'Right?'

'My father doesn't make empty threats.'

'Ah yes, your father. Don't think I've forgotten that key nugget of information in the panic of this wedding nonsense. As if things weren't hard enough here, now I've got Mr Hastings' golden boy watching my every mistake too.'

'I'm many colours in the eyes of my father, golden is not one of them,' he says without looking up from the display he's fixing. '*You* know that.'

'I don't—'

'You remember when you said you don't care who he is...'

'I don't care who he is.' I sigh and push a hand through my hair and accidentally dislodge my black bow headband. 'I *don't* care, Bram. I care about the fact you didn't tell me.'

'Cleo, can we not?' This time, he looks me directly in the eyes. 'I know you want to yell at me. I know you want to thump me, but not here, okay? Not now. Not with certain "I spy with my little eyes" watching.' His eyes flick in the direction Tabby went, making it clear that anything she overhears will *not* stay between us. 'Tonight, if you'll still come over. You can shout at me then. You can hit me then, I promise.'

'Scheduled violence. Something to look forward to.' I can't help smiling and I see the smile in his brown eyes when he looks at me. 'Although I don't think there's much point in me coming over. We can't cater your sister's wedding. This is all over, no matter which way you slice it.'

'Keep calm. Let's not panic.' He moves back to standing opposite and then winks at me. 'Don't throw the baby out with the carrots or hatch your chickens before they can count. It's not over until the big-boned bullfrog sings.'

'Your mixed sayings come out more when you're panicking and trying to pretend you're not.'

'I don't know how you know that.'

'You've let me see behind your hat.'

'There's nothing behind my hat but blue hair.' He gives me that megawatt Hatter grin, but today, I can see how much is hidden behind it. There is so much more to Bram than blue hair, hats, and immense control over a deck of cards. I'm starting to realise that all of those things exist *only* to hide the real person – a softer, quieter side who's been hurt once too often.

12

The gate to Bram's house opens as I pull up to it that night, and he's sitting on the steps outside, waiting for me. He lifts a hand in greeting and I do the same through the car windscreen as I stop under the magnolia tree and park on a carpet of fallen pink blossoms.

The early-evening spring sun is behind me as I get out of the car and crunch across the gravel. I'm unsure of everything now. I don't even know if I'm angry at him. The panic of being expected to cater a wedding has obliterated everything else. It feels like weeks since I found out who his father is, not mere hours.

'Hi.' He holds a hand up to shade his eyes as he squints up at me. He's got a zip-up grey hoodie on with the sleeves pulled up to his elbows and the hood half-up, partially covering his longish hair where it frames his face, soft and wavy now after a shower.

'Hi, Bram Hastings.' I climb the stone steps and sit down beside him.

He groans and buries his head in his hands. 'I'm sorry, I'm sorry, I'm sorry. You can hit me now, I don't mind.'

Without lifting his head, he holds his right arm out so it's in front of me, but instead of hitting it, I trace my fingertips along his skin, letting my fingers rub across the fine dark hair covering his strong forearm. 'I don't want to hit you. I want to know why you didn't tell me.'

'Oh come on, really?' His chin is resting on his other arm, almost on his knees, but his eyes are trained on the spot where my fingers are touching. 'You were wary of me from the start because I'd *phoned* him. If you'd known we were related, you'd never have let me in.'

'And wasn't that a huge...' I was going to sarcastically snap 'mistake' but I stop myself. It doesn't feel like it was a mistake to trust him. No matter who his father is, *he* has done nothing but build me up and help The Wonderland Teapot to thrive.

He tilts his head to the side and meets my eyes, and I know he's heard the unsaid word and recognised that I didn't say it. 'His shadow is large and impossible to get away from. My whole life, I've had people befriending me because of who he is, because they want me to "put in a good word", or for a million other reasons that all revolve around him. The other night when you said you didn't care who he was, my heart kind of leapt and did a fluttery thing. I wanted that to be true, but it never is. That shadow looms too large for anyone to ignore.' His voice sounds strangled and quiet, and he's talking to the concrete of the steps rather than to me. 'I know I should have told you, but honestly, I liked you not knowing. If you liked me, I wanted you to like me for being a good Mad Hatter, not because you thought I would have some influence over your lease. And if you hated me, I wanted you to hate me for being me, not because of who my father is.'

I can't help noticing the anomaly in those two options. Like him for being the Mad Hatter or dislike him for being himself. Why is there no option for simply liking him as he is?

As I'm thinking about it, I realise my fingers are still on his forearm and pull them back quickly, and he jolts in surprise, like he hadn't noticed either. 'I meant what I said the other night. I *don't* care who your father is, Bram. I care who *you* are. Your father's shadow has bully written all over it. Who he is has no bearing on who you are, other than to ensure you're the complete opposite of him.'

His smile starts off small and gradually widens until he's beaming wider than any Mad Hatter grin he's ever thrown my way, but for once, it's a completely genuine beam that makes it impossible not to return until we're both sitting on his steps, smiling at each other.

There's something about him that's infinitely trustworthy. From the nervous habit of card shuffling to the instant slip into character when Mr Hastings refused to shake his hand. It's clear that Bram's been on the wrong end of his father's boorish behaviour many times. 'Why'd you do that with the confetti today? And don't say it's because you're obnoxious, because *you* aren't. You must've known it would only make him angrier...'

'Because I'm sick of being told there's something wrong with me.' He says it instantly and then stops and thinks over what he's said. 'If I know someone doesn't like me, I want to be *more* me. I want to wind them up. I want to drive them crackers. I want to give them a reason to hate me. When I'm told that I'm too much, I want to *be* too much.' He lets out a long sigh. 'I'm an adult. I don't need my father's approval, but sometimes I want it. I want something I do to be good enough. I've tried, *so hard*...' His voice cracks and it sounds so aching and desperate that it makes my heart leap into my throat. 'But I'm never, ever going to be who he wishes I was, so I may as well be ornery and cantankerous. It's easier to be hated for a character I play than for who I am.'

I didn't intend to take his hand, but suddenly I'm holding it, clasping it between both of mine. 'So your level of annoyingness is based solely on how annoyed people are with you...'

'The sign of someone who had a screwed-up childhood and has a plethora of deep-rooted issues, I'm sure.'

He says it with such a frivolous tone that it makes me smile, but it also confirms something I've been trying to figure out. Bram has been nowhere near as annoying lately as he was at first, and I hadn't yet worked out whether it was him being less annoying or my tolerance level growing. 'I've noticed that, you know.'

'The plethora of deep-rooted issues?'

I laugh. 'No. That you haven't been anywhere near as annoying as you were at first.'

'You haven't been anywhere near as annoyed with me as you were at first.' He moves his hand in mine until our fingers line up and then slots them together and squeezes. 'I'd go so far as to say you might even like me, just a little bit.'

It makes me laugh out loud, because I know he doesn't mean it in *that* way, and because it's unequivocally true. He's impossible not to like when you get to know him. 'Nah. Not *at all*.' I'm grinning as I say it. 'Not even the teensiest little bit. No siree.'

He's laughing too. He knows I'm joking, and I know how good he is at reading people. There's no point even trying to hide it.

His eyes gleam as he disentangles our hands and reaches over, clicks his fingers from somewhere behind me, and pulls a tulip out from behind my ear.

'Bram!' I want to be mad at him but it's impossible to stop smiling. 'I hate it when you do that!'

'Yeah, I know,' he repeats, that familiar mischievous glint in his eyes again. We both know that's exactly why he does it.

He holds the tulip out to me and my fingers brush against his as I take it. His hand lingers just a moment too long against mine and it sends a little shiver up my arm when he pulls away, and I fight the urge to chase after it and catch hold of it again.

I twirl the stalk between my fingers. I don't know where he got it from; the tulip planters are at the bottom of the steps and I'd have seen it if it was already here. I let my fingers stroke over the pinky-white satiny petals. I know I shouldn't ask, but I can't stop myself. '*Did* you have a screwed-up childhood?'

I can feel his eyes on me but I keep my focus intently on the tulip, because if I look at him, I'm not entirely sure I won't hug him.

It takes him a long time to answer. He's obviously considering his words carefully and probably weighing up how much he wants to share, and I'm moments away from standing up and pretending I didn't say anything before he speaks again.

'Things cut deep in young children, and the way to mess a kid up is to constantly question why he's like he is. I spent my child-hood being dragged around to a steady stream of child psychiatrists and psychologists while my father insisted that they needed to diagnose me with something, anything, because he wanted to know there was really something "wrong" with me, but I never fitted into any of their parameters. None of their tests defined me.' His voice is barely above a whisper and I'm certain he's never told anyone this before. 'I was shy, I didn't like being told what to do, and I never wanted to be anything like my father. That wasn't an acceptable life choice in his eyes, and he needed to believe that there was a label to explain it, rather than put up with me being...' he shrugs, at a loss for how to finish the sentence.

I reach over and push his half-up hood the rest of the way down. 'A spectacular nut.'

My hand trails over his shoulder and he reaches up to cover it and give it a quick squeeze. He mouths a 'thank you' but no sound comes out.

His hand stays on mine and his eyes close and he lets out a long sigh, looking like he's enjoying the sun on his face, and I take a breath too, force myself to exhale and loosen my shoulders for what seems like the first time all day. 'It's so beautiful here.'

'Yeah, it is. I don't always remember that.' He looks at me and his lips tip up slowly into a gentle, vulnerable smile and I can't help smiling back because this feels so peaceful and like we could sit here for the rest of the evening and that would be absolutely fine with us both.

A distant car horn breaks the reverie and Bram sits upright, blinking as the sun glints down on us.

'What did your father mean about someone else being offered the tearoom?' I've got so relaxed that my muscles protest at being used again when I push myself upright.

'I don't know anything about that. First I've heard of it.'

'Oh come on, you know everything about everything that goes on at that council.' I look at him expectantly but his face remains blank. 'Was it Tabby? Is that what she's doing – extending the olive branch, so to speak? Showing your father that she can play nice so she's first in line when I inevitably fail?'

'You're not going to fail,' he says, and although I appreciate the boost of his confidence in me, it's also a display of his ability to swerve a conversation subject.

'Come on, Cleopold.' He reaches across and slides his hand over my knee, the heat of his palm lingering through my leggings. 'We've got a wedding to cater.'

With a squeeze, he lets go and vaults to his feet and holds out a hand to pull me up.

'No, we haven't.'

''Course we have.' He pushes his hand closer to me when I ignore it the first time.

'Bram, I made that Battenberg three times in one afternoon to get it right-ish!'

'Then it's a good thing we've got plenty of time to practice.' He's still holding his hand out and I reluctantly take it and let him pull me to my feet. 'Because my father *is* a bully and we're not going to let him win. Between us, we *are* going to provide Laura with everything she wants for this wedding. I'm not going to let you lose The Wonderland Teapot because of me.'

'It's not really your fault, you know,' I say as I follow him into the house, even though I've been roundaboutly blaming him for most of the day. 'No one could've known that would happen today. The caterer pulling out, your father happening to be in the tearoom when Laura found out...'

'Her happening to try an amazing slice of Battenberg,' he adds, and I give him a scathing look.

'It was like the fates aligning in a really, really bad way.'

'So let's kill two stones with one bird and actually do it. See this as a crash-course in baking. All the practice pieces can be sold in the tearoom, and by the end, you will be a master of the flour, queen of the stand mixer, and I will knight you with whisks as Cleo Jordan, owner of The Wonderland Teapot on Ever After Street. Because, between us, we've got this.'

It makes me think of the thing he always says – that we're in this together.

Just like we have been from the very beginning.

* * *

'Laura said you know what she likes.'

'She likes what most people like.' Bram is standing in the doorway of the pantry in his kitchen, looking at well-stocked shelves. 'She likes Nutella.' He gets a jar out and plonks it on the unit.

'Jaffa Cakes.' A box of them follows.

'Cherry Bakewells.' He adds a box of them to the ever-growing pile on the kitchen countertop. 'Cadbury's Creme Eggs and just about everything in the chocolate aisle of any supermarket. We just need to make that into wedding food. Any suggestions better than Cherry Bakewells smeared with Nutella and garnished with a Jaffa Cake? Because I'd totally eat that, and as a bonus, no one will ever have had it at a wedding before, or ever again.'

His sense of humour cuts through the panic I'm feeling and the much-needed laugh makes me relax a bit and actually look at the pile of things in front of us. 'What about chocolate-hazelnut muffins made with Nutella?'

'My mum used to do that when we were little, that's perfect.' He scribbles it down on a list and adds something else. 'Macarons. She loves macarons and they're hard to find round here.'

'I can't make macarons! They're delicate little patisserie things! You saw me trying to wrap that Battenberg in marzipan the other day, it was like trying to hit a Highland cow's backside with a banjo.'

'Macarons are surprisingly easy – you just need to be good at piping, and *you* are excellent at piping.'

I go to protest again, but I decide to listen to him instead. If he believes in me... maybe I can embrace this rather than running away from it. I've hidden away enough in the past couple of years, and I don't want to let Mr Hastings chase me away from the one thing that's made it worthwhile getting back out into the world. My spark in the kitchen *has* been coming back lately, and if I could really make macarons... 'We could do them in stacks of pink and purple and put a rice paper Cheshire Cat head on the top and a tail on the bottom. On theme for the tearoom *and* something Laura loves.'

'See?' He nudges his elbow against my arm and looks down at me with a bright grin. 'You were made for this. Don't let my father destroy your creativity, because that's your strong point. That's what made your application stand out from the crowd. Combine that with our joint baking ability, and that's how we win – with imagination and a sunny spring in our can-do step.'

No one has ever made me feel more *can-do* than he does. 'Okay, what do you suggest we make with this?' I wave a hand towards the pile of stuff he's put on the kitchen unit.

Instead of a sensible suggestion, he tears into the packet of Jaffa Cakes and offers me one.

'Arguably a good answer to any question.'

He laughs and stuffs a whole one into his mouth. 'I do have some ideas, but they're more for the tearoom in general. You want to hear them?'

'Of course.' I like that he phrases it as a question. Most people are only too quick to force their opinions on you, and he makes me feel like I have a choice.

'I think you're going too traditional. You want to bake your nan's tearoom staples like lemon drizzle and Victoria sponge, but I think that's doing a disservice to what you've created with the atmosphere there. If the tearoom was mine, I would embrace the bonkersness. We need to make things that people are going to talk about. That people are going to remember. And this is how.' He holds an open hand towards the things on the unit. 'By using things people already love and making something new with them. Nutella muffins are just the start. What about Cherry Bakewell cupcakes? Or Creme Egg cheesecake?'

'Jaffa Cake brownies?' I suggest.

'Yes!' He nudges me again. 'Laura would absolutely love any of those at the wedding, but it's the sort of thing you should bring into The Wonderland Teapot too. No one is going to remember a bit of Victoria sponge, but when people talk about Ever After Street, someone *is* going to say to their friends, "Oh my God, I had the *best* slice of Terry's Chocolate Orange cake there, you have to try it!"'

I think I lost the thread of this conversation at the mention of Creme Egg cheesecake, and I steal another Jaffa Cake to mop up in case I'm drooling. He's like a walking Pinterest board. He's so animated as he talks that he could almost be a cartoon character. His enthusiasm is contagious as he gesticulates with his hands, his singular dimple deepening with every sentence as his smile grows. A really, *really* gorgeous walking Pinterest board.

'And right now, I think we should test one of the endless possibilities by making some Nutella muffins.'

'I don't have a recipe.'

'Don't need a recipe. You have your experience and instincts. You just need to trust yourself. And I can help. I've made muffins many times.'

Is it that simple? I could go online right now and grab one of countless recipes from the internet, but for once, I don't want to. I want to do what I used to be able to do – go into a kitchen, use a basic recipe that I knew by heart, and add things to it to make it extra-special. Measuring by sight and guesswork, tasting along the way, and never being bothered if the results weren't perfect. I haven't felt like that in years, but tonight, I do.

I can't help grinning at him. 'You had me at soft, gooey, chocolatey, hazelnutty goodness.'

* * *

'Yoghurt keeps muffins moist.' Bram whisks together melted butter, eggs, and yoghurt, while I measure out sugar, flour, bicarb, and cocoa powder and suddenly stop stirring when I remember something.

'Yoghurt! *That's* what my mum used to put in her cakes to keep them fluffy and light. It increases the moisture without increasing the fat content. She always used to tell me that, but I'd forgotten.' I look over at him. 'Thank you. That's the first time I've thought of that in years.'

His smile is warm and genuine. 'See what happens when you *don't* think about it?'

When he brings his bowl over to mine and pours the wet ingredients in, I go to mix them and his hand instantly covers mine on the spatula handle. 'Gently.'

He's noticed my tendency to beat up ingredients rather than fold them in. He steps up behind me and all I can concentrate on is the heat of his body and the sense of his height behind me.

'This okay?' His voice is right beside my ear as his fingers wrap around mine on the wooden handle and force me to move it slowly.

I make a noise that could best be interpreted as 'more than okay'. His closeness has obliterated all sensible thoughts. It's been a while since I had a gorgeous man get this close, and Bram is extra gorgeous and extra close.

'This isn't a punching bag that you take your frustrations of the day out on.' His chin is resting on my shoulder as he looks at the bowl we're sharing now, his voice low and calm. 'Overmixed batter makes tough and chewy muffins. Doesn't matter if it's still lumpy.'

If I turned my head even slightly, I could kiss his cheek. His stubble grazes my neck with every movement, and his exuberant aftershave has taken over the scent of chocolate in the kitchen.

I let him take the lead with the spatula, telling myself I'm absorbing his expertise, but my entire focus is on every point where his body presses against mine, and the space where his hand covers mine feels like it's burning with tingly heat.

'We're overmixing this batter, aren't we?' I whisper when an abnormal amount of time has passed.

'We might be.' His chin presses against my shoulder. 'Got to admit I'm struggling to care.'

'Me too.'

'Consider this a theoretical lesson. I'm telling you what to do in theory but showing you what *not* to do in practice.'

I laugh and lean back against him the tiniest smidgen. I'm starting to think the biggest hazard when it comes to baking is getting too close to Bram in the kitchen. 'There's a bag of chocolate chips over there that we should have mixed in at least five minutes ago.'

'Yeah.' He glances at them and then sighs and steps away to reach the bag, and I instantly miss the closeness.

I pour them in and he moves further along the unit to line a muffin tin with paper cases and then slides it down to me, and I spoon in equal amounts of the chocolatey batter.

We clean up while they cook, and when they're done, Bram slices the tops off and uses a mini scoop to score out a hole from the middle of each muffin and passes them over to me, where I splodge a spoonful of Nutella into the middle, put the top back on, and dust them with icing sugar.

'Cheers.' We take a muffin each and he knocks his against mine in a toast, and we peel the cases back and take a bite.

'They're amazing.' I put a hand up to cover my mouth because they're too good not to say it instantly. The Nutella has started to melt with the heat of the muffin, creating a mix of soft, gooey, hazel-nutty chocolate cake. 'Now we just have to do it a hundred and fifty more times. With several different things. And get them all ready in time for one day.'

He flashes both dark eyebrows at me. 'What, that? Easy.'

'Easy,' I echo, although there's something about Bram that makes things feel much less daunting than they would if I was alone.

13

'What are they?' Tabby peers into the front of the display case as I stand behind it, using tongs to arrange the muffins onto a three-tier stand in the centre.

'Nutella muffins. Bram and I made them last night.'

'Don't you make all of this?' She waves a hand towards the other things on display, including a coffee walnut cake from the super-market that I've unwrapped and decorated, cherry tarts with added fresh cream and heart sprinkles, and flapjacks with card suits iced onto them.

'Well, yeah, but—'

'It's the first joint effort.' Bram comes in from out the back and finishes the answer when I get flustered at the slip-up. 'First time we've made something together. The first of many.'

I meet his eyes across the shop and he winks at me, but I feel my cheeks burning under Tabby's analytical eyes. 'Would you like one?'

'Ugh, no, calories!' She frowns at me with such horror that you'd think I'd offered her a poison apple rather than a chocolate muffin.

'They're a trial for Laura's wedding,' I say, in case she gets the wrong idea about why Bram and I are making things together.

'Oh, the wedding!' She clasps her hands together. 'It's going to be a fairy-tale day. I've got so much planned for the hen night. I'm doing a pampering session for all the ladies to show them what I'd do at my wellness retreat. The mother of the bride is going to be there. Just about the only person in the universe who has influence over dear daddy Hastings. When she sees what I can offer, she'll put in a good word for me. Maybe one day we'll be neighbours on Ever After Street after all.'

'At least there are no calories in acupuncture needles,' I say to cover how nervous that makes me. *Is* she the person who was offered this shop before me? What if Mr Hastings' wife singing Tabby's praises and waxing lyrical about literal wax treatments really could influence him into considering that Ever After Street needs a wellness retreat instead of a teashop?

Luckily customers don't seem to agree because it's a busy morning – so busy that I have to put Tabby on tea-making duty, and Bram runs himself ragged between bringing dishes to customers and entertaining visitors. He flutters around cards, spinning them, plucking them from mid-air, making things disappear and reappear in different places, tricks that no one can explain logically, and there's something about his smile when people like what he does. It's impossible not to watch him, even when I'm supposed to be concentrating on the orders for chicken mayo sandwiches, hot buttered crumpets, and cream teas.

I'm overjoyed when the first person orders a Nutella muffin and a teapot of sparkly tea, and Bram's eyes are dancing as we both covertly watch her from opposite sides of the tearoom.

Until she digs a fork in and her face contorts in disgust. 'Excuse me, I think there's something wrong with this. It's so salty. I can't eat it!'

'Salt?' I say in confusion as she waves me over.

Bram hurriedly finishes a card trick and comes over too. 'There's no salt in it whatsoever.'

'Oh, there very much is. That's disgusting!'

My confusion is mirrored on Bram's face and we give each other a clueless shrug. He takes the muffin away, while I offer the customer something else but end up refunding her entire order when she refuses, looking like she might be scarred for life by the muffin experience.

'There's salt in these.' By the time I've finished, Bram's taken another muffin from the display case, put it on a plate and pulled it apart. 'Look at that. Those grains in the Nutella and all over the top. Someone's put salt in this.'

'How can someone have put salt in it?' I get a fork out and gather up some of the cake and can't contain the shudder when I shove it in my mouth. 'That's like taking a bite of a tub of Saxa.' I go to spit the mouthful into the bin, and Bram tries a bit too and quickly follows me.

'I don't get it. They weren't like this last night.'

'Of course they weren't like this last night.' His dark eyes scan the tearoom. 'Someone's sabotaged them. Someone's thrown a load of salt all over them.'

'No! Who? And why?'

'Gremlins?' he suggests seriously.

'Gremlins?' I picture the cute creatures from the eighties' movie. 'I *don't* think we've been invaded by gremlins, do you?'

He raises an eyebrow. 'Well, on the off chance that it *wasn't* gremlins, there are only three of us here and it wasn't you or me. That somewhat narrows it down.'

'Tabby? Why would she do that?'

'The question isn't why, the question is whether she's done it to anything else.' He's at the display case, pulling out plates and serving platters and peering at them. 'No one else has complained about anything, right?'

I shake my head.

'Then hopefully they're fine and it was just the muffins because of what we said this morning.' He scrunches his fingers for a fork, and when I pass one over, he spears one thing after another and puts them in his mouth one at a time before putting the plates back in the display case. 'They're fine. So are they, and those.'

'Why would she do that?' Tabby is on her lunch break and I can hear her moving around upstairs and repeat my earlier question, unable to believe that *anyone* would do this on purpose. Maybe an accident that she was too embarrassed to own up to? The thought that this could be deliberate, that there's someone out there – or, more specifically, *in here*, who wants to cause this kind of harm sends a shiver down my spine, and makes me feel apprehensive and unsafe, and like I can't trust anyone.

'Oh, who knows with that woman. Probably to get at me because she knew I'd had a hand in making them. Trying to convince my father that a wellness retreat would be a better option than a tearoom in this spot. Just trying to make life difficult. The possibilities are endless. This is why they say never work with children, animals, or exes.'

I think about what I thought last night, about someone being offered this space and then having the offer rescinded when I came along. What if that really was Tabby? It'd be something she'd hold against me. Something she'd want revenge for.

'Want me to go and have it out with her?' Bram offers.

I glance upwards, where the upstairs floorboards are creaking. 'No. There's enough animosity between you already. I'll talk to her later.'

* * *

'Salt? I don't understand. Why would there be salt in them?' Tabby is either completely clueless about the suspected muffin sabotage, or she could win an Oscar for her innocent look.

'Someone put it in,' I say when I corner her in the staffroom before the end of her lunch break.

She regards me for a minute. 'Oh, and let me guess, Bram suggested it was me.'

'Well, there are only three of us here and it wasn't me or him.' I repeat his words from earlier.

'Yes, quite convenient. You can't honestly think I'd be that stupid, can you? Why would I do something that would be so obvious? Don't you think *I'd* know that *you'd* know it was me?'

I go to refute it, but it's quite a good point actually. There *are* only three of us here. You'd either have to be totally daft or an evil genius to do something so obvious when you knew you'd be the first suspect, and I don't think Tabby is either. She's a bit spoiled, but she's not stupid and she's not horribly cruel. I actually think she's found working with Bram harder than she expected it to be.

'Maybe a small child got behind the counter when none of us were looking and liberally doused everything with salt. Or maybe you should look a bit closer to home.' A sinister tone has crept into her sickly-sweet voice.

'What does that mean?'

'Well, rather than being blinded by that ridiculous hair and offensively bright jacket, you should take a step back and objectively consider who is most likely to have ruined your muffins. Who made them?'

'Bram and I did, together.'

'And you saw *everything* he put in them, did you? You had eyes on him at *all* times?'

'Yes! Well, no, but I'd have noticed if he'd dumped half a tin of salt in them! And we tried them! They were perfect last night!'

'Right, and after that, did you leave him alone with them? Who handled them last? Who's been alone in the tearoom this morning?'

The answer to all those questions is Bram. Of course it is. Last night, I took stuff out to the car while he loaded the muffins into cake tins ready to bring in this morning. I didn't watch him every second – why would I? 'That's ridiculous. How would he know I wouldn't have one for breakfast and find out? And why? What would Bram have to gain from sabotaging anything around here? If I lose The Wonderland Teapot, he loses his job as the Hatter.'

'He'll find another one. People like him always bounce back. You don't honestly think dear daddy Hastings would let him be jobless for long, do you? This'll be his idea of a practical joke, you mark my words.'

'He's not a practical jokey kind of person. Bram does magic tricks, he doesn't pull pranks.'

'Same thing.' She reaches over to squeeze my shoulder. 'You're young and naive, Cleo.'

'I'm thirty-four! And you're only two years older than me, you're not exactly a wizened old tortoise are you?'

'You forget that I have five years' worth of experience with Bram. You've only known him for a few weeks. You're taken in by his sense of humour, but that wears thin *very* fast, especially when you're an adult and he has eternal Peter Pan syndrome. The attention-seeking manchild who point-blank refuses to grow up. He's the class clown. Disrupting lessons and causing havoc, and the more the other students find him funny, the more he acts up to impress them.' She squeezes my shoulder again and I'm torn between being annoyed at being patronised and trying not to show how much my interest is piqued. I like Bram. He doesn't seem like a manchild, he seems like someone who's been hurt and has created a shield to stop himself being hurt again, but she's right too – realistically, she does know him better than I do, and there's a horrible, gnawing niggle of doubt in my mind.

'And he knew full well he could blame the salt on me.' She goes back to talking about the muffins. 'He doesn't want to work with me any more than I want to work with him. He's trying to get me fired.'

'No, he's not like that. He's not bitter about the way things ended between you.'

'Things didn't end between us – he ended them out of the blue. *I* thought we were happy. It left me reeling. It's taken years for me to put my broken heart back together. I was part of his family and he tossed me aside like the past five years of our lives had meant nothing.'

I don't know whether I want to get into this or not. It's nothing to do with me, and I don't want to get in the middle of whatever happened between them, but I can't help myself burrowing. 'That's not what I heard...'

'I'm allowed to have standards! A wedding day is the most important day of any woman's life. I'm not wrong to want to marry a man who *doesn't* turn up wearing flipping eyeliner or cracking some lame joke and embarrassing me. Our wedding photos would have been with us for the rest of our lives. I didn't want him to look like...' She waves a hand towards the stairs. '*That.*'

'Surely the person you're marrying is more important than what they look like.'

'And I think he should have compromised to make me happy. His family had become like my family. We had spent five years together. We'd gone on holidays together. Shared important life events. They were my in-laws in all but an official capacity. And suddenly, gone. Over. Now I feel like I'm doing something wrong by even contacting them. Laura's been like a sister to me for years, and now she can't invite me to her wedding without being torn over upsetting him. I don't have a close family of my own, and losing them broke my heart.'

I bite my lip because I really feel for her. The things no one tells you about the consequences of a break-up. When two people have been together for that long, it isn't just *them* that splitting up affects.

'Daddy Hastings always thought my influence was good for Bram. And now look at the state of him without it.'

And just like that, my hackles are bristling again. She can switch from making me want to give her a hug to making me want her to drink a shrinking potion and shrivel down to ant size in one simple sentence. Bram has done nothing but help me since I met him. He doesn't deserve that. 'He's—'

'He's a mess, Cleo,' she interrupts before I can defend him. 'Squatting in his father's house, dressing like a toddler who's got into their parents' wardrobe and make-up case, doing magic for a living, and before now, running a carousel. It's not exactly blazing ambition, is it?'

'He's playing a character in the tearoom. He's ambitious with what he does. The tricks he can do are something else. People can do what they love and be happy. Not everyone needs to be rich and famous.'

'But everyone should want bigger things. Like you. I might think this place is a bit childish, but it's good to see a young woman with a vision and the drive to make it happen. Have a little more faith in yourself and you won't need his help, and trust me, everything is better when Bram Hastings *isn't* involved in it.'

I take that thinly veiled compliment and use it to appeal to her better nature. 'Okay, so businesswoman to businesswoman, level with me. Any means necessary to succeed, right? Even a spot of sabotage? You can be honest with me, Tabby. I'd prefer the truth... because I can't help but think Mr Hastings offered this place to you, and now you want it back.'

'What?'

I explain, and to be fair, she seems totally confused by the revelation that Mr Hastings offered the building to someone else and then changed his mind.

'That's odd. Mr Hastings *never* changes his mind about anything. He's very set in his ways. And he's far too professional for anything of the sort. I'm sorry, but to put it in words you understand, you're barking up the wrong raspberry bush. I have zero idea about this building being given to anyone else, and even less interest in trying to sabotage anything you're doing here. I champion women in business. My only interest is in showing Mr Hastings that I'm a team player and ensuring I'm front and centre of his mind when the next empty space comes up on Ever After Street.'

'Well, one thing's for certain, it won't happen again. No one will be unattended with any cakes from now on.'

'You just make sure you're looking in the right place, Cleo. Because one thing magicians are good at is misdirection – ensuring you're looking at the side of the stage while the trick is being done right in front of you.'

It sets a cold seed of dread growing in my chest. She *does* know Bram better than I do. What he told me about their break-up was only his side of the story. There is always another side.

Her comment about Bram not being on my side has been playing on my mind since she made it yesterday. I don't *know* that he wouldn't do something like this – what if Tabby *does* know that he would?

14

'How's life at The Wonderland Teapot, Cleo?' Ali from the 1001 Nights restaurant asks.

It's a Monday morning and it's my first Ever After Street meeting as a shopkeeper, even though I've got to know everyone throughout the months of helping Marnie. Lilith, who used to own the tearoom, would provide tea and cake for all the shopkeepers, so Bram and I have brought along a plateful of Cherry Bakewell cupcakes – vanilla sponge with chopped almonds and cherries in it, with a white peak of almond flavoured icing and a cherry on top. It's really a test to see if our twist on the classic will go down well with Cherry Bakewell lovers, and the meeting is constantly interrupted by moans of pleasure whenever anyone tries one.

We're gathered in the clearing in the middle of Ever After Street, surrounded by little white fences and flower beds, with seating and verges of grass for picnicking on. I glance at Bram, who is reclining along one of the picnic benches with his yellow boots up on the table and he grins at me.

I try to ignore the little flutter of butterflies flashing around inside and answer Ali. 'It's really good.'

'You have plenty of customers going in and out,' Mickey, who runs The Mermaid's Treasure Trove, says.

'I have people warning me that I'll have to let their wedding dresses out if they eat any more of your cakes,' Sadie, the seamstress from The Cinderella Shop adds. She makes wedding dresses for all the brides who have flocked to get married at the castle since she and Witt opened it up for weddings and receptions.

I can't help blushing. I've been working so hard, practising at Bram's every night, making batches of anything we can think of to incorporate well-loved British treats, and selling them in the tearoom the next day, gradually reducing the amount of supermarket-bought goods on offer and increasing the number of genuinely homemade ones.

'Children are always talking excitedly about it. At the carousel, I've seen a huge increase in kids happy because they're about to go in.' Joshy is the new carousel operator, a young lad of about twenty who's taken on Bram's old job. He's more of a balloon-animals type of children's entertainer than his predecessor, and also impresses both children and adults by singing made-up songs in his extraordinarily deep voice. 'And lots of nans and granddads warning them that they've got to have their ride first and then eat cake. The other way around tends not to end well.'

'Tell them about the wedding,' Marnie prompts me. 'It's totally unfair. Someone should tell that awful Mr Hastings where to shove his bullyish ultimatums.'

She's the only person I've told about the wedding catering job and how I can't get out of it without losing the tearoom, and I hadn't intended to tell the others because I feel small for not refusing and standing my ground, but how can I run the risk of Mr Hastings following through on his threats?

'Bullyish?' Lissa, the curator of Ever After Street's fairy-tale museum, can't hide her ears pricking up at the hint of a good cause to get behind.

'Ultimatums?' Imogen, a middle-aged lady who runs Sleeping Beauty's Once Upon A Dream – a lovely little shop full of all your nighttime needs, like sleepover kits, fancy pyjamas, bath bombs, soft and cosy blankets – sits forward, clearly wondering what's been going on when words like that are thrown around.

I sigh and tell them everything about Laura's caterer drop-out and Mr Hastings' threat. 'I don't have any choice. He made it clear that if I don't do it, my time at The Wonderland Teapot will be terminated, and I don't want to lose that. I love it. I love it. I've always loved *Alice in Wonderland* and I love getting to share that, I love how many people ask me about it and how many have said they're going to read it because of me, I love Bram, I—' I choke on my own words. 'I love *working with* Bram,' I amend as quickly as possible. 'Everyone who comes in loves the madness of the Hatter. I feel like I've been waiting all my life for this job.'

I'm trying not to meet his eyes, but I can't resist a peek to see if he heard the unintentional blunder that I'm hoping *no one* heard. His cheeks have gone as red as mine, and the twinkle in his eyes looks like he's trying not to smile but he can't quite stop himself.

'That's totally unfair.' Lissa folds her arms. 'Complain to someone higher up. He can't be allowed to treat employees like his own personal minions. That's preposterously unprofessional.'

'There *is* no one higher up. Mrs Willetts saw it happen, but no one has any authority over him. Speak out against him and you get fired. He's a one-man power-hungry inflated walking ego.' Bram gives me a nod at the throwback to what I said before I knew who he was.

'Of all people, I don't think *you* can say that.' Lissa fixes him with a look that answers my unspoken question of whether I was the *only* one who didn't know Bram's surname.

'You don't need to get out of it. You need to show him that you won't bow down to his coercive tactics.' That's Franca, who works at The Nutcracker Shop on Christmas Ever After. 'Why don't we help? Mr Hastings didn't specify that *you* have to do every little thing, did he?'

I shake my head.

'Well, why don't we all chip in? I make a great lemon meringue pie. My colleague from the festive clothing shop is a whizz with Christmas cookies, she makes them for us year-round. I'm sure she'd be delighted to make some wedding-themed ones instead.'

A few others from the festive end of the street murmur agreement. They're a little bit separated, and not all of them join us for the Ever After Street meetings, especially at this time of year, although we join forces when Christmas comes. Last year, they held the first Christmas market at the castle and it was unexpectedly popular, like a fairy-tale winter wonderland.

'We can all help.' Ali claps his hands together. 'I own a restaurant. If anyone can help with wedding catering, I can. You should have come to me straight away!'

Mickey whisks a pen and a notepad from her bag. 'Right, let's make a list of what's needed and then divvy it up between us. It won't be so overwhelming then. Having to cater an entire wedding is outrageous, but if everyone makes a batch or two of something, it'll be much easier, and Mr Hastings need never know.'

'Oh, no, I couldn't... You'd all deserve credit where it's due.'

'Cleo.' Marnie wraps an arm around my shoulders. 'You deserve to keep your place on this street, and *we* deserve to have you and The Wonderland Teapot. Let us *all* show that horrible Mr Hastings that nobody puts *our* baby in the corner.'

I'm not sure if it's just a good moment for a *Dirty Dancing* reference, or if she means I'm the baby of the street as the newest arrival, but I can't help feeling flushed with warmth that they're even offering.

'You know what they say – many hands make the sticky-fingered skeletons in the closet dance for joy.' Bram has pulled his feet off the table and sat upright, and I look over at him, silently asking if he thinks this is a good idea, and he gives me a nod like he understands what I've managed to convey with my eyes.

Within five minutes, Ali has agreed to make a vast selection of salads and pasta salads. Mickey is doing vol-au-vents and Lissa is on mini sausage roll and mini cheese roll duty. Imogen has volunteered for mini quiches. Franca is making a few lemon meringue pies and arranging for her colleague to make love-themed short-bread cookies. The Cherry Bakewell cupcakes have convinced everyone that Bram and I are the best choice to stick with cakes and other baked goods made from Laura's favourite things, and Marnie and Darcy have agreed to help us with those. I'm so overwhelmed with how easy they've made it that my eyes are welling up. This absolutely crushing thing that's been hanging over me in the week since Mr Hastings' visit is suddenly so greatly reduced that I can feel myself sagging in relief, even though I also have to make enough sandwiches to give a hundred and fifty people plenty of options.

Bram comes to stand next to me and slings an arm around my shoulder. 'I can't believe I didn't think to ask for help. I should've known this lot would spring into action at the first sign of difficulty.'

'Do you think Laura will mind?'

'Not at all. No one need ever know.' He's left the stack of hats in the shop, and he tilts his head until his blue hair is leaning against mine, the hairsprayed spikes catching on my loose blonde strands. 'And if anyone did ever know, then no, she wouldn't mind. Her original caterer wouldn't have done it alone, he'd have worked with a team of people. Even my father couldn't object to us bringing in help. A 150-guest wedding is a *lot* to dump on anyone. And you have friends here who want The Wonderland Teapot to stay as much as I do. You don't have to do everything alone. It's okay to share the burden.' He squeezes my shoulders pointedly, holding me against him for a long moment, and I exhale and tell myself to breathe, because it feels like I haven't since Mr Hastings walked in the other day.

Bram's head turns until his lips touch my hair, not a kiss, just a reassuring gesture that makes me feel good and turfs out the doubts that have been lingering since I spoke to Tabby last week. There's no way he's anything but genuine.

Seeing as he's the one person who knows what Laura likes, he's in-demand, and Mickey asks him about allergies, and then Lissa comes over to ask him about cheese preferences, and he drops his arm from around me and steps away to fend off enquiries, reaching over to scribble things on everyone's sheets, so popular that it's like he's signing autographs.

'Haven't had this much fun since I won third place at the last tea tossing competition,' Bram says when he's started to look like he needs some space.

'What's a tea tossing competition?' Ali asks, sounding as confused as everyone else looks.

'You know when you spill a cup of tea and it sploshes so far across the unit that you couldn't throw it any further if you tried? Well, I like to consider it a competition. How far can I toss the tea today? One point for covering the oven. Three points if it goes under the microwave. Bonus points for the floor too. People still talk fondly of the great tea toss of 1983.'

Our co-workers think he's lost the plot. Imogen is looking at him like he's barking mad, but I think about what he said about being shy. He got uncomfortable being the focal point then and said something daft to deflect attention. I can see him playing up his character and hiding behind his Hatter shield. 'You really are a nuthatch, aren't you?'

'I am a handsome blue and orange bird with awesome eyeliner skills, yes. Thank you for the compliment.' He takes a bow and then stands back up and winks at me.

'Surprisingly it was.' I can't help smiling as our eyes meet and his mouth tips up lopsidedly, making his dimple dip his left cheek, and making me feel warmer than the spring sunshine heating the back of my neck.

When the last of the cupcakes are gone, Bram goes to collect the cake cases and plates.

'Is he always like that?' Imogen whispers to me as I start gathering up empty cups and teapots and loading them onto one of the trays we brought with us.

'He is.'

'I don't know how you put up with it. Every conversation is one-third normal and two-thirds nonsense. It's like spiralling down a rabbit hole and wondering what the heck he's going on about.'

I laugh out loud. It's one of the most accurate descriptions of Bram I've heard so far, and it makes me remember how I felt about his unique approach to conversations at first. 'Surprisingly, you get used to it. You even grow accustomed to it.'

As if he can sense we're talking about him, he looks over and grins at me and my stomach does that fluttery thing again.

'Very, very accustomed to, hmm?' Imogen's eyes flit between us, and I walk into a table because I'm too busy smiling at him to watch where I'm going.

He's the personification of Wonderland. Slightly mad, quite nonsensical, and... somewhere you want to go back to again and again.

* * *

That afternoon, it's all going too well... until a customer starts screaming and clawing at his mouth. 'Hot! Hot! Hot!'

There's a couple who have come in and ordered sparkly tea; the wife has had a lavender and thyme scone with lemon curd, and the husband has just taken a bite of his Jaffa Cake brownie. He spits it back onto the plate and tries to scrape the remainder off his tongue.

'Water! Get us some water!' the wife shouts.

'Yes, of course!' I was on the other side of the tearoom chatting about *Alice in Wonderland* with a curious customer, and my heart is racing as I dash into the food prep room, grab a jug, and turn the cold tap on.

'Milk,' Bram shouts after me, having gone over to find out what's going on. 'It's better at taking heat away.'

I fill another jug with milk and race over with them both, trying to ignore the watchful gazes of *every* other eye in the tearoom, and of course, it's busy this afternoon so there are a lot of eyes watching this poor man having a terrible experience with his Jaffa Cake brownie.

The man guzzles milk straight from the jug, his face bright red and sweating, as his wife fans her hand in front of him, trying to cool him down.

It's happened again, hasn't it? Someone must have put something hot in the brownies. Bram and I made those brownies last night, and we ate a couple together, and there was nothing spicy about them. Just warm, fudgy, orangey gorgeousness. And after Tabby's warning the other day, I made sure that *I* was the one who loaded them into cake tins ready to bring in this morning.

The customer is panting, blowing out air through pursed lips, and his wife is mopping sweat from his brow with a napkin. She asks if he's okay and he nods. My panic recedes. Although I still have an underlying fear that I will one day accidentally kill a customer, today is not that day.

'What are you playing at, you idiots?' The angry man stands up and pokes a finger into Bram's chest. 'I could have been killed!'

'Tad dramatic?' Bram tries to diffuse the situation with humour, but the man is furious. 'What if I was allergic? Chilli wasn't mentioned on the ingredients when it's clearly the main one!'

'It's not supposed to be!' I edge closer because I'm concerned by how much angrier he could get.

'This is an accident, I assure you.' If Bram is disturbed by the man jabbing a finger into his chest, he doesn't show it. 'They're not meant to be spicy in any way. The responsibility is mine alone.'

'Bram...' I say, because we made them together.

'No. I made them. I obviously made a mistake somewhere. I'm very sorry. I'll ensure it doesn't happen again.'

'We made a mistake in coming to this dreadful place! Our feelings will be reflected in a review and a very stern letter to your boss!' The man has every right to be angry, of course he does, but his level of anger is really quite scary.

'We will, of course, give you a full refund, and a—' I was going to offer them a voucher for their next visit, but they look like they'd rather visit the surface of the sun than come here again, so I leave it. The wife gives me her debit card to refund while the man gathers up their shopping bags and stomps out the door, slamming it behind him.

'Sorry,' the wife apologises as I hand her card back. 'It really was a very nice scone.'

Bram hears it too and can't hold back the giggle. When she leaves, he leans over and whispers to me. 'My money's on her being the culprit because she wanted to see him suffer.'

The laugh relieves some of the blinding panic and gives me a moment to take a breath, which I haven't done since the man's first screech. When I hold my hands out in front of me, they're shaking.

'Don't worry about it.' Bram notices too because he reaches over to slip his fingers around mine and give them a squeeze. 'Every silver lining has a cloud and every cloud has a soft and squishy centre.'

He lets go of my hand and turns to make an announcement to the rest of the diners. 'Nothing to see here, ladies and gentlehamsters. Just a little Wonderland magic gone wrong. Jaffa Cake brownies are off the menu for today while we gather up the gremlins that have got into the kitchen. If anyone would like a refill of sparkly tea to calm their nerves, it's on the house.'

I raise an eyebrow at him, and he leans over the counter again. 'The longer they stay and enjoy something, the more likely they are to forget about that... interruption.'

I think the redness of that poor man's face will be imprinted in everyone's minds forever, as will his scathing review, because that will undoubtedly be on the internet for the rest of eternity and no one will need to use their mind's eye to remember it.

I do a couple of teapot refills as customers take up the offer, although most of them peer warily at the display cabinet like a cake might be about to leap forth and bite them, and unsurprisingly, absolutely no one wants another cake, and probably never will again after that incident.

'Well, that was fun. Haven't enjoyed myself so much since I tried plucking my eyebrows with a lawnmower.' Bram clears their table and when he returns to the counter, he gets the plate of brownies out of the display case, breaks one apart with a fork and takes a mouthful.

His face turns red and his eyes start watering. 'Flipping 'eck.' It makes him cough. 'Someone's put hot sauce or chilli or something in the Jaffa Cake brownies. Don't try them.'

I ignore him and take a forkful, and immediately regret it. My mouth blazes so hot that it feels like my teeth try to retreat back inside my gums. Sweat prickles my forehead, my eyes are streaming, and even spitting the cake out isn't enough to stop the burning sensation.

'This is ridiculous! No one's been alone with the cakes today! We set everything out and then we locked up when we went to the meeting. What have we got, a ghost who's good at sleig—' I cut myself off abruptly and cover it by choking on my burning tongue again. I was going to suggest a ghost who's good at sleight of hand, but while I don't think we've got any haunting issues, we *have* got a magician who's an expert at it. If anyone could have snuck a bottle of something in, concealed up a sleeve, and doused the brownies with it when no one was watching...

I bite my burning lip as I watch him bending over the sink, trying to run tap water through his mouth. He couldn't have... He wouldn't... Why would he? If The Wonderland Teapot goes, so does the Mad Hatter. He'd have nothing to gain, unlike Tabby, who despite her acting ability, I'm *sure* must be the person who Mr Hastings considered to take over this shop before me. And Tabby was suspiciously early this afternoon. She was waiting outside when we got back from the shopkeeper meeting. If there's one thing Tabby *never* is, it's early. She's got the hen night to demonstrate to Mrs Hastings how wonderful a wellness retreat on Ever After Street would be – is she trying to ensure that the tearoom has got a few scathing reviews beforehand to give her extra ammunition?

'What have I missed?' The Queen of Hearts in question reappears at the bottom of the stairs. 'What was all the shouting about? So much for peace and quiet on my tea break.'

I go to tell her but Bram gets in first. 'I'm sure you know exactly what that was all about. I'm surprised you didn't come down to revel in your win.'

'Oh, let me guess, *someone* has done *something* to... whatever those things were.' She gestures to the plate of smashed up brownies on the counter in front of us. 'And you're trying to blame me, even though I haven't been alone with your silly cakes for a moment today. I got here after you, remember?' She locks eyes with me. 'Let's hope *some* of us aren't stupid enough to fall for your... embellishments. Trusting you, Bram, is a mistake that any woman only makes *once*. Now, if you'll excuse me, some of us have work to do. We can't *all* toss around playing cards and call it a job.'

'I don't—' He goes to protest, but there's a child measuring their height against one of the wooden chess pieces and she's looking at Tabby's ballgown and red bouffant wig with wide, adoring eyes, and Tabby swishes over to say hello.

He makes a noise of frustration and then schools his face and pastes his Hatter grin back on. 'I think it'll take a week for the skin on my lips to regrow. Note to self – buy lip balm. Are you okay?'

I'm surprised by the question. I don't know if he means the hot brownie or the scene the man made, and the answer to both is... yes *and* no. I nod instead, and then even though I shouldn't, I reach out and let the back of my hand brush over the soft T-shirt covering his chest, right where the angry man jabbed his finger. 'Are you?'

'Me? I'm fine. Been intimidated by plenty of people worse than that in my life.'

I get the feeling he means his father, but before I have a chance to think about how much I want to hug him, his hand covers mine and he lifts it to his mouth to press a kiss to my fingers. 'Thank you though.'

He doesn't drop eye contact and the intensity in his dark eyes makes my knees feel wobbly and I'm glad I'm standing near enough to the counter to brace my hip against it. My heart is suddenly pounding again, and I'm feeling flushed for an altogether different reason this time.

'Why did you take responsibility for that?' You wouldn't think my mouth could be dry when I've just swallowed so much water, but it comes out hoarse and I have to clear my throat and try again. 'We *both* made them.'

'He seemed angry enough to complain to someone, somewhere, so better for me to get in trouble than you. Don't worry about it.' He drops my hand again when a customer comes in, and goes to greet them with a levitating playing card trick.

'He's so good, isn't he?' Mrs Moreno says as she comes up to the counter and orders a cup of sparkly tea and her usual toasted teacake.

'He's as mad as a box of frogs,' I say with a smile, trying to forget everything else and concentrate on the customers who *haven't* just witnessed a potential poisoning on the premises.

'And you wouldn't have him any other way, right?' She looks over her shoulder to where Bram is now with another customer and has produced a playing card from nowhere and turned it into a rose with a snap of his fingers, only for it to vanish and then turn up again on the other side of the table moments later.

'Right,' I say. Because he *is* as mad as a box of frogs in the best way possible, and he's many other things too, and yet the only question I keep coming back to is him taking responsibility for the brownies. Is it because he's kind… or because he *is* responsible?

15

'You okay, Bram?'

'Fine.' He lifts a hand to reassure me without looking up, probably because he knows that if he looks at me, I'll see how ill he looks. It's 4 p.m. on a Wednesday, just over a week after the fiery brownie incident, and for the past hour or so, Bram has not been looking good. And although he insists he's fine, he's gone from Mad Hatter to Quiet Hatter. He's been getting paler and paler until his face is so white, a ghost would look healthier, and he seems to be using the backs of chairs or the walls to keep himself upright as he moves around the tearoom.

It's the after-school rush time. There's always an increase in customers when the school day finishes. Parents and kids come up to the counter, picking out baked goods from the display case and tea or the soft drinks we've started offering for youngsters, squash or lemonade, served in mason jars with 'Drink Me' tags tied around them. Bram loves kids, he thrives on making them gasp in awe, but at the moment, he's leaning listlessly against the back wall, looking like he's having trouble staying vertical.

'Bram?' I say again, between customers, not wanting to draw attention to him.

'I'm fi—' Instead of finishing the repeated rebuttal, he pulls a chair out and sinks down in it, laying his arm across the empty table and putting his head down on it, unable to hide the groan that such a small movement elicits.

I nearly cut my own fingers off as I make an order for Brie and cranberry sandwiches and keep poking my head round the food prep room door to check on him, and as soon as I deliver the tray to the woman and young girl, I go and sit down in the chair opposite him.

One hand is on his belly, holding it protectively, and I can hear the angry gurgling noises his stomach is making. I reach over and slide my hand over his other hand where it's curled into a fist on the table. 'What's wrong?'

'Something I ate,' he mumbles. 'You know what they say – the proof of the pudding is in the food poisoning.'

'You've only eaten my caramel cake all day. And a cheese sandwich at lunchtime.'

He groans like the mention of food is making it worse.

'Do you want to go and sit upstairs? Can I get you some water or something?' I ask, despite the fact he doesn't look like water is going to solve this problem.

'Don't think I can move without throwing up. Just gimme a minute, it'll pass. Don't worry abo—' The sentence is cut off with another groan and I can *hear* how violent that stomach cramp was.

'I'm going...' He lifts his head and points upwards. 'Bathroom. Staff puking in the tearoom is a really bad look.'

Even when he's feeling like death warmed up, he still makes me smile despite the worry for him. He pushes himself up to his feet, looking wobbly, and hesitates for a moment. I didn't think it was possible for his pallor to go any paler, but now he goes from white to almost translucent and suddenly dashes behind the counter and up the stairs, the thump of his feet reverberating through the café from how fast he takes them.

I follow him as far as the bottom of the stairs, but the bathroom door has slammed shut and the tap is running to drown out any other noises that might be audible, and it's Tabby's day off, so I can't leave the tearoom unattended.

I take the caramel cake out of the display case and lift the cloche off. Bram has had at least three slices today. I baked it last night, and early this morning, a customer complained that it was a bit doughy, but he refused the refund I offered him so I thought the cake couldn't have been *that* bad. Because it was something I baked by myself, Bram has been trying to make me feel better about the moany customer by nabbing a huge slice at every chance he's had, and at least three other people have ordered slices today too, and no one else has complained, although one woman did leave a big chunk on her plate. Usually we've been making batches of small things, and it felt like a big step to make a whole cake, by myself, displayed under a cake dome, ready to be cut into slices if anyone ordered one, and I decorated it with strips of Galaxy Caramel bars and drizzled warm caramel over the top. There's a third of the cake left and I take it out the back and break it up with a fork, and although the top part is cooked, the 'soggy bottom' is very, very soggy indeed. The lowest parts of the cake are barely cooked.

No wonder he's feeling ill. What about the other customers who have eaten this today? Are their stomachs rebelling in the same way?

I look up the stairs again. I want to go after him and see if he's okay, but it looked like that was only going to end one way, and there's not much I can do to help with that.

I keep going to the bottom of the stairs, but the bathroom door is still closed and the tap is still on after twenty minutes have passed, but at least the tearoom is quieter now.

Marnie and I have partnered up with the friendship dates she runs, where she matches her customers up and sends them here to get to know each other better, and two women nattering about their favourite books are the only customers left, and when they eventually leave, I shut the door behind them and flip the sign over to 'closed' even though it's not five o'clock yet, and run straight upstairs.

'Bram?' I knock softly on the bathroom door. 'You okay?'

'I'm fi—' His denial is cut off by the sound of him retching, and guilt presses down on me. Are all the other customers having this reaction too? Are there, right now, three other people heaving into toilets because of *me*?

Why did I ever think trying to run a tearoom was a good idea? This is exactly what I feared would happen, but I never imagined it would happen to *my* Hatter. I've made someone ill, and not just someone, but someone I really... care about. It's bad enough to think that strangers might be ill after eating my cake, but it's even worse when it's Bram.

I'm about to ask if he needs anything but I think better of it. There's only so many things a person can need when they've got their head over a toilet bowl. 'I'm around if you need anything.'

I want to stay and do something, *anything*, to make him feel better, but no one wants someone hanging around outside the bathroom door, listening to the dulcet tones of them being ill, so I go back downstairs and start cleaning up, collecting plates and cups and taking them through to the sink in the food prep room. I wipe down all the tables and set all the Wonderland props to rights after a day of being played with by kids and used as selfie props by adults. The playing card roses in a vase on each table frequently end up squashed where people fiddle with their cardboard petals, so I squish them back into shape, and when there's still no movement from upstairs, I start washing up, and then I dry up and put everything away in the cupboards ready for tomorrow.

I go back upstairs and knock on the bathroom door again. 'Bram?'

'I'm fine, Cleo.' His response is mumbled and he does *not* sound fine. 'Just go away.'

There's not much more I can do downstairs, so I sit at the desk in the corner of the staffroom and cash-up the takings from the till.

It's after six before the toilet flushes for the last of many, many times tonight, and the bathroom door unlocks.

I jump up and clearly startle him because a very clammy looking Bram lets out a yelp and overbalances on wobbly legs and grabs onto the bathroom doorframe to hold himself up. 'What are you still doing here? I thought you'd gone home!'

'I couldn't leave you by yourself, could I?'

'I wish you had,' he mutters. 'There were some extremely unpleasant... sound effects... coming from that bathroom. No gentleman wants a lady to overhear *that*.'

'I've given you food poisoning, Bram. We left gentlemanly and ladylike things behind long ago.'

'You don't know it was the cake. It could've been dodgy cheese at lunchtime. Maybe I've developed a sudden allergy to dairy products. Maybe it's another gremlin-related incident.'

We both know Tabby wasn't in today, and no matter the niggling doubts she's put in my mind, it's not like he's going to have eaten something that he *knew* had been tampered with, is it? 'You didn't see the state of the partially raw cake I just pulled apart downstairs.'

I didn't think it was possible for his face to go any paler, but at the mention of the cake that caused this, his skin takes on a decidedly green tone and he glances back at the toilet bowl longingly.

The sickness has made his eyes water and his eyeliner has run, leaving big splotches of black around his eyes and I wish I could hug him, but I doubt he's feeling like being crowded, so I keep my distance. 'What do you need?'

'There's a spare toothbrush in my bag, you couldn't grab it for me, could you?'

There's something about a man who cares so much about his oral health that he carries a spare toothbrush. There's a cabinet of staff lockers in one corner, but Lilith lost the keys to them years ago, so now they're just storage cupboards, and all of us leave our stuff in the staffroom, and Bram's camo-print bag is on a chair near the desk. I rifle through the array of pockets and zippered compartments, pulling out packs of cards and other tricks of his trade, and oddly, a spray bottle of squirrel repellent. It's so bizarre that it stops me in my tracks.

The bathroom is around a corner from the main staffroom so he can't see me as I pull it out, wondering what other mysteries of the universe he's got in here. Does he really have so much trouble with squirrels that he needs to bring squirrel repellent to work with him? This is bizarre, even for Bram.

'It's in a white toiletries bag...' It doesn't sound like he suspects I'm snooping through his things, but it makes me realise that he soon will if I don't get a move on. I rummage through the endless compartments until I find the toiletries bag and take it to him.

'Thanks, beautiful.' He goes to take the bag and then his hand freezes in midair when he realises what he's said, and his complexion is so ashen that it's actually a relief to see the redness of a blush smudging his pale cheeks.

'Sorry,' he mumbles. 'I'm not... My mind's not... not thinking clearly, I didn't mean to say that.' He salutes me with the toiletries bag and disappears back into the bathroom, but then he pokes his head back out again. 'I think it, but I didn't mean to say it.'

My cheeks redden too because I'm so surprised by the simple compliment. I didn't know Bram saw me like that. I dress as Alice during the day, in my white pinafore and blue dress. My blonde hair is always down and held back by a black bow headband, and when I see him in the evenings... Well, after a long day at work, I'm certainly not dressing up, so I typically go to his house in jogging bottoms and oversized T-shirts, so it doesn't matter if I get them coated in flour or spattered by whatever batter we're mixing. But 'beautiful', in a moment when he doesn't have his walls up... It feels special. Significant.

I glance at the closed bathroom door, and before I realise what I'm doing, I've gone back over to his bag and pulled out that bottle of squirrel repellent again. There's a picture of a squirrel on the front with sizzle lines around it, and when I turn it over and read the back, it explains that squirrels don't like the spiciness of this spray. The ingredients list only two things – cayenne pepper and water.

Cayenne pepper. We never found whatever was put into those Jaffa Cake brownies last week. No hidden bottles of hot sauce or jars of chilli powder lurking around the place, but this... I swallow hard because this makes my insides burn more painfully than a forkful of that brownie did. Surely this is *it*. This is the smoking gun. And it's in Bram's bag.

Why *else* would he have a spray of burning hot spice with him at work? And it's not like he's been out and bought it today to repel squirrels at *home*, because it's half-empty, and I have a horrible feeling about where the other half went.

I pace around, listening to the sound of the tap running as Bram cleans his teeth. I keep the spray in my hands, twisting it between them, trying to think of a reasonable explanation. Maybe it's a prop or a trick? There's a *lot* of stuff in his bag and he can produce seemingly anything from the multiple pockets on his trousers. Magicians carry a lot of *stuff*. Maybe it's just part of that?

Yeah, it sounds a bit unlikely in my head too.

This time, *he* makes *me* jump when he emerges from the bathroom. He holds the toiletries bag out to me because he doesn't look like he can walk that far himself without keeling over, and I shuffle over awkwardly to take it, keeping the squirrel spray concealed behind my back. I feel guilty that he trusts me when I've just snooped through his things, and I slide it back into his bag alongside the toiletries bag. He's obviously forgotten it's there. He doesn't realise what I've just seen.

I go to say something, to confront him over it because the evidence is right there, but he looks *so* ill that I can't do it. What I want to do is take him in my arms and hold him. It's *my* fault he feels this bad. I cannot bring myself to metaphorically kick him when he's already down.

He's splashed his sweaty face with water but it's done nothing to remove the smudged eyeliner, and he's leaning against the wall by the doorframe, looking like it's the only thing keeping him upright. Everything about him looks leeched of its usual colour. 'That's it. I'm never cooking anything again.'

'Of course you are.'

'I've given you food poisoning, Bram! And probably a few other people too!'

'Well, that's not so good, but I wouldn't worry about it. Very few people would associate cake with food poisoning.'

'Parts of that cake were raw! Trust me, it will be an easy association to make. Didn't you realise it wasn't cooked properly?'

'No, I thought it was fudgy and delicious.'

The caramel threw me off. The skewer coming out with gooey stuff on it made me think it was just that and not still-raw cake batter. 'I'm beginning to think this place is doomed. Something seems to go wrong at every turn. If it's not salt in the muffins or chilli in the brownies then it's salmonella from undercooked eggs in the cake.'

'Actually, it's raw flour that's the number one culprit in food poisoning from baked goods. The processing that the plants go through to convert them from grain doesn't kill any germs they might have picked up while growing in the fields. If flour hasn't been cooked, it can have all sorts of nasties in it.'

'I will never look at a bag of flour in the same way again. Murderous stuff.'

He laughs and then groans because laughing must've been painful, and I chew my lip in worrying for him. 'What can I do for you?'

'Nothing. Honestly, I'm fine. Just go home. I'm not leaving the vicinity of a bathroom yet, so I'm going to stay... right... here.' He limps to the wall opposite the bathroom door and slides down it into a sitting position. His green jacket and stack of hats are dumped in the staffroom, so he's just wearing his usual black combat trousers and a T-shirt that looks like the innards of a kaleidoscope. He leans his head back against the cool painted surface, and I reach down and press my palm to his forehead. 'You're burning up.'

'I'm freezing,' he says as a shiver goes through him.

'So you've got a temperature. That's not good, Bram.'

'I'm fine. Honestly. Just go home. Or go back to mine and make something; you can take my keys; it doesn't matter if I'm not there.'

'You think I'm going to leave you alone in this state?'

'I wish you would,' he mutters without opening his eyes.

'I've given you food poisoning, Bram!' I repeat incredulously because he seems to have forgotten. 'I don't want to come in tomorrow morning and find your internal organs on the bathroom floor.'

He laughs. 'I'll be fine. My stomach's... rebelled and got... everything... out.' He's obviously choosing his words carefully and trying not to venture into TMI territory. 'I'm going to sit with this lovely wall for a while and wait for the room to stop spinning and my insides to stop twisting themselves in knots. I just want to be left alone.'

'Well, we don't always get what we want.' I step over his legs and sit down next to him. I wriggle my back against the wall and try to get comfortable.

He rolls his head along the wall until he's blinking heavy-lidded eyes at me. 'Cleo, don't. I'm a mess. It's bad enough thinking about what you might've heard coming from that bathroom. I might need it again in a minute. Just leave me alone, honestly.'

His skin is still so pale that I can almost see through him, and another shiver wracks his body, and I reach over to feel his forehead again. There's no thermometer in the shop, but he's burning hot. 'I need to cool you down.'

Even though he's boiling to the touch, his teeth are chattering, and I get up again and get my phone to google what to do for a high temperature. I get a glass of water in case he wants to sip it, soak a tea towel in cold water, and grab his lime green jacket and sit back down beside him. 'Do you want to lie down?'

'Here?' His eyes are closed and raising an eyebrow takes a Herculean effort.

'Yeah. Come on.' I shift over to give him space and pat my lap. 'Put your head down and get... well, comfy might be pushing it, but comf*ier* than sitting upright.'

He laughs. 'Nooo, I can't. My hair still bleeds blue dye. You'll get a stain on your Alice dress.'

'I don't mind.' I reach over and let my fingers rub over the back of his hand where it's resting on his lap. 'Save yourself the energy of trying to protest and let me at least give you a pillow to lie on.'

He forces both eyes open and rolls his head along the wall to look at me again, and he goes to protest, but I give him such a stern look that he stops, sighs, and shifts around to lower himself down onto his side and rest his head on my thighs. Once I can reach the back of his neck, he lets me pull the hair up and lay the cool damp tea towel across his skin, and the online advice says I can cover him with something light, so I pull his jacket over and spread it out across his body. 'This okay?'

He sounds like he doesn't have the energy for more than a noise of consent.

'Close your eyes. Doze off if you need to. I'm not going anywhere.' I hold my hand against his forehead again, which still feels warm, and from there, it's kind of natural to brush my fingers through his hair.

He makes a noise that's a cross between a groan and a moan of pleasure. 'That's the nicest thing I've ever felt.'

There's something so refreshing about how he says exactly what he feels. His body was stiff and tense, but the tension melts away as he relaxes, so I keep doing it. His blue hair has got a line of dark brown roots growing through now. It started off in hairsprayed spikes this morning, but has now deteriorated into a chaotic mess of spiky bits and mussed-up bits sticking out in every possible direction and then some extra directions for good measure, and I scrunch my fingers in it, stroking my fingertips along his scalp, brushing it back off his too-hot forehead, and he snuggles into the jacket and shifts around to get more comfortable, letting out that little noise of contentment again, and it makes something inside my heart turn to goo.

I don't think Bram lets people take care of him. He keeps his Mad Hatter shield up all the time, and if anyone says something that might cut a bit too deep, he'll say something silly or throw a handful of confetti or make a playing card appear out of thin air, anything not to let someone see they've hurt him, and this is a side that he hasn't let anyone see for a very long time.

He's half-asleep already. His breathing is shallow and his arm is stretched out, his fingers limp where his hand is resting on the floor, but he's still shivery, and I continue playing with his hair, letting my fingers work through the remaining hairspray, stroking through the bright blue strands, and loving every little sigh of bliss and every time he turns into the touch, and the way relaxation seeps through his shoulders, the rest of his body sinking into the carpet too.

I didn't realise how much I care about him. There's nowhere else I'd rather be than right here, making sure he's okay, or at the very least, that he's not on his own if he isn't. Even when he's not fully awake, his stomach is making *very* angry noises, and I feel so horribly guilty because I'm responsible for this. My mind goes back to the other customers who ate that caramel cake too. I have no way of getting in contact with them to see if they're currently feeling as bad as Bram is, but I suspect they probably are.

I've still got my phone in my pocket and without taking my fingers out of his hair, I scroll one-handedly through social media while he dozes, checking for mentions of Ever After Street, and refreshing the review site in case anyone has posted something about food poisoning.

This could be the end of everything. Guilt over not making sure, double-sure, that cake was cooked mixes with panic that my one mistake could finish The Wonderland Teapot when it's barely started. I feel *horrible* that I might've caused other people illness, and as well as scrolling reviews, I read pages of info on how to ensure things are cooked properly and place an order for a food thermometer because I'm determined to ensure this doesn't happen again.

I lose track of time. I know it's passing because I can see the edge of a window in the main part of the staffroom and where it was daylight when I first came up here, darkness has long since fallen outside now. All that seems to matter is Bram's head on my lap and the way his hair twirls around my fingers, and as much as I don't want it to, that bottle of squirrel repellent keeps popping into my mind.

I'm at war with myself over it. Should I have confronted him straight away? Does it just tie in to that niggling worry that was already sitting in the pit of my stomach, the one that says if *anyone* could sabotage cakes without being noticed, it would be a magician. Or is it something completely innocent? Maybe he has squirrels nesting in the car or something... Maybe he had to repel a squirrel on the way out this morning and it was easier to shove the bottle into his bag than take it back to the house? Maybe he is followed by gangs of vengeful squirrels everywhere he goes and spray bottles of repellent are his only defence?

It's certainly a possibility...

There's no way he would've done this. *Why* would he, for a start? He has nothing to gain by sabotaging things here. If he wanted anything to go wrong with this place, he could've just left me serving supermarket-bought cakes and not tried so hard to help. Or he could've taken that information straight to his father and watched me be fired on the spot. He hasn't. He's gone out of his way to help me rediscover my love of baking. The man is letting me use his kitchen night after night. Why would he do that if he wanted this venture to fail?

'What are you thinking about?' Another hour or so has passed before his hoarse voice disrupts my spiralling thought pattern.

'You're awake?' I whisper without knowing why I'm whispering. Neither of us left a light on earlier, and now the staffroom has fallen into darkness.

'Not really. Somewhere in between.' His voice sounds scratchy and thick with sleep. 'With you doing that to my hair, I might be in heaven. Do you think they have stomach cramps in heaven?'

I burst out laughing so hard that it shakes him too, and then I scrunch my fingers in his hair by way of apology and tuck it back gently, enjoying the way his eyes slip closed again and he shifts to get more comfortable.

'You didn't answer my question,' he murmurs after a few minutes.

It's the perfect opportunity to bring up the squirrel repellent. I wasn't going to, but he's so relaxed that his body is practically a blue-haired puddle, and if there's ever a moment to get the truth out of him, this is it.

The more I try to think of a way into the conversation, the harder it seems. 'Do you have a lot of trouble with squirrels?' I eventually blurt out. Great work, Cleo. Totally subtle. He's going to know instantly that I've been through his bag.

'Squirrels?' He sounds thoroughly confused. 'I thought I was awake, but this is clearly some bizarre fever dream. As random questions go, that really is quite random.'

I reply by raising an eyebrow. His eyes flick up to my face and then he sighs. 'I can honestly say I've never had trouble with a squirrel in my life. Does that answer your very strange question?'

He doesn't seem to have made any connection between my question and the bottle in his bag, and it's not the right time to push it. 'I guess so.'

'Where did that come from?' he asks after a while in silence.

'I don't know. Thinking about you, I guess, and Tabby, and the... gremlins.'

'You think the gremlins are squirrels? Because I was thinking actual gremlins, you know, the "don't get them wet, don't feed them after midnight" type... Squirrels are clever, but I'm not sure they've got the dexterity or presence of mind to add salt to muffins or hot sauce to brownies...'

Does he really not get it? Is his mind so fevered that he *hasn't* put two and two together as to why I'm asking about squirrels?

'You never told me what she said when you confronted her...' His leading tone suggests he's waiting for me to fill in an answer.

'She denied it,' I say eventually. His eyes are still closed and my finger pads skim his forehead where I'm brushing his hair back, debating whether to tell him the rest or not. 'She actually suggested it was you.'

His dark eyes fly open and his body stiffens. 'Of course she did. And let me guess, you believed her.'

'No. Of course I didn't believe her.' It's a lie and we both know it. The bottle of squirrel repellent floats unbidden into my mind, but something doesn't sit right about it, and I realise it hasn't changed anything. I still don't believe he could be responsible for the sabotage.

His head has shifted on my thigh and I can sense his eyes looking up at me, and it feels like he can read every thought, so I keep letting my fingers stroke through his hair.

'I don't think you'd be doing that if you did,' he says eventually and then sighs too. 'It wasn't me, Cleo. Of course it wasn't. And I'm not going to defend myself. I spend so much of my life defending my choices, and you make me feel like I don't need to, and I'm not going to do it with you. You either believe me or you don't. Either way is fine.' He sounds beyond exhausted and weary, like he knew this was coming. 'You know what they say – you can lead a horse to water but you can't teach it to fish.'

'Make it drink!'

'Ah, no, but you can make it thirsty. If it needs to be led to water, it's probably already a bit on the parched side.' His face screws up like he's given this some serious thought.

'I'm not sure if you're one of the greatest philosophers of our time or just a complete nuthatch.'

'Can't I be both?'

I was trying to suppress my giggles, but this makes a full laugh burst out, and I contort myself until I can lean down and kiss his forehead. 'Yes, you can.'

Long moments pass in which I'm grateful for the darkness because he can't see how red my cheeks have gone, although his head is still on my thigh, and I'm so embarrassed that even my thighs are blushing. Why did I do that? What possessed me to kiss his forehead like that? It's a protective, motherly instinct because he's not well, I tell myself, even though my maternal instincts are usually similar to that of an iguana.

'We didn't lock the back door, you know.'

'What, now?' I say, because no matter how confused I am by the random observation, I'm glad of the subject change. 'I can run down and do it...'

'No. Last Monday. I thought I'd locked it when we went to the shopkeepers' meeting, but when I went out of it later, it was open. Anyone could have come in while we were outside with everyone else.'

'And Tabby *was* suspiciously early that day.' I realise what he's saying. On the day that *something* was done to those brownies, Tabby *could* have come in and done it without us knowing. And so could anyone else, for that matter. It doesn't narrow it down, but surely it's more likely than Bram being involved, because we were together at the Ever After Street meeting that whole time.

'She was telling me about your break-up,' I say casually when silence has settled over us again. 'About how close she was to your family...'

'Yeah, she was, but...' He pushes out a long breath. 'What am I supposed to do – invite my ex for Christmas because my sister got on with her? Have her round for Sunday lunches so my family can have a catch-up? Break-ups don't work like that. What if there was someone else?'

My heart is suddenly thundering in my chest and it feels like my whole body is pounding. There's no way he can't feel it too. '*Is* there someone else?'

He shifts over onto his back until he can look up at me, and when our eyes meet, he reaches up to tweak the black bow of my headband and rubs his fingers over the velvet material. His arm touches mine and the spot is burning heat, and it has *nothing* to do with his body temperature. 'You're the only woman in my life, Alice.'

It's physically impossible to take my eyes off his. He doesn't mean it in *that* way, but it still makes my breath catch. It's nice to hear that. It's been a while since I felt special to anyone.

He drops his hand with a sigh. 'Relationships end, and unfortunately, other facets of those relationships get caught in the crossfire. I know she's bitter, I know she thinks I ended it out of the blue, but I didn't. I ended it after years of being picked at and criticised. It's not wrong to want to be with someone who wants to be with *me*. Tabby didn't. She knows that, really. Besides, she's seeing someone now. She's moved on. I've never tried to stop her keeping in touch with my family, but it's awkward, and it's always going to be awkward. I don't want to hurt her, or them, but I don't want to pretend we're still friends, because we're not. I don't want to spend time with someone who made me feel the way she did.' He sighs again and shifts back onto his side. 'Families should come with an instruction manual.'

'Tell me about it.' My mutter makes him glance up at me.

'Will you tell me about your mum?'

'How about you go back to sleep instead?' I suggest, scrunching my fingers through his hair again, and then sigh when he gives me the same look that *I* gave *him* earlier. 'There's not much left to tell. It was a fractured relationship. In the handful of times I saw her over the years, I never let her get close. I never opened up to her because I thought she'd leave again. I thought we'd have a big emotional reunion, and then she'd go back to her life in Greece without a second thought for me, so I kept her at arm's length, and yet, I'd always thought we'd repair the relationship somehow. That I'd go out there or she'd come here, and everything would be forgotten and we'd go on mother-daughter shopping trips and go out for lunch together and do all the things that I spent my life watching my friends do with their mothers, and when she died, the grief was really about the fact we'd now never have a chance to do that. And regret, too. I wished I'd made it a priority to go out and see her. I was always resentful that she wasn't there while I was growing up. I held it against her. She sometimes invited me to visit her and I always had something better to do because of that petty resentment.'

He doesn't say a word as I speak, but he's taken hold of the hand that's not in his hair and he's playing with my fingers, running his fingers up and down them, pressing his fingertips against my nails. Soft reassurance and gentle encouragement, like he knows I've never told anyone that before.

'When she died, I felt like something was broken inside of me. It suddenly seemed so childish and stupid to have pushed her away and put my fear of being hurt again above the chance to reconnect with my mum, and now the chance was gone. I didn't know what to do with the unexpected emotions. At first, I channelled it into starting up the tearoom, and when that fell through, it made me want to back out of the world, to get away from people and shut myself away and stop connecting with anyone because I clearly couldn't be trusted to handle relationships and other people's feelings.'

His fingers slot between mine and curl over and he pulls my hand up until he can press his lips to the back of it, which makes *me* feel overheated and shivery and very glad I'm already sitting down.

'I'm sorry,' he says gently. 'Grief comes in different forms and I don't think anyone would know how to handle that kind. You seem like you're coping better now?'

I let out a bitter laugh, because some days, it still feels like swimming against a tide of emotions that are going to drown me if I stop kicking my legs for half a second, and other days, especially in the last six weeks, it's got easier to face the world each day. Doing something I *love*, getting to live a Wonderland fantasy every day and seeing how happy it makes other people... It's made me feel like life is worthwhile again.

'It'll probably sound weird, but finding Ever After Street and connecting with Marnie made a huge difference, and then I got to know the other shopkeepers too, and they all made me feel like I belonged here. They *wanted* me to get a shop here. Feeling unwanted was something I'd been struggling with my whole life, and feeling like they wanted me kind of made me understand that and confront it.'

'It's a powerful thing, feeling wanted,' he murmurs. 'Not many people understand how it affects someone to grow up feeling unwanted or not good enough.'

I know it's a sentiment he understands all too well, and I squeeze his fingers between mine, and for tonight, it feels like the only thing either of us *wants* is to sit right here with each other.

It's later still when he stirs again, shifting and groaning at the ache of lying on a hard floor for so many hours. He disentangles his hand from mine and pushes himself up into a sitting position, holding still for a long few moments in case any internal organ is going to object to the movement.

My backside is aching so much that it went numb hours ago

and I get myself onto my knees and lean forwards to see how dark it is outside the staffroom window. Pitch black. My phone screen tells me it's nearly 10 p.m.

Bram scrubs a hand over his face and winces at the brightness of my phone lighting up our little corner of the room.

'Your colour looks better. Earlier you looked like a ghost. Now you only look like a zombie who's been dead for about five years.' I reach over and press my palm against his forehead. 'You feel... less warm. How do you feel?'

'Like I might make it home tonight after all.'

'I'll drive.'

'Cleo—'

'You're in no fit state to get behind the wheel, and I'm not leaving you alone, end of story.'

He doesn't agree immediately, but he's obviously exhausted, and after it takes both of us a good few minutes to get him onto his feet and he's clinging onto the wall and panting just from that small exertion, he relents. 'My car's in the car park round the corner. Keys are in the front pocket of my bag.'

It feels like a teeny-tiny win. 'You don't need to be a fun and frenzied Mad Hatter all the time. Sometimes you can just be Bram, and that's okay.'

He waits for me to meet his eyes and then swallows before he speaks. 'I always am with you.'

It warms me inside and that fluttery feeling comes again, especially at the intensity in his dark eyes when he doesn't drop eye contact. I know I've seen the real, unguarded Bram tonight. The one who's quiet and vulnerable without ever losing his sense of humour. The one who manages to be just weird enough to make me feel at one with my own weirdness. The one who wants to be loved *for* who he is – not in spite of it.

Eventually he blinks and looks away. 'Sorry, I must look an absolute fright.'

'You're beautiful, you know that,' I say without thinking.

He scoffs. 'I've got blue hair, I wear eyeliner, have got both ears pierced, and wear clothes that make me look like I get dressed inside a box of Liquorice Allsorts every day. "Beautiful" is *not* a way to describe me.'

'Yeah, but underneath all that. Your playful brown eyes and killer smile. That dimple.' I reach out and touch his singular dimple, the pad of my index finger pressing against the first hint of five o'clock shadow on his cheek. 'And you. Just *you*, Bram. Superficial things aren't what makes someone beautiful.'

It's like an out-of-body experience. My voice doesn't sound like it belongs to me. The words sound like they're coming from somewhere else, some*one* else. It's like his honesty when it comes to feelings has rubbed off on me and it doesn't even cross my mind *not* to be so embarrassingly open with him.

'I've been so fevered tonight that I might not remember some of our conversations, but trust me, I'll remember this one.'

'Please don't.' At least it's still too dark for him to see me blush, although I'm surprised the red glow from my cheeks hasn't illuminated the room.

'I'll tell myself you're just trying to make me feel better.' He uses the wall for stability, and I haul his bag over my arm and tuck his jacket over the top of it, and keep a hand on his shoulder as we go down the stairs, him in front of me.

At the bottom, he holds a hand out. 'For safety.'

That's all it is, I tell myself as I slip my hand over his. For safety. To make sure he doesn't walk into anything in the darkness.

He laces his fingers with mine and squeezes. 'For safety.'

He's quiet in the car, his eyes closed, his head resting against the window, and once we're inside his house, whatever reserves of energy it took to get this far swiftly drain away, and I keep an arm around him to make sure he stays upright as he toes off his yellow boots, stumbles to the living room and sinks onto the sofa. He tries to protest as I plump up the cushions and make sure he's comfortable. I find a bucket in the kitchen and leave it beside him, just in case, and put a glass of water on the coffee table. He's not feeling as hot now and there's a cream-coloured knitted throw over the back of the sofa, so I pull it down and cover him with it.

And because I can't help myself with this man, I tuck it over him and lean down to kiss his forehead. 'Goodnight, beautiful.'

I'm not leaving him alone, so I text Marnie to let her know I won't be in the caravan tonight and curl up in an armchair on the opposite side of the massive room. There's another snuggly cream throw over the back, so I pull that over me and huddle under it, and when I close my eyes, all I can think about is his smile and his soulful brown eyes, and how nice it was to simply *be* with him tonight.

16

It's daylight when I wake up to sunlight streaming through the Georgian-style arched windows and Bram crouched beside the armchair, gently shaking me.

'Cleo.' He sounds panicked, and it takes me a few moments to remember where I am and what happened that led to me waking up in Bram's living room, contorted like a pretzel where I've sunken into the armchair and folded in on myself. 'It's late and no one went to the supermarket *or* made anything last night.'

I grip his hand where it's on my knee. 'How are you?'

'I'm fine.' I have to squint in the brightness but he doesn't look fine. He looks like he's just fallen off the sofa himself. There are dark circles under his eyes that aren't just from the smudged eyeliner. His skin looks sallow and you wouldn't think there were many more directions for his hair to stick out in, but it's invented a whole new compass. 'Neither of us set an alarm last night. It's gone 8 a.m.'

That makes me sit bolt upright and look at the clock on the living room wall. It *is* really late, and it's too far to walk to Ever After Street from Bram's, and my car is still at Marnie's.

He offers to drive me back, but he looks too drained to make it down the hallway, never mind drive anywhere, so I call a taxi and tell him to take it easy, leave it at least twenty-four hours before eating anything, and drink some water. I stand on the steps outside his house waiting for the taxi to arrive, feeling like I'm doing the walk of shame even though spending the night at Bram's was completely innocent, and when the taxi arrives, he walks me to the end of his driveway and insists on paying the fare.

In my panic to get back to the caravan, shower and change into another Alice dress, I'm still a discombobulated mess when I fall through the tearoom door. It's after nine and there's a customer waiting outside, and the only cakes on display are ones that didn't get sold yesterday, and a few emergency back-up packets of French Fancies and Cherry Bakewells that I mercifully hadn't opened yet, and anyone looking will immediately clock that they're made by Mr Kipling and not by me, but it's the best I can do for today.

It's another one of Tabby's days off and, without Bram, I'm a frazzled frenzy by 11 a.m. As I'm on my own, it's sod's law that *today* is the day that every human in Herefordshire has decided to visit Ever After Street and pop in for a cup of sparkly Wonderland tea, and I've already sold out of crumpets, I'm running low on teacakes, and the display case is looking alarmingly bare. Even the bread for sandwiches is going to run out before the day's end at this rate.

I haven't had a chance to reply to Marnie's texts yet, and when she pops over at lunchtime to check on me, she's shocked by the length of the queue and the amount of customers waiting far too long for their orders.

'You need help, Cleo.' She dashes a plate of tea and sandwiches over to a waiting customer, even though she's got Darcy minding A Tale As Old As Time on *his* lunchbreak, and then comes back to get another one. 'I'll put a call out in the shopkeepers messaging group and see if anyone's not busy.'

It's the kind of day when *everyone* on Ever After Street is busy, and I'm surprised when, less than twenty minutes later, Franca from The Nutcracker Shop at the year-round festive end of the street arrives, bearing packets of teacakes and crumpets. 'One of the pleasures of owning a Christmas shop on a warm spring day is that people aren't thinking about nutcrackers. Which is unusual because *I'm* always thinking about nutcrackers. I haven't had a customer for hours, so I was out the back carving anyway; it makes no difference if I close up for a bit. Where'd you want me?'

She's already gone through to the back room, put the food on the unit, donned an apron and tied her hair up, and I'm so grateful that I could cry. Except crying over sandwiches is frowned upon and might bother some customers, so I hastily add crumpets and toasted teacakes back onto the menu board while Franca rushes to take orders to waiting tables, chats to customers to distract them from how long they've *been* waiting, and most importantly of all, boils the kettle to make *me* the first cup of tea I've had all day.

You can say many things about Bram, but one of them is that making sure there is always a cup of tea nearby is his top priority, and I've never realised how much I appreciate that until today.

Franca stays for a couple of hours, but by mid-afternoon, it's quietened down enough that she goes back to The Nutcracker Shop. It's good to see The Wonderland Teapot so busy, but I'm missing Bram *so* much. How alive the tearoom feels because of him, and how he makes *everything* feel better. No matter how busy we are, he never loses his cheeky grin and positive attitude, and his sense of being in control of everything makes me feel in control too, and today, I can feel all the threads slipping out of my grasp. Even with Franca's help, it makes me wonder how I would ever have managed without him.

I've been thinking about him so much that I think I'm halluci-nating when, just after 4 p.m., the door opens and Bram walks in.

I'm spreading butter on a plate of bread-and-butterflies for a young girl, while simultaneously making the tea her father has ordered, and also keeping an eye on the tearoom when the door opens and I catch sight of a flash of blue.

'Bram!' If I didn't have hygiene gloves on, I'd have rubbed my eyes to make sure I'm not seeing things. 'What are you doing here?'

He flashes me a bright, smiley grin and holds both hands up in a surrendering gesture. 'Before you say anything, I'm not an on-duty Mad Hatter, I'm an off-duty friend.'

I raise an eyebrow. 'You're not supposed to be here.'

'I like being here,' he says with a shrug, and I can't help smiling at his simple honesty.

'Good afternoon, Mrs Moreno.' He greets our regular customer, who's sitting at a table, eating her usual toasted teacake while watching her grandson on the flamingo croquet. 'Those teacakes would have nowhere to go without you.'

The old lady regards him and it clearly takes a moment before she recognises him because he looks *so* different to his usual character.

'Oh, I didn't realise that was you. I wondered where you were today. My grandson was looking forward to seeing his favourite Hatter.'

'I'd like to believe I'm the only Hatter around these parts.' He tips his baseball cap to her, waves to the grandson, and then slips in behind the counter.

I don't intend to smile *quite* so widely, but there's something about his presence that makes the weight of the day pressing down on my shoulders feel lighter somehow. 'You're supposed to be taking the day off. You know, to rest and recover?'

Apart from the baseball cap, he's got his grey hoodie on over a white T-shirt and black jogging bottoms, his hair is washed and smooth, curling at the nape of his neck and around his ears, and if I wasn't in the middle of handling food, it would take all my willpower not to reach up and tuck it back. 'Go home. Watch Netflix.'

'I've seen Netflix.'

'All of it?'

'Feels like it sometimes.' His dark eyes are twinkling as they hold my gaze, and I have no doubt that he knew I'd protest and he came fully prepared not to let me.

'How are you feeling?'

His laugh is a low snort. 'Like I've been for a spin in a tumble dryer on the highest heat setting. But other than that, great. Peachy. Fit as a candlestick maker's dog.'

'Then you shouldn't be in wo—'

'You want me to feel better and seeing you makes me feel better.'

I roll my eyes. 'Very funny.'

'Look, I had another nap after you left this morning. I took a long bath, and then I wandered around the house going stir crazy and missing you. Thought I'd poke my head in and see if there was anything I could do without actually working.' He strains his neck and looks around the doorway to the back room and lets out a low whistle. 'And judging by that heap of washing up, there definitely is. I'm not customer-facing today, but I can tackle *that*.' He rolls his sleeves up. 'If that gets any higher, we're going to have to fill in a shedload of paperwork to have it declared a new mountain, so let me help. Okay?'

It's like he's waiting for permission, although if I said no, there's no way he'd listen.

'O-Okay.' The word stutters as it comes out because it's hard to concentrate on anything apart from the look in his dark eyes, the effervescent scent of his aftershave, and the heat of his body where he's standing closer than he was moments ago…

...until the father who is still waiting for his tea and his daughter's bread-and-butterflies and squash clears his throat and we both jump.

'Sorry, sir, Alice is just sorting out some gremlins.' Bram nods towards them. 'My fault entirely. We won't keep you a second.'

He touches his hand to my hip, and in one swift movement, lifts the peak of his cap so he can lean down and kiss my cheek. It's the briefest peck, but it makes my head spin like the black and white spirals so associated with Wonderland. He's usually cleanshaven but he's got a couple of days' worth of stubble now, and it makes him go from sexy to *hot*. Very, very *hot*.

He's got the sense to step into the back room and put some space between us, and I give myself a shake and go back to the bread-and-butterflies, tea, and squash order.

'He's a breath of fresh air, isn't he?' Mrs Moreno says when I've delivered it to the waiting table.

At first I think she means the father who's jabbing angrily at his phone, but my eyes follow hers to the clink of china from the back room and the whistling that's started up. 'That he is.'

He's a breath of something, all right. And the relief I feel just from seeing him is astounding. I love how simple he makes everything, even the washing up. Usually, between us, we manage to keep on top of it, but that hasn't been an option today, and I was dreading tackling that later.

And along he comes and simply takes care of it without question or complaint. And it makes me think again about what happens if I get this tearoom. What if I get to work with this spectacular nut for longer... and what if I don't?

* * *

The tearoom isn't closed yet, but it's mercifully quiet enough to catch my breath and appreciate the constant out-of-tune singing from the back room.

I know he knows I'm there, but I lean my head against the doorframe and watch Bram for a few minutes before speaking. 'How are you so happy?'

'Why shouldn't I be happy?' He's got bright pink rubber gloves on, and he glances up at me with a smile. 'I'm alive. I have a roof over my head and a job I love, and I feel well enough to come in. What do I have to complain about?'

'If only more people saw the world the way you do.' I can't get my head around his attitude sometimes, and yet, I *love* it. He's so positive about everything, and it rubs off on others, whether they want it to or not.

'Happiness is a choice. If you've got two sinks full of washing up to do, eleven piles of laundry to iron, hoovering to do and a lawn to mow, you can sing and dance your way through it and enjoy yourself, or you can grunt and groan and moan all the way through, and neither way makes it go any faster, but one is infinitely more enjoyable than the other. No one's life is perfect. Everyone is unhappy in some way. In fact, the only thing that makes some people happy is complaining about it and dragging others down too. I don't ever want to be that person. It's a privilege to be able to do chores. Some people can't. Some people would kill to feel well enough to run the hoover through the house. If we have a roof over our heads and food in our bellies, we have it better than most. Some of us are even lucky enough to have people who care about us...' He looks up and meets my eyes. 'And that makes us extraordinarily fortunate. People get so caught up in little niggles and forget the bigger picture. Many of us don't realise how lucky we are just to live. And sometimes the most powerful thing anyone can do is realise that.'

The bell above the door tinkles as a customer comes in, but I turn back to Bram quickly before I go to greet them. 'You know what I said last night about you being either one of the greatest philosophers of our time or a complete nuthatch? It's the first one.'

He lets out a loud laugh. 'I'm still fine with it being both.'

'You wouldn't be you if you weren't a bit bonkers too.' I bite my lip as I consider it. 'And that would be unthinkable.'

The width of his smile makes my knees feel weak. I don't think he expected me to say that, and it's probably a good thing there's a customer, because otherwise, I wouldn't be able to stop myself going over to hug him.

I never realised just how much I needed someone like him in my life. After the past couple of years of hiding away, being alone and ensconced in a ball of grief, regret, and injustice, growing lonelier and more bitter, resenting the world, and hating myself for the mistakes I made when it came to my mum and the trust I put in my ex, what I needed more than anything was a different perspective, and I never thought the barmy Mad Hatter who knocked on the door all those weeks ago would give me that, but he makes me feel glad to be alive again.

What I needed was someone who, by the sheer size of their presence, doesn't let you dwell on negativity, who is so bright that it's impossible to feel dark in their company, and Bram is that in spades. More than anything, he makes me want to give this tearoom everything I've got and remain a part of this special street full of wonderful people.

The customer orders tea and tuna and cucumber sandwiches and then there's a rush as Marnie's after-school reading group leaves A Tale As Old As Time and parents bring children in for an evening treat in the twenty minutes before closing time, and I feel like I'm herding sheep as I shuffle after them to shut the door and turn the sign over to closed. It has been a *long* day.

I tidy up the tearoom and take the next batch of washing up out to the back, where Bram is still in his pink Marigolds, waiting for it, and no matter how much I try to tell him he doesn't need to, he grins and ignores me. By the time I've wiped down all the tables, mopped the floor, and cashed-up for the night, he's washed every dish, as well as dried it and put it away, cleaned every countertop, and now he's sitting on the unit, his head leaning against one of the cabinet doors, looking half-asleep.

'What are you doing here, huh?' I say gently. 'You should be at home.'

'I don't know. Just wanted to see you. Spend time with you.'

I love how he wears his heart on his sleeve. He says things aloud that other people wouldn't dare to vocalise. It doesn't seem to cross his mind to be dishonest about anything.

'How are you feeling?' I go over to stand in front of him and reach up to fit my hand against his forehead. He takes his cap off and ducks his head to give me better access. I'm no longer worried about his temperature, it's just an excuse to touch him, and I'm sure he knows that.

'I'm fine. Just tired, and really, really hungry, but my twenty-four hours before eating again isn't up until tonight.'

I can't feasibly get away with holding my hand to his forehead for any longer, but as I reluctantly drop my arm, he reaches out and catches hold of my hand, his fingers folding around mine and squeezing. 'Thank you for last night.'

'Bram, I gave you food poisoning!' I don't know how many times I've repeated that, but he doesn't seem to have understood it. 'It's not something people usually express gratitude for.'

'Well, thank you for making last night better than it would have been if you weren't there. I felt pretty rough and you made me feel better than I would have otherwise, and that was no easy feat. No girl wants to see a guy like that, so thank you.'

He jiggles my hand and then lets go to run a hand through his hair and tug awkwardly at the back of his neck. 'I need to say something else as well.'

There's a serious tone to his voice that makes me take a step back and look up at him.

'When I opened my bag this morning, I understood why you asked the squirrel question. I'd never seen that before in my life, Cleo. I don't know how it got there. I know what you must be thinking, but it isn't mine. Someone else must've put it in there.'

'Tabby wasn't even in yesterday.'

'It could've been there for days. I don't look in my bag from one day to the next. I only went in there this morning to get the toothbrush out. Without working lockers, my bag was in the staffroom. Anyone could've opened it...' He sighs long and hard, sounding just as fed-up as he did last night. 'I meant what I said – I can't make you believe me and I'm not going to waste energy in trying. You either do or you don't, and nothing I say will make any difference to that. And it's okay if you—'

'I believe you.' I wasn't sure myself, not really, but he looks so utterly wretched that it's impossible *not* to believe him. There's something about Bram that's infinitely trustworthy, especially now, when he's not playing a character, and trusting that I'll trust the real him.

He holds his hand out to me, inviting me to slip my fingers over his again, and when I do, his curl tightly around mine, and he uses his grip to tug me nearer and holds his other arm open, silently asking for a hug.

Hugging him, *properly* hugging him, is the one thing I've been desperate to do since the moment he started looking so ill yesterday afternoon, and I take my hand from his and push his knees apart on the counter so I can stand between his legs and reach up to slide both arms around him, and I get a delicious little thrill when he bends to meet me and pulls me tight to him and one of his legs hooks around mine to hold me in place.

He lets out a long and deep exhale and I can feel the tension draining from his body even as his arms tighten around me, and after a day of stress and worry and being rushed off my feet, I can feel myself sagging against him. His hands spread open on my back and his stubbled jaw grazes against my neck as he tries to get closer. My knees are braced against the lower cabinet door, and my hands naturally find their way upwards, cupping the back of his head, and my fingers slide down to play with the ends of his hair, and it sends a shiver through him, and he makes a little contented noise.

And we just... don't move.

Long minutes pass and I could happily stay put for many, many more. It's the kind of hug that shuts out everything outside of his arms, and each one of my senses is consumed by him. The touch of his body, the sound of his breathing, the scent of his aftershave, and I'm so relaxed that I could fall asleep standing here. His body is deadweight against mine, his arms around me are heavy, and even his hands on my back have gone limp.

I squeeze him tighter and he mumbles something incomprehensible and snuggles in closer. And the thought of making him *this* comfortable makes my heart swell. I know he's not good at letting people get close, and neither am I. This is the closest I've been to anyone in years, and I thought it would feel scary, but the *last* thing I want to do is disentangle our bodies.

It takes me a long time before I whisper again. 'Are you asleep?'

'No, just having a really long blink.'

I laugh and go to pull away but he curls tighter around me. 'Don't go yet. This feels too good.'

'Yeah, it does.' The words hang in the air like a decoration. So real that I could touch them. It *does* feel good, in a way I never expected it to. I never intended to let anyone in again. Love hasn't been on my radar in recent years. After my ex, I was glad to be alone. I'd forgotten what it's like to fall for someone.

And then Bram burst into my life in an explosion of colour and card tricks and he's got under my skin without me even noticing, and suddenly I *care* about him. I *like* him. I like spending time with him. I get butterflies as I drive towards his house in the evenings. If today is any indication, I *miss* the living daylights out of him when he's not around.

I've spent the majority of the past twenty-four hours with my hands on him in some way, and it's felt *good*. And this hug, it's like we're the only two people in the universe, and everything is right with the world, as long as neither of us ever moves.

It feels like waking up when he finally starts to stir, grunting with stiffness where his body has been curled so tightly around mine, and he looks kind of dazed and blissful, squinting at the sudden brightness of the kitchen light. 'That was probably the nicest hug I've ever had.'

I laugh, because there he goes with just blurting things out again. And yet there's something refreshing about it too. Bram doesn't play games. He says what he feels in the moment and worries about it later. Or, actually, doesn't worry about it later, unlike me who lies awake at night replaying conversations where I made myself look foolish that day in my head, and it makes me want to be more like him. Being happy for people to think whatever they want of him, and being secure enough in himself for it not to matter. 'Ditto.'

He smiles, that stupidly wide smile that brightens up the whole room and makes his singular dimple dip his cheek and his tired eyes shine, and it's impossible not to smile back, and... I really want to kiss him. I'm at just the right height to slide my hand along his jaw and cup his face. It would take nanoseconds to push myself onto tiptoes, and I take a breath, trying to steel myself to find the courage to do it, and... and then his stomach lets out a growl of hunger, making his cheeks flare red as he giggles with embarrassment.

I shake my head to clear it. 'I'm coming home with you tonight. You can eat something later so I'm going to make you a piece of toast and a cup of tea and *nothing* else. I don't trust you not to go home and bake a batch of brownies and eat the whole lot.'

'You're coming home with me so you can bake something for the shop tomorrow. Get back on the horse before the stable door has bolted... No, that's not right. You know what I mean. Don't let this one incident knock your confidence.'

'I don't think I should ever bake again.'

''Course you should.' He reaches out and takes my hand again. 'And I'm going to be your first tester.'

'No you're not. You can't still have faith in me after that.'

'I still have faith in you after that. You were made to do this. This job lights you up. You just need to get a teensy bit better at identifying whether something is cooked or not.'

I burst out laughing. At least we can agree on that.

17

As the wedding gets closer, the one thing that gets stronger is how much I love Ever After Street and want to stay here, no matter what. I *love* my tearoom. I've bought some copies of *Alice in Wonderland* from Marnie and put them out on a shelf, and it's a joy to see customers pick them up and flick through them while drinking their sparkly tea.

It's the sense of community too. I only met Marnie last year but I feel like I've known her my whole life. I love my Ever After Street colleagues. I feel like there are people I can turn to at any time with any question or query, and people to help out if needed, like Franca did last week.

And then there's the help with the wedding. It's Thursday evening, three days before the big day, and Marnie, Darcy, and I are in Bram's kitchen, the four of us forming a tag team with the Nutella muffins and Creme Egg cheesecakes. We've got over a hundred and fifty of each to make before Sunday, and with the help of a battalion of airtight containers, they'll still be fresh enough by the big day.

Bram's put a nineties' music playlist on, and we're all singing along and dancing around the kitchen, and none of us are any good at singing *or* dancing, so the self-consciousness has gone, and we're just enjoying ourselves, according to Bram's policy of making tasks fun. And it's brilliant. What seemed like an overwhelmingly impossible undertaking has become a fun evening with good friends.

He and Darcy are making the cheesecakes and Marnie and I are working as a team on the muffins, and I'm having one of the happiest evenings I can remember in recent times, and it's all because of one man.

I meet Bram's eyes across the kitchen, and he beams at me, tips an imaginary cowboy hat in my direction, and then line dances back over to the counter to the tune of 'Cotton Eye Joe'.

I tap my foot as I stir the third batch of muffin mixture, and Marnie steps closer and nudges me with her elbow. 'He's smitten.'

'Don't be daft.' I try to ignore the little quiver that sets off in my chest.

'He hasn't stopped smiling since we arrived, and coincidentally, he hasn't taken his eyes off you since we arrived either. And neither have you, for that matter.' She nudges me again and whispers, 'I'm starting to think that you and I only paired up to ensure there was no canoodling over the muffins.'

'Canoodling!'

I don't realise how loudly I've said it until Bram and Darcy both turn to look at me.

'…is a great word.' I try to save the sentence, which fails when Bram raises both eyebrows with a cheeky grin, and it makes my face flare so hot that it could be used to cook the muffins if we run out of oven space.

'This is fun.' Darcy, who is still limping as he recovers from a broken ankle at the end of last year, swipes another piece of the cut-up Creme Eggs the boys are using on the other side of the kitchen. 'Why have we never done this before?'

'I didn't think anyone from Ever After Street would want to hang out with me. You know who my father is,' Bram adds when Marnie and Darcy both look at him in confusion.

'I didn't,' Marnie says. 'I only ever dealt with my own landlord.'

'Me neither,' Darcy confirms.

'Yeah, but... guilt by association. He makes life difficult for a lot of people on our little street. If you rent from the council then he's an ogre to his tenants. If you rent from a private landlord then he still makes life difficult, and if you own outright then you still have his strict guidelines to follow, as you two know.'

The shopkeepers of Ever After Street helped Marnie buy her bookshop last year, and Bram is referring to Mr Hastings' constant monitoring of her business, and the stringent hoops she has to jump through if she wants approval to make the slightest change. Trust in the shopkeepers who work on Ever After Street is not Mr Hastings' strong point.

'I'm also not great at letting people in,' Bram continues quietly. 'I know I'm not everybody's cup of Cream Soda. I dress strangely. I wear eyeliner and jewellery. Not everyone likes magic – some people find it downright creepy. I'm weird, I know that.'

'As Cleo once said to me about Darcy – all the best people are,' Marnie says. 'And it's certainly true in our case.'

They make eyes at each other across the kitchen, and I meet Bram's gaze and grin at him, knowing he'll have recognised the Alice quote too.

'I don't think it's about being weird,' I say. 'I think it's about finding people who are on the same wavelength of weirdness as you are until there's so much weirdness that it kind of cancels itself out and you're just normal with each other.'

'The weirdest sentence that makes perfect sense to me.' Bram smiles at me again. I might've thought he was a bit weird at first, but now I think he's perfect just as he is.

Darcy's taller than Bram and he slings an arm around his shoulder. 'You were always kind to me when I refused to accept kindness. No one knows better than me about looking weird.' He indicates his facial scarring that he kept covered for so long, and although he no longer wears the disguise he used to wear, it's no secret that he still struggles.

'Aww. Thanks, mate.' The playlist song changes to 'Kiss from a Rose' and right on cue, Bram clicks his fingers and produces a playing card rose from thin air and holds it out to Darcy.

He doesn't have his usual cargo trousers on tonight and seems to have nowhere to stash any trickery. For a moment, I wonder if it's more feasible that he has actual magic powers.

'I have no idea how you did that. That's incredible.' Darcy pokes at the rose like it might disappear in a puff of smoke at any second.

Bram blushes and I realise something. He's himself tonight. He's not doing a Hatter act. He's letting two... well, not strangers because I know he *knows* Marnie and Darcy, but not well enough to call them friends. He's letting them see the real him. The shy side who's scared of rejection. He separates the parts of himself. He mostly only does magic when he's got on his loud, untouchable front, and I think it's taken more than he'll admit to let *my* friends in and trust that they won't ridicule him.

'I haven't had Cream Soda since I was a kid, but you're definitely my cup of it,' Darcy says. 'We should do this again sometime. Maybe without the chaos of a few hundred things to bake, but still...'

Bram blushes and makes an excuse about checking things in the oven, and maybe it's a good thing we're not alone tonight, because that blush makes me want to wrap my arms around him, press my lips to his red cheeks and make sure he knows that the people who make him feel like he's barely tolerable are far, far outnumbered by people who think he's bloody brilliant.

It's hours later when the final batch of cheesecakes has been slid into the giant fridge. It's dark outside, and seeing as none of us have had a cup of tea since early afternoon, Marnie's making an emergency cup while I set out muffins on a plate for us all to test. 'I can't believe it's nearly 10 p.m.'

Darcy is cleaning the kitchen countertops while Bram loads the dishwasher. 'Time flies when you're having kittens.'

I can't help giggling. His mixed-up idioms have become the highlight of my day, and that familiar urge to hug him twinges again. It's definitely a good thing we've got chaperones tonight.

He smiles back at me, but it's cut off by the ring of his gate security camera, and he dries his hands and goes to answer the video screen beside the door.

'It's my father,' he calls in from the hallway. '*He* will be the one having kittens if I refuse him entry and I don't fancy cleaning *that* mess up.'

Marnie's eyes widen. 'Should we hide? It's supposed to be you doing the wedding catering. We don't want him to know you've had help.'

'No caterer would work alone. The one they hired would've had a team of staff. He *should* see what an unreasonable demand this was. I *want* him to know that we couldn't do this alone,' I say, touched that she thought of it.

Bram is still watching the video screen in the hallway. 'Judging by the garment bag, he's here to talk to me about my clothing choices for the wedding on Sunday. Again.'

Mr Hastings huffs and puffs his way up the stairs to the door when Bram opens it, a garment bag draped over his arm as he indicates Darcy's truck in the driveway. 'Am I interrupting something, Abraham?'

Bram steps back from the door and invites him in. 'It's 10 p.m. and we're busy. Why would you be interrupting anything?'

If Mr Hastings detects the sarcasm, he doesn't acknowledge it as he smooths down the garment bag over his arm before he spots me lurking in the kitchen doorway.

'Oh, Miss Jordan. It's you.' He sounds like he'd be more thrilled to find a giant slug in the hallway, chomping on the skirting boards.

'We're preparing for the wedding,' Bram says. 'We had to call in reinforcements seeing as Cleo is not a caterer and your black-mailing has forced her into doing the impossible.'

'Blackmail is such a strong word. I merely asked her to do us a favour, and I thought it might be nice for you to be involved in your sister's wedding. You hardly spend any time with the family these days. You push us all away.'

'You push me—'

Mr Hastings cuts off Bram's comeback. 'Besides, I thought nothing was impossible. Isn't that what the quote on your wall says, Miss Jordan?'

'We didn't say it was impossible,' Bram answers before I have time to come up with a witty retort. 'But we are quite busy. I assume the garment bag is for me?'

'I wanted to make sure you have something suitable to wear on Sunday, Abraham.'

It irks me hearing Mr Hastings use his full name. It *isn't* his name and it feels like a little niggling way of insulting him.

'I have something suitable to wear.' Bram sounds so weary that I suspect this is approximately the seventh time they've had this conversation.

'Well, why don't you show me and I'll be the judge of that?'

'Because I'm not four years old. I don't need my clothing choices to be policed by you.'

'We've been over this, son. This is the most important day of your sister's life. You need to put her first and put aside your own choices for one single day, unlike what you put poor Tabby through when she was trying to plan *your* wedding.'

'I have my clothes. Cleo can vet them later to make sure they're suitable. You can trust her judgement even if you don't trust mine.'

'Yes, well...' Mr Hastings looks me up and down, like I'm hardly a candidate for fashion advice, with my hair tied in a messy knot, a baggy T-shirt that takes the place of an apron, and there's probably flour smeared across my face. He turns back to Bram. 'Take this anyway. It's a suit – understated and sophisticated. I'm just trying to help.' His eyes linger on Bram for a moment, like he wants to say something else, but then he sighs and his gaze returns to me. 'I'm glad you're here actually, Miss Jordan. I have a letter for you in my car. I was going to drop it by the tearoom in the morning, but you can save me a trip. If you'll accompany me outside...'

He shoves the garment bag at Bram, and then jerks his head to indicate that I should follow him.

'Let me hang this up and I'll be out too.' Bram takes the garment bag and catches my eyes as I follow Mr Hastings.

'I fear you think me unduly cruel, Miss Jordan.' Outside, Mr Hastings stops at his posh car but doesn't open it or look at me. 'I dread to think what my son has told you, but you seem to have achieved the impossible and formed a mutually respectful connection with him.'

'Oh, we're not...'

'He listens to you. It's been years since he listened to me. He just won't...' Mr Hastings makes a noise of frustration. 'If he could just look... normal. Get a proper job. Something with security. Long-term prospects. A pension plan. There's no future in bleedin' card tricks, is there?'

'What he does is so much more than card tricks. He's exceptionally talented. He makes people believe in the impossible, and doing that makes *him* happy.'

'I had a future all lined up for him,' Mr Hastings continues as though I haven't spoken. 'In-demand qualifications. A well-paying job. And he goes and throws it all away to toss around cards and throw confetti. I only want what's best for him, and I don't understand what *he* wants from life. I don't know how to make him see...'

'Maybe it's you who could see it from his point of view,' I say carefully, feeling hideously out of my depth. Mr Hastings obviously needed to vent, and he's chosen to do it to *me*, but he's still my terrifying boss. Does he *really* want my input on this? 'All he wants is what any of us want – to be happy and to be loved.'

'I *do* love him. I *do* want to see him happy. I just...' He sighs and shakes his head. 'The distance between us is growing and I don't know how to reach him. I try, but all I end up doing is pushing him further away.'

'Just because he's different to you doesn't make him wrong. There's plenty of space for both of your viewpoints, but—'

We both look up as the door opens and Bram comes out.

'I know what it's like to lose a parent without making amends,' I say quickly. 'Any compromise is worthwhile before it's too late.'

''ello, why are my ears burning?' Bram bounces down the steps, suspicious eyes looking between us.

'I was just getting an update on the catering from Miss Jordan,' Mr Hastings says. 'Which brings me nicely to my point. I wanted a word about some complaints we've received.' He opens the passenger door of his car and extracts an envelope from the glovebox, and hands it to me.

I tear open the ominous-looking brown paper, glad the outside floodlights are bright enough to read by.

Food Safety Warning is stamped in big red letters across the top.

Due to a number of complaints received about the quality of food served at your establishment, the local authority deems it necessary to complete a food safety inspection. An inspector will arrive onsite at nine o'clock on 31 May. This appointment is non-negotiable.

If shortcomings are found, steps must be taken to ensure these incidences do not occur again. If serious issues are found, then we will be forced to insist that you cease trading with imme-diate effect.

Please ensure you are following correct hygiene protocols and that your business is closed on the given date and you are available to answer the food safety inspector's questions and co-operate fully with our investigation.

Bram is reading it over my shoulder and he scoffs. 'This is ridiculous.'

'We've had some complaints about The Wonderland Teapot.' Mr Hastings scuffs the toes of his shiny shoes against the gravel, looking uneasy. 'There are reviews talking about salty muffins. A complaint about brownies. Even a case of food poisoning, so I hear.' His eyes flick to Bram. 'It all seems to be coming back to you, Miss Jordan. I've tried my best to help, but this really can't be ignored any longer.'

I'm surprised Bram told him about the food poisoning. I don't blame him, but considering how often he's taken responsibility for things that were my fault, I didn't think he'd rush to tell his father about that.

'The council's food safety team will send an inspector to have a look around. While I'm sure it's not your doing, we have to take these things seriously and handle them with empathy. If you *aren't* doing anything wrong and these complaints are merely fiction-alised, you've got *nothing* to worry about.'

'You can't blame Cleo,' Bram says. 'Things have happened that are beyond anyone's control. It's a new business. There are gremlins sharpening their teeth.'

His father gives him a scathing look and Bram rolls his eyes. 'Metaphorical gremlins. I don't think there are *actual* gremlins.'

At least he clarified that because there are times when I haven't been sure. Mainly, I appreciate the way he sticks up for me, no matter what.

'Gremlins or not, Abraham, I don't appreciate having my ear chewed off by the head of the environmental health department, or the insinuation that I am not keeping on top of the eatery establishments in my jurisdiction.'

'It's impossible to prove,' Bram says.

'Impossible or not, the establishment must take full responsibility, financial liability, and learn from mistakes made. If you're not willing to comply, Miss Jordan, maybe you don't belong on Ever After Street after all.'

'I'll comply.' I pull myself up taller and puff out my chest.

'Jolly good. I wouldn't have expected anything less.' With one final look at Bram, he walks around to the driver's side of his car. 'My apologies for interrupting your evening. As you were.'

I hold the letter out in front of us. 'You can't make that disappear with an abracadabra, can you?'

'No, but *you* can make it into a paper rose, and one day we'll display it in *your* tearoom when this is nothing but ancient history.'

Mr Hastings gets into his car and starts up, giving us a wave through the windscreen as he reverses with a spray of gravel.

'Don't take it personally. If there's one thing people are always going to do, it's complain. What we need to do before that inspection is find a way to prove Tabby tampered with those cakes and that it wasn't something we did.'

'And if we can't?' I sigh. 'And even if we can, what difference does it make? *I* should have been overseeing things. Having a staff member tampering with the cakes is just as bad. I'm the one who's taken my eye off the ball. And either way, does it stop *me* being shut down? Does it change the fact that people have been ill after eating at *my* tearoom?'

'Yes. Yes, it does. Because she's not *your* staff member. She's employed by the council. She's *his* responsibility. Lie down with dogs and... you have a great time. Dogs are brilliant. Who wouldn't want to lie down with them?'

It makes me laugh even though laughing is the last thing I feel like doing. He's said it in his nasally Hatter voice, just high-pitched enough to let me know he's bothered by this too.

Maybe it's a sign from the universe. I feel like everything has been against me from day one, apart from Bram. Maybe this was never meant for me. Maybe I was stupid to attempt to take on my own tearoom with no experience. Marnie still needs an assistant at the bookshop and I bet Bram could get his job at the carousel back... I sigh because the thought spiral is getting me down, and I step back until I can nudge his arm instead. 'Are *you* okay?'

'Yeah.' He glances down at me. 'I have a suit for Sunday. A perfectly normal grey one with a tartan waistcoat and a tie. He won't find anything to complain about. But I've been winding him and Laura up by threatening to wear wild outfits and they don't realise that the more wound up they get, the more I wind them up. He doesn't understand the concept of teasing.'

Even *I* know that about Bram, and I've only known him for two months.

'He doesn't mean any harm, not really. He's just trying to make sure I don't look like me. He bought me a box of dark hair dye last week. I've heard the "that hair is going to be in your sister's wedding photos for the rest of her life" speech three times in the past two weeks. *I* offered to not be in the wedding photos if it offends them that much.'

We're standing underneath the magnolia tree and still watching Mr Hastings' car reversing slowly towards the gate. I reach up and stroke Bram's hair back from where it's covering his ear, and then whisper into it, 'Never change.'

I hear his breath catch, and his arm goes around my waist, low on my back, his fingers curl into my hip on the other side, and he holds me against him. I let my hand slide over his shoulder and then rest my head on it as we watch Mr Hastings' fancy car reverse through the gate.

'You mean that? My life is full of people who wish I was different.'

'I think he's trying, in his horribly misguided way. I think he wishes he understood you better, but he doesn't know how.'

He lets out a sigh and his head drops to rest against mine and it feels like he simply breathes for a few moments, and I appreciate the calm stillness because any meeting with Mr Hastings is always fraught with tension for *both* of us.

'How long before Marnie and Darcy realise we've been out here canoodling?'

'No canoodling!' I smack his arm and he laughs, making that single dimple dent inwards, and without giving myself a chance to second guess it, I use my grip on his shoulder to pull him down while I push myself up on tiptoes and brush my lips across it.

His fingers touch his cheek like he isn't sure what just happened. 'That was definitely canoodley.'

I blush. 'You have a way with words, Bram.'

'Usually the wrong way, except when I'm with you. Nothing seems wrong when I'm with you.'

I look up into his eyes and can't imagine being anything but honest in this moment. 'Same.'

His mouth twitches as he tries not to smile. 'Hmm. Curiouser and curiouser.'

18

It's Saturday night and the wedding is tomorrow. After Bram and I stocked the tearoom this morning, Marnie and Franca have run it for the day while we finished off the last few batches of Jaffa Cake brownies, Cherry Bakewell cupcakes, Cheshire Cat macaron stacks, and checked in with everyone else who is making things. It was 9 p.m. when I said goodbye to him and wished him luck for tomorrow, because he dreads family events and I won't see him until the reception.

After a shower and changing into my pyjamas, I snuggled down in bed and... tossed and turned. And now it's nearly midnight and I'm annoyed at myself because I've got to be up at the crack of daylight tomorrow. I wanted an early night, but sleep is just not happening. I turn over and squash the pillow into a better shape, like that is solely responsible for stopping me sleeping, and just as I've closed my eyes again, I jump out of my skin when there's a knock on the caravan door. Adrenaline shoots through me and my heart is instantly pounding. Marnie's got a special knock and that's not it. Who on earth would be knocking on my caravan door at this time of night?

'It's me, Cleonidas.' Bram's voice comes through from outside.

I scramble out of bed so fast that my legs get tangled in the duvet. 'Are you okay? What's wrong?' I call out as I flail across the small space.

My heart is still hammering but with worry now. I expect to find him horribly injured or with news that something dreadful has befallen the cakes we've made for the wedding, but when I yank the door open so hard that it nearly comes off in my hands, he's standing on the driveway with a cheerful grin on his face.

''ello.' He holds up a picnic basket. 'Fancy a midnight picnic?'

'Bram! It's midnight!'

'*Yeeeah.*' He draws the word out, sounding as confused as he looks. 'The clue is in the title? *Midnight* picnic? Be a bit pointless at 11 a.m., wouldn't it?'

'I could've been asleep!'

'Were you?'

'Well, no, but...'

'There we go then. You know what they say, the best things in life are unexpected.'

'Free! The best things in life are free!' I snap, still trying to persuade my heart rate to calm down.

'Well, a midnight picnic is both free *and* unexpected. Bonus points.' His grin is so wide that it's absolutely impossible to be annoyed at him.

I shake my head fondly. 'You really are a nuthatch, aren't you?'

His grin gets even wider. 'When someone says it like that, I take it as a compliment.'

I'm above him in the caravan, looking down, and it makes a change to be taller than him, and the sight of his smile makes me want to take his face in my hands and pull his lips to mine. It was definitely a compliment.

'If we stand here for much longer, it's going to be a 1 a.m. picnic, which doesn't have quite the same ring to it. Can I come in while you get ready? It's freezing out here.'

'And you want to go for a picnic in this weather?'

'Yeah, why not?'

'Because...' I trail off. *Because* it's so unusual. Because it's not what other people do. Because it's so unexpected. All qualities I *love* about Bram. Who the heck wants to be normal when you can be someone who turns up at midnight for a picnic?

He grins at me like he can read every thought going through my head, and I step back to let him in. He knew where I'm staying because he gave me a lift home one night, but I didn't invite him in because... the caravan is so embarrassing. It's cramped and damp and I'm convinced it smells of mould, and I have too much stuff and it's a squash for one person in here, never mind two, plus the fact that I'm in my mid-thirties and still can't afford a place of my own, especially when he lives in the nicest house I've ever seen...

'*Nice* pyjamas.' He reaches out like he's going to touch them and then stops himself.

They're pink and purple striped fleece bottoms and a cream long-sleeve top with the Cheshire Cat on the front. 'If I'd known you were coming, I'd have worn something less embarrassing.'

'Where would be the fun in that? Pyjamas are perfectly acceptable midnight picnic wear.'

I think about it. On the one hand, they're *pyjamas*, and on the other, there is no such thing as a bedroom in the caravan, just the sofa that folds out into a bed, so there's no door to close where I could feasibly get changed in private, and I'm not undressing in front of Bram.

'This place is amazing.' He's looking around as I debate what to do. He pokes at one of the window frames, and then reaches up to wiggle a dodgy bit of the roof. 'You sure this is a caravan and not some mobile science laboratory where they study different types of rust?'

It makes me laugh, even though I'm mortified too. 'It's over fifty years old. You'd be a bit rusty and leaky if you were over fifty and had people living in you!'

'Touché.' He laughs too. 'It wasn't an insult. I love it. It's so you.'

Other people say things like that and they're derogatory, but with Bram, it's a genuine compliment. He looks at the framed watercolour painting of Alice that Marnie had commissioned for me at Christmas, admires the handmade colourful bunting strung across the windows, and then starts poking through the open craft box on the only available work surface. 'It's alive with *you-ness*.'

It's mostly alive with woodlice, to be fair, and that thought makes me decide *not* to get changed before he discovers those as well. I grab my coat and take hold of his arm to gently but firmly drag him outside and half-push him down the two steps. 'Okay, that's enough caravan exploration for one night. Do you have somewhere in mind for this midnight picnic of yours?'

He lets me turf him out without a fuss, and waggles his eyebrows in answer to my question. 'I do.'

'Are you going to enlighten me?' I shove my feet into a pair of shoes and lock up behind us.

'Wasn't planning on it.' Instead, he holds his hand out, openly inviting me to slip mine into it, and when I do, he laces his fingers between mine and squeezes. 'For safety. It's dark. I know where we're going and you don't.'

'For safety.' I return his hand squeeze and let him lead the way through silent streets, subconsciously edging nearer to him with every creak of a branch in the forest and every car whizzing past on a distant road.

'I love your caravan. It's so full of personality. It must be nice to live somewhere that's totally your own. My house sucks the colour out of anyone who crosses the threshold.'

I squeeze his hand. 'No, it doesn't.'

He tugs my arm closer to his body. 'I would so happily live there. Anywhere that feels like *mine*. I know my house looks impressive, but *anyone* could live there. The caravan is so unmistakably you. I'd swap in a heartbeat. There's only so much you-ness you can inject by buying colourful tea towels.'

I want to say something nice, like he's so bright that his presence lights up the entire building anyway, but I decide to stick with focusing on the quiet of the night and watching where I'm going so I don't accidentally fall into a ditch.

We seem to be skirting round the back of the forest that surrounds Marnie's neighbourhood, and heading towards... 'It *is* Ever After Street!' I exclaim when we come to the car park and round the corner to the main street. 'What are we doing here?'

He makes that smug little noise again but clearly isn't going to share anything yet.

Ever After Street is magical at this time of night. The streetlamps are alight with a warm orange glow, and Witt and Sadie's castle lights are glinting on the hill in the distance, but every shop is dark and there's nothing but the sound of silence. This place is *never* quiet, with so many shops and their visitors, a lot of them of the excitable small-human variety.

'Right.' Bram extracts his hand from mine and turns to face me. He's still holding the picnic basket, but he puts one hand on my shoulder and moves me into a position so I'm standing by the white picket fence surrounding the area with flower beds and picnic tables in the middle of the street. 'I need to go and do something, and I need you to stay right here for a second so you get the full effect, so just don't move, okay?'

From my shoulder, his hand runs down my arm until he lifts my hand and transfers the picnic basket into it. I grunt at the unexpected weight because he says, 'Don't jostle that, there's a *very* unstable cake in there.'

'Half the time, I think you *are* a very unstable cake,' I mutter, still unable to work out what he's up to.

'Awwww. That might be the nicest thing you've ever called me, Cleonie.' He winks at me as he walks backwards for a few steps, and then turns and jogs away, his footsteps echoing against the paving stones.

Within moments, the darkened carousel bursts into life, flooding Ever After Street with a rainbow of coloured lights and vintage organ music which plays an instrumental selection of classic Disney songs, and I stay put until Bram comes back towards me, his arms spread wide and an equally wide smile lighting up his face.

'You said you always wanted to go on the carousel but were too self-conscious when it's full of kids. I believe that no one is *ever* too old to have fun and wanted to prove that. In private. And with cake.'

The fluttering that fills my chest makes me feel all giggly and bubbly inside. I can't remember when I said that to him but it was weeks ago, and he still remembered and went out of his way to do something so special. 'I didn't think you worked at the carousel any more.'

'Joshy let me have my keys back for one night only.' He takes the picnic basket carefully from my hand, and there's still a little sparkle as his fingers brush against mine, and an even bigger spark when he settles the basket in his hand and then he holds his other hand out to take mine again. 'A midnight ride on the carousel awaits. But first, cake. Follow me.'

The carousel is going round on its own, filling the street with the music of 'In A World Of My Own' from *Alice in Wonderland*, as Bram leads us over to the grassy area beside it, sets down the picnic basket and spreads a gingham blanket out.

I sit down on it, and he kneels and opens the basket. 'We should celebrate what we've achieved this week.'

'With an unstable cake?'

'With an... Unbirthday cake.'

My mouth falls open in surprise when he lifts a cloche-covered cake stand out of the basket and uncovers it to reveal a familiar pink cake. It's an exact replica of the cartoon Unbirthday cake the Mad Hatter gives Alice in the film, and it's just like the one my mum made for me, so many years ago. I remember telling him about it when we first met, but I never thought either of us would be able to recreate it.

I didn't intend to get emotional but my eyes have welled up. It's a flashback to a day, many years ago, when everything was right with the world and what I wanted from life was so clear. It's almost like being back there, a little girl again, with my mum and nan, waiting for my dad to come home from work. Making a wish that life would always be like it was in that moment.

Bram's chewing his lip, looking unsure of himself, like he's still undecided whether this was a good idea or not.

'It's perfect.' I let out a breath. '*How* did you do that? *Why* did you do that?'

At least that explains why it's unstable. The cake tapers down so the narrow part is at the bottom and the wide part is at the top – as topsy-turvy as everything else in Wonderland – and he's decorated it beautifully with pink fondant, beads of white royal icing, and blue flowers.

'It's your Unbirthday.' He beams at me. 'It's my Unbirthday too.'

'It's our Unbirthdays 364 days a year.' I can't help giggling at how cheerful he sounds. 'Why tonight? After doing nothing *but* baking cakes lately, tonight you decided to use your free time to... bake another cake?'

'I wanted to surprise you. I know this cake means a lot to you, and I know this is the kind of thing you want to do in the tearoom, so it's a prototype too. It would be incredible to have these on display, and if people book their Unbirthday parties in advance, we could make them one of these for that extra special touch. And I think there's a way to make smaller, individual ones too, for everyday use. If we use pudding moulds so the base tapers down, slice the cake in half and fill it with buttercream and then ice it, each one would be a mini version of a proper Unbirthday cake in a single-serving size.'

'Do you know how...' I stop myself because I was going to say 'how special you are?' but I can't just blurt something like that out.

He meets my eyes in the darkness, his face coloured by the neon lights from the carousel behind us, and a tiny smile plays across his features, like he's heard the rest of the unfinished sentence, then he blinks and looks away.

'...how much I didn't intend to talk about work tonight?' He finishes the sentence for me. 'Sorry, I'm getting carried away. The tearoom excites me in a way nothing has for years, and once I get started... Well, you know shutting up isn't my strong point.'

I reach over and slide my hand across his knee. 'I love it too. It excites me too. All I want is for it to be mine. To have the security of being my own boss and not being answerable to someone else, with no threat of it being taken away at a moment's notice.'

'You will. Because every Unbirthday cake comes with an Unbirthday wish.' He gets a candle out and pokes it into the top of the cake, then produces a little box of matches, strikes one, and leans over to light it.

I can't help grinning at the unintentional throwback to what I did at the interview, all those weeks ago.

'Go on.' He pushes the cake towards me. 'Make a wish.'

I go to protest, to say I'm a tad too old for believing in wishes, but Bram is the kind of person who makes anything seem possible, so I hold his gaze for a moment, and then close my eyes and blow the candle out.

I wish for life to continue being as magical as it's felt since I met you.

He's still smiling at me when I open my eyes. 'Pretty sure I just felt a sprinkling of fairy dust. Now you know it will come true.'

'You don't know what I wished for. I could've wished for something random, like a badger to walk by.'

'Ahh, I've got a pretty good idea. Although I'm going to get really suspicious if we see any badgers tonight.'

He hands me a paper plate and a plastic fork, and gets out a cake slice knife, and I can't help watching his skilful hands as he cuts a reassuringly *massive* slice. You know a man is a keeper when he doesn't skimp on cake slices. He transfers it onto the plate I'm holding out and it's so comically heavy that I nearly drop the plate at the weight of it.

I can't help looking at the smile lines around his eyes as he cuts a piece for himself too, and I think about how when I first met him, I thought he was someone who smiles and laughs a lot, and it makes me appreciate how much he's made me smile and laugh over the last couple of months, and how flipping lucky I got that day I opened the door to find the Mad Hatter outside, and of all the Mad Hatters in all the world, mine turned out to be *him*.

'Always time for tea.' I blink back to reality to find he's pulled out a Thermos flask and is holding out a steaming cup of tea in a plastic mug, sounding like it's not the first time he's tried to get my attention.

I take it from him and he pours another one out for himself and then holds it up to toast against mine. 'Cheers to...'

There seem to be an equal amount of things to celebrate and dread. The catering has gone so incredibly well that, minus any Mr-Hastings-related curveballs, surely, *surely* he will consider the trial passed. Then the tearoom will be mine. And my love of baking has come back with a vengeance. The wedding catering has left me with no choice but to get over my hang-ups and get back in the kitchen. Things I've *known* for years but had forgotten have come back to me, and I've rediscovered the joy of baking, rather than being scared of something going wrong, and it's been wonderfully fun, all because of Bram. But there's the sabotage too. The inspection this coming Friday... but I don't want to think of negative things tonight. He's gone to so much effort to make this night truly beautiful, and I want to revel in it rather than run myself mentally ragged on a collection of 'what ifs' and worst-case scenarios.

'All things Wonderland.' He fills in the answer, like he can tell I'm struggling to come up with one.

'And to people who bring a touch of magic into the world.' I clink my cup against his pointedly, and he smiles like it's the best answer he could've hoped to hear.

I dig my fork into the cake. 'Oh my God, Bram. *How* do you do that? That is *gorgeous*.'

It's the most delicious melt-in-the-mouth rich vanilla cake, with soft buttercream and sweet fondant, like a birthday cake you can eat on any day of the year. A perfect Unbirthday cake.

He blushes, and it's not just the red lights reflecting from the carousel. It's stopped turning now and the music has stopped too, but the lights are still shining, illuminating the outlines of the carousel, like a giant nightlight lighting up our little picnic area, and it's by far the most romantic moment of my life.

We finish our cake and tea without really saying anything. He's quiet. I get the impression he's thinking about something, and I don't want to push him if he's not ready to talk. 'This is like a fairy tale. Never imagined we'd have Ever After Street all to ourselves or a private showing of the carousel. Thank you for doing this.'

'I wanted to thank you. I think my little sister getting married has made me a bit reflective, so can you bear with me being soppy and weird for a minute?' He gives me a smile, but it's muted enough that I know he's struggling to come up with the right words. He holds his hand out across the blanket and I slip my fingers into it, and his thumb rubs over the backs of them. 'Thank you for liking me.'

'Br—' I go to admonish him for saying something so daft, but I stop myself because he asked me to bear with him without interrupting.

'After Tabby, I didn't think I'd ever let anyone into my life again. I thought I'd rather be alone forever than go through that again. And then you appeared and it just happened. I never even thought about opening up to you – I just *was* open with you. It's a hollowing, lonely feeling to perpetually be told that my preferences and judgements aren't good enough. For a long time, I've hidden behind magic tricks and a wild and loud persona, because the real me isn't good enough for some members of my family. I've tried to tell myself that I'm enough just as I am, but I've never really believed it, until you came along. I carry my father's list of my faults around like a metaphorical chain hanging from my neck. Tabby reinforced that chain and made it stronger and heavier. You've torn it apart. Day by day, you've taken every link out. So many times, I've thought about giving up – doing what he wants, becoming who he wishes I was and giving up on myself, and every day you've reminded me of why I won't do that. You've made it all feel worthwhile because I know you like me, and you have *no* idea how long it's been since I felt that anyone would ever accept me. Hanging out with Marnie and Darcy the other day and being accepted as I am... that was *wonderful*, and I never would have done that without you. My father has made me question everything about myself, to the point where I never thought I'd trust my own judgement again, but you've given me back confidence in my own authority. Thank you.' He's looking at our joined hands as he speaks. His voice is shaking, and I think my nails are slicing into his fingers where my hand is curled so tightly around his.

'You have no idea how much I needed you.' I didn't realise I was going to cry until tears fill my eyes. 'For the past couple of years, I've hidden away and avoided the world. I may as well have not existed. I didn't know how to get out of that rut. When I started helping Marnie out at the bookshop last year, it was great while I was there, but then I'd go home and slip back into the rut again. Every time I was at home, it got harder and harder to go out again. And then I burnt the kitchen and got evicted and Marnie was the only person I could turn to, because I've pushed everyone else away. It made me realise that I wanted to *live* life again. The Wonderland Teapot was a last-ditch attempt to force myself back into the world, to do something I'd always wanted to do, and even that, she had to push me into. And then there was you. You've filled every day with so much joy. You've reminded me of who I used to be and the things I used to love, and you've made it okay to be childish and silly and find joy in simple things. You've helped me so much. Baking at your house every evening hasn't given me a chance to go home and dwell. You've never made me feel belittled for living in a caravan, or ridiculous for trying to take on a tearoom with no kitchen and long-forgotten baking skills. You've simply believed in me. You've made life happy again.' There are tears rolling down my cheeks and his eyes have filled up too. 'So don't you dare thank me for liking you, because it's impossible *not* to like you. God, I so much *more* than like you. Everything about you is exactly as it should be. You're human sunshine.'

Before I realise he's going to move, he's scrambled across the blanket and pulled me into the tightest hug. I kneel up to meet him, wrapping my arms around his body, my hand automatically finding its way to his soft hair and tangling in it.

His breath shudders against my shoulder. 'If I live to be a hundred, no one will ever say anything that nice about me again. Thank you.'

His lips brush against my neck, and he curls even tighter around me, and I breathe him in. The butterflies that have been flitting around inside me since he knocked on the caravan door go still, like they've been soothed by the warm blanket of his body, because everything about being in his arms feels right, and I never want to be anywhere else.

My fingers play with his hair, stroking down to the nape of his neck and back again, making him shiver, and his hand has slid under my coat so his palm is spread open on my back, holding me as close as physically possible, his skin burning hot through the thin material of my pyjama top. His other hand is entwined in the knot my hair is in. I've never known anyone who can put so much emotion into a hug as Bram does.

'Cleo,' he murmurs after a few long minutes. 'We need to get up and ride the carousel right now, because if we don't, I'm going to kiss you...'

The typical Bram honesty makes me smile. I want to. Leaping leopards, I want to. I've never wanted anything *more*. It would be so, so easy to pull back now and kiss him, but at the same time, I freeze up. Everything seems so up in the air. He's such a huge part of the tearoom, and there's so much uncertainty with the inspection next week, and he's all tangled up in that, and kissing him would make things even more complicated than they are already, and...

I hesitate for long enough that he releases me and pulls away, getting quickly to his feet.

'Bram, don't,' I say hoarsely, but I know him well enough to know that he's not going to kiss someone unless they *want* to kiss him, and I didn't respond quickly enough to make that clear.

'I promised you a midnight ride on the carousel and it's... well, it's not midnight any longer.' He holds his hand out to pull me up and I squeeze his fingers as I slip mine into his, hopefully tight enough to make him realise that I hesitated for so many reasons and none of them were because I didn't *want* to kiss him.

'Sorry, Cleo. I say so many stupid things, can we just write that off as one of them?' He drops my hand faster than ever before. 'We should... you know... enjoy this. I had to bribe Joshy to give up his keys for the night with a Reese's peanut butter cup cheesecake all to himself, so choose your noble steed.'

The interior of the carousel is brightly lit and I can see how red his face has gone, and instead of pushing it, I place a hand on the nearest horse and inelegantly clamber on.

'Be right back.' The carousel is operated by a control panel in the centre, a fair few horses away, and he winks at me with a familiar cheeky wink, and it eases the weird tension that's sprung up between us and sets the butterflies soaring again.

I wrap my hands around the pole my horse is mounted on and watch as he turns his keys and the carousel judders into life. 'When You Wish Upon a Star' plays as we start turning slowly and my horse moves gently up and down. I can't take my eyes off Bram, using the poles to keep his balance as he walks back along the moving carousel.

When he reaches me, he swings a leg over the horse next to mine and grins at me, and I appreciate how awkward things could've got after that kiss comment, and how he didn't make them so.

Maybe I shouldn't touch him again, but it's been impossible not to touch Bram for a while now, and tonight isn't any different. I take one hand from the pole and reach out for his, trying to ignore the flutter of excitement when he instantly leans over to hold my hand between the horses. We're smiling at each other as the tinny song plays, and considering the carousel is the *only* thing illuminated on Ever After Street, nothing is brighter than his smile.

I let go of the pole with my other hand and spread my arm out wide, letting the night breeze drift through my fingers. 'I'm flying!'

'Wrong movie. That's *Titanic* and it didn't end well.'

It makes me laugh so much that, never mind flying, I feel like I'm soaring, and it's nothing to do with the up-and-down movement of the crankshaft the horses are attached to.

When the song ends and the carousel stutters to a halt, he asks if I want to go again, and again, and we're on the fourth ride before I realise I have to do something. There's magic in the air tonight. This is a big, important moment, and if I don't do *something*, I'm going to regret it for the rest of my life. Bram says whatever he feels without hiding anything, and he deserves to know how special he is, without skirting around it or shying away.

This time, when the carousel has started moving and he walks back, I reach out and grab his hand before he can get back to his horse and tug him over to me instead.

'You okay?' He wraps a hand around the pole, right above mine so the side of my hand presses against the side of his.

I reach up and pull him down for a hug, and he slides one arm around me and keeps hold of the pole with the other hand, and the hug makes him laugh because I'm moving up and down while he's standing still.

My mouth is suddenly dry and I have to wet my lips and swallow before any words will come out. 'Thank you for tonight,' I murmur into his ear. 'This is spectacular. *You* are spectacular.'

I can feel his face shift as he smiles. 'You missed the "nut" out.'

'Yeah, that too, but no. I meant spectacular. In *every* way.' I turn my head until I can press my lips hard against his cheek, and his breath catches. He pulls back just far enough to meet my eyes, silently asking permission to kiss me, and if the width of my smile wasn't answer enough, my horse chooses that moment to glide upwards, smashing my lips against his.

'I knew I loved this carousel for a reason.' His words are pressed against my mouth as my hand tightens on the back of his neck and his fingers curl into my lower back.

It's a soft, sweet, gentle kiss, nothing more than a press of lips on lips. I think we're both nervous, both excited, and the fact that he's standing still and I'm on a horse that's moving up and down makes it... absolutely impossible to kiss properly. Our mouths are pulled apart and then rammed back together, but neither of us are willing to part for long enough for me to get off the horse *or* wait for the carousel to finish. Every time he makes a noise of disappointment and his lips chase after mine, and then find them when the horse unceremoniously pushes my face into his, until we're both just clinging onto each other and laughing ourselves silly, and somehow it sums up our topsy-turvy Wonderland relationship so well that there couldn't have been a more perfect first kiss.

'Oh, thank God,' Bram says when the carousel mercifully comes to a stop. 'I can honestly say I've never had a kiss quite like that before.'

It feels good to feel so wanted that he can't take his hands off me as I shift on the horse, swing one leg back over it until I'm sitting sideways and can wrap my legs around his body and pull him closer until we can finally, finally kiss properly.

This time, there's nothing soft and gentle about it. My nails are digging into his shoulders, and he's holding me so tightly that I can feel his heart racing. I get a thrill because every time my fingers graze across his skin, he shivers and goosebumps chase after every touch. I'm dizzy and it's definitely not just from the four rounds on a carousel.

His fingers are digging into my body as he tries to pull me impossibly closer. He makes little noises of happiness against my mouth, and his tongue is hard, pressing, his teeth nippy, and I lose myself so desperately in giving in to the feelings I've been pushing down for weeks now that it feels like the ground under us is moving so much that we could be on a rollercoaster, not a carousel.

We're both panting when we pull back.

'Now, *that* was a kiss,' I murmur.

Even his giggle sounds dazed. His forehead is resting against mine as he gasps for breath. 'Am I awake?'

I blink my eyes open to see his are still closed and there's a blissfully soppy smile on his kiss-reddened lips. 'If you're not, I'm not.'

'Pinch me. Because I've been dreaming of doing that for a while now, and if this is a dream, the sooner I wake up, the sooner I can start getting over the disappointment of it not being real.'

'I'm not pinching you!' I love that, even in the middle of the best kiss *ever*, he still makes me laugh. I lean up and press my lips to his again and he sighs into it, his full weight resting against my horse like his body has completely melted.

'The two hours I spent making that Reese's cheesecake last night were worth every second.'

I laugh out loud. 'Oh, Bram, you know how to make a girl feel special.'

He leans down and touches his lips to the corner of my jaw, just below my ear, still breathing hard. 'So are we...'

'Are we...?' I repeat.

I love that even when we're so close that I can *feel* the heat as his cheeks redden, he still blushes. 'Are we... doing this? Are we in... *this*... together?'

'I'm in if you are.'

'I've been "in" since the day in the shop when my father came in, and you had every right to be angry, but instead you reached over and squeezed my hand. I've fallen fur-over-whiskers for you every day since then.'

'Since the first time I came to your house and realised how different *you* were to the character you play. When we left to go to the supermarket and you tucked your hair under a hat because you didn't want to be looked at. I realised we weren't so different after all.'

When he kisses me this time, it's a mix of the softness of the first time and the passion of the second time, and when we pull back, I'm light-headed and fizzy inside, desperate to kiss him again, to never *stop* kissing him, and I can't help giggling about what anyone would think if they caught sight of us.

'Never thought the best kiss of my life would be in the middle of the night while sitting side-saddle on a carousel horse, wearing Cheshire Cat pyjamas.'

'I've never seen sexier pyjamas in my life.' His fingers run up and down my outer thigh, teasing the fleecy material. 'And the best kiss of your life, really?'

I smack at him.

'Instead of giving me an ego, that gives me a challenge – to outdo myself every time I kiss you from now on.' He kisses me again. 'And just so you know, it was the best kiss of mine too. Even the split lip from the moving horse. I've never had a more enjoyable reason to buy Bonjela before.'

I cannot stop laughing. If I couldn't sleep before, God only knows how I'm going to sleep after this.

I let him go long enough for him to restart the carousel again, and the tinny music of 'A Dream Is a Wish Your Heart Makes' fills the night. Instead of getting on his own horse, he stands next to mine, stealing kisses every time it glides low and I cling onto the pole with one hand and don't let go of his hand with the other, and when the music stops and the horses come to a halt, neither of us makes any attempt to move, and it's by far the most magical evening of my entire life.

19

The Ever After Street castle is easily the most romantic place I've ever been. It's such a real-life Disney castle that the only thing it's missing is a pumpkin carriage parked outside. On Sunday morning, it's decked out in wedding finery. Darcy is the gardener here and he must've been putting extra effort into growing pink and white roses because displays of them line the walkway and white rose petals cover the ground. In front of the castle is an archway made of brown willow branches interspersed with green foliage and pink and white roses, and inside, the castle has been decked with twinkling fairy lights, every pillar wrapped with garlands of roses, and sprays of wisteria hang from above.

The wedding itself is taking place in a nearby church this morning, and then guests are coming here for the reception, and while Laura and her fiancé get married, the rest of the Ever After Street team have come to set out the wedding buffet. There's no vehicle access to the castle, so Darcy lent me a wheelbarrow to push up the many, many boxes of cakes. Ali has brought wheeled trolleys from his restaurant, and Mickey and Lissa are weighed down with bags containing stacks of filled Tupperware.

The reception is taking place in one of the ballrooms and Laura wants all the food set out as a buffet for guests to help themselves to. The dancefloor is at one end of the giant room, the guest tables are in the middle, set out with lacy tablecloths and vases of roses, and place cards for all the coming guests. The bride and groom and both sets of parents have one long table of their own, and the buffet tables are at the opposite end, furthest away from the door.

Bram's at the wedding this morning, and I wonder if he's as tired as I am. After a *lot* more kissing last night, it was past 3 a.m. when he walked me home, and I was absolutely right about not being able to sleep after he left, except this time it was because my whole body was fizzing with tingly excitement. Because, for the first time in a long time, everything felt *right* with the world, and I probably dozed off about an hour before my alarm went. But every moment of last night was a *thousand* per cent worth every gallon of coffee I have to guzzle today.

I wouldn't know where to start with setting out a buffet, but Ali is an expert. He allocates a table for sandwiches and savoury foods, a table for cakes, and a table for nibbles and snacks. He's brought tons of silver platters, and as Witt and Darcy put the finishing touches to the décor, Sadie, Mickey, Lissa, and Marnie form a chain of passing boxes to each other, while Ali and I arrange things nicely on the vintage serving wear the castle has in abundance, and by the time we've finished, there's the noise and chatter of the first guests starting to arrive.

The others duck out a side door, but I've left my wheelbarrow in the entrance hall, so I retrace my steps to collect that, and as I exit the ballroom, I walk headfirst into Mr Hastings' enormous chest.

'Ahh, Miss Jordan, just who I was looking for.'

Despite the more human side I saw the other night, there's something about his drawling voice that fills me with dread. Whereas Bram fills a room with light, Mr Hastings has the same impact as a cloud crossing the sun, and I'm instantly on edge, despite the fact I've done what he wanted me to. Between all of us, we have *somehow* catered this wedding.

'Me?' I gulp then repeat the question in a less squeaky voice.

'Yes. I wanted to say a resounding thank you for all your hard work. I must admit that when I offered you this challenge, I had my doubts, but fair play to you, you've come through for my family when we needed you.'

A dark-haired woman who I'm guessing is Mrs Hastings is with him, her hand through his arm, and she smiles kindly at me with twinkly brown eyes just like Bram's.

God only knows what they think of me. I didn't intend to be seen. I'm not here as a guest and I'm certainly not dressed as one. I've got on food-dye-stained jeans and a T-shirt with a hole under the armpit, because as soon as I've set out the buffet, Bram's given me his spare key and left the recipe for the mini Unbirthday cakes in his kitchen and I'm going to try making them.

'Laura is absolutely delighted,' Mr Hastings is saying. 'And I've just had a little look-see myself, and it looks like a wholly professional job, and Abraham assures me that it will all taste as good as it looks. I'm not a man who goes back on my word, Miss Jordan, so I'm delighted to offer you the tearoom lease on an eighteen-month rolling contract. Congratulations.'

He reaches out to shake my hand and when I'm too surprised to respond instantly, he takes my hand and shakes it without waiting for permission.

I didn't expect this at all. Not *today*, not before anyone has even eaten any of the food we've made, and I mouth at thin air like a stranded goldfish a few times before any words come out. 'Oh, wow. Thank you. Thank you very much.'

Why am I one quiff away from sounding like Elvis Presley? Mr Hastings is still pumping my hand up and down so hard that it's like he's shaking around the thoughts in my brain and jumbling them all up. I know this was the deal *he* made, but I still expected him to change his mind or put up more hurdles, and I don't know what to say...

Except that I thought this moment would feel euphoric, but it feels like a bit of a hollow victory. *I* haven't catered this wedding. There's no way in hell that *I* could have, but *we* have managed it, between Bram and me and all our friends on Ever After Street, it's *us* who have done it. It feels like I've conned him in some way, like I'm taking credit for everyone else's work when I shouldn't be, even though everyone knew that the whole point of doing this was to help me get the tearoom.

I feel a bit... wrong. Like I did after the interview when the only thing that swung it for me was the rose cupcakes that I let them believe I'd made. I've got what I wanted, but I don't feel like I deserve it.

Mr Hastings finally lets go of my hand, and waves a stern finger at me. 'You make sure you don't give that pesky inspector anything to concern himself with, okay?'

'Of course not.' I paste on a smile. Is *this* the catch? Is this the niggling feeling I have in the pit of my stomach that something is about to go horribly, horribly wrong?

'Now, no more work today, it's a day to celebrate my daughter's happiness.' He gives me a nod and goes to drag his wife away, but I stop him.

'Mr Hastings?' I wait for him to turn back towards me. 'Thank you for sending Bram to work with me. I think your son is the most wonderful person I've ever met. He makes the world a better place. A brighter, happier, funnier place. None of this would've happened without him. He deserves to be loved for who he is, even if you don't always approve of his choices. There are worse things a child can do than not follow *your* path in life. You should be very proud.'

Mr Hastings frowns, probably not wanting the reminder of his candidness the other night, but clearly getting the insinuation *and* the fact it's none of my business, but Mrs Hastings looks like she can't stop her smile getting wider.

She extracts her arm from his and reaches out to shake my hand. 'Bram's told us a *lot* about you. It's so nice to finally meet you in person. I look forward to getting to know you better and can't wait to try this wonderful buffet. Mrs Willetts has been raving about your rose cupcakes for weeks.'

Oh, *those*. 'There won't be any of—'

'Come along, dear, we mustn't loiter, guests are wanting to get in.' Mr Hastings doesn't let me finish my feeble explanation about the lack of rose cupcakes. 'I'll stop by with the paperwork this week, Miss Jordan. Cheerio.'

I take it for what it is – a dismissal, and that's fine, because someone could've tripped over my unattended wheelbarrow by now.

I hurry through the hall towards where I left it when Bram catches hold of my arm and pulls me aside. ''ello.'

'There's a wheelbarrow.' I jerk my head in the direction I was heading.

'Darcy's already taken it.'

'Oh thank God. The bride landing arse over teakettle in a wheelbarrow is a previously unknown wedding tradition that we *don't* need to start.' I finally look up at him and every thought disappears from my mind instantly. 'Wow. You look incredible.'

He's blushing as I take in his grey suit, white shirt, red tartan waistcoat and shiny grey tie that looks like it's been gradually loosened over the course of the morning. 'So do you.'

'I'm wearing jeans and a T-shirt!'

'Exactly.' He grins, and it's almost impossible *not* to kiss him, but there are people around us. Witt and Sadie are checking in coats and directing people to the bathrooms. People are admiring the castle. The suits of armour. The portraits of Witt's family that he's recently had restored. We get bumped into by a woman who's looking up at the mural-painted ceiling and not at where she's going, and then gives *us* a glare for being in the way.

Bram leans down and whispers, 'But more importantly than that, I hear a celebration is in order.'

'How'd you know that?' I look at him in surprise.

'I've just shared a car with my father. He told me what he was about to do. Come with me.'

'Why?'

'Well, firstly because I really need to kiss you but there's cousins, aunts, uncles, and God-only-knows-what-relations *everywhere* who interrogate me about my love life at every family gathering, and if they catch me snogging you then I'm never going to hear the end of it, and secondly because I'm not the only one who's over all the moons in the Milky Way that you're joining Ever After Street on a more permanent basis. This way.' His hand slips down my arm until he entwines our fingers and gives me a firm tug towards the stairs, but skirts around them to where there's a door underneath, the entrance to the staff kitchen. Instead of going in, he shuffles us until we're mostly out of sight under the stairs, and then slips his arm around my waist and leans down for a hug. It's brief and I can tell he's hyperaware of being spotted, and when he pulls back, he touches his lips to mine for the briefest peck.

There are footsteps outside our little nook and he steps back and laces our fingers together again and pushes open the door, and I'm immediately greeted by the burning smell of a party popper bursting and a chorus of people shouting, 'Congratulations!'

'Welcome to Ever After Street!' Marnie calls. 'For real! For good!'

'You're one of us now!' Darcy says.

'What are you all doing in here?' I look around the room. All of my friends from Ever After Street are huddled in the big staff kitchen, sitting on benches, tables, or the units themselves. It's like an impromptu surprise party, and from the smirk on Bram's face, I'm guessing he's responsible for it.

Ali is at the table with a kettle and a pile of teacups. 'Bram showed me how to make sparkly Wonderland tea. It seems like the perfect way to celebrate. Cheers!'

He holds up a cup of glittery tea in a toast and everyone else does the same.

'You did it, Cleo.' Sadie pats me on the shoulder as we slip further into the room and Ali beckons us over for a teacup each that he's already sprinkled with edible glitter.

'I didn't...'

'We've had fun.' Mickey cuts off my weak protest. 'And we've helped secure the absolute perfect tearoom for Ever After Street. It was totally worth making over a hundred vol-au-vents for.'

'You and Bram have worked harder than anyone. It's *your* win, Cleo, and it's well-deserved. Cheers.' Lissa clinks her teacup against Mickey's as Ali hands one each to me and Bram.

'Shouldn't you be with the wedding party?' Darcy asks him as we head towards one of the picnic-table style benches, weaving past Imogen and Joshy, and Franca knocks her shoulder against mine with a smile.

'I'd rather be here with you lot,' he says with a shrug, making me smile at his simple honesty again. Life would be so much easier if more people had Bram's honest approach to it.

'I see why...' Darcy raises an eyebrow at our joined hands.

'Thanks, everyone.' Bram lets me sit down first, and when I do, he flops down beside me and rests his head on my shoulder. His blue hair is held down with styling product, but the ends at the back of his neck are making a break for freedom, so I let my other hand play with them and goosebumps rise across his skin. 'I know this was about The Wonderland Teapot, but you've all helped to make my little sister's big day really special, and my whole family appreciate that, even if my father has a tendency to go about things in the wrong way.'

'We were doing it to help our Cleo,' Mickey says.

I've never been anyone's 'our' anything before and it soothes my frazzled nerves more than the hot tea. I hit it off with the Ever After Street girls from the moment Marnie introduced me to them when she was organising the book festival last year, and it feels like they've become true friends over the past few months.

'As soon as we met, we knew you belonged here in one way or another. I'm just glad you found the perfect way. Congratulations, and here's to many happy years of spreading Wonderland sparkle on our little street.' Lissa lifts her teacup to toast me too.

I'm getting choked up as I try to think of what to say to get across how much their kindness means, from gathering here to congratulate me to giving up so much of their time this week to help with the wedding catering. I swallow hard and take a deep breath. 'I can't thank you enough for all your help. There's no way I could have pulled this off without every single one of you. You've all gone *so* far above and beyond that I can't even wrap my head around it. None of you will ever have to pay for a cup of tea again. I owe you all so, so much, from right now and back to the very beginning. I know it was one of you who persuaded the council to look at my application, even though it was received after the cut-off point.' My money has always been on Mickey or Lissa, they've both worked here for years and are likely to have some sway with the bosses, and Lissa is always at the head of any protest and backing any underdog. I give them both a knowing look, but neither owns up, and nor does anyone else.

'So what's the first thing you're going to do now it's yours?' Franca asks.

'Take on your first employee, presumably.' Marnie nods towards Bram, and I can feel his face shifting into a smile where his cheek is leaning on my shoulder.

I turn my head and murmur against his forehead. 'What do you say, will you be my Mad Hatter on a more permanent basis?'

He lifts his head and grins at me. 'Depends. Do I get cake for breakfast every day?'

'Whether I say yes or no, you eat cake for breakfast every day anyway!'

He laughs and squeezes my knee. 'Then I'll be your Mad Hatter for as long as you want me to be.'

The others all do a collective 'awwww', and I'm grinning so widely as I clink my teacup against Bram's and we both take a sip. He leans his head back on my shoulder, and I sink down a bit lower to make him more comfortable.

The butterflies turn into small, flying, fire-breathing dragons at the thought of being responsible for employees now too. I don't know much about running a business and now I've *got* to earn enough of an income to cover the rent *and* pay other people too. And how can I ever be Bram's boss? He's un-boss-able. And surely I'll need to take on someone else as well. We've had plenty of times where the tearoom has been too busy for the two of us to keep up with. 'At least I can fire employees too now, and the first thing I'm going to do is fire Tabby.'

'She's hilarious,' Marnie says. 'I don't think she's ever even *seen* Alice, never mind read the book. She only seems to know one line – *off with their heads!*'

'She might not be a fan of reading *or* Alice, but at least with her gone, we'll know there will be no more sabotage incidents.'

Everyone sits forwards in anticipation of gossip, and I tell them about the salted muffins and spicy brownies that, contrary to popular belief, have *not* been caused by gremlins. 'None of you know for sure if she was offered the tearoom before me, do you?'

'Offered the tearoom...?' Lissa asks in confusion.

I explain about Tabby's plans for a wellness retreat on Ever After Street. 'Mr Hastings apparently gave the tearoom to someone else and then changed his mind and rescinded the offer. Any of you know who that was? I'd like to know I'm firing her for a reason...'

A wave of clueless shrugs and head shakes go around the room. No one seems to know what I'm talking about, but I didn't really expect them to. It's the sort of thing Mr Hastings would keep to himself.

And then one voice cuts through the bamboozlement. 'I thought it was you, Bram.'

Every eye in the room turns to Joshy, who looks surprised by the sudden attention.

'Didn't *you* leave the carousel to take over the tearoom? Isn't that why your father hired me?'

'No, to help me with the tearoom,' I correct him. Joshy's young, he's got his wires crossed...

...But Bram instantly sits up. Rather than lazy and languid, he's now as stiff as a robot that hasn't been oiled.

And just seeing him look *that* uneasy sets off a swirling squall of a thunderstorm inside me.

'Wait, no, that's not right, is it? On the first day...' I think back and it gives me a sudden and overwhelming urge to put as much space between me and Bram as possible. I slide along the bench so hard that I nearly fall off the other end as I turn the thoughts over in my head. 'The first day, you'd already left the carousel. You said your plans had fallen through but they'd hired your replacement, so you were at a loose end... That's why you were available to play the Mad Hatter...'

I watch his Adam's apple bob as he swallows. He looks around the room before looking at me, but his eyes flick away the second we make eye contact. It's probably the first time I've ever seen Bram lost for words, and it leaves me with the foreboding kind of goosebumps. A haunting chill. The 'this cannot be happening' feeling of being in a horror film. It can't be him. He *can't* have been lying all along.

'At the interview, Mrs Willetts asked your father about "something", and he said *it* wouldn't be a problem. When you handed me your phone on that first morning, he said, "good luck with *it*". I thought it was just sarcasm, but it wasn't, was it? In both instances, he was talking about *you*.' I shake my head, trying to clear it, but the thoughts are swirling so loudly that it's like being inside a spinning washing machine. 'It can't be you. Of all the people who could've been offered that tearoom, it can't be you. Tell me it's not you, *please*.'

He sits forward and goes to run a hand through his hair, but realises it's stuck down so slides a hand across it instead and pulls awkwardly at the back of his neck. 'Any chance we can have this conversation in private?'

In that one simple sentence, he's given me all the answer I needed. 'What that means is there's a conversation *to* have. That wasn't supposed to be your answer. You were supposed to say, "Pfft. What? No, of course not, I left the carousel for some completely different and totally unrelated reason." *Why* aren't you saying that, Bram?'

'Cleo...' He reaches a hand out towards me but it ends up hanging limply in mid-air.

I scramble onto my feet before he can get any closer and start pacing. Except there are so many of our colleagues packed into this room that there's barely space to move, and 'pacing' involves taking two steps between Marnie and Franca and back again before I walk into Sadie. It feels like the world is crumbling in on itself, and I'm right back to where I was two years ago. Adrift in a bank, with a business plan and a bank manager who was waiting for *two*. Phoning and phoning my ex, desperately pleading for him to answer, telling the staff that he must've been in a car accident on the way because there was *no* chance he wasn't coming. Checking the traffic reports to see if there were roadworks that he could be stuck in, and he'd *obviously* forgotten to charge his phone... And then the slow, seeping realisation that he really wasn't coming. I always imagined it was like a bride would feel on her wedding day if she was left standing at the altar. And this feels the same. Watching the dream splinter before my eyes. Let down by another man who I'd put my trust in. The *only* person I've trusted, the only person I've let into my life at all in years. All the doubts that Tabby has instilled converge at once overwhelm me.

'Why don't we go for a walk?' Bram's eyes flick to mine but again, he looks away at the exact moment our eyes meet.

'I'm not going anywhere until you explain this.' I fold my arms. I want his explanation *now*. Not in ten minutes' time when he's had a chance to concoct some reasonable story as we have a pleasant stroll through the castle grounds. Now.

He takes a deep breath and exhales for so long that his lungs must be burning. I see him look around the room and he eventually sighs in resignation. 'Lilith couldn't continue because of her health, her family kept the tearoom going for a while but it was temporary, they had their own jobs to get back to, and she eventually reached a deal with the council to buy the building from her. My father had an empty tearoom with no one to run it, so he threw it open to applications, and *none* were suitable. He had thirty applicants, and not one of them was the right fit. I was at his office when he was looking through them, and I took a chance. I was ready to do something different from the carousel, and I *love* baking, so I took a massive leap of faith and said, "Let me do it." I thought he'd laugh, but he didn't. He said yes. I thought he was finally trusting me with something – something big. I thought he was finally treating me as an adult, allowing me a shop of my own. He's always made fun of my baking, joked that I'd never be any good, it's not a "manly" enough job, and I felt like he was giving me a chance. He was finally believing in me. The applications hadn't closed, but he'd given up on finding anyone, so we put the plan into action. He hired Joshy, I started planning what I'd do with the place, and then another application came in, and it blew *everything* out of the water. Everyone had always said there should be *Alice in Wonderland* representation on Ever After Street, but nothing had ever come of it. And there you were with your Wonderland Teapot idea – the *perfect* fit. Exactly what this street needed. That's all there is to it.'

'That's not all there is to it though, is it? You've lied to me from the very beginning. You must have resented me. It was going to be *your* shop, and then suddenly you were downgraded to working *for* me. Washing up, waiting tables. What an insult that must've been.'

'Not at all. Cleo, *you* wash up. *You* take food to waiting customers. I would've been doing that no matter what, just like you do. It makes no difference. People don't realise how lucky they are to have the ability to do menial jobs. It's nothing to complain about.'

I've always loved his attitude, and I never, ever expected to be questioning whether it was genuine or not, because I'm suddenly doubting every word Bram has ever said. 'Why did you help me? Why let me use your kitchen? If you wanted to take over the tearoom, you could've just left me serving supermarket-bought cakes. I'd have slipped up eventually and been found out.'

'I didn't want you to slip up. I wanted what was best for Ever After Street. You had the imagination to come up with everything in that tearoom, but you'd lost your spark. And this was your dream. It was an opportunity for me, but it was a lifelong dream for you. I didn't want to stand in the way of that. Yeah, I was angry at first. He pulled the rug out from under me by going back on what was planned. He offered me the Hatter job as a consolation prize. I'm not going to pretend I wasn't upset. Disappointed. But I believe in making the best of things. What good does it do to be bitter and resentful? Throwing a tantrum wouldn't change anything... and I didn't want it to. *Alice in Wonderland* was inspired. I couldn't have come up with anything like that. I know I should've told you, but I didn't, and now it's too late to change that.'

He's not wrong there, and I appreciate the way he tackles things with head-on candour, but that also makes this even worse. 'You're so honest, Bram, about everything. You blurt out whatever you're thinking, but this... this one major thing, you kept quiet about. I even asked you outright and... you didn't tell me. You *told* me you didn't know anything about it.' I thought Bram was different. I thought he was the one person in my life who could be relied on to say things as they are, and I can't get my head around the fact that he isn't.

He rubs his eyes with the heels of his hands and his words are muffled through them. 'I knew what you'd think.'

'What I think is that all along I've thought Tabby was sabotaging what we've been doing because she wanted the building... but if she didn't... if she *hasn't*... who has?'

He sighs and looks up at me. 'Oh, come on, really? How many times do we have to go through this?'

'Until it makes sense! Why would anyone sabotage our bakes? The only possible explanation is that it's someone who wants The Wonderland Teapot to fail so they can step in when it does. Who *else* would be lurking on the sidelines, waiting on tenterhooks for me to crash and burn?'

He gets up and tries to pace too, and a couple of people move aside to give him more space. '*Why* would I do that? I'm not going to be accused of something I haven't done. And if you don't believe me, that's up to you. I can't prove it either way so there's no point in trying. I've done nothing but help you, and if you can't see that...' He sighs and turns away, a wobble in his voice. He's clearly hurt and it makes my heart constrict and the urge to go and slip my arms around him dances just out of reach.

Am I being too harsh? I've never doubted him for a second, but now, everything is blurred. He's been dishonest about something so important, and now I'm questioning if there was a hidden agenda behind *everything*. I've once again started to rely on someone who's turned out to be unreliable. Last time, my plans fell through because my ex let me down, and I *still* haven't learned the same lesson. Staying at home and shutting out the world was the right idea – I should've stuck with that.

'Since the moment I walked in on that first morning, the *only* thing I wanted was for it to succeed, because it's brilliant. Because you're brilliant, and because you belong on Ever After Street.'

'We agree with that.' Marnie nudges me kindly. Bram and I are both het-up: both our voices are rising, I'm wringing my hands together and he's pacing with angry stamps, and she's trying to defuse matters.

I take a deep breath and let it out slowly. The past two months are playing out in my mind like a DVD stuck on repeat, except it's like I've watched the film without understanding the dialogue and suddenly someone's put the subtitles on. 'You even told your father about the food poisoning. Which you had every right to do, obviously, but I was surprised.'

'No I didn't. I don't tell my father anything.' He fixes me with a hard stare. 'But *you* told Tabby.'

I think back to what he means. After the food poisoning. The day both Tabby and Bram were fully back in work and I wanted him to take longer off. I was worried about him, I kept checking to make sure he was okay, and Tabby noticed and asked why I was so bothered. I said he hadn't been well, and she'd jokingly said, 'It wasn't food poisoning, was it?' and I'd laughed just a tad too hysterically, and my overcompensation was clearly enough to tip her off.

'I've done nothing but throw myself headfirst into this and I've *loved* every minute of it. I've loved every minute with you. I've been... God, I've been *so* happy with you. I've looked forward to seeing you every morning.' He shakes his head and sits down again with a sigh. 'And this is what you think of me. For the past couple of months, I've been so secure because we've had each other's backs. So comfortable in my own skin because *you* liked me. And this one thing... you're going to let it make you doubt everything you know about me?'

'One thing *you* lied about!' I snap at him, even though it makes my stomach plummet with guilt. Do I really doubt everything I know about him? The beautiful soul I've got to know behind the loud character, something he's never hidden from me... I *can't* believe there was anything false about that, and yet, it doesn't fit with the bitterness he's just admitted to. He was angry at first. Resentful. He never showed a hint of that to me. He hid it behind his sunny Hatter smile. How many other things have been hidden behind card tricks and mixed-up sayings that made me laugh out loud while he was seething on the inside? 'Don't try to make me feel like I'm doing something wrong by not trusting you when you haven't been honest *and* have let me carry on believing that all the problems were down to your ex on a quest for revenge, and not...' I trail off. I can't bring myself to say outright that he is the saboteur. It doesn't sit right, despite all this.

'Well, unless the tearoom really is full of gremlins, it *has* to be one of the three of us, and it wasn't me or you.'

'How can I ever believe that?' I say quietly as sad realisation hits me. This changes everything, whether I want it to or not. The one thing I thought I knew about him was that he was too honest for his own good, but he's let me down – as people *always* do. I *want* to believe him, but I *can't*.

'Because you know me better than that.' His eyes are damp and it makes my heart jump into my throat and feel like it's beating there. I'm *still* fighting the urge to hug him because it's natural to comfort someone you care about when they're upset.

I hadn't realised how much this would hurt him. I didn't *want* to hurt him. I know he's let me in where he's always kept others at arm's length. I know he's opened up to me, but that doesn't excuse what else he's done. It doesn't change the outright lies. And it doesn't take away the main thought that's filling my brain. Was he trying to help me – or was he trying to make sure that he won't be second choice next time?

Silence falls. I can see the others getting twitchy. They want to say something, do something, *anything* to disperse this awkwardness. Lissa goes to speak and then thinks better of it. So does Darcy, but he also reconsiders before any words come out.

With hindsight, maybe this *was* a conversation Bram and I should have had in private to spare the others witnessing the supernova explosion of our relationship.

'There you are! I've been looking for you everywhere!' After a few endless minutes of uncomfortable silence, the door opens and Mrs Willetts bursts in. 'After a heck of a delay and many panicked phone calls, the wedding cake has finally arrived and Laura wants to cut it immediately and pose for photos. Hurry up, Bram! You too, Cleo! Laura wants to thank you personally and asked me to send you in if I found you. Should've known I'd find you together.' She waggles her wiry eyebrows, clearly not having a clue what she's just walked in on.

Bram pinches the bridge of his nose. 'It's not a good time.'

'Your family will have my guts for garters if I let you miss the cutting of the cake. I can handle your father, but I'm *not* tangling with your sister on her wedding day. Now, come on, off with you.' She pushes at his shoulder hard enough to get him moving, and he looks back at me.

I have no intention of getting involved in this and I'm about to tell Mrs Willetts to tell Laura I've already left when her age-spotted hand wraps around my wrist in a vice grip. 'You too, Cleo, you're not getting out of it that easily.'

I feel like Bram and I are naughty children being marched to the headteacher's office as she drags us through the vast hallway and towards the wedding party's ballroom, and no amount of wriggling persuades her to free either of us.

We're both still protesting as she pulls us into the ballroom and the three of us make enough of an entrance that every eye in the room swivels towards us, and the only thing that finally makes Mrs Willetts let go is the squeaky sound of wheels on the wooden floor from behind, and a shout of, 'Coming through!'

All three of us dive in different directions as a trolley is wheeled in, carrying the most beautiful wedding cake. It's four tiers high with a plastic bride and groom on the top, and decorated with cream coloured butter icing and delicate iced pink roses and has green leaves around the base of each tier as iced rose petals float down the sides to the tiers below.

Also on the trolley are custom-made stands displaying matching cupcakes in a waterfall formation. Matching *rose* cupcakes… Oh no. Oh *no*. It can't be. Not *those* cupcakes.

It's all right, I tell myself. No one will know. Only Mr Hastings and Mrs Willetts were at the interview. They won't recognise them. I don't know if the other man is here as well, but he wasn't overly interested at the time. No one will remember a few cupcakes so many weeks later. Of course they won't.

'Oh, hurrah!' Mrs Willetts squeals in delight. 'Finally, your rose cupcakes! I knew you wouldn't withhold them at a wedding. I've been wanting another one of these since the day we met. You don't mind, do you?' She helps herself to one from the stand and peels the case off eagerly.

'Oh, I, er...' I stumble over my words, trying to think of an excuse to sidle out quickly, but as I turn around, I'm standing face to face with the woman I bought that cake stand and those cupcakes from two and a half months ago.

'Oh, it's you.' She raises a finger in recognition. 'I don't remember all my customers, but it's impossible to forget someone who buys half the display. What a small world to run into you here.'

'Oh, Cleo, you really have outdone yourself. These are divine.' Mrs Willetts is making such noises of pleasure that some of the nearby guests are looking quite alarmed.

'Ms Baxter made those, Mrs Willetts,' Laura says kindly. 'She's made them as a gift to complement the wedding cake. Isn't that lovely?'

'Now don't be silly. I gorged myself on these cupcakes when Cleo brought them to her interview in March. I've been wait—' She cuts off the sentence halfway through like the previous two sentences have just caught up and I can see the calculation happening behind her eyes as she adds them together.

I've never *seen* cake turn to stone in someone's mouth before, but Mrs Willetts suddenly looks decidedly ill and shoves the cake onto the nearest table as she realises exactly what has gone on here.

Judging by the deathly silence in the room, and the many, many pairs of eyes that I can feel burning into me, she is far from the only one who has just put two and two together.

'Well, we won't keep you from your busy day, Cleo, but I'd heard you weren't staying and I wanted a chance to thank you in person before you left.' Laura leans across her table, almost conspiratorially, like she's also realised what's about to happen and is giving me an excuse to run away.

But it's too late. Mr Hastings has stood up and made a hand gesture, and a minion whisks a cupcake from the display stand and deposits it into his outstretched hand.

'Ah, yes, I recognise these very well. Aren't these cupcakes the one and only reason we offered you the tearoom in the first place?'

'They're not the *only* reason, Dad.' Bram speaks from beside the door. 'Cleo's proved herself over and over again. Whatever happened at that interview is irrelevant now.'

He's realised too. And I feel warm inside that he's still defending me, even after everything that's just happened.

'Well, no, but they were certainly a deciding factor. We appreciated the demonstration of her talents and the effort she'd gone to in making them for us. It showed enthusiasm and motivation to make her idea a success, and the cakes were absolutely delicious and sure to be very popular.' Mr Hastings picks off a bit of icing just like he did at the interview. 'Let me get this straight, Miss Jordan. You purchased these from Ms Baxter's bakery and passed them off as your own during your interview, intending to fool us into believing they were a sample of what would be on sale in the tearoom. Why not make your own?'

'I couldn't.' I say it quietly, hoping it will let him know that I don't want to talk about it.

Laura is biting her lip, looking like she's trying to think of a way to intervene, but Mr Hastings is undeterred. 'Louder, please, Miss Jordan. I'd like to know the reason behind this deception and at a volume I can hear, if you don't mind.'

'I couldn't,' I repeat. There's no getting out of it now. May as well go the whole hog. 'I was a terrible baker. And I got kicked out of my flat and I'm living in a caravan on my friend's driveway.'

Murmurs race around the room. Whispers at every table.

Who would do such a thing?

Caught out!

Well, I won't be going there again!

People are talking about me in every direction. Muttering. Gossiping between themselves. A camera flash goes off to commit this moment to memory forever.

And it's all too much. The display of cupcakes is between me and the door. And Bram's by the door. If I make a run for it, I'm going to have to get round that massive trolley. If I make it, I'm going to have to get round him. There's no option but to stand my ground.

It started off with just my knees knocking inside my stained jeans, but now every part of my body is shaking as I turn back to Mr Hastings. 'I drove past Ms Baxter's bakery on my way to the interview. I stopped and bought a platter of cupcakes. I didn't intend for you to think I'd baked them myself, but you did, and I let you carry on thinking it because everything in my life had been going wrong, and I desperately, desperately wanted that interview to go right. I love Ever After Street and I didn't want you to say no, and I thought you would if I tried to explain—' I'm getting choked up. So many words are trying to get out at the same time that I'm stumbling over my sentences and probably making even less sense than this makes anyway.

'Cleo, maybe we should go somewhere more private?' Laura says pointedly. 'This is between you and my father. I only wanted to thank you for your work today.'

But I'm on a roll now. Instead of shaking knees, a catharsis has come over me. It's long past time this truth came out. 'Don't thank me for something your father blackmailed me into doing. Something I couldn't have contemplated without your brother. And you...' I turn to Mr Hastings. 'I am *not* a wedding caterer. I run a tearoom, not cater buffets for a hundred and fifty people. You had no right to force me into doing this under the threat of being fired and losing my tearoom.'

'Oh, you lousy sod!' Mrs Hastings smacks his arm. 'You said she wanted to do it!'

'I couldn't do it! Until a couple of months ago, I couldn't bake anything. I'd lost my love of baking. Every time I went near a kitchen, everything went wrong. But that's different now.' I look around the room until I settle on a pair of familiar dark eyes, lurking in the corner by the doorway. 'Because of Bram. Your son has done everything possible to help me. Hours and hours of patience – talking, reminiscing, helping me to remember what I used to love, and reminding me of who I used to be, endless trips to the supermarket for ingredients, and for the cakes that I couldn't bake myself in the beginning, and unlimited access to the kitchen in *your* house, because what Bram did was believe in me so hard that I ended up believing in myself. But the one thing I didn't do is cater this wedding. *We* did. Bram did. Marnie and Darcy did. Sadie did. Mickey and Lissa did. Imogen from the Sleeping Beauty shop and Franca from the festive end of the street. Ali from 1001 Nights has gone above and beyond. And all of them have done it to help me when I don't deserve it. All of them have let me take credit for *their* work so we could play you at your own game and trick you into letting me become a part of *their* street. I don't deserve any thanks, but the people who do are... right outside.' I peer around the open doors to see quite a few friends have followed us and are gathered around the doorway, trying to get a look at what's going on without drawing attention to themselves.

'Come in, all of you.' Laura beckons everyone in. 'Take a cupcake at the very least. Have a seat if you can find one. There's endless champagne.'

It's lovely of her to invite these people who are strangers to her to share in her wedding party, but I use the influx of friends coming in to fade into the crowd and sneak out.

Marnie catches my hand and squeezes it, her eyes silently asking me if I'm okay as I slip past her. She goes to come with me, but Darcy is behind her and Ali is crowded behind him and she gets pushed forwards while I shuffle behind Ali until the door is within sight.

I squeeze past Mickey, and then Bram is right there, too near, and I turn around so my back is to him, and hope I can get through the door without having to see him. I scrape my chest on the door-frame because it's too much of a squash with people still coming in, and then finally, at last, I'm in the much emptier entrance hall, and I can breathe again.

I put my hands on my knees and take deep breaths, adrenaline coursing through me. The past few minutes feel like an out-of-body experience. Did I really say all that so publicly? I can't believe they all know... I can't believe this is over. Because that's *it*, isn't it? The end of The Wonderland Teapot and all the dreams that live there.

'Cleo!' Bram must catch sight of me because he calls my name, and then I hear him shouting, 'Excuse me! Let me through!'

He's obviously stuck inside the doorway too, but I don't wait to hear any more. I dash from the castle as fast as I can.

Usually I love everything about this beautiful old building and this place, but for today, I want to run away from Ever After Street, and never, ever come back.

20

'I miss his hugs.'

'I know. You've told me 15,698 times this week, and it's only Tuesday afternoon.' Marnie wraps her arm around my shoulder and gives me a squeeze.

'He was the best hugger.' I know I'm annoying her. I'm annoying myself, but I can't stop thinking about Bram. Every inch of The Wonderland Teapot reminds me of him. Every customer who comes in either looks for him or asks me where he is. The third child this week has just left with their parents, disappointed that they didn't get to see magic today.

'I can't work out how he does it, can you?' Mrs Moreno says, unaware that when she asked where the Mad Hatter was, my bumbled explanation of 'he's not in today' really meant 'he'll never be in again' and that I've got my lip clenched between my teeth to stop tears forming in my eyes as she waxes lyrical about him when I take her toasted teacake over. 'I always think I'll catch him out if I watch closely enough, but I never do. Maybe he's got actual magic powers, do you think?'

'It's a distinct possibility,' I mumble, and then I have to go and hide out the back to get my emotions under control, and when I look up, Marnie is leaning against the doorframe, looking worried. 'Why don't you answer one of his texts?'

'I did answer one of his texts. I told him to go away.'

'And?'

'He went away.'

She laughs and then schools her face when I must look like I'm mere seconds away from wailing.

We've opened The Wonderland Teapot again today. I was at such a loss yesterday morning, the day after the wedding, I didn't know what to do or where to go, so I did what I've been doing every Monday morning since March – I put on an Alice dress and a black bow headband, added the pair of shiny black shoes that I've worn so much they don't even pinch my toes any more, and came to work.

No one from the council has said that I shouldn't. No one has confirmed that I've been fired from the tearoom, although it's probably a safe bet to assume that I have. I'm expecting a 'cease and desist' visit from Mr Hastings at any moment, or one of his minions if he can't stand the sight of me himself, but no one has come. The postman has been and gone, and yet another day has passed without a letter arriving that tells me I'm sacked and currently trespassing on council property.

So I carry on, even though everything's in limbo, and the tearoom is missing a Mad Hatter. Marnie's insisted on not leaving me to handle it by myself, so she's bought a Cheshire Cat jumper and a cat ears headband, persuaded Darcy to look after A Tale As Old As Time, and spent the past two days helping me.

A father comes in with two little boys who want an Unbirthday party, and Bram's absence is felt like a sinkhole in the middle of the tearoom. I push two tables together in a corner and put some props out to make it look like a Mad Hatter's tea party. Colourful teacups glued together in stacks. Broken teapots with clay mushrooms sprouting from them. Colourful plates and a table sprinkled with confetti. But I never realised how impossible it would be to have a Mad Hatter's celebration with no Mad Hatter.

I try to be fun and carefree, but I'm not loud. I can't do magic. I mess up pulling a playing card out of my pocket, never mind making one appear in mid-air. I sing the boys 'The Unbirthday Song' but Bram's lack of self-consciousness made me less self-conscious too, and without him, I'm crowing an out-of-tune disaster.

He's left a bag of confetti, and I blow it over the boys. One of them gets glitter in his eye and starts bawling. One of them misses the playing card arch with the hedgehog ball on the flamingo croquet and has a tantrum, and the dad is busy dealing with the glitter-in-eye incident, and there's no one to distract him from the tantrum with a magic trick, and I try to handle it by attempting to... persuade him not to have a tantrum. It does not end well. Technically it ends with him kicking me in the shin, which is fair enough, really. When the dad and two boys leave, it does not look like they'll come back, ever.

I never went to his house and never got the Unbirthday cake recipe on Sunday, but I've been using Marnie's kitchen to bake. It's been days since I needed to use any of my supermarket-bought back-ups, and even *that* makes me sad because Bram worked so hard to make me believe in myself and now he's not here to share it with.

'Oh, thank God,' I murmur as I see off the last customer at 5 p.m. the following day and turn the 'open' sign over to 'closed'. Wednesday was no more successful than Monday or Tuesday were.

'How can you mope in a place that's as happy as this?' Marnie starts clearing the tables and I pull on Bram's bright pink rubber gloves and make a start on the washing up.

'It's not though, is it? It was Bram who made it happy. With me it's just... doomed to failure, like everything else I get my hands on.'

'I don't think it's the *shop* that Bram made happy, do you?' Even though I'm in the back room and she's still on the shop floor, I can *hear* the all-knowing raised eyebrow.

'It's like a break-up but we never actually broke up, and I'm not even sure you *can* break up if you only kissed someone for the first time less than ten hours *before* said break-up.'

'No, but you've been emotionally attached to him for a lot longer than ten hours. And he has to you. I've never seen anyone so happy simply to *be* around another person. I've known Bram for a while now. He's bright, loud, hilarious, and always, *always* putting on a front. He's worked on that carousel for nearly two years and none of us have ever got to know him because he's *never* let anyone see behind that front. Apart from you. And me and Darcy when we came over the other night. And you've done that. I don't know anything about his life or why he finds it so hard to let people in, but he's let you in far enough to let you bring other people in too, and that means something.'

'It means everything, but look at what he's lied about...'

'Maybe, but there's no way he sabotaged those bakes. He was so dedicated the other night when we were there. He worked harder than any of us.'

'That was for his sister's wedding.'

'It's not his style, Cleo. He'd make things disappear, not pour bloody salt onto them. And honestly, I believed everything he said the other day. It's obvious how much he believes in this place *and* in you. I think that obliterated whatever was supposed to come before.'

The problem with Bram is that everything he says is infinitely believable, and at least some of the things he's said have been infinitely untrue, and I don't know how to marry up those two contradictions. 'So why didn't he tell me? When I asked him about who was given the tearoom before me, and if it was Tabby and her wellness retreat, he said he didn't know.'

'And you've never let a little white lie continue for longer than it should have because you were scared of the consequences if the truth came out?'

'No,' I huff and plunge my hands into the sink because I don't want to admit she's right.

She appears in the doorway with another tray full of crumb-filled plates. 'Don't make me bring up the rose cupcak—'

'I know, okay?' Those rose cupcakes will haunt my nightmares until my dying day. More than anything, I wish I'd been honest about them from day one. Maybe none of this would've happened then. Maybe they'd have said no, and Bram would've continued with his plan to run the tearoom, and I... would never have met him. I don't know which is the worst option.

The bookshop is overrun with customers on Thursday and Darcy's got a gardening group at the castle, so Franca comes to help out instead, and there's still no word from *anyone*. No one has come with any paperwork. No one has demanded I return their keys and vacate the premises immediately, and I'm not brave enough to phone the council and try to speak to Mr Hastings. I'm not keen on speaking to him at the best of times, and having caused a scene at his daughter's wedding and been exposed as a lying liar who lies *and* takes credit for other people's cakes, these are definitely *not* the best of times.

The week creeps closer and closer to the inspection on Friday, and surely the only explanation for why I haven't been fired yet is that Mr Hastings doesn't know that The Wonderland Teapot is still open, and when word does get back to him, I certainly will be.

* * *

'He texted me last night.' Marnie pushes her phone so close to my face that I take a step backwards before I can read it.

> I know she hates me, and I know it's unspoken best-friend law that you have to hate me too, but I don't know who else to turn to. Please help me, Marnie. I'll do anything to fix this.

> Oh, this is Bram, by the way.

Seconds later, another one, and then a couple more.

> You'd probably figured that out already.

> Unless you have several best friends going through romantic crises, that is.

> I don't usually send this many text messages in a row. I'll leave you alone now.

It gives me a little thrill that he hasn't given up yet. He hasn't texted me since I told him to go away, and I keep checking my phone, unsure of which one I'm dreading more – that he will text me... or that he won't.

It's Friday morning, the day of the food safety inspection, and although the tearoom has to stay closed today, Marnie's got Darcy looking after the bookshop again so she can be here for moral support. The text on her screen makes my heart beat faster because he still wants to fix things. 'I can't deal with this right now. The inspector will be here at any—'

'Are you Miss Jordan?' Before Marnie and I have got inside, a young man wearing a suit and carrying a briefcase appears from nowhere. He shows an ID card and pushes past us to enter first, and then mutters when he walks into a chair because I haven't got as far as getting inside to switch a light on yet.

He's got a laptop with him, and is utterly uninterested in anything as tedious as making conversation, despite my best efforts. He even refuses the cuppa that Marnie offers him, although maybe that's sensible considering he's only here because of complaints about the quality of our food.

He looks over the food safety documentation, inspects the condition of the main shop, and I hover while he goes to look around upstairs. He inspects *every* surface to check on the quality of the cleaning, and even looks in the cupboard under the stairs to check for adequate cleaning supplies. He checks every seal of the display unit, and every joint in the counter where bacteria could lurk. He checks the temperature of the refrigerator and the cupboards and takes photographs of the inside to go with the photos he's taken of *everything* else.

'Your toaster crumb tray needs emptying,' he says when he's inspected every millimetre of the food preparation room.

'Everyone's toaster crumb tray needs emptying,' I say, hoping it might elicit a smile.

No such luck.

'I've never even *seen* my toaster crumb tray,' Marnie offers.

Still nothing. I can't stop my mind going to how Bram would've handled this – if anyone could've got a smile from the uptight man, he would have. I don't know why I care if he smiles or not. Is he any less likely to order us to be closed down if we make him smile?

He's been here for over an hour when he finally says, 'Right, Miss Jordan, now I'll need to see the kitchen where you make the food, and your arrangements for transporting it.'

I don't know why, but that was the last thing I expected. 'Well, the sandwiches are made right here. So are the drinks. And things are toasted here.'

'Toasted teacakes are very popular.' Marnie tries to back me up but the scowl doesn't slip from his face.

'And everything else? You serve cakes and baked goods, so I understand? They're made in your kitchen at home, presumably, and then transported in?'

'They're made... um...' I can't mention Bram's kitchen *now*, can I? After everything that's come between us, I can't rock up with a food safety inspector like nothing's happened.

'She's actually using my kitchen now,' Marnie says.

He jumps on it like a hawk that's been gliding above ground, waiting to grab an innocent vole going about its day. 'Is there a problem with your own kitchen?'

'No. Not at all. It's just... um... I no longer have access to the kitchen I've *been* using, and...'

'We live together.' Marnie wraps an arm around my shoulders in solidarity. 'My kitchen is her kitchen. *Our* kitchen.'

No one needs to know that she means I live in the caravan. He'd have a field day if he saw the kitchen in *that*. And the woodlice would have a field day if they saw him.

His suspicious eyes flick between us. 'Right, and this really should have been made clear before now. How am I supposed to check on your handling practices and food monitoring equipment? How can I possibly inspect your food preparation area if your food preparation area is not *here*?'

'I didn't know you didn't know that.'

'We'll now need to make a second appointment for a further inspection of *those* premises, and I do warn you, Miss Jordan, although I see very few issues with these premises, there is room for improvement in your food safety management practices. There seems to have been no staff training in food hygiene provided whatsoever—'

'There are no staff!' I interrupt him. 'It's just me now. I'm alon—'
I get choked up and can't finish the sentence.

'As the manager, you should be carrying out four-weekly
reviews and daily checks. I see no evidence of these in your paperwork. Furthermore, I don't know what exactly is going on here, but
it seems like you're trying to hide something, and I'm afraid I have
absolutely *no* confidence in your management skills, and as I can't
complete my inspection today due to your omissions in information, I cannot confidently allow you to continue trading at this time.
We shall make a further appointment to inspect your kitchen, and
following that, I'll update my food hygiene score and we'll go from
there.'

This is it – my worst fear. The realisation that I am not good
enough to do this. The imposter syndrome that's finally been
proved right. Listening to Marnie and Bram tell me I'm good
enough is one thing, but the moment a professional health
inspector claps eyes on me, they'll realise the truth – that I'm
fooling everyone, including myself, by thinking I can do this, and
probably putting public health at risk too. What did I expect to
come from this? Is this why no one has told me to stop this week –
because it was blatantly obvious what was going to happen today
anyway? This dream was going to die this week one way or another
– it may as well be in the most humiliating way possible.

My thoughts are cut off by a hammering on the front door, and I
glance through from the back room, but I can't see who's there.

I swallow hard. 'Probably an eager customer wondering why
we're closed. They'll go away in a minute.'

Marnie meets my eyes when the hammering comes again. 'You
may be surprised to realise how popular this place is. There will
probably be loads of people knocking to come in before the
morning is out.'

'I need to type up my report before I leave, Miss Jordan, and I can't hear myself think. Please ask them to leave, and make sure to prominently display a "closed until further notice" sign to prevent confusion.'

The hammering is insistent and whoever it is doesn't seem to be going away. I steel myself for letting a disappointed customer know that we won't be reopening, unsure of how I'm going to do it without sobbing, and walk across the shop floor on unsteady legs.

'I'm sorry, we're closed,' I shout without opening the door.

Instead of replying, a hand bangs on the glass again, even louder this time. I can see the outlines of two figures outside through the frosted glass.

'We're closed,' I say again, more forcefully this time.

One of them hits the flat of a hand on the door again, even though they can surely see I'm standing here now, and there's no way they didn't hear what I said.

I put the chain on for safety and open the door just wide enough to tell them to go away, and then gasp in surprise.

Bram and Mr Hastings are standing outside.

''ello,' Bram says with his high-pitched voice and bright Hatter grin.

'It's not a good time,' I hiss, both overjoyed to see him and frustrated at the truly horrible timing.

'You've got seventy-two clocks in there. It's a good time by one of them.' He flashes the wide grin my way again, but now I know how much he hides behind that grin, I know the difference between his real smile and the one that's part of his character.

'The food safety inspector is here, and it's not going—'

'And that's exactly why *we're* here. We're not going away so you may as well open up.'

I glance between him and Mr Hastings, who would look less unimpressed if he'd recently swallowed a wasp. There's nothing to do but let them in.

'Thank you.' Bram's wearing jeans and a grey hoodie, there's no product in his blue hair and it's curling around his ears, and he tips his baseball cap to me as they come through the door.

My nerves were already shot this morning, but seeing him, having him near enough to touch again, and seeing that familiar 'I'm up to something' twinkle in his brown eyes makes my heart thud harder and I can feel my pulse beating in my fingertips where I'm clenching my hands together. 'What are you doing?'

The inspector chooses that moment to emerge from the back room with his laptop open in his hands. He stops in his tracks when he sees Bram's father. 'Oh, Mr Hastings. I didn't expect to see you today, sir. Is there a problem?'

'Yes, there is,' Bram says to him. 'We've come to stop the investigation. The incidents you're investigating were deliberate acts of sabotage. They bear no impact on The Wonderland Teapot's food safety standards. They could not have been prevented by good practices. They were caused by an individual who no longer works here. The problem has been resolved. There's nothing to investigate.'

I suddenly realise what he's going to do and grab his forearm with both hands. 'Tell me you haven't taken responsibility for this. I know you want to fix things, but this isn't the way.' That's exactly something Bram would do – claim it was him even though it wasn't.

'Taken responsibility...' He glances down at me and blinks for a few moments. 'I thought you thought it *was* me.'

'Of course it wasn't you.' I don't realise how vehemently I knew that until the words pop out of my mouth. 'It's the furthest thing from something you'd do. It wasn't you, Bram. I know that. Don't you dare say it was.'

'You thought it was me the other day...' He raises a dark eyebrow and his lips are twitching like he's trying not to smile.

'I was angry and upset and shocked the other day. My mind went automatically to the worst places, but I know you better than that. There's no way...'

He holds my gaze for a moment, losing the battle against not smiling and letting his lips tip up just enough to dent the dimple in his cheek, and then he does a cheerful shrug. 'You're right – it wasn't me. Dad, if you will...'

Mr Hastings looks between him, me, and the inspector, and

then huffs, like he's got no choice in the matter. 'I take full responsibility for the incidents that occurred here. When I hired Tabby, I told her about what had happened with Bram – about promising him the tearoom and then finding someone better suited. I told her how guilty I felt over it and how strained things had been between us and how I had made it worse by going back on my word to him. Tabby misinterpreted my meaning – she thought I was asking for help, and took it upon herself to "get the tearoom back". She thought that if The Wonderland Teapot failed, the tearoom would be Bram's again, and she would have helped me out – and I would owe her a favour she could cash-in at a later date.' He turns to me. 'I'm sorry, Miss Jordan. I had no idea what she was up to until Bram figured it out this week.'

I'm surprised, of course I am, but it's the kind of surprise that makes perfect sense and answers so many questions. It's a relief too. I wasn't imagining it. It wasn't because I'm in over my head. It wasn't gremlins. And Bram wasn't involved. I glance up at him. That's the main source of my relief. Bram *wasn't* involved.

'Allow me to get this straight, Mr Hastings,' the food safety inspector says. 'You're accepting responsibility for unsafe food being served to the public, without the proprietor's knowledge, and that all the issues mentioned in the complaint were caused by someone... who thought she was doing you a favour?'

Mr Hastings gives him a brisk nod. 'No one else is at fault. I should have checked up on Tabby. When I heard the first complaints, I should have made sure there was nothing untoward going on, but I let it slide. Hold me fully accountable.'

He scratches his head. 'How on earth am I going to word that in my report? *May* I report it, sir? I do have to be honest and—'

'Yes, of course you do.' He flicks a finger towards the laptop. 'Let's have a look at that report, lad, see if we can't figure out perhaps the kindest way to mention it.'

Marnie's trapped in the back room by the two of them, and she makes eyes at me over the inspector's shoulder, texting someone on her phone, probably Darcy for rescue.

I glance up at Bram again and he drops his head to rest against mine and murmurs into my hair. 'I'm sorry I didn't figure it out until this week. After you left the wedding, Tabby mentioned something about me having the tearoom again now, and the "again" stuck in my mind because *no one* knew, and I realised that the only way she could've known was if he'd told her. It took me a few days to work out exactly what went on and why.'

I've still got my hands wrapped around his forearm and I lean up to whisper. 'What about the food poisoning? *That* wasn't an act of sabotage, that was a mistake I made.'

'I think that's something that can be shared on a strictly need-to-know basis, and I see no one in this room who *needs* to know, do you?'

I can't help smiling as I squeeze his arm. '*You* have every right to shout it from the rooftops.'

'Nah. Mistakes happen. And we still don't know for sure that it wasn't dodgy cheese. Did you know that food poisoning can occur weeks after eating the offending item? There's no proof it was *that* partially raw cake. And you more than made up for any mistakes that night. Don't worry about it.'

I knock my arm against his in a silent thank you. Not just for that, but for doing this today too, especially after everything.

Mr Hastings is leaning over the counter from one side, the inspector is leaning over from the other side and they're sharing the laptop screen.

'How'd you get him to do this?' I'm surprised Mr Hastings has admitted all this so easily, and I get the feeling that Bram has had to do more persuading than he's letting on.

Bram shuffles us further away for a bit more privacy. He gets his phone out, taps the screen and then hands it to me. It's showing a photo of a man with hair in alternating neon green and magenta pink spikes, so sharp that they look like you could impale yourself on them, along with facial tattoos and a few piercings. 'Told him that would be my next look and I'd do the hair dying in his bathroom.'

I laugh. *Really* laugh. Some might call it a guffaw. And once I start, I can't stop. I have to duck my head against his upper arm and turn away in an attempt to get myself under control. My eyes are still watering with tears of laughter when I turn back and make the mistake of looking into his eyes, and see them twinkling back at me, a smile playing across his lips.

The tension of the past few days leaves me in a flood and I suddenly know we're going to be all right, and the relief makes me take leave of my senses. 'I love you, you absolutely spectacular nut.'

He blinks like he's trying to process what he's heard, and slowly, oh-so-slowly, a smile spreads across his face, and his eyes change from twinkling to sparkling. 'Really?'

I've never blushed so hard that it interferes with my ability to speak before, but my cheeks are burning *so* red that I don't think I can open my mouth. 'N—'

I want to deny it. *I* didn't even realise I felt like that until the sentence popped out, but it's unequivocally true. Day by day over the past couple of months, I have absolutely, whole-heartedly, undeniably fallen for *everything* about Bram, including but not limited to, his fondness for confetti and enjoyment of producing things from behind people's ears, the way he sings misheard lyrics with complete confidence, and the way he makes every aspect of life feel bright and exciting again.

'Don't get me wrong,' he says quickly. 'I'm head over heels in love with you too, but I'm not sure if I just had an auditory hallucination because of how desperately I hoped you might feel the same.'

In answer, I throw my arms around his neck and pull him down for a hug, loving the noise of surprise he makes, and even though my back is to the rest of the shop, I can *feel* three gazes on us. Marnie lets out a cheer.

Bram plants his legs apart to keep us upright as his arms wrap around me and he hugs me as tightly as it's physically possible to hug another person. My fingers automatically slide up to play with his hair, and his body relaxes against mine as he lets out a long exhale. 'That's the best feeling in the world.'

I can't help grinning at his typical Bram openness. I've spent the past five days fearing that I wouldn't get to hug him again and this feels so good that my eyes are threatening to well up and I have to take a shuddery breath that isn't as deep as it should be because he's holding me so tightly.

'And just in case you think he's completely heartless, he did genuinely feel awful when he realised how far Tabby had gone. We had a heart-to-heart talk with no egos and no expectations. I don't think he ever realised how serious I was about taking over the tearoom and I didn't realise that it wasn't personal when we saw your application. I don't know what you said to him the other night but I know you said something, because that chat felt like the first time he'd ever *heard* me speak. Our father-son relationship isn't magically mended, but maybe it isn't a completely lost cause either, and this is the first time I've felt like that in years, so thank you.'

I hold him impossibly tighter. There's so much I want to say, but it's not the right time when we've got an audience of three, but it's been too many days since I had a hug and I'm not ready to let go yet, no matter who's watching.

Marnie's cheer alerted the inspector to her presence, and he's stepped aside to let her out of the food preparation room, and she comes over. 'Hate to interrupt, but if you don't need me any more, I'd better go and relieve Darcy from bookshop duty.'

I reluctantly disentangle myself from Bram and give her a hug instead. 'Thank you for being the *best* best friend ever.'

'Text me later, I want details! A *lot* of details!'

I let her out and lock the door behind her, and when I turn back, Bram has gone to join his father and the inspector at the counter.

'I trust you've found nothing of concern in your investigations?' he asks, his tone suggesting that he's expecting the answer to be no.

'Well, not really, but...'

'The toaster crumb tray needs emptying,' I interject.

Bram looks over at me and then at the inspector. 'Allow me.'

The inspector and Mr Hastings watch in amusement as he goes out to the back room, empties the toaster crumb tray into the bin and washes his hands, and comes back with a hilariously smug Hatter grin on his face. 'There we go, you can strike that one off your long and elaborate list. Was there anything else?'

'There's a bit of cracked grouting in the splashback behind the sink, and...'

'Right, grouting. I can do that. And...?'

'Previous food hygiene scores are exemplary, I'm sure there'll be no problem going by them for the time being.' Mr Hastings doesn't give him a chance to add anything else.

'And *our* kitchen is available for inspection at your convenience,' Bram says.

I meet his eyes across the room and he gives me a subtle wink, and my heart flutters at what he means. That things are okay and we can go back to how we were.

'I'm sure you're very busy today.' Mr Hastings reaches over to pat the inspector on the shoulder. 'We wouldn't want to hold you up any further. Is that everything you need for your report?'

The inspector ums and ahhs for a minute, but clearly doesn't fancy trying to argue with Mr Hastings. Even if he's slightly less heartless than I thought he was at first, I doubt many council employees would want to get on the wrong side of him.

The inspector packs his laptop and gathers up his things, and the three of us follow him to the door and wave him off.

'I'd better get back to work too.' Mr Hastings starts patting down his pockets as if to make sure he hasn't left anything behind. 'That was quite an eventful morning.'

'I'm sorry about the cupcakes and the scene at the wedding, Mr Hastings.' I've been debating with myself whether to bring it up, but if there's one thing we need in The Wonderland Teapot, it's a bit more honesty on all sides, including mine, and I finally blurt it out as he goes to open the door, and he turns back to me.

'And I'm sorry too, Miss Jordan. I made a mistake in sharing our private business with Tabby. I acted as if she was still my daughter-in-law without ever truly understanding what had happened between her and my son. Given how insistent *Bram* was about us making this right, I suspect we may be seeing more of you in our family life.' He glances at Bram uncertainly, like he's making sure he's used the right name, and then reaches out to shake my hand. 'And I really do apologise for my part in this debacle. I hope The Wonderland Teapot will continue to thrive for many happy years on Ever After Street.'

He shakes Bram's hand too, and we stand together in the doorway as we watch him walk off down the street and then both realise at the same moment that everyone has gone and it's just the two of us. He grins at me. ''ello.'

'Hi.' It seems a daft thing to say when I've been standing next to him for the past twenty minutes and just confessed my love for him.

He reaches out for my hand. 'Can we talk?'

I can't slip my hand into his fast enough. 'I didn't realise how much I'd miss you.'

'Me too. I mean, I always knew how much I'd miss you, but life has been extraordinarily dreary since Sunday. I've come to rely on your hugs like oxygen. If I could *not* have to go another day without hugging you, ever, it would make me very happy.' His cheeks go gorgeously red and the tightness that was still clenching around my chest and shoulders suddenly lifts, and we're just smiling at each other again. He jiggles my hand and tugs me towards the nearest table. 'Tea?'

'Always time for tea.' I can't resist the opportunity to make use of his favourite quote.

He's about to go and start making it when I clamp a hand on his shoulder and push him downwards because the circles under his eyes are so dark that it looks like he's still wearing eyeliner, even though he isn't. 'Sit down. You look exhausted and you've been making me tea since the moment I met you. Let me.'

I boil the kettle and throw a teabag into two glitter-sprinkled mugs as quickly as possible, and then carry the tray over and set it on the table between us.

'Cake?' He looks at me expectantly, like serving tea without cake is one of the most scandalous crimes a person can commit.

'I don't have any. I didn't make anything last night because I was too scared of it being "inspected" and I couldn't very well let him inspect supermarket-bought cakes.'

'Ah, but I do. I always come prepared.'

'Prepared for situations where you might need cake at a moment's notice?'

'Exactly.' He flashes the Mad Hatter grin at me and beckons me to sit forward and leans closer so he can reach a hand across the table and his fingers hover in my peripheral vision.

'Bram, if you're about to pull a cake out from behind my ear, I won't be responsible for my actions!'

He laughs, but instead of a cake, he pulls a card out from behind my ear and hands it to me. The Ace of Hearts. I can't help smiling as I turn it over between my fingers and watch as he gets a cardboard cake box out of his bag.

He opens it out on the table and inside are two cupcakes in the shape of teapots, covered with lemon-coloured fondant icing and decorative green piping, with a fondant handle formed on the side. 'They need better decoration, which is where you come in, but I thought they'd be really fun and Wonderland-ish in the display case. And I was trying to be productive while I couldn't sleep last night. Thought I might have to bribe you to talk to me, and cake was my best bet.'

I go to grab us two plates and he lifts the cupcakes from the box and passes one over. I pop a bit in my mouth and can't hide the noise of pleasure at the sweet lemon-and-lime taste, and he sips his tea, and it's blatantly obvious that we're both putting off the actual talking part of this conversation, but neither of us seem willing to face it head-on.

'He hasn't got away with it,' Bram says eventually, without needing to clarify who he's talking about. 'Plenty of his colleagues were at the wedding – they heard everything you said and were far from impressed to hear he's been using his position to bully employees. He's got questions to answer for an internal investigation and he's been "relieved" of some duties, and Mrs Willetts has been appointed as co-councillor for the Ever After Street area to ensure everything is handled fairly in the future.'

'That's good. Almost as good as this cupcake.' I eat another piece and take a deep breath. 'Bram...'

'I'm so sorry I didn't tell you about the tearoom,' he blurts out before I get any further. 'It wasn't meant to get as messy as it did. Yeah, I was going to take this place on, and yeah, I didn't expect someone else to come along at the last minute, but I believe things happen for a reason, and I was okay with that. At first, it was irrelevant, I didn't expect to get close to you, and I didn't think you needed to know. And then my father used it as blackmail material, and the sabotage incidents started, and suddenly it became a big deal, and I was right in the middle of it, and I didn't know what to do. And then the other day, when it came out, I froze up. I could feel you slipping away and I didn't know how to stop it happening. I was exposed and vulnerable and I didn't have my usual shields up, and in front of so many people... My shutters came down and I turned defensive. I could feel everyone in that room turning against me, and I panicked. It was like my father's shadow had crept in and eclipsed yet another part of my life.'

'I was wrong to doubt you.'

'I lied to you, Cleo. You weren't wrong to doubt me.'

'I was wrong to doubt you in front of so many people, then. By the time I realised that it really *was* a conversation we should've had in private, it was too late. It was just... I didn't expect to hear that, and the shock took over all logical thought.'

His hand is lying on the table, and I reach over and give it a squeeze, deciding to voice something I've figured out in the last few days. 'It *was* you who persuaded your father to look at my application, wasn't it?'

His eyes flick up to mine like he didn't expect me to know that and then flick back down to our joined hands and he nods.

'Even though you knew what might happen? You knew there was a chance he'd go with my idea?'

'Yeah. I meant what I said about wanting the best for Ever After Street. I know the council have to go with the best option, and I *knew* that was you – you were so much more of a better fit than I ever would've been.'

'Why didn't you tell me that the other day? It would've made a difference.'

'I didn't want you to know.' He sighs and shrugs at the same time. 'I have a thing about people liking me – you know that. If you liked me, I wanted it to be because you liked me, not because you thought you owed me something. The other day, I wanted you to know I was telling the truth because you trusted me, not because I suddenly pulled an ace from my sleeve.' He looks up and winks at me. 'And I'm weird, sometimes that's the only explanation you need.'

'And I love every single weird thing about you.'

He lets out a loud laugh and smiles like he couldn't stop himself if he wanted to and pushes his chair back to stand up. 'Okay, you don't get to say things like that without letting me kiss you. May I?'

'If you think you need to ask permission every time you kiss me, we've got a probl—'

Before I've finished the sentence, he's pulled my chair out, turned it to face him, and crouched down in front of me. One hand is on my thigh and the other slides upwards to cup my head and he crushes our lips together.

I let out a happy sigh and one leg hooks around him to keep him close as our mouths meet. The force of the kiss has knocked his baseball cap off and his mouth is hot and he tastes of tea and the sweetness of the cake. His hands are everywhere, and mine are all over him, clawing at him, unable to pull him close *enough*, like the emotions of missing him so much in the past few days finally break loose.

I can feel the glitter on our lips from the mugs, and this has got to be the sparkliest kiss ever, which is somehow really fitting for someone who's made my life sparkle since the moment I met him.

My hand tangles in his hair to pull him closer, and he grunts into the kiss as he nearly overbalances, using one of his legs to push himself up a bit higher, get a bit closer, kiss me harder, and then harder again, but this time it's with such force that my chair tips backwards and I squeal and grab the table to stay upright, breaking the kiss.

'You know it's a good kiss when someone nearly gets injured.' He's still crouching as he makes sure all four chair legs are safely on the floor, and when I start giggling at how lost I got in that kiss and how abruptly it ended, he starts laughing too. His hands are on my knees to keep himself upright and he's gasping for breath as much as I am.

He leans forward so his forehead rests against mine, breathing hard. 'God, I've needed to do that again *so* badly since the carousel the other night.'

'Me too.' My fingers play with his hair while the other hand runs up and down his back, and every shiver it elicits makes me grasp him tighter.

'This is probably not the ideal time to bring up my dad again, but he did ask me to say something,' he says between pants. 'The lease is still yours if you want it.'

I'd been hoping that was the case, and at some unknown point this week, I've also worked out what my response would be. 'I don't.'

'What?' His eyes fly open, his head shoots up and his body stiffens instantly. 'Cleo, come on, you hav—'

'Not alone.' One hand is holding his shoulder, and the other is stroking through his hair and he watches me with eyes that turn from shocked to hopeful. 'Not without you. I want us to go into this together – to take over the lease as partners, both of us.'

His legs give way and he slips over and sinks down to sit on the floor with a thud, shaking his head in surprise, both hands still holding onto my knees. 'Seriously?'

'I can't do this without you, Bram. The theme might've been my idea, but you've brought it to life. Without you, it would just be a decorated tearoom, but *you* make it Wonderland. I want us to be "in" this together for real. Equal partners.'

His eyes meet mine, like he's silently asking me if I'm serious, and I hold his gaze, watching as his smile gets wider and wider.

'I just have one very important question...' He lifts my hand and brings it to his mouth, pressing his lips against the back of it and letting his dark stubble graze against my skin. 'What are your thoughts on mixing business with pleasure?'

I laugh out loud and it turns into a whimper when he repeats the motion. 'I could be persuaded on the merits of it.'

He lets out a whoop and gets onto his knees and leans over to kiss me again. It's gentler this time, but his elbow is digging into my ribs, he yelps when his knee crunches against the floor, and it's such an awkward angle that it makes me laugh again, even though every kiss with Bram makes everything inside me soar with happiness.

He pulls back, laughing too. 'One day we'll have a kiss that doesn't result in mortal injury.'

'Where would be the fun in that?'

'My thoughts exactly.' He gives me a seductive grin and leans over for another kiss, and then sits back again without letting go of my hands.

'I had another idea too,' I start. 'When you talked about the shop you used to run and showing kids how to do magic, it was obvious how much that meant to you. You know better than anyone how much of an impact magic can have on a young person. What if, once a month or something, you hosted some kind of workshop to show youngsters how to do some of the things you do? Pass on your knowledge to the next generation?'

He blinks for a few moments, seemingly lost for words. 'I would *love* that.'

'Me too.' I take a deep breath. 'So, what do you say? Will you be my Mad Hatter on an eighteen-month rolling contract?'

The phrasing makes him laugh and he thinks about it for a moment, his face contorting as he gives it serious thought. 'On one condition... Come and stay with me. At least park your caravan on my driveway. You know how many empty rooms I have, and if one of those happened to be more appealing than sleeping in a caravan... I'd love you to be there, and you'd have easy access to the kitchen where it seems we're going to be spending a lot of time... I'll say yes if you will.'

I've been spending so much time at Bram's lately that it doesn't require much thought, and Marnie's neighbours aren't very happy about the rusty old caravan cluttering up their road, although Marnie's neighbours aren't *quite* the deciding factor here. 'Good job you're impossible to say no to, isn't it?'

'Yes!' He does a victory punch and scrambles to his feet, pulling me with him until we're both upright and he wraps me in his arms and hugs me so tightly that he lifts me off the floor and I squeak and cling onto him.

Endless minutes pass as he rocks us gently, pulling back only enough to share the occasional kiss, until my entire body has melted against his and everything that's felt wrong in my life for the past few years is suddenly right again, because it led to here, and this is exactly where I was supposed to end up.

'If you believe in me, I'll believe in you,' he murmurs against my ear.

He always does have a way with words. It's something the unicorn says to Alice in *Through the Looking-Glass* and it's such a perfect fit for us, and it has been since the very beginning, except unlike Alice, I'm not about to wake up and discover this was all a dream, because even in my wildest wishes, I couldn't have imagined a future so rainbow-coloured with brightness, and a spectacular nut who makes the whole world feel like Wonderland every day.

ACKNOWLEDGEMENTS

Thank you, Mum. Always my first and most important reader! I'm eternally grateful for your constant patience, support, encouragement, and belief in me. Thank you for always being there for me – I don't know what I'd do without you. Love you lots!

Marie Landry, my best friend and my absolute favourite spectacular nut! There are so many in-jokes and nods to us in this book, but none is more intentional than the line Cleo says to Marnie – "Thank you for being the *best* best friend ever." I am so lucky to get to call you my best friend and I'm grateful every day to have you in my life! I love you to bits! A huge thank you also to Nancy Landry for the constant love and support, even from half a world away!

Thank you to Bill, Toby, Cathie, and Bev for your continued love and enthusiasm. Thank you to Jayne Lloyd and Charlotte McFall for being such wonderful friends, and an extra special shoutout to Kirsty Oughton for always being so lovely!

I want to say a massive thank you to everyone who I chat to on social media, who I've connected with thanks to books, and to all of you who show me so much support and kindness on a daily basis. A big shoutout to some Facebook groups who support me tirelessly and are an absolute pleasure to be part of. A huge and heartfelt thank you to all the members and admins of Vintage Vibes and Riveting Reads, The Friendly Book Community, The Spirituality Café, Chick Lit and Prosecco, Book Swap Central, and Fiction Addicts at Socially Distanced Book Club. If you're a booklover looking for somewhere to brighten your day, lift your spirits, and make you feel like you've found a group of people who understand why we always buy more books even though we need scaffolding to hold up our current to-read pile, please find your way to these groups! You will be glad you did – although your to-read list may not!

Thank you to my fantastic agent, Amanda Preston, and my brilliant editor Emily Ruston, along with the rest of the wonderful and hardworking Boldwood team and the lovely Boldwood authors! It's a total joy to belong to Team Boldwood!

And finally, thank *you* for reading! I hope you enjoyed falling down the rabbit hole into The Wonderland Teapot and sharing Cleo and Bram's story. It was imagining these two and the goings-on inside a Wonderland-themed tearoom that turned Ever After Street from a standalone book into a series, so this one will always have a special place in my heart. I hope you'll come with me for the next book, where we'll be joining Franca in The Nutcracker Shop at Christmas! There are always many more happily ever afters to come!

ABOUT THE AUTHOR

Jaimie Admans is the bestselling author of several romantic comedies. She lives in South Wales.

Sign up to Jaimie Adman's mailing list for news, competitions and updates on future books.

Visit Jaimie's website: https://jaimieadmans.com/

Follow Jaimie on social media:

X x.com/be_the_spark
f facebook.com/jaimieadmansbooks
instagram.com/jaimieadmans1

ALSO BY JAIMIE ADMANS

The Gingerbread House in Mistletoe Gardens

The Ever After Street Series

A Midnight Kiss on Ever After Street

An Enchanted Moment on Ever After Street

A Wonderland Wish on Ever After Street

WHERE ALL YOUR ROMANCE
DREAMS COME TRUE!

THE HOME OF BESTSELLING
ROMANCE AND WOMEN'S
FICTION

 WARNING:
MAY CONTAIN SPICE

SIGN UP TO OUR
NEWSLETTER

https://bit.ly/Lovenotesnews

Boldwood

Boldwood Books is an award-winning fiction publishing company seeking out the best stories from around the world.

Find out more at www.boldwoodbooks.com

Join our reader community for brilliant books, competitions and offers!

Follow us
@BoldwoodBooks
@TheBoldBookClub

Sign up to our weekly
deals newsletter

https://bit.ly/BoldwoodBNewsletter

Made in the USA
Middletown, DE
19 October 2024

62916884R00175